Me Without You

Me Without You

Kelly Rimmer

bookouture

Published by Bookouture

An imprint of StoryFire Ltd.
23 Sussex Road, Ickenham, UB10 8PN
United Kingdom

www.bookouture.com

ISBN: 978-1-909490-39-0

This book is a work of fiction. Names, characters, businesses,
organizations, places and events other than those clearly in the
public domain, are either the product of the author's imagination
or are used fictitiously. Any resemblance to actual persons, living
or dead, events or locales is entirely coincidental.

ACKNOWLEDGMENTS

I'll forever be grateful to Oliver Rhodes for seeing the potential of this story long before it was realised, thanks for your guidance and encouragement. Thanks also to Emily Ruston, editor extraordinaire, for so many brilliant ideas and improvements to the "rough diamond" we started with.

To the dear friends who read and re-read various drafts and so generously provided feedback and encouragement; Tracy, Melissa, Penny, Shelly and Cath—thank you.

My sisters, Mindy and Jodie; thanks for being my personal writing cheer squad since my first late-night storytelling sessions when we were insomniac kids. And to my baby brother Rick (who secretly loves my cooking), thanks for always having my back.

To Mum and Dad, who have taught me that real love is a beautiful, complex thing—thanks for believing in me.

My husband Dan—where would I be without you to distract me with cricket chat whenever I wanted to talk myself out of trying? Thank you for providing random motivational quotes, distraction-free minutes (and occasionally even hours) and most of all, unquestioning support.

CHAPTER ONE
Callum

It was absolutely *not* love at first sight.

I saw a filthy bare foot out of the corner of my eye. I tried not to look, but facts are facts—bare feet in public places are inexcusable, and at that point I hadn't realised what the body the foot was attached to was like. I'm sure I grimaced, but I did try to keep my eyes on the laptop I was working on. Evidently I failed because she caught me staring.

'My eyes are up here,' she said, but she sounded amused and I glanced up to see if I'd misread the tone.

That's how we made eye contact. And that's when I fell in love with her—so maybe it was actually love at second sight.

Lilah was all kinds of wonderful, in ways words could never quite capture. She was barely five feet tall and so skinny it seemed she'd break if you held her too tightly. That day, her deep auburn hair was in a glossy bun without a single flyaway and I remember thinking of the joke I'd heard about corporate types thinking hair that moved was a sign of weakness. Lilah somehow knew how to wear a plum suit with chunky wooden accessories and still appear flawlessly professional.

There was something so wrong with the polished top half of her image juxtaposing the homeless-esque foot situation. Although I was embarrassed to have been caught staring, I just had to ask.

'Why aren't you wearing shoes?'

'Listen, buddy. I stood for eight hours today. In stilettos,' she informed me. She gave the women around her a *can you believe this guy?* glance.

'That's no reason to be barefoot now. Anyway, if you'd worn more sensible shoes, you would still have clean feet.'

'Oh, so *that's* the answer.' The sarcasm was softened by a laugh. 'Tomorrow when I walk into court and the judge asks me why I'm wearing my runners, I'll tell him some guy on a ferry told me to.'

'One of the many, many things that completely baffle me about women is what you'll put yourselves through for rules that only women care about.' I'd had the argument with nearly every woman I knew at some point. It never ended well.

'Rules only women care about?! I once got fired because I refused to wear make-up to work,' the woman beside Lilah chimed in. Almost before she'd finished the sentence, Lilah had passed her a business card.

'You should call my firm. We can help you with that,' she said, but her attention was back to me in an instant. 'Are you seriously suggesting to me that the reason women dress professionally for work is to impress other women?'

'I'm all for professionalism. You can see I'm wearing a suit, and I do every day I'm in the office. But if someone suggested to me directly or indirectly that I had to wear nipple clamps to get ahead in my career, I'd see through it. If your shoes hurt your feet, wear less elaborate shoes. Simple.'

It was at this point, possibly belatedly, that I realised I had about ten sets of angry female eyes pointed in my direction. I twisted my neck to see how far away Manly Wharf was.

'Thinking about swimming away from the argument?' Lilah asked.

'I know I can't win. Men aren't allowed to challenge the institution of womanhood.'

'Mate, if you're *going* to challenge the institution of womanhood,' the man beside me muttered, '*don't* do it on a boat at sea against a lawyer who just spent eight hours standing in high heels.'

'Wise words,' Lilah agreed.

'I'm not wanting to be argumentative,' I said, although clearly I was. 'I genuinely don't understand why women feel they have to put themselves through pain to look good. You're a beautiful lady, Miss...?'

'Ms.—and it's none of your business.'

'Ms. None of My Business,' I repeated. 'You'd be equally as beautiful and professional in a pair of flat leather shoes as you were today in your stilettos.'

'Thank you for your kind, if somewhat patronising, words.'

The interaction was probably drawing to a close, but there was no way I was going to get off that ferry without finding out who she was. I had been waiting a very long time to feel as fascinated by someone as I was by this mysterious lawyer, even with her filthy bare feet.

'And what area of law do you practise in?'

'Guess.'

'Oh.' I'd done a few law subjects at uni, but it felt like centuries ago, rather than decades. 'Corporate?'

'Nope.'

'Property.'

'No.'

I looked at her again. Something about her outfit suggested she fit ever-so-slightly out of the ordinary corporate grind.

'Ah. It's got to be family law.'

'No!' She laughed again. Her laugh was delicate and musical—exactly the sound you'd think a woman as beautiful as Lilah should make when she laughed.

'Employment?'

'Wrong again.'

'Criminal.'

'Nope.'

'What other areas *are* there?'

'Only the most important and dynamic.'

'Copyright law?'

She looked at me suspiciously.

'Are you in the entertainment industry, sir?'

It was my turn to laugh.

'Marketing.'

'Even worse. I can see that, with that capitalist head on your shoulders, you're not even going to spare a thought for the planet that supports you. Typical.'

The penny dropped.

'You're an environmental lawyer, out to save the world.'

'Finally!'

'Sorry to be obtuse. I just thought environmental lawyers wore hemp T-shirts and had dreadlocks, but now that you mention it, the bare feet should have given it away.'

'I can't help but wonder…' she said, but stopped midsentence as if she'd thought better of whatever she was about to say. In hindsight, knowing Lilah, it was probably a ploy to test my interest level, rather than an actual hesitation.

'Yes?' I prompted. The truth was, I was hanging on her every syllable.

'Oh, nothing.' She flashed me a smile and my cliché of a stomach did a flip-flop. 'Just wondering how you're going to turn this banter on its head and ask me out for dinner.'

'I was just wondering if he was going to make you go home and put sensible shoes on first,' the lady next to her laughed.

'I'm wondering if you should invite the rest of us as back-up—I think you might be outwitted,' the man beside me said under his breath. There was general chuckling from the area around us, but Lilah and I had locked gazes, and the sound washed over me like the canned laughter of a sitcom.

'Tonight?' I asked.

'I don't go on dates with marketing guys.' Her tone was playful and I knew she would.

'I have an herb garden on my kitchen windowsill.' It was a total lie, of course—I didn't even *have* a window sill at that point, given that I'd torn out most of the kitchen during a renovation I'd never quite gotten around to finishing. It didn't matter—my desperate pitch inspired further laughter from our audience, and Lilah grinned at me.

'Oh, well, in *that* case...'

✿ ✿ ✿

We stepped off the ferry together, as the crowd began dissipating into the mild Manly twilight. Lilah had an oversized handbag on her shoulder that I could see held a laptop, and I had several hours' work that I had planned to finish before morning. I didn't believe in destiny—I still don't—but somehow I knew to pay attention to the moment, as if I had just started a once-in-a-lifetime journey.

'So, you're an evil marketing genius,' she prompted. We were waiting to cross the road to the Manly Corso and the late peak-hour traffic was still heavy.

'Something like that. I did spend today planning ways to trick children into buying poison.'

'Lace it with sugar.'

'We've been doing that for years. My new technique is to lace it with sugar *and* cocaine—I'm always thinking of new ways to keep them addicted.'

The joke fell a little flat. She gave me half a smile out of pity. 'Why marketing?'

'Why anything?' I shrugged. 'I like the challenge of changing people's minds.'

The light turned amber and the flow of traffic slowed, then stopped. We surged forward automatically with the crowd to the Corso, because that's what people in Manly seemed to do. The Corso was lined with stores and restaurants, and the other end of the street opened up literally on the sand. Day or night, summer or winter, there was always a stream of bodies being funnelled along the Corso, drawn by the pull of the beach.

'Did you fit these torturous stilettos into that handbag somewhere?' I asked. I was hesitant to mention her bare feet again, but I couldn't imagine any restaurateur being pleased with a barefoot patron, even though we were only a few hundred metres from the ocean.

'Nope, they're safely under my desk at work, resting up preparing for more torture tomorrow. How about I show you my favourite place?' she suggested. Then, reading my mind, 'There *are* places in Manly that don't mind that I'm a filthy hippy.'

'You run around barefoot often enough to know that?' I asked.

'Life is too short to be uncomfortable. If my feet hurt, I take my shoes off. If my bun annoys me, I pull it out. Which reminds me.'

She stepped against the shop to her right and passed me the oversized handbag, which I took mutely. It felt a little bit like she was so magical that any move she made was going to startle and amaze me, and my senses were on high alert. I watched as she removed several pins from her bun and unwound her hair down past her shoulders. It sprang and bounced with the movement of her hands and fell near her waist. The tight bun had shaped it into loose waves. She shook her head to loosen it further and then smiled at me. 'That's better.'

I still wish I could have stopped at that very moment and taken a photo of her on my phone. Darkness was falling and the artificial glow of the shop we stood beside illuminated the shroud-like fall of her hair. Her blue eyes sparkled like the ocean off Manly on a sunny day and a soft smile was on her lips. I amused her.

'Ready?' she prompted. Had I been staring? I wasn't sure. The whole encounter was beginning to feel surreal. A fleeting thought breezed past my consciousness. Had I ever fallen in love? Was this what it felt like?

'Let's go,' I said. I was achingly conscious of the pounding of my own blood in my ears. As I turned away from her to continue our walk towards the beach, she laughed again.

'My handbag really suits you. Do you think sometime soon we should swap names?'

I passed her back her handbag and hoped she didn't notice the warm flush creeping up my neck.

'I'm Callum. Callum Roberts.'

'Well, hi, Callum-who-lets-barefoot-strangers-pick-him-up-on-the-ferry,' she grinned. 'I'm Lilah Owens.'

'I picked *you* up,' I protested.

She grinned again. 'Sure you did. Whatever makes you feel comfortable.'

Lilah. The name seemed perfect for her. I tried it on in my mind—*Lilah Roberts*—then mentally shook myself, horrified. I didn't want to get married, ever; it wasn't in the game plan.

My parents had taught me a lot of things about love and marriage—the most important lesson being that those things were *not* for me.

'Where *are* we going?' I asked, to distract myself from the uncomfortable train of thought my mind had taken. I had a sudden urge to take charge. I'd been everywhere worth eating at in Manly, and I tried to figure out somewhere suitable. It needed to be informal because of the feet situation, but romantic—dim lighting? A decent wine list? Some mood music perhaps? Turners?'

'Eww,' she grimaced, clearly not impressed with my suggestion of the reputed best gourmet restaurant in the suburb. 'No, we're going to Giovanni On the Seaside.'

'The pizza place?' I was confused. We'd crossed the road and were walking side by side along the Corso now, towards the beachside road that housed Giovanni On the Seaside. It was a casual pizza place, with outdated décor, a low price menu and only a few tables—most of the business was takeaway.

'Not highbrow enough for you?' She was teasing me—or maybe testing me.

'It's absolutely fine.' It was also kind of near my apartment, which seemed a bonus. 'I didn't pick you for a pizza girl.' Mainly because she looked like she'd never eaten a mouthful of junk food in her life.

'Doesn't everyone love pizza?'

'I suppose they do. What's the case you're working on?'

'Well, today I was in court, trying to get an injunction granted to stop the development of a new mine.'

'Why is the mine a bad thing?'

'Most mines are bad things.' Anyone else using that tone would have seemed arrogant. Lilah just seemed confident.

'This one is supposed to sit just beyond a national park. There are three endangered species with habitats within a few kilometres of the site. It's just too risky.'

'Will you win?'

'I should.'

Good thing I wasn't the judge. I'd never have a hope in hell of concentrating on detail if she was arguing before me.

'And what do you do in your spare time, Captain Planet?'

'I cook a little. But mostly, I knit.'

I couldn't tell if she was joking or not.

'Jumpers?'

'Booties, mostly. For the babies I'm going to have.'

Definitely joking.

'I'll bet you have a nursery set up and everything.'

'Two, in case I have twins.'

'Are you going to deflect every question I ask you?'

'Are you going to ask me stupid first-date questions all night?'

'If you were stuck on a desert island, what three things would you take?'

'A GPS, a satellite phone and my laptop.'

I could smell the ocean, and the hint of pizza on the breeze. Giovanni On the Seaside was there before us, but suddenly I was hesitant. As Lilah moved to step inside, I gently caught her by the elbow and turned her back towards me. She raised an eyebrow.

'I'm not sure I can take you to this casual little pizza place for our first date.'

'And why is that?'

'I think you deserve better.'

'Well, aren't you sweet?' The bravado actually softened a little bit and she gave me her first genuine smile of the night.

'But trust me, Callum, I'm a fussy eater, and there's a dish here I just adore.'

The gentle breeze stirred her hair, and a lock fell over her eye. I reached down and tucked it behind her ear and saw her swallow. It was a strange chemistry that hummed between us—uncomfortably intense, but somehow innocent and pure in spite of the river of sexual undertone. I wanted to kiss her already, and I knew she wanted me to. For the first time in my entire life though, I wanted to savour every second and prolong each step of the journey.

'Sounds like a meal I can't afford to miss.'

The cheeky grin was back, and the moment ended. Lilah pulled away and stepped inside.

❄ ❄ ❄

The restaurant was half empty but the menu was packed. I'd been there before but hadn't found any particular dish worth braving the exhaustive menu for. Lilah knew exactly what she wanted though.

'The vegan thin crust, please.'

'Vegan?'

'It means no meat, no egg, no dairy. No animal products at all,' the helpful waiter informed me. I was genuinely confused.

'How does that work in a pizza?'

'Cashew cheese is bloody amazing,' Lilah informed me.

'*Cashew* cheese?' I winced. 'How is that even a thing?'

'I think we better share the *large* vegan thin crust,' Lilah said, taking my menu from me.

'But I was going to order the extra meaty meat lovers, with extra meat, and a side of meat.'

Her gaze challenged me.

'I'm not an evangelistic vegan by any means. But if you've never even heard of cashew cheese, don't you think the least you should do is give it a chance?'

She could have suggested we share a plate of dirt and, with a flutter of those eyelashes, I'd have asked for a sprinkling of gravel on top.

'I can always swing by the steakhouse shop on the way home,' I muttered.

'So, you aren't above flirting with a stranger in public but you *are* scared of a meal without a dead animal in it.'

'Multiple dead animals. I'm an overachiever.'

'You live near here?'

'My apartment is back a few blocks.'

In other circumstances, I'd surely have missed the subtle way her eyebrows rose or the gentle curve of her lips. She was thinking about coming home with me. We locked gazes again for just a moment before she corrected her posture and tossed her hair away from her face.

'I love Manly,' she said. 'I love the scent of the ocean on the night air, the delight on the backpackers' faces when they get off the bus, and most of all, the fact that the CBD is in another universe.'

'I actually have a very unhealthy love affair with Sydney itself,' I admitted. 'I lived in the CBD until last year. The energy fuels me.' More than that; the energy had fuelled my creativity, and I felt somehow that it was the city that had inspired me to work as hard as I had over the years. The city, and the feeling that my career really was the sum total of my life's worth, so I had better make it count.

'So why did you move?'

'I started to suspect that you can't be *on* all of the time,' I said. 'It was wearing me thin, the constant bustle. I didn't want to move too far away, and the idea of jogging on the beach before work then catching a lazy ferry across the harbour was enticing.'

'Do you jog on the beach before work?'

'Not as often as I thought I would.'

'And you catch the fast ferry.'

'If you can afford to buy property in Manly, you don't have time to catch the slow ferry,' I sighed.

'That's very sad—but I suppose it's true.'

I'd never understood what it was like to be so enchanted by someone that I could genuinely not tear my gaze from them. I'm sure I'm an appalling listener—I'm invariably self-absorbed, a reality I'm sure my many exes would attest to. But with Lilah, I didn't want to miss a word.

'I inherited my grandmother's house when she passed away,' she said quietly. 'I went into commercial law first, made a bucketload of money, and thought I could quell my do-gooder leanings with some half-arsed tending to the enormous garden my grandparents cultivated when they were alive. It's a few acres of fruit trees, right near the ocean at Gosford, the most beautiful place I've ever been—but within a few months I'd just about destroyed it.' She laughed. 'I had no bloody idea what I was doing, but the very idea had just seemed so… romantic.'

'Reality versus expectation,' I surmised.

'Exactly. Now the older couple across the road tend the orchard, and they've planted a substantial market garden too, and in exchange for caring for it properly for me they sell the produce at farmers' markets on the weekends. And I visit every now and again and gorge myself on fresh fruit and veg. The only way the dream worked was to let go of the expectation.'

'I think that's what I've done with my Manly move, actually.' I surprised myself with the depth of the realisation even as I said the words. 'It is what it is. Even if it's not the leisurely life I'd imagined, that's okay.'

'Did you grow up in the city?' she asked.

'Cronulla. How about you?'

'Oh, we lived all over the place.'

'Do you have family in Sydney now?'

'Mum has a place at Gosford. Dad passed away a while ago.'

'I'm sorry,' I hesitated. 'My parents are both gone too.'

'I have a theory that even if you are ninety when your parent dies, it must still make you feel like a child all over again.'

'I think you're right.' I hated—still hate—talking about my parents' deaths, especially to women, and most of all to women I was interested in. It was just such a tale of wonder and love, and they always got this miserable look of longing on their faces. By the time I reached the depressing end of the tale, I either felt like I was breaking their hearts or that they'd missed the point and only saw it as entirely romantic, which annoyed me even more.

'Have yours been gone for long?' she asked.

'It's a bit of a long story.' I wasn't fobbing her off, not exactly. This just wasn't the sort of tone I wanted to set for the meal. Before I could figure out how to change the subject, she rested her elbow on the table, her chin on the back of her hand, and she flashed me a soft smile.

'I'm not in any rush.'

Maybe three times I'd talked about my parents with women I'd been seeing, and maybe three times I'd walked away from the conversation feeling irritated. Once upon a time I'd asked out a woman I met at the gym, and when the conversation turned around to our parents and I told her about mine, she'd actually *cried*. I'd wrapped up dinner early and gone home alone. I remember resisting the urge to snap at her, to point out what *should* have been obvious—there was no *happy ending* to the tale.

I suspected Lilah might have a different reaction to the story—I'm not sure why, maybe it was an instinct. I started talking about it before I even decided to.

'Mum was American. She and Dad met in New York. He was twenty-one, and a few years into his career as a journalist. He took an extended break to go looking for adventure, and somehow he wound up over there. They bumped into each other in a supermarket, the canned vegetable aisle I believe, and were inseparable from that moment on. Mum used to say that they literally didn't have a moment apart until he went back to work a few months later. She followed him back here, they were married within a few weeks, set up a house and just generally got on with being blissfully happy.'

'A fairy tale.' Lilah didn't look impressed. 'Where's the wicked witch? There's always a wicked witch.'

I grinned.

'A hippy *and* a realist. I like it.'

'I want to be optimistic and believe in the good of the human race, but the reality is, as a species, we suck. So where did it sour. Divorce? Infidelity?'

'Oh no, they really were blissfully happy for forty years. I was born, my twin brothers, numerous cherished dogs and cats came and went, they bought and paid off their home, took fabulous holidays quite regularly and flourished in their careers until they retired at a sensible time—and, worst of all, I never once saw them speak a single disrespectful word to one another. It was an unbelievably stable family—I had literally only had one bedroom until I moved out when I went to uni.'

'What a frightful fucking childhood.' She raised an eyebrow at me. 'You poor thing.'

'Don't worry, it *did* sour.' It always felt like a thunderstorm rolling in, remembering the loss. I tried to keep it light. 'Mum died of a stroke, very suddenly when she was sixty. She was as fit as an ox, and then a minute later, she was gone. A week later, Dad dropped dead too. They said it was a heart attack.'

'But you know it wasn't.'

Her words caught me by surprise.

'Yeah, I *know* it wasn't. There was nothing suspicious about his death—he just stopped living. They'd built their whole lives around each other—when Mum went, Dad had nothing left. Hell, I'm surprised he lasted a week. That's the problem with fairy-tale love—and there's your wicked witch. True love is just a synonym for desperate dependency.'

'I don't even believe in true love—what utter bullshit that concept is. And your story isn't sour—it's beautiful. They had forty years of happiness, and a great life together. Your mum went quickly, and your dad subconsciously chose to follow. I'm sure it was horrendous to lose them both like that, but at the end of the day, just like your move to Manly, it is what it is. Besides which, you and your brothers are the product of their relationship, so in a sense, their union lives on.'

It was my first taste of blunt Lilah, and for a moment I wasn't sure what to make of her. I leant back in my chair and surveyed the beautiful contradictions—the empathy in her eyes, the hard lines around her mouth. It suddenly struck me that Lilah was *listening* to me—really listening, as if I was a subject that commanded an intense focus. Her dismissal of my grief stung a little, but this was tempered by the surprise of her full attention.

I've used romance to market products a hundred times, feeding the public with the line that you can meet someone, and they can understand you and you can understand them, and together the world will be an easier place for the both of you. We usually dress it up as sex in an ad campaign, but at the end of the day, people are looking for connection, and that's why sex works so well as a sales tactic.

And there was me, who'd understood the concept intellectually for as long as I'd been an adult, sitting in a slightly dingy pizza shop at nearly forty years old and maybe wanting that for myself for the very first time. There had been lovers, even girlfriends, who had passed through my life without ever really knowing me, and when they moved on, I was left unchanged. Even if Lilah stormed out of the restaurant midway through our pizza, I had a feeling that wouldn't be the case.

'I have just revealed more about my family to you than some of my lifelong friends know. And you've just been more brutal to me than any of them ever were, even though I still do enjoy a good wallow on this very topic even a decade later.'

'You just need better friends,' she told me, and we both laughed.

The pizza arrived, silently slid onto the table between us by the effectively invisible waiter, and Lilah waved her hand over it.

'Survey the wonders of an environmentally sustainable approach to food, my friend.'

It did look like a regular pizza, except that where meat should have been, there were chunks of pumpkin and olives. I sighed and reached for a slice, the largest slice, and somehow it felt too light in my hands.

'The next time I pick up some filthy stranger on the ferry, I'm sending her home for a footbath and some shoes so we can go somewhere with real food.'

'Literally every single time *I* pick up a stranger on the ferry and bring him here, he complains when I make him eat the vegan thin crust.' She slipped a slice of pizza onto her plate and grinned at me. 'Bon appetite!'

'Why be vegan?' I asked her, after my first few bites. The pizza was surprisingly tasty, but not substantial. I knew I'd be starving within a few hours.

'The cashew cheese hasn't convinced you?' She feigned shock. 'It was a revelation when I first tried it.'

'A revelation enough to abandon pretty much every delicious food known to man?'

'I spent a bit of time in China a few years ago. I was travelling with a friend, and one of his uni buddies was working in healthcare in an isolated village. A bunch of elderly people in that village were still amazingly healthy—but their grandchildren were all obese and sick. It all came down to diet. Even as available healthcare improved, more meat and dairy crept into what they were eating, and so in spite of what *should* have happened, the new generation was in serious trouble health-wise, while the old guys carried on.'

'So that was enough to inspire you to give it all up?'

'Not even a little bit.' She grinned at me. 'I went on to Europe, then months in Central America before I finally came back and committed to a plant-based lifestyle. But, yes, I have completely eschewed animal food products since then. My carbon footprint is at least nine tonnes a year less than yours.'

'And that's a good thing, right?'

Lilah rolled her eyes.

'That's a good thing.'

'Was this when you were at uni? A gap year?'

'Oh no, this was only a few years ago,' Lilah said as she reached for more pizza. 'I took a year off work and went to see the world.'

'I keep meaning to do that.'

'What's stopping you?'

'I have absolutely no idea. My brothers are in Melbourne and Paris; from time to time they email me and ask me when I'll visit. There's nothing much keeping me here other than my job. But, you know, there are a bunch of things I just can't get around to, and a holiday is one of them, even though I know I really need to go see them both, or meet them half-way, or, I don't know… something.'

'Life is short, you know.' The blue eyes twinkled. 'I could *very* easily have thrown you overboard on that ferry today and you'd never have seen your brothers again, or ever caught a glimpse of the Eiffel Tower.'

'I've seen it on Google Earth. It didn't seem that great.'

'I saw Paris the first time when I was nineteen. My then boyfriend and I backpacked over the summer holidays. We lived off baguettes and cheap cheese and slept in flea-ridden backpacker hostels. When I saw the Eiffel tower, I was with the man I thought I'd marry. It was like a dream.'

'I thought you didn't believe in true love.' I was irrationally, embarrassingly jealous.

'Who said anything about true love? It was my first taste of sex that didn't end in tears and I thought that was special. We sat and watched the snow fall on the Eiffel Tower and shared some cheap food and snuggled and it was *the* most amazingly romantic moment.'

'So, where was the wicked witch?' I prompted.

'Back at the hostel. Later that night, I caught them going for it. Next to me while I slept. On the same bed—they were even under the same *blanket*.'

I winced, and she giggled.

'It's a great story, isn't it?'

'Is it real?'

'Every disgusting detail.'

'So the takeaway message is "go to Paris with someone you love—but sleep with one eye open?"'

'No, Callum. The takeaway message is "just go to bloody Paris." It's not that hard.'

'You sound like my HR manager.'

'Oh, well, if you won't listen to the HR manager, I'm wasting my breath.' Lilah laughed again, then reached for the menu on the table. 'For someone who's not impressed with cashew cheese, you ate pretty much the whole pizza.'

She was right—and I was still ravenous.

'Oops.'

'More pizza?' she suggested, then flipped the menu over and turned it around to display the wine list. 'Fancy a red?'

❄ ❄ ❄

It took me about one hour with Lilah to realise that she lived and breathed her job. Up until that moment I'd have said I did too, but Lilah's job was a cause, and mine was a career. The difference was crystal clear.

'Do you remember hearing in the media last year about the fight for that tree over near Shelly Beach?'

'Vaguely,' I lied. If I'd heard about it, I hadn't paid enough attention to remember it. I'd probably seen an article here or there and dismissed it as hippy rubbish.

'That was my firm, my case. A developer wanted to knock down a tree on the edge of the reserve so that he had an un-obstructed ocean view from his kitchen sink.'

'I didn't even know there was a reserve over there.' Her eyes widened and I grimaced. 'Sorry. And this case was a big deal?'

'A big deal… are you kidding me?' Her face fell. 'You didn't even *hear* about it?'

'I'm sure I heard about it.' Another lie, and not a very convincing one this time because she tilted her head at me and narrowed her gaze. 'I just don't remember the details.'

'The whole community got involved, Callum. There were fundraising events every weekend to pay our legal fees! There were public meetings and protests just down the block from here! How do you miss six months of controversy right on your own doorstep?'

'Wait a minute. All that was for *one* tree?'

'It was only one tree, but it was two hundred years old. And, remember, the tree's only crime was to grow directly in front of the view some corporate fat cat wanted to enjoy two weeks a year when he holidayed here.'

'You spent six months working to save one tree.'

'You're missing the point, Callum. Yes it was *one* tree. But it represented something to this community, and we stopped *one* guy and his big fat chequebook from demolishing it. And you know what? In a hundred years' time that developer will be long gone and the tree will still be there. And we *did* that.'

There was a joy in her eyes, a shining pride and determination, and even speaking about the case was so exciting to her that she'd become fully animated—gesturing wildly with her hands as she explained it to me. When Lilah spoke about her work, there was real meaning to it all—some kind of cosmic importance that I'd never come close to, and even she seemed to get caught up in the wonder of that. She was saving endangered species and fighting for compensation and opposing dangerous mining practices. When she had success at work, the ecosystem was protected or people's lives genuinely improved. When I had success at work, sales were made and products shifted. The generational impact of her profession would be fathomless and positive; the generational impact of mine was probably obesity and a sense of poverty and need, regardless of how wealthy people really were.

The stark contrast should have been confronting, but there was something magnetic about that kind of passion. Maybe it was the confidence it took to commit to something so fully, or maybe it was just the enthusiasm that radiated from her. Whatever it was, I was completely enthralled.

'I'll show you,' she said suddenly.

'Show me what?'

'The tree. You'll understand when you see it.'

Lilah and I had finished both the bottle and the second pizza, and the restaurant had begun to close around us. It was time to move on, and I had been hoping to leave with her, but I was thinking we'd head *towards* my apartment, rather than *away* from it.

'Now?'

'Yep.'

'In the dark?'

'It's a fifteen-minute walk and there's a path the whole way. I could find my way there blindfolded. Couldn't you?'

'Actually...'

Her eyes widened, then narrowed.

'Please don't tell me you've never been there.'

'Well, I know it's there; it's just that the main beach is closer and I've heard Shelly Beach is tiny.'

'You've got to be kidding me. You live in Manly and you've never been to Shelly Beach?'

'There are plenty of things here I haven't done.'

'What *have* you done? You're never going to make it to Paris if you can't even get yourself to Shelly Beach. Come on.'

'But… you don't have any shoes.'

'Why would I need shoes to go to the beach?'

'So you don't tread on a syringe?'

'Oh, Jesus, Callum, if I avoided risks that remote, I'd never do *anything*,' Lilah laughed, even as she shook her head at me. She was already reaching for the bill and I moved to take it from her.

'Oh, let me—'

'I wasn't going to pay.' She shot me a pointed glance. 'I'll pay half.'

The stubborn determination in those wide-blue eyes told me not to bother protesting.

'Of course.'

We stepped from the warmth of the restaurant into the semi-darkness of the street. There was a chill to the air, and as I moved to protest one last time against the late-night trek, Lilah silently slipped her hand into mine. My words died before they even left my mouth and I automatically closed my fingers through hers.

It was such an innocent gesture, and of course it was nothing—nothing compared to the intimacy I'd shared with other women, or even the intimacy I was already hoping to share with Lilah at some point. But her hand in mine, the fragile softness of her skin, the warmth of our palms together… it was breathtaking. I looked down into her eyes and the promise and the excitement that simmered there. We shared a smile. I'd have stood there for longer, enjoying the peaceful simplicity of being connected, but Lilah apparently had other plans, tugging gently at my arm as she led me towards the ocean.

'I can't understand how someone could live in this suburb and have never snorkelled in Cabbage Tree Bay. You know it's an aquatic wildlife reserve, right?'

'I do now.'

Lilah half-laughed, half-groaned.

'It's the only aquatic reserve in Sydney. And people come from all over the world to see it; there are nearly two hundred aquatic species in the reserve including five that are endangered. Have you ever been scuba-diving?'

'No... I wouldn't mind giving it a try though. I love photography; I thought one day I might try some underwater.'

'There are dive schools right here in Manly; you don't even have to leave home.' I could hear the confusion in her voice, and I actually understood. My own inertia had been bewildering me too. It was like I couldn't get myself into gear to do even the things that I desperately wanted to do, and so what I *did* do—sometimes *all* I did do—was work and procrastinate.

'So you scuba-dive too?' I asked her.

'Actually I don't enjoy it. I've done it and it makes me feel claustrophobic. But that doesn't mean it's not worth trying. '

We'd come to a road, and stopped to wait for a break in the traffic. Our hands were still entwined between us. We each walked with our laptop slung over our outer-most shoulder.

'What *do* you do to relax, Lilah?' I asked her.

'Relax?' she repeated. 'Isn't this relaxing?'

'Running towards a beach in the middle of the night with an environmentally uneducated near-stranger is relaxing?'

'*Strolling* towards the beach in the moonlight with a *new friend* is relaxing. Are you one of those people who think you can only relax while you're still?'

I laughed.

'Actually, yes.'

As we wound our way away from the commercial precinct and towards the reserve, shop lights faded to street lights which then faded to the light of an almost full moon. The transition was steady but subtle, and along with it came a new quiet, the bustle of traffic and voices giving way to the sound of waves and words spoken more softly.

'Have you really not been over here? Not ever?' she asked.

I'd never even been to the main beach at night, let alone the secluded smaller beach that Lilah was hauling me towards. I'd seen the path and vaguely understood that it led to a tiny beach, but hadn't been interested enough to walk it myself at any point.

'I genuinely have not. Is it really that fantastic?'

'You'll see for yourself in a few minutes. Well, you'll see the night-time version.' After a few steps, she glanced at me. 'I don't get that. How can you live so close and not go exploring?'

I shrugged.

'I'm exploring it now. I like to wait for adventure to find me. It's safer that way.'

'There is nothing safe about that,' she assured me. 'It sounds like you're at serious risk of dying from boredom.'

'I'm not bored,' I said. There was a thread of defensiveness in my tone and I hastened to add, 'I'm content. Isn't that what you're supposed to strive for in life?'

'It depends on who you ask.' She stopped suddenly and pointed in front of us into the darkness. 'There's the rock pool down there, so we're halfway.'

'Do you do things like this often?'

'Like what?'

'Late-night environmental education sessions with dates.'

'Well, for a start, I don't go on *dates*,' she laughed. 'I'm not quite sure what happened back there on that ferry actually. I'd normally have shot you down in about a millisecond.'

'I'm really glad you didn't.'

It was a funny thing to be walking in the moonlight, hand in hand with her, the clear night sky above us and the waves crashing onto rocks below us. If I'd had six weeks to prepare a special night and an unlimited budget to create atmosphere, I could never have topped it. It was as if the night itself was gently nudging us, pushing us nearer to each other. Even as we neared our goal, I noticed that our footsteps had actually slowed and we'd each relaxed our joined arms, as if we'd been holding hands and walking in step for decades.

Then the beach was before us in the moonlight, the sand surprisingly bright against the darkness of the rocks around it.

'Where's this tree—' I started to ask, but Lilah let go of my hand and ran ahead of me, down towards the water.

'Beach first,' she called back. 'Come on!' I laughed and shook my head, watching as she sat her handbag on a flat rock and then sprinted down towards the water, her hair blowing behind her like a jet stream. Then I winced as she failed to slow down even as she neared the water's edge.

'Lilah, that water is going to be freezing!'

'I'm not going swimming! But you can't go to the beach and not stand in the waves—it's against the law you know,' she exclaimed.

'Well, you *would* know.' I muttered, although I knew she wouldn't be able to hear me; she was now well ahead of me. The beach was sheltered and the waves were low. Lilah dropped her pace at the last minute but splashed her way into the water anyway. I sat my laptop down beside hers, and then walked slowly across the sand.

'Okay, no shoes was strange, but this is certifiably crazy,' I informed her.

'Are you kidding?' She turned back momentarily to give me a pointed look I couldn't miss even in the darkness. 'You're not coming in?'

'Not coming in? Of course I'm not coming in!' I laughed.

Lilah spun around, so that her back faced the bay. She edged backwards until the waves were lapping mid-calf, and then extended a hand towards me.

'You're coming in, Callum.'

'Seriously, it's not happening.' The very idea of it had me shivering. I laughed at the determination that marked her face and her stance. 'I'm enjoying the view from here—there's no need for me to get wet.'

'There's *every* need for you to get wet,' she frowned. 'You can stand there and watch me enjoy it, or you can take your damn shoes off and try it yourself. You know this water covers seventy per cent of the earth's surface, right? Take two tiny steps in front of you and you can temporarily be a part of something that's nearly as big as the earth itself.' She extended her hand again, her grin both playful and patient. 'It's really that easy, I promise.'

'It's *freezing*.' I somehow decided that it was time to point out the blatantly obvious to someone who knew even better than I that I was right. Maybe I was running out of excuses.

'It's not so bad once you're used to it.' She gestured towards me, beckoning me. I hesitated, and then was startled to realise how close I was to diving in after her. My resolve, or maybe my sanity, resurged and I took a determined step back and shook my head.

'I'm *not* coming in. I'll get sand in my shoes!'

'Yes. You will.' she agreed. 'But tell the truth, you already *have* sand in your shoes, don't you?'

I squeezed my toes and felt the grit beneath my socks.

'But...'

'Let me put it another way.' She dropped her outstretched hand to her thigh then drew it slowly back up her body to plant it on her hip. Her body language shifted, her hip jutting towards me, her shoulders arched back, her chin dropped. 'Do you want to kiss me?'

If she hadn't already, she now had my full attention. Lilah slowly tossed her hair back from her face and there was no missing the way her expression morphed from teasing to downright taunting.

'Well?' she prompted. She had me and she knew it.

'You are awfully confident, Lilah Owens.'

'I can read you like a book. You want to kiss me and I'd love you to kiss me. But I can also see that deep down inside you want to paddle too, so I'm not getting out of this water until you're in it. If you *really* want to bring this exhaustive night of flirtation to an end, you're going to have to take off the bloody shoes and come on in.'

I groaned and bent down to roll my trousers up to my knees then remove my black leather work shoes. Next I folded my grey socks up and stuffed them inside. My feet made their first contact with the shock of the cold, coarse sand and I gasped.

'This kiss had better be worth it,' I muttered.

She cheered playfully as I neared the water's edge. The coarse sand became finer, and I yelped as my foot hit water for the first time.

'That's *freezing*.'

'Oh, please. If you think this is cold then you've obviously never been to Russia.'

As soon as she had my hand, she dragged me a few steps further into the water so that it now passed my ankles.

'Well, you lured me in here with the promise of a kiss…'

'I was actually going to peck you on the cheek and run away,' she grinned, but the smile faded as we automatically stepped closer together.

'*Was* going to?' My voice was dropping. Lilah rested her hand on my chest and our gazed locked, the playful moment coming to an abrupt end.

The waves were splashing around my calves, and somehow all of her nonsense about standing within something as large as the earth itself seemed sensible and amazing. I reached to touch her cheek with the back of my forefinger, then turned my hand to cup her face as I bent all the way down to kiss her. It was a gentle kiss, a reverent kiss, although I daresay it wouldn't have stayed that way for long had an unexpectedly large wave not drenched me to my thighs in icy cold water.

Lilah burst out laughing and dragged me back towards the shoreline. Being so much shorter than me, she was now wet well and truly to her backside. I was laughing like I hadn't done in as long as I could remember, chuckling with that kind of breathless joy and shock that steals away your words. She collapsed onto the sand and I sat heavily beside her. But for the fact that my toes felt like ice and the bottom half of my trousers were dripping, I might have suspected I was having a particularly trippy dream.

'Whoops,' Lilah said.

'You were right,' I laughed. 'That was magical.'

She pulled her handbag down off the rock beside us and sat it behind her, then lay all the way back to use it as a pillow.

'Your suit… the sand…' I started to protest, but she pulled a face that suggested I was missing the point again. I sighed and copied her, propping my laptop case behind my head.

'Look at the stars,' she said. 'Don't you hate how the light pollution of the city washes them out like that? You can't even see the Milky Way from here. My place at Gosford is only ninety-odd kilometres away, but it's like a whole other sky. I've been sitting on my deck late at night and I've seen shooting stars that pop like camera flashes.'

I felt for her hand against the cold sand and entwined our fingers again. It struck me that she saw the cloudless night sky as a pale imitation of its potential, but right beside her I was staring at exactly the same view, stunned by the spectacle of it. I tried to remember if I'd ever stared up at the stars as a kid. I could remember Dad dragging me camping with him and the twins a few times—surely I'd looked up at least once. Or maybe I hadn't, because it seemed as if I was seeing the enormity of the night sky with brand new eyes.

Lilah sighed heavily beside me then moved closer, but at the same time I tried to snake my arm around her and we giggled together like teenagers as we awkwardly collided. Eventually she settled so that her head was resting on my chest. Finally, I managed to slide my arm all the way around her. She was slight, and the weight of her in my arms was like nothing at all, especially compared to the weight of the moment.

'We're going to catch hypothermia and die,' I said softly.

'And your final words will be, *I so wish I'd gone to Paris,*' Lilah murmured.

I chuckled and felt the answering rumble of her chest against mine. For a few minutes, we lay like that in the cold sand, staring at the stars and enjoying the closest thing to silence a person can find in the city. Eventually Lilah turned to rest her chin on my chest and stare up at me. I brought my other hand up to touch the thick softness of the wild mess of hair around her shoulders then brushed my fingers over her lips.

And then she stretched up so that her face was over mine and she kissed me.

This was a different kiss to the one we'd shared in the water. Slow and almost wondrous, it was the physical equivalent of our soft conversation as we'd walked from Manly to the beach. We were learning one another, and the freezing sand against my back and my wet trousers and feet faded into oblivion as the warm glow of the kiss took over.

When Lilah relaxed away from me a few moments later, I felt dizzy, like things had spun out of control. Something was happening between us, something I didn't have words for yet, but something very real. Lilah settled back into her previous position, now using her forearm on my chest as a pillow, and stared at me. Her gaze was quizzical and questioning.

'Have you ever had sex on the beach?' she asked, but her tone was more curious than suggestive. I raised my eyebrow at her and propped myself up a little more so that I could maintain eye contact without doing a mini sit-up.

'Nope.'

'I have,' she said, and wrinkled her nose. 'What were you saying about reality versus expectation? Sand, friction and certain body parts are not a great combination.'

'I'll bet you were stranded on a dessert island with a handsome sailor or some such adventurous combination.'

'Actually, I was in Fiji,' she laughed softly. 'I was only a little bit stranded though. Mum was singing on a cruise liner and I flew over to spend a few days with her between her cruises. It was only after I'd landed that she realised her ship was docking in Port Villa, which is actually in Vanuatu, so I was in the right region, but the wrong country. My then boyfriend and I had three days sitting around Denarau with not much planned.'

'So you made your own fun.'

'Something like that,' she agreed, then sighed. 'I have terrible taste in men. That guy was an idiot.'

'Maybe you've matured with age. You've made all of the right choices tonight.'

She laughed softly.

'Do you want to head back?'

I wanted to scoop her up in my arms and sprint back to my apartment, and at the same time, I didn't want the moonlight encounter to end.

'Didn't you bring me here to show me a tree?'

'Ah! So I did.'

I rose and helped Lilah to her feet, and we both dusted the sand off ourselves—as much as was possible given it had pretty much coated us where we were wet. Lilah led the way back up the beach and when she was on the path again, pointed up into the hill behind us. I could see the bright lights of houses along the rise. With the wide mouth of the bay behind us, I well understood someone wanting to maximise their view. I wouldn't tell Lilah that though.

'There,' she said, pointing to the silhouette of a Norfolk Island pine jutting out into the greyed night sky. I recognised it only because there is an iconic line of the same pine all along Manly beach, but the truth is, it's probably the only species of tree I know by name. It was taller than the other foliage in the area, and formed a skeletal silhouette against the glow of a very large house behind it. 'That's the tree. Now do you understand?'

Truthfully, I did not understand, not even a little bit. And I knew that even if I visited during the day, I'd still fail to see her point. I'd probably still side with the property owner, who clearly had money to burn even to own a patch of dirt with such a view, and had probably worked hard enough that he deserved to enjoy a sparkling water vista if he ever did his own dishes.

What I did understand, though, was that anyone with the determination to believe so completely in something, and the will to fight for it like Lilah clearly had, was *not* going to understand my lack of comprehension. So I whistled, as if I was as awed by the tree as I was by her, and I shook my head slowly.

'That's a real beauty. Two hundred years old you say?'

'We think so, yes.' She stared in silence for a moment, as if paying her respects. 'I *knew* you'd understand if you saw it. Some things you just have to experience for yourself, don't you?'

My gaze had wandered back down the hill, and landed on her face.

'You're absolutely right.'

❊ ❊ ❊

Just like I couldn't remember agreeing to go to the beach, I couldn't remember discussing where we were walking to, but I knew our goal was my apartment. We walked faster this time, perhaps spurred on by the rising heat between us, or maybe even the practical discomfort of dripping clothes and a cold winter's night. Our conversation came in bursts, a short sentence and a short response, and then only the sound of our breath as we walked at a slightly uncomfortable pace.

When I finally opened the door to my apartment and we stepped inside, Lilah immediately dropped her skirt onto the floor in a shower of sand. I sat my keys onto the hallstand and tried to contain my shock and delight.

She gave me that quizzical glance I was already becoming familiar with, as if my reaction was the only strange thing that was happening at the time, and wandered further into my apartment wearing her suit jacket and underpants.

'You weren't kidding when you said you were mid-renovation, were you?' she remarked. She bent to run her hand over the heavy wooden coffee table I'd paid a fortune for, inadvertently giving me a delightful view of her sand-sprinkled thighs and buttocks. 'Nice coffee table. Where's the bedroom?'

❊ ❊ ❊

The next day I woke up excited and it felt strange. Life wasn't exciting to me anymore, and it hadn't been for a long time. Lilah really had been wrong when she said I was bored, and I certainly wasn't unhappy—I'd just achieved everything I wanted to, and then I'd fallen into a holding pattern.

Lying there, with the scent of Lilah on my sheets, I felt something within me coming back to life. It was the tinniest green bud on the starkly bare branch, but it was still there, and I knew that it could flourish into something remarkable.

I realised as soon as I opened my eyes that she was already gone. Lying in bed, I scanned the room for some physical sign that she'd really been there, but the shirt by the door... the jacket by my bed... her handbag in the space where my built-in-wardrobe would go one day... it was all gone.

I showered and dressed for work, forcing an inner monologue about the day's meetings and deadlines so the disappointment didn't have any room to rise. I had artwork to review with one team, a pitch presentation I needed to start, and a new client to court. I needed to talk to HR about filling that copywriting position and write the performance management plan for the researcher who was giving me headaches. The board meeting was only a week away and I still wasn't sure if I should recommend adopting the proposed IT budget for next year. So much to do, so little time, especially after a totally unproductive night.

It was only as I stepped onto the ferry and caught myself scanning the peak-hour crowd for a glimpse of her that I acknowledged the heavy feeling in my gut.

I didn't want to be Lilah's one-night stand—but the worst thing was, I hadn't *expected* to be. I'd been caught completely off guard, and it stung that I'd made myself vulnerable enough to feel so disappointed after just one night.

CHAPTER TWO

Lilah

26 August

It's seven a.m. and I find myself at the café near the court-house. I sat outside, as if early morning sun rays might find me, even though experience tells me that the skyscrapers all around me will block them. This patch of cement only sees sun for an hour or so at noon, and only in summer, because the monstrous tower across the road is at just the right angle to block direct light altogether in winter. And knowing all of this from years of arguing at this court house and having brunches and lunches at this very café in between sessions, I sat out here anyway. I'm not sure if that makes me an optimist or a slow learner.

I've been sitting here looking at the blank page of this journal for a few minutes, trying to remember how to start. It's been five years since I wrote in one of these books. They were busy years, years with zero time or tolerance for the kind of self-absorbed navel gazing I once did in these things. I bought this particular notebook nearly six months ago, on a bad day, when I was sure I was about to get sick again. It's always there, right at the front of my mind, and that wasn't the first time that I'd convinced myself that the remission had ended and the nightmare had returned. The bad day passed and I stayed well, but I kept the journal on my desk at home—a visible reminder every time I walked past. I can't afford to take the beauty of life for granted, because I'm living mine on borrowed time.

Journaling has been my solace and companion during the troughs of my life, but more than that, it was always a simple way to take the intangible essence of myself and make it tangible. Thoughts are like vapour—they disappear in the wind. But words on paper... well, that can be forever, or close enough to. I can write my soul here today, and come back tomorrow to check—is that still who I am? I suppose when I've felt lost in time, my journal has been an odd type of compass.

Ah, prattle. That's what I used to do on these pages, I'd let the thoughts drain from me like I was bleeding out and the paper was absorbing my essence. I stopped writing because it felt like a self-indulgent waste of time, and time was something I could not afford to waste.

I'm running on virtually no sleep between the late night with Callum and the insanely early morning I had studying up for court today. I've been sipping today's green smoothie—extra kale and wheatgrass. I felt I needed the vitamin boost. And all of these thoughts are just a way to postpone facing the real reason I've come running for this journal again: I'm feeling unsettled. I don't do unsettled, not these days, when everything is in place and organised and I know exactly what it is I'm here to do.

I only agreed to have dinner with Callum because I was caught off guard. Shit, I could easily list a dozen reasons why now is not the time to start a relationship. That judgmental look he cast me on the ferry really got my hackles up, and the next thing I knew, I was genuinely enthralled in the dinner conversation.

Yes, there was a moment late that night when, lying in his arms in the darkness of his half-renovated apartment, maybe it was nice to daydream about seeing him again. We could meet for a casual coffee, or a drink together at the bar on the ferry one evening. We could talk for hours again, make love at his place. This time I'd stay and we could wake up together and he could explain to me how he managed to live in that godawful unit. It reminded me of Grandma and Pa's house, during the second week of my renovations. The first thing I saw when we stepped inside was the wall of paint samples. He's obviously had ideas over time about what the colour scheme might be: in perfectly straight columns and rows, he's painted tiny patches. There are dozens of them now, all perfectly ordered, line after line of indecision.

The kitchen is in pieces, there's a jagged hole in the ceiling in the living area where he obviously intends a light, and the skeleton of a built-in wardrobe rests against a wall in the bedroom. It's all functional I suppose, but definitely mid-job. When I renovated, I couldn't wait to get it all done and enjoy the final product. But Callum openly admitted that he'd left it like that for months? Bizarre.

What was it about Callum that had me so fascinated? He's exactly the kind of guy I have historically avoided like the plague. He has a fancier haircut than me, for a start, with his curls sitting just-so atop his head and the back and sides perfectly short. Plus, I'm pretty sure there was product in those curls. *Product.* For fuck's sake, *I* don't even use product. And was his chest genuinely bare or had he *waxed* it? And even if I give him the benefit of the doubt and assume he really is some kind of six-foot hybrid of masculinity and just-so locks and hairless skin, he still smelt like he'd just stepped off an after-shave ad. Maybe it was his shampoo or deodorant—or both. Whatever it was, it was no doubt laden with methylchloroiso-thiazolinone and sodium laureth sulfate and God only knows what else. I should probably have warned him that he's dous-ing himself with industrial chemicals that will mess with his endocrine system and fry his cell-aging process.

The worst of it though was the whole corporate-capitalist thing. It seems crazy when I think back to what I was like when I was working in corporate law myself, but I can't help but loathe that whole lifestyle now. Work harder to earn more money to buy more things so that companies can pay their staff more money which they can use to buy more things? It's madness.

At times when he spoke last night, I'm sure I could hear his life straining at the seams, wanting to burst open from the cage he's contained himself in. I saw in Callum the same confused dissatisfaction I once felt myself when I was stuck up to my eyebrows in the corporate lifestyle. Maybe the only reason I'm still thinking about him today is that he triggered in me some need to rescue him, because he reminded me of myself, once upon a time.

Shit. Who am I kidding? I really liked him. I liked the square set of his jaw and the surprise in his smile just about every time I spoke last night. I liked his quiet confidence, and the hint of wild creativity that's hiding somewhere in there under the suit, just waiting to be unleashed on the world.

And probably most of all, I liked how safe I felt in his arms, like I was coming home after an exhausting, madcap adventure and I could finally rest. I liked showing him my tree, and dragging him into the water. It would be fun just to share hours with him, to watch the startled pleasure on his face as he smashed his way out of the rut he's stuck in.

In another life, I'd have been giddy like a schoolgirl right now figuring out how to bump into him again. Instead, I'm one day into what is potentially a lifetime of driving to work so I *don't* see him.

It wouldn't be fair to either of us. I just wish it was. Oh, to just relax and enjoy the blind naivety that Callum does. I wish I too could believe that the years will be generous, that there's time to frit away, waiting for life to come to me. I wish I had the space for flirtations and silly love affairs with men who use hair product. If only I could just throw a few nights or weeks into this thing and see where it took me. It wouldn't have to be happily ever after—happy *for now* would do.

CHAPTER THREE

Callum

I was frantically busy at work, which was business as usual. The directors liked to keep the workload at burnout pace, which was probably why I'd been at Tison Creative since my internship. Junior staff were disposable assets, and if you happened to survive long enough to get a promotion, the pressure became a way of life.

I was the conduit between the creatives and the business at Tison's. When new work was on the horizon, it was me who took the phone call and then later presented the pitch. And I was good at that, bloody good actually. I loved standing before rooms full of suits and trying to change their minds, in the same way that I loved managing campaigns to change the public's mind. There is something very addictive about making people's thoughts line up with yours. I've often wondered whether, if I'd been religious, I would have been one of those television evangelists, getting rich converting people to my way of thinking.

Once we had secured a job it was my role to manage the flow of work all the way through to the final invoice. I passed the tough messages downwards and the hopeful messages upwards. So, it was my job to send the email that cancelled all planned leave during the election campaign, to fire the graphic artist who'd been caught chatting on infertility forums during business hours, and to announce the board's decision to take on the cigarette company's account. There have been times during my career at Tison's when I have been able to walk from the elevator all the way to my desk in the corner office without a single person smiling or even acknowledging me. I have never been at work to make friends, and that's probably why I only had one there.

His name was Karl Dickson, and he was one of the senior designers and an all-round nice-guy. The yin to my work yang—well liked, friends with everyone, good at remembering the details of people's lives and enjoying small talk with them at the water cooler. He had arrived at Tison's with the ink on his degree still wet around the same time I did, and we'd climbed the corporate ladder side by side over the past eighteen years. Karl lived on the creative side of the marketing divide, which was probably how we'd wound up friends—we were never directly competing. I imagine if we'd gone head to head for a position or even an account in the early days, our friendship would have imploded pretty quickly. Instead, we'd shared nearly two decades of life, and although we rarely saw each other outside of work now that he was a husband and father, he was closer to me than my brothers.

We had a morning ritual, when our schedules allowed it. Sometime between nine and nine thirty a.m., we'd meet by the ridiculous pot plant outside my office. It was a plastic palm tree in a plastic pot, and I'm sure someone thought it would make the work environment more appealing, but, at least to me, it represented everything that frustrated me about Tison's and our work there. The plant never grew, it couldn't die—it seemed to have absolutely no purpose other than to fill the space. I suppose in that sense it was the perfect place for me to meet with the one human being in the office I had

actually formed a friendship with. Beside the pot plant was a
stairwell, so we'd walk the ten flights of stairs to the café at the
bottom of our building and catch up on any news of the day,
work related or other. Karl was happily married these days,
but once upon a time we'd hit the town together after work
and then met back at the pot plant in the morning to swap
offensively shallow tales from the nightclub scene.

We both grew up though. Karl grew up into a loving husband and father. And I grew up too, purely because my job
took up all of the available space in my life and I no longer
had time for juvenile games. Besides which, these days, even
if I did manage to have dinner or more with a woman, I had
at last achieved enough maturity not to brag about it.

The morning after Lilah, though, the words spilled from
my mouth like lava from a volcano.

'I met the most amazing woman last night.' The door
hadn't even shut behind us as we stepped into the stairwell.
Karl was in front, about to begin the long walk downwards,
but he turned to stare at me, his expression stuck somewhere
between disbelief and bemusement.

'On a Thursday?' He laughed out loud. 'Shouldn't you
have been at home working?'

He began the descent down the first flight of stairs, and I
pulled the door shut and followed him.

'I met her on the ferry. She wasn't wearing shoes. I asked
her why. We got talking. Went out for dinner and connected
in a way I didn't even know was possible. Then we went back
to my place. I woke up and she was gone.'

'For someone who finally broke a dry spell, you don't look
very happy.'

'She was gorgeous: smart, witty—the whole package. And
then she just disappeared while I was asleep.'

'You can't tell me you've never been the one to disappear,' Karl shrugged. 'You got laid, and you didn't have an awkward morning after. Sounds win-win to me.'

'Except for the part where I don't have her contact details and I'm assuming since she didn't leave them she's not hoping to hear from me again.'

My words echoed around me in the stairwell and I heard how petulant I sounded. As he turned the first corner to the floor below us, I saw Karl grinning to himself.

'I think someone is smitten.'

'Fat lot of good it's going to do me.' I was outright sulking now. There was no hiding it.

'Google her.'

I'd googled her on my phone on the way to work. Apparently either Lilah Owens, lawyer, kept an incredibly low profile—or she'd given me a false name. I had a sneaking suspicion it was the latter. With another search, I quickly found the public outcry and then the media coverage of the tree at Shelly Beach being saved, and even a reference to a bunch of lawyers who'd worked on the case, but the name she'd given me wasn't mentioned anywhere.

'That's a little too stalker-ish for my liking,' I lied.

'So your game plan is to—what—hope you run into her on the ferry again and she doesn't jump overboard to get away from you and your crappy sexual performance?'

'My sexual performance was fine. And something like that.'

That was precisely my plan. In fact, I was already formulating my next move. The only common ground I really had with her in our day-to-day lives was the ferry, and so I was going to stagger my ferry trips as much as possible and try to bump into her again. A phone number, or even her real name, would have been easier, but in the absence of those things I was going to have to find a hidden well of patience.

❄ ❄ ❄

As the morning wore on, my thoughts turned to the conversation I'd had with Lilah about visiting my brother, Ed. I opened my email and began to construct a message to him.

I had a sister-in-law I'd never met, whose name I could never remember, and embarrassingly she'd been married to my brother for several years. They'd invited me to the wedding of course, but it had been a whirlwind romance and they'd only given a few weeks' notice. I vaguely remembered trying to shuffle a few things at work and realising that it wasn't going to happen, and informing Ed via email that I wouldn't be there. I had a feeling our infrequent communications became markedly more so after I missed his wedding.

Ed, I really need to come see you and meet...

Lizette? Suzette? Hell.

...your lovely wife. When's a good time to visit?

I sent the email. Ed replied almost immediately and suggested the European winter which was months away, and I was thrilled—it was far away enough that I could postpone taking any action for some time. I forwarded the email to William, my brother in Melbourne, with a vague note about catching up on the phone sometime and maybe arranging to go to France together.

And then, feeling as if I'd at least achieved one thing for the morning, I shut my laptop and went to find lunch.

There's a shopping centre underground near my office, and I almost always sat in at the food court to eat. Generally I read the newspaper at the same time.

I'm not sure why I did something different that day. I remember the blue skies beckoning as I walked from my office to the food court, and so I got a takeaway lunch instead.

I thought I'd walk up George Street and find myself a sunny spot on Martin Place, an open air pedestrian-only plaza entirely framed by sandstone buildings. There were even a few small trees here and there and I thought yet again of Lilah. I wondered why she hadn't even woken me before she left. Had I said something to offend her? I'd been so sure she felt the connection between us too—had I been wrong? Or would she just turn up again if the mood took her? Would I hear the intercom sound one night and find her on the other side of the door as if she'd never left?

When I first saw her step from the taxi, I assumed I was imagining her. There are nearly five million people in the city of Sydney; surely I wouldn't be lucky enough to bump into her two days in a row. But there she was, just around the corner from my office, wearing in a dark grey suit this time with her hair again trapped within the confines of a too-tight bun. She stepped out of a taxi and began to powerwalk towards a lobby.

'Lilah?'

Her eyes widened when she turned towards me, and I saw her sharp intake of breath. I couldn't quite read the expression on her face—but it wasn't delight; if I had to guess, I'd say it was probably closer to dismay. There was a sudden drop in my guts, that feeling you get when a plane hits an air pocket and dips without warning.

Her companions, a younger man and woman, had been trailing behind from the taxi and came to an uncertain stop beside her. Around us, the buzz of the city continued, car horns sounding and engines roaring past. But the sight of Lilah filled my field of vision, and all I could think was that I'd come so close to eating in the damned food court, and I'd have missed the terrifying exhilaration of this moment.

'Wait for me in the boardroom.' Her tone was sharp, and her colleagues silently obeyed. And then we were alone—at least it felt like we were, even though George Street is the busiest street in the city.

For far too long we stared at each other. It was becoming apparent to me that Lilah was trying to figure out what to say. Should I be embarrassed to admit my heart was pounding with a flight-or-fight response? I'm not afraid of confrontation and never have been. It wasn't fear of the discussion that was affecting me; it was a stone-cold fear of rejection.

'I met this lady on a ferry once,' I said, or rather blurted, just to end the taut stretch of time since one of us had spoken. Lilah raised her eyebrows.

'You did.' She was unsurprised. Unimpressed. And, worst of all, the set of her expression was still hard. I pressed on.

'She was incredible. Best night of my life. Then she disappeared.'

'That is a terribly sad tale.'

'That's not the worst of it. I'm pretty sure she lied to me about her name.'

'The wench.' Lilah didn't deny it, and didn't look at all surprised that I suspected her subterfuge. She clucked her tongue in mock-sympathy. 'How traumatic for you. I hope you've recovered.'

'Hard to say. I still cry myself to sleep but at least I'm eating again.'

'Tell me, Mr…?'

'You can call me Mr Lonely,' I said. I realised that she was engaging in my game, which meant that in spite of the tight way she'd crossed her arms over her chest and the hard line of her mouth, she hadn't entirely closed the door on me.

'Mr Lonely. Tell me, did you and this amazing woman discuss a golden future together?'

'I thought at least some analysis of the likely success of such a future was warranted.'

She raised an eyebrow.

'Are you *sure* you're not a lawyer?'

'Why did you sneak out?' I heard the frustration in my tone and knew I needed to keep it in check. There was another moment of silence, briefer this time, but once again made awkward by the fact that she was obviously formulating a way to get rid of me.

'I told you I had court today. I had to leave early to prepare, to make up for the night I spent naked with you instead of reading.'

'Then why did you give me a false name?'

'I always give false names to men I pick up on ferries. That way if I don't want to see them again, it's easy to avoid them.' She flashed me a charming smile and I could almost have forgiven her then and there. Her words sunk in. I didn't want this conversation to be light-hearted anymore. I wanted answers.

'Are you really telling me you didn't want to see me again?'

'That's not what I said,' Lilah corrected me carefully. 'I said I gave you a false name *in case* I didn't want to see you again. We did have a really great night together.'

'Now you're lawyering me.'

'Callum,' she sighed impatiently. 'I am really not the relationship type. I thought it would be like ripping off a band-aid—over within an instant.'

The day was far too beautiful for a potentially painful conversation like this one, but even more than that, I'd *noticed* the beauty of it. For too long I'd gone through the motions, days and weeks and months and maybe years blurring into one another in a monotony. And yet this day was different to the one before it; the cycle of sameness had been shattered. I wanted to point these things out to Lilah and impress her with the depth of my thoughts. Instead, I knew I was fighting for the chance to share such things with her and to have her share her equally random thoughts with me. I'd take what I could get, from both this woman and this conversation, even just a coffee together every now and again, or the promise to smile at each other if we saw one other on the ferry.

This encounter just had to end with the chance of a continued connection.

It *had* to.

She'd shifted her attention to the revolving door beside us, and I glanced there too. *Davis McNally*. Was this where she worked, or was she there for a meeting?

It was time for a different approach, before she skittled through the doors and disappeared from my life forever.

'I think,' I said quietly, 'you were scared.'

'A little,' she admitted easily. Again I was surprised, and she shrugged her shoulders. 'I told you, we had a great night together. We really connected, and you're right, I've never clicked with someone like that before. But like I said, Callum,' she drew in a determined breath, 'I am *really* not the relationship type.'

'Well, Lilah,' I paused. 'Is it Lilah?' She hesitated, and I decided to press on. 'I'll do you a deal. Give me one dinner and I'll leave you alone.'

'You had one dinner.'

'One more dinner.'

'You *will* leave me alone—you have no choice; you don't know who I am,' she pointed out. Before I could think of my next argument, she turned on what I assumed was her most determined tone, 'So that deal is actually pretty shit, given that I already have what you're offering. No, you're going to have to argue this case on its own merits. Tell me *why* I should have one more dinner with you.'

Because I need to get to know you. One way or another, I'm going to be marvelling at how I felt last night for the rest of my life.

'I'm not the *relationships type* either,' I mocked her gently. 'I'm not looking for a wife. I'm not even looking for a girlfriend. I'm looking only to spend some time with you. End of story.'

She didn't seem impressed.

'One more dinner.' Was I pleading? Surely the whiny tone was getting close. 'Maybe you'll bore me to tears and the next time we run into each other on George Street I'll jump in front of a bus to avoid speaking to you.'

She was staring at the ground beside me, contemplating my offer I suppose. I was an anxious child waiting for approval and acceptance, literally holding my breath as she turned the request over in her mind.

'One more dinner,' she agreed. I smiled at her. She pursed her lips and her eyebrows nearly met. 'Don't go getting clingy.'

'I smiled. How is that clingy?'

'Let's do this tonight then,' she exhaled, as if she was suggesting we get a distasteful task over and done with, but I suddenly realised she was as excited about this as I was. It wasn't in her tone, but it was sure as hell in her eyes, the shared sense of relief that we'd found each other. 'How about *you* pick the restaurant this time, and I'll try to wear shoes.'

'Deal,' I said, once the celebrations in my brain had eased off and I could speak again. 'And who exactly am I having dinner with?'

'Lilah,' she said firmly. 'Lilah who will meet you at the five p.m. ferry tonight.'

'What if I break my ankle and can't make it? How will I contact you?'

'Send one of your evil advertising minions to give me a message.' She was glancing again to the revolving door, and

I knew I'd pushed my luck already. No, finding out her real name would have to wait. But that was okay. I could be patient, as long as there was a chance. 'I'm sorry, Callum, I really have to go—we're on a break from court and I need to get back to my team and prepare for the afternoon session. I'll see you at five?'

'You will,' I said, and she nodded curtly and disappeared through the revolving doors. I watched her go then turned back towards my office, the grin on my face so broad that I felt the stretch in my cheeks.

❋ ❋ ❋

The day was now a certified write-off. I sat in my office with the door closed, interspersing brief sprints of essential work tasks between long stretches of daydreaming.

When the time finally clicked over to four, I gave up on work for the day and left the office. I'd meant what I'd said to Lilah about Sydney energising me and there was something particularly inspiring about Friday afternoons. So many suits, all rushing—towards home, towards a bar, towards the park. I disappeared into the crowd and emerged when I spotted some flowers in a window. Maybe the gesture was quaint, maybe it was antiquated, but I needed to *somehow* express that I was enthralled.

And at five p.m., I was waiting at the turnstiles when she appeared. It was a long way off dark yet but the shadows were beginning to grow long, and a cool breeze was coming off the harbour. She'd let her hair out and the wind was stirring it. I had to remind myself to breathe. Belatedly, it occurred to me that environmental types might not appreciate cut flowers. I looked from her rapidly approaching figure to the bouquet in my hand and contemplated tossing them into the nearest bin.

Too late. She was right before me.

'You bought me flowers,' Lilah said. She was surprisingly, *blessedly*, pleased. 'How sweet. Thanks, Callum.'

I had to clear my throat to speak.

'You said you'd wear your shoes. It seemed the least I could do.'

She grinned at me and to my delight reached up to plant an innocent kiss on my cheek. I caught a hint of her shampoo as she brushed passed me. Lemon? Some hippy nature stuff for sure. The sand and the brine from the night before had been well and truly washed away.

'So where's dinner? Somewhere more impressive than that *last* crappy place, I hope.' She was teasing me and I loved it.

'You haven't abandoned the vegan lifestyle today, by any chance?'

'Sorry, can't say I have.'

'I guess that means the steakhouse is out.' I gestured back the way she'd come, away from the ferries. She seemed surprised.

'We're eating in the city then?'

'Prepare to be amazed.'

❄ ❄ ❄

I'd found a vegetarian restaurant in Surry Hills that had some rave reviews online, and as we sat side by side in the back of a taxi travelling there, Lilah chatted freely about her day. The tough girl I'd bumped into on George Street was gone, replaced again by the free spirit I'd been so captivated by the night before.

'Law is kind of like playing a board game with a lot of really detailed rules. It's the kind of game where you have to spend years studying just to make a single move, and then you play for months at a time before anything happens.'

'That's a great analogy. I majored in law at uni,' the taxi driver interjected.

'Really! How did you end up driving a taxi?'

'Well just like board games, some people who try to tackle the law are really good, and some people aren't. The people who aren't don't pass the Bar exam, and live on their father's couch for a decade before he buys them a taxi and kicks them out on their own.' The taxi driver and Lilah laughed. I marvelled at the instant rapport she seemed to form with people—with the small crowd she formed on the ferry in our first discussion, with the waiter at the pizza place, and now with this guy—not to mention me. Every person Lilah met was more potential new friend than stranger. I wondered what it would be like to live life open like that.

She had never been to the restaurant I'd chosen and seemed impressed that I'd found it. The pleasant glow of my success faded quickly when I picked up the menu.

'What the hell is tempeh?' The restaurant's website had said Australian vegetarian cuisine, but half of the dishes may as well have been Greek to me.

'Fermented soy.'

'Sounds delicious.' I shut the menu with a shudder. 'How about you just interpret this thing and order me something I'll actually recognise?'

And so, over a bottle of red wine, we shared several dishes. There was something called cauliflower steaks—a most misleading name, given that it was essentially just barely cooked chunks of cauliflower rolled in herbs, and marinated gluten pieces with various other stir-fried vegetables.

'Gluten is healthy now?'

'Provided you don't have celiac disease, it's fine,' she informed me wryly.

All in all, the food was nice enough—but the company was divine.

'You said you moved around a lot growing up,' I prompted her. Lilah was leaning on her elbow on the table top, and every now and again I saw her entwine a strand around her finger then smooth it down over her shoulders. She was relaxed and chatty, and I again enjoyed the full focus of her gaze on me.

'Mum is as free a spirit as you'll ever find. I was born in India, but by the time I was thirteen we'd lived in seven countries.'

'Yikes!'

'Yikes is right,' she chuckled at my surprise. 'That must appal you, Mr I-had-the-same-bedroom-until-I-was-an-adult.'

'*Appal* is the wrong word. *Amaze* is better.'

'It wasn't amazing. I had some great experiences, but when I was about to hit high school, it suddenly seemed to occur to my parents that I could barely read and didn't know how to keep friends.'

'I'm assuming you learnt to read, given your profession. So they hastily settled down?'

'Oh, no,' she laughed again and reached for her wine. 'They left me with my grandparents. Dad wasn't nearly as flighty as Mum, but by then he was just used to doing as he was told.'

'What did they do for work? How did they manage to move so much?'

'Mum is a musician. A singer, actually, and quite a good one, but she was chasing her big break right up until a few years ago. She would spend a term here and a term there, teaching or doing theatre or just lining up for endless auditions. Don't get me wrong; she had some great successes— but then there were some spectacular failures, like the year we spent in Hollywood. That whole year, she was at auditions pretty much every day without scoring a single role. So on we went. Dad, on the other hand, was a sensible horticulturalist and he brought in at least some money even when she couldn't.'

'That's an interesting combination. Did they meet at school?'

'No. Dad was a few years older than Mum; they met when he came to do a job at my grandparents' house. Pa hired him to tend the orchard one spring and he and Mum hit it off. Dad loved to be busy, so wherever we went he found something to do to bring home some money, even if it was packing shelves.'

'And your grandparents? Hippies too by the sounds of things?'

'Oh, hell, no. They were salt-of-the-earth-type people. They just happened to live on a big patch of land up near Gosford. They actually despaired over my parents' lifestyle and were more than happy to take me under their wing when the time came. They were the most patient people I've ever met. Grandma pretty much tutored me up until I could handle myself at school and Pa was an incredibly wise, gentle guy. He also happened to be a very successful lawyer. He was a partner in a general practice in Gosford, so I spent a lot of time there after school waiting for him and fell sideways in love with the law.' She shrugged. 'The rest is history.'

'Do you see much of your mother?'

'I speak to her most days, and I do go to Gosford pretty often to see my place up there. Mum and I are pretty close actually.'

'You don't resent—' I hesitated. She shook her head; there was no need for me to finish the sentence.

'No, I don't. Maybe I did when I was younger, but life's too short to hold on to that kind of thing. They made some funny choices—but, God, so have I. I just don't have a kid to inflict them on.'

'Yet?'

Again, she shook her head.

'I'm not having children.'

'Why not?' I asked.

I wasn't sure I wanted children either, but I knew I'd probably want to consider the idea if I ever settled into a stable relationship. Maybe, if we got that far, just maybe I'd change her mind. Lilah pursed her lips. I saw a crease form between her eyes as her gaze sharpened. She didn't even like the question.

'Not everyone wants children,' she said finally.

'Most people do.'

'Plenty of people don't. And there's no shortage of excellent reasons why a person would choose not to have them.'

'I agree. I just wondered what *your* reasons were.' I shrugged. 'I'm not even saying that I *do* want them, but I know why I'm hesitant.'

'Children are disastrous for the environment.'

'Mostly because they grow into adult humans—right?'

'Exactly. And there seem to be far too many of those already. It's not just that… I don't know. It's just a decision I made a long time ago and it's one I'm entirely happy with. What about you?'

'I don't plan on getting married, but if I ever did really settle down with someone, I'd probably think about kids.' I shrugged. 'I certainly don't have my heart set on them. How old are you, anyway?'

'Guess.'

'Well, to be completely honest with you, I am pretty good at judging ages and I feel like tonight is going pretty well and I don't want to risk that by guessing correctly.'

She grinned at me.

'How old are *you*?'

'I'm just on the right side of forty.' Not by much, granted. 'You're thirty.'

She laughed.

'Oh, please. That wasn't even a convincing guess.'

'Thirty-one.'

'It's going to take nine more guesses to get it right at this rate.'

'Twenty-two?' I offered, and she grinned.

'So we're about the same age then. What month were you born?'

'December.'

'Early or late?'

'New Year's Eve, actually.'

'Ah, Mum would say we're a terrible match.'

'Why is that? Star signs?'

'Actually, because you're younger than me.'

'What's your birth date?'

'Twenty-third of July.'

'You just had a birthday.'

'I did.'

'And that means I'm younger than you by, what, all of five minutes?'

'Five minutes is still five minutes. At this point I'm on the wrong side of forty and you're on the right side so...' She shrugged those skinny little shoulders. 'Well, I gave you one more dinner. I guess this is where it comes to an end.'

'Are you joking?' I was hoping she was, but her expression was deadpan. She suddenly grinned.

'Your place or mine?'

I didn't miss a beat on that one.

'Yours.'

'Ah,' I could see she regretted the offer instantly. 'Is now a good time to reinforce that whole thing we decided about *just one dinner?*'

'You can remind me in the morning,' I suggested as I motioned for the waiter to bring our bill.

❀ ❀ ❀

Lilah's unit made my unrenovated bargain look like a shack. It was only a few blocks from mine, but where my home was on the ground floor of a 1970s red-brick box, hers was on the top floor of a near-new development right on the ocean. I looked out from my kitchen into a laneway, but the balcony off Lilah's living areas skimmed the top of the pine trees that line Manly beach.

Her home was beautiful, although there was a slight discord in the mix of modernity and comfort items from her past. There were glossy white tiles and bright red leather couches, mingled with rainbow-speckled Peruvian throws and pillows. Modern wallpaper adorned one wall in the living area, a black-and-white chevron print, but this surface was then cluttered with randomly framed photos of Lilah and idyllic scenes across the world in a completely disorganised fashion. I suppose the artist in me cringed a little at the chaos of it all, but the rest of me was delighted. I was right there, in her home—and that meant that I knew where she lived.

'When someone comes home with you, do you ever feel like the dynamic changes?' She went straight to the kitchen and retrieved two glasses and a half-empty bottle of wine. 'I mean, you're *here* now. Am I host, or am I lover? Do I offer you a snack, or rip your clothes off?'

'You should definitely go with whatever impulse overtakes you,' I said, as calmly as I could given the mental image she'd just generously provided. Lilah walked past me, towards the bright red couches, and I noticed her feet.

'Your shoes are already off.'

'Of course,' she sat the bottle on a glass tabletop and curled up in the corner of the L-shaped lounge. 'Don't you take your shoes off at home?'

'Yes… but…' I laughed and shook my head, 'I didn't even notice you do it.'

'I usually do two things when I walk in the front door,' she informed me. 'I take my shoes off, and I take my bra off. The only reason I didn't do the latter is I thought you might want to do it yourself later.'

'Very kind of you.'

'I do try.'

'So, last night was pretty amazing.' I sat on the couch beside her and reached for my wine.

'It was,' she agreed.

'I was confused when you were gone in the morning.'

'And I was confused by how you live without a real kitchen.' I noticed that she'd deflected my question, and for a moment I contemplated trying to steer it back to her early morning disappearing act. I didn't want the conversation to get awkward though. I was *in* her home—wasn't that enough for now?

'I'm going to renovate it.'

'Like you're going to go to Paris?'

'Exactly.'

'What else are you *going* to do?'

'Don't you have a work-in-progress list?' I shrugged.

'My work-in-progress at the moment is finishing this wine. That's about as long as I leave things undone if I want to do them.' She sipped her wine then glanced at me. 'Maybe I can understand that you're too busy with work to go visit your brother. But seriously, that unit? What's the go with that?'

'I bought that place because I thought it'd be a fun weekend project. I had visions of spending my weeknights up a ladder and laying floorboards.'

'But?'

'But then I bought tiles for the bathroom and got them home and they weren't right,' I sighed. 'The tone was wrong, too warm for the paint I'd bought, so I took them back and was going to get some samples and try again.'

'And that was it?'

'No, I got a bunch of sample tiles, but none of them were quite right either. And by then I'd run out of steam for the bathroom and I started ripping out the kitchen. I just want it to be *right*. What's the point of a project like that if it's not perfect? Besides which, I still have everything I need there—there's no real rush.'

'The thing that amazed me most about your unit was that it's a total disaster zone; it actually looks like you're mid-construction on a house build, but yet there's not a speck of dust in it.' Lilah laughed. 'Don't look too closely here—you'll be mortified; I only wash up when I run out of clean plates.'

'Apparently it's only the big jobs I can't get around to finishing. I don't like mess.'

'When I was a kid, I went through a brief phase when I thought I'd become a cleaner, which is hilarious now that I can't even keep this place clean,' she said. 'I was probably seven or eight, we were living in New York at the time and the lady Dad was working for had a live-in housekeeper. I used to go with him to work and while he tended the garden I'd sit in that great, big house and watch the housekeeper potter around. She was always dusting... she'd dust from front door to back over the week and then start at it all over again. The house was like a mansion compared to the little bedsits we were living in and it was full of the most beautiful things I'd ever seen. I couldn't ever imagine having enough money to buy those things myself, so I thought... "Well, if I can score myself a domestic job, I can still at least *see* the beautiful things."'

'Your apartment is amazing,' I said. 'Do you wish you could travel back in time and bring seven-year-old Lilah here for a visit? She'd surely be impressed.'

'No fucking way. I'd leave her there.' Lilah shook her head fiercely. 'I wouldn't want seven-year-old Lilah to realise how fragile life is, or how unsatisfying those beautiful things would be, or even how tumultuous the next few decades would be for her. Can you imagine being innocent enough to think that being an underpaid live-in housekeeper would be the most amazing job in the world? Not a chance that I want to lose those moments or the simplicity of those thoughts, not for anything. Those years were some of the best.'

She turned her gaze on me, and it was suddenly probing.

'Did you dream of being a marketing guru when you were that age?'

'No,' I grimaced. 'You know when you're a kid, and everyone asks you what you want to do when you grow up? I used to hate that question. I always felt like adults were mocking me when they asked it. I *knew* I wouldn't be an astronaut, or a fireman, or a racing car driver. '

'Well, what did you want?'

'Honestly?' I looked into the plum depths of the wine, then back to the focus of her blue gaze. 'It's a bit embarrassing, but I wanted to be a photographer. Dad worked at the newspaper and I'd visit with him sometimes and the photographers would let me look at their cameras. I thought they were the most mysterious technology—to be able to take a moment, and lock it in time forever.'

'Jesus, you scared me,' she grimaced. 'I thought you were going to say you wanted to be a serial killer or a circus clown. Photography isn't embarrassing. Why didn't you do it?'

'I kind of did. I did a minor in photography and visual arts at uni. I just… it's not a very practical career, is it? Most people dream of some kind of art, but day-to-day… being an adult is more about paying the bills… making a life for yourself.'

'Those two things aren't mutually exclusive,' Lilah frowned. 'You can make a life for yourself and skip town every time the electricity bill arrives. And you can pay your bills and miss life altogether. My parents flitted about like they were carefree butterflies most of their marriage but I'll tell you one thing: they had a bloody fantastic life.'

'Was it *really* that fantastic? Surely you all missed the stability of home?'

'There was *no* home,' she laughed and shifted, so that she could lean against me and stretch her legs out on the lounge, her long red hair splayed over my arm and my lap like a blanket. 'I was born on the road, so to speak. I didn't understand what it was like to put roots down, or to feel settled. Every now and again we visited Grandma and Pa back in Gosford, but even so, I barely knew them at that point.'

'I just can't imagine it.' I shook my head. 'When my parents died, and when my brothers and I sold that house… I felt like I'd lost a part of myself, like it—like it had been my anchor, and then I was adrift.'

'There is something really, truly beautiful about having a place to call home,' Lilah agreed softly. 'But surely it's got to be a base to return to, rather than an anchor. Ships only use their anchors between journeys, don't they?'

'You can't always be on a journey.'

'Of course you can,' Lilah murmured. 'Life is a journey. You don't have to travel, but you always have to be going somewhere or you stagnate.'

A silence fell, and my thoughts turned towards the moment we were sharing. Both of our wine glasses were empty, and we'd shared plenty of wine at the restaurant too, but in the strangest way I felt like I was more drunk on the chat than I was on the wine. I couldn't remember ever talking like this, relaxing into a conversation with a woman and just letting the words run free. But even if the words ran out, I'd have been equally content just to sit there with her and watch for her next move.

'Do you have this effect on everyone?'

'What effect?'

'I feel like you're this teeny, tiny whirlwind, and in two dinners you've managed to jumble up every single thing I thought about my own life.'

'In a good way?'

'I think so.' I ran my fingers through the lengths of her hair for a moment, until she sat slowly and lowered her glass onto the floor beside us. She turned to me and rested her hand on my shoulder. Staring into her eyes, and with her staring right back into mine, a sudden sense of my own smallness escaped me. 'Aren't I boring to you?'

Lilah leant forward and swept her mouth ever so gently over mine.

'No, you're not boring,' she smiled as she whispered. 'Maybe you're a little maddening.' Another kiss, longer this time, soothing any offence her words might have caused. 'And maybe just a wee bit judgemental when it comes to people who don't like shoes.' The next kiss was longer still, and deeper, and when she broke away from my mouth she leant her forehead against mine and closed her eyes as she whispered, 'But I barely know you, and even I can see that there's so much more to you than all that. How could I find you boring?'

❊ ❊ ❊

I woke before her, and as soon as I did, I realised that the very best part about waking up at Lilah's apartment was that she had absolutely nowhere to run to escape me. When she stirred in my arms and I saw her eyelids flutter open, I could imagine waking this way every day for the rest of my life.

I love you, I'd whisper, and she'd whisper it back and we'd share a stinky-morning-breath kiss. There'd be extraordinary beauty in the ordinary intimacy of our life together, and I'd never feel disconnected again.

The thought was startling and I wondered where it had come from. Lilah was a beautiful, fascinating woman. I'd known plenty of those before and never even considered that I should settle down with one of them, let alone after a single night. The thought was uncomfortable, and I shifted to give her a brief good-morning kiss and asked, 'How did you sleep?'

'Like a fucking log,' she stretched and smiled at me again. 'Even though you snored.'

'I'm pretty sure that was you.' I was stark naked; there was no way I could hide my blush. I *had* slept deeply, much deeper than I could remember sleeping in a long time.

'Don't be embarrassed. Unless my neighbours complain, then you can be embarrassed—and they might; you snore *loud*.'

She was teasing me again. I kissed her forehead.

'What do vegans eat for breakfast?'

'You do realise vegans are not a whole other species. We eat food too, not just at night, but at all times of the day. Let me have a shower and I'll whip you up some fakin' bacon.'

❄ ❄ ❄

We sat out on the balcony. In the darkness the night before, I hadn't realised that it contained a veritable forest of herbs and pot plants in various states of health. Some were not just dead, they were starting to compost. There were random-sized and coloured pots in every available space, including two long grey rectangles fixed to the top of the balcony edge.

'I didn't inherit Dad's green thumb and there's no Leon and Nancy here to tend these ones,' she sighed when I asked her about the skeletal plants.

'Leon and Nancy?'

'The caretakers at my Gosford house. They're amazing. I could take these dead plants up there and they'd be harvesting them in days.'

'What's your real name?'

It genuinely slipped out; I suppose there was a great deal of curiosity dammed up behind the question by then and the pressure just grew too great, but I had planned to raise the issue with at least some subtlety.

She stirred her coffee. I don't know why she was stirring it—there was no sugar, just a splash of almond milk. The stir-ring seemed to take a very long time. Eventually she looked at up me.

'Saoirse Delilah MacDonald.'

'Seer-sha?' I tried to repeat the word the way she'd said it, but it was completely new to me. She gave me a knowing look.

'My point exactly. It's Gaelic—spelt S-a-o-i-r-s-e. Which is fine if you're in Dublin and it's a normal name, but we're not in Dublin and in spite of us moving every five minutes, we never so much as passed through the place. So I spent the first two decades of my life being called *Sao Iris* which isn't even close. '

'Sao Iris,' I laughed. 'Where did the name come from?'

'Dad was Irish; his mother was Saoirse. She died just before I was born so they seemed to think it was fitting, but I suspect Mum regretted it pretty quickly. For as long as I can remember, she just called me Lilah.'

'Saoirse,' I repeated correctly this time. 'It's actually a beautiful name.'

'It is, and it means liberty or something along those lines. I don't dislike it—I still use it professionally.'

'You told me your surname was Owens?'

'Mum's maiden name, my grandparents' surname. I was worried you'd track me down and I wasn't sure I wanted to be tracked down. Actually, I was pretty sure I *didn't* want to be tracked down.'

'So why the change of heart?'

'Who says I've had a change of heart?' It was Lilah's turn to laugh. She was wearing only sunglasses and a dressing gown but appeared totally at ease. 'I don't know, Callum. *This* is great—these last few nights have been amazing—but nothing has changed. I'm just not looking for a boyfriend.'

I thought about this for a moment. Below us, the waves rolled into the beach, and the sound filled the silence, which meant I felt comfortable to contemplate her words a lot longer than I probably would have otherwise.

'I have lost count of how many women I've slept with,' I said, when I'd formed the right sentence in my mind. 'I'm not proud of that; I guess in some ways I'm ashamed of it. I used to be the one who did the walk of shame, who gave the false name, who didn't call when I said I would. I don't think I believe in marriage or monogamy. And I'm not saying all of that to be anything other than honest, because I appreciate that's exactly what you're doing here too.'

Even behind the dark glasses, I could feel her eyes on mine. It boggled my mind that we could share such an intimate discussion after only a few nights together and that I would feel not even a hint of embarrassment.

'I don't know where this is headed, Lilah. But can't we just share whatever path it takes while it lasts?' I was impressed with how casual I sounded. The truth was I felt so nervous I had put my coffee down so that she wouldn't see me shaking. If she asked me to leave, and not to contact her again, I wasn't sure how I'd handle it.

It was her turn to sit silently for a painfully long moment. This time the ocean didn't fill the silence at all, and I felt exposed and in danger. When she finally reached across and took my hand, I could have done a cartwheel over the balcony.

'Okay,' she said slowly. 'We'll take it day by day.'

CHAPTER FOUR
Lilah

Sunday 30 August

So. Apparently I have something like a lover for the first time in five years. And, also possibly new for me, I no longer have anything like a spine.

Callum has just left, after spending two days and nights with me. *Two nights.* I distinctly remember promising myself Friday night that I would not sleep with him again, that we would keep it to dinner, and then I would immediately resume my new commute via car and never speak to him ever again.

This time I can't blame it on being caught off guard. Yes, maybe I went overboard on the wines at dinner, but it wouldn't have made much difference if I'd stuck to water.

There are no awkward silences with Callum. When the conversation fades, I can sit with him and be at ease. These last few years I have felt like there is always something to prove, another fight shuffling to the top of the queue demanding my full attention—as if I owe the world something just for being here. It is busy in my mind, too busy even to journal until now, but when he is with me I am fully in the moment. The rush of thoughts slows, and I forget all of the good reasons why we can't have a future, because the present is just potent enough to distract me from them.

We talked Saturday morning and I tried to explain to him that I just couldn't see him anymore. I didn't try very hard, because when push came to shove, I didn't want to convince him at all. So we agreed to take it moment by moment, and I made another promise to myself. After lunch, I'd send him home, and I'd do some work.

But then we decided to go for a walk along the Corso. We were any young-ish professional couple walking hand in hand, just going for a casual stroll with our takeaway coffees, making the most of the weekend. We walked through the farmer's market and while I bought some vegetables, Callum snuck into a takeaway shop and emerged with greasy hot chips and fish cocktails for morning tea then laughed at my disgust. And then I tried on hats and jokingly posed for him. He watched through the store window then he pantomimed a fashion photographer. It was so silly, ridiculous actually, but we laughed so loud that other people glanced our way and I saw one older lady flash me a knowing smile. She thought we were in love, and I wondered if she was thinking of a long-lost love of her own. This is what people do, isn't it? They meet someone who makes them laugh, and they laugh together, and the years melt away.

And all of these deliciously ordinary things these last few days have been so much fun. I own so many hats that it's ridiculous and I can't remember buying a single one of the others, they are just an instrument I use to try to avoid the freckles that I know I *can't* avoid. The black felt bucket hat I bought today will be different. This one holds a memory.

He went home then just to get some spare clothes, and later we decided to go for a run along the beach together.

I was confused when he put his runners on. Apparently he wears shoes, even when he runs on sand, which quite frankly seems insane to me. It's a pretty well-established fact that the human foot has evolved to run bare. When I said as much, Callum clutched his expensive running shoes to his chest in mock-horror and pointed out that he hadn't mentioned my bare feet *all day* so the least I could do was let him wear his shoes.

And so we did the length of the beach, me at my top speed, him barely jogging, allowing me to keep up. We talked as we ran, and he told me about how he'd long been thinking about training for a marathon, and how he'd once loved to do long distances on the weekends, but he'd really let that go when he started his new job. I could hear the frustration in his voice, even as he jogged. He's a man with a dream or two or ten, and the barriers between him and those dreams are all in his own mind. Callum thinks his job defines him, and anything outside of that is not important enough to be prioritised. I reckon if he could make one single step towards one single goal, he'd suddenly know that he's so much more than that, and the chains would fall right off him.

It was a nice idea, to run together, but Callum being so much taller than me, not really all that practical. After one length we separated and he ran ahead to do his second lap. I watched him run away from me, extending his stride to eat up the metres. I ran on the hard wet sand close to the water like I always do. He ran further up the beach, right at the edge of the dry sand. As he powered away from me I let my toes get wet and focused on the splash of cool ocean water up my calves. Even though I've lived right on the water for most of my adult life, I am still always aware of the scent of sea salt. In the same way that the scent of baking bread takes me back to Grandma and the scent of gaudy perfume reminds me of Mum, briny air takes me home.

The beach is so busy on the weekend afternoons, which is why I love to run at this time of the week—so many families together, splashing in summer or building sand castles in winter. People are happier in groups. I've always known this to be true even through these recent years when I've been alone by choice. But yesterday, I chose to be in a pack again and it felt amazing. Even when Callum was hundreds of metres ahead of me, he was there *for* me, and I loved it.

It was good. Far too good, and far too easy, which is why when afternoon became evening it seemed only natural for us to go get some dinner. He told me he was dying for a steak and so we walked to one of the restaurants just down from my place and sat out on the street as dusk fell.

It's been five years since I ate meat, and the truth is that I very rarely miss it. And then there are times where the sight and scent of it claws at me and I feel like just sitting my environmental objections down under the table for a few minutes and digging in with gusto. If I'd asked for a bite, Callum would have offered me one—in fact he would have loved to share it with me and I'd have heard about it all night.

But of course, I didn't share the steak and I can't share a steak, because that's not the life I've chosen. I wish I could understand why I can resist *that* temptation but Callum himself seems a whole other story.

We were finishing our meals when a musical duo started to play. It was just an acoustic band, a sole guitarist and a woman perched on a stool, singing soft ballads to the assembled diners. The woman's voice was beautiful—liquid silk and raw honey, deeper than Mum's voice but the same sort of acrobatic tones. Callum was trying to flag a waiter down to ask if we could move to an inside table, but instead I pulled his arms around me and we started to dance.

He told me later that he doesn't dance, but he could have fooled me, there on our improvised dance floor. Maybe he hesitated a little at first, and I expected him to, given that we were at the front of the room by then standing right before the singer, and everyone else in the restaurant was sitting down eating. There wasn't even much room between the musicians and the tables, but we made it work. The guitar and the voice and the lyrics spoke of longing and the sounds weaved their way around us just like the moonlight did last night, and all we had to do was shuffle gaze to gaze. I always wondered if relationships could really be like that, where if a moment lined up just right, you could stand in a crowded room with them and feel only their presence.

We raced home after that, tearing at each other's clothing like teenagers as soon as my front door shut behind us. In these last few nights together, it hadn't been like that—sex with Callum the first few times was very mature lovemaking, us showing off our skills and mastery of the art, both of us restrained as we learnt each other's rhythms and tastes. But this was different; it was primal and hasty and one hundred per cent instinct. There was no playful giggling and no midcoital comments or instructions. Our impromptu dance session had become a kind of tantalising foreplay, and I suppose feeling just a little safer in each other's company, the undercurrent of sexual tension between us was finally unleashed.

I only realised this morning how the days had bled into each other, how *one last dinner* Friday night had already turned into Sunday morning. I promised myself I'd fix this, before it got any worse, and I dragged myself away from him and out of my bed to be fully alert and awake for when he woke. I decided I'd make him a cup of coffee, be politely aloof, and then remind him that I had been saying all weekend that I needed to do some work and the time had come.

But then he slept, and he slept, and he slept, and noon was fast approaching. And then I started banging around the kitchen to wake him up. But when he finally stepped out of the bedroom, he was oblivious to how rude I'd been and hadn't even noticed the noise, and he grabbed me by the waist and kissed me until I was breathless. Then of course I forgot that the plan had been to shoo him out the door, and he asked me to go see a movie with him, which apparently was enough to convince me I should. While I was simultaneously getting dressed and cursing myself for my hopeless inability to nip this thing in the bud, Callum did a horrible job of julienning some carrot sticks for me so I'd have a snack at the theatre, noting that he'd realised that I wouldn't eat buttered popcorn. In spite of his terrible knifemanship, the gesture was so sweet it nearly floored me.

When the evening began to descend and it really was time for Callum to go home, when I could no longer put off the work I needed to do for tomorrow and when he too became distracted by the preparation he needed to do for the week, I walked him down to the lobby and we kissed goodbye.

I wanted to ask him to stay. All I had to do was ask. I could see how much he wanted me to, and he'd have said yes in a heartbeat. At least I had the willpower to resist *one* impulse this weekend.

He told me he'd call me tomorrow and I forced myself to tell him I had a busy week ahead of me but that I'd call him instead when I had some time.

Now here I am, less than an hour later, and I'm feeling something that's an awful lot like *missing*. I've tried to busy myself: I watered the pot plants and even did my dishes, but there was no way I could focus on work. So I'm sitting on the balcony with the ocean breeze in my face and this journal on the table before me.

And next to the journal is my mobile phone, and my hands *really* want to call him and tell him to come back...

CHAPTER FIVE

Callum

I lay awake for much of the night after I left Lilah, wishing that I'd had the balls to ask her to sleep over with me again and reliving the days we'd spent together in my mind. It seemed obscene to make it to nearly forty years old without ever feeling as alive as I had in one single weekend with her, and unfair that the weekend had passed so quickly.

I looked for her on the ferry in the morning, and was disappointed that she didn't happen to be there. She'd given me her mobile number as we parted, but I was determined not to use it too quickly—besides which she'd *asked* me to wait for *her* call. I didn't want to scare her off.

Karl was waiting at the pot plant at nine. As I stepped out of my office, he scanned my face, and then grinned.

'So, it went well then?'

I tried to play it cool.

'Yeah, we spent some time together over the weekend.'

'And?'

'And what?'

'Is she really as amazing as your first impression?'

I laughed.

'Even more so.'

'Well, colour me surprised.' He stepped into the stairwell and I followed him. 'I honestly thought you'd be a bit mopey today.'

'Mopey?'

'Sorry, bad choice of words. You were already mopey. I thought you'd be cast free from the mopey-ness, into a whole new level of mopey-ness.'

'Why do you say that?' I was amused, and maybe just a little offended too.

'This whole Lilah business reminds me a lot of that psychology training we did last year, on branding and first impressions. I seem to recall you inflicted it upon us, actually. Do you remember it?'

'Vaguely.' I did. I didn't like where he was going with the conversation though.

'Consumers form a strong opinion of a brand in the first ten seconds of exposure to a design. So if the design is great, they'll love the product, even if the product isn't a good fit for them, and it takes repeated exposure to the negative aspects of the product to show them otherwise.'

'Ouch, Karl.'

'I also wondered if half of the appeal of Lilah was that she was unreachable because she disappeared on you. The thrill of the chase and all that.'

'If you're going to verbally beat me to death, you'd better be buying the coffees today.'

Karl laughed. 'No, seriously Callum, I'm glad it's working out for you. It won't hurt you to settle down a bit and have something to go home to.'

'She's pretty determined this isn't going to be a long-term thing but I'll enjoy it while it lasts.'

Karl fell silent. He was walking a few steps in front of me, but as he rounded a corner he glanced back up at me, and then grinned. 'You are pretty bloody smitten, aren't you?'

'You'll understand if she sticks around long enough for me to introduce you.'

❋ ❋ ❋

I made it all the way to bed Monday night without contacting her. It was a feat of endurance given how many times I'd picked up my phone during the day. Just as I shut my eyes, one last impulse overtook me. I picked up the phone from my bedside table and drafted a text message.

I know you've got a big week on, I just wanted to say the weekend we shared was amazing and I'm thinking of you.

My finger hovered over the abandon button, and then I sighed and hit send anyway. It was late, and I didn't expect her to respond, which made the ding of the phone a few seconds later even more gratifying.

Thank you, Callum. Want to share a ferry in the morning?

Manly Wharf is behind a small, upmarket shopping centre. The bargain supermarket is nestled between overpriced boutiques and cafes, as if it was striving for balance somehow—pay too much for your chocolate and coffee, and we will reward you with cut-price flour and sugar. I found Lilah waiting in line at a coffee bar at its entrance. We were both carrying black umbrellas due to the heavy cloud cover above but Lilah also had a small suitcase on wheels.

'Are you going away?'

For a moment she seemed confused, then she followed my gaze to her suitcase and laughed.

'That's just documents I was reading last night for a case. Way too much text to try to get through digitally. Have you ever read so much on a screen that when you look away you see the electronic glare like a curtain over the real world?' I laughed and nodded before she grimaced, 'I had an injunction granted last week and I have a feeling the bastards are about to try to get it overturned.'

'Go get 'em, tiger,' I said, and she reached up and planted a kiss right on my mouth. I was surprised and delighted, and we shared a grin. Over our heads, thunder rolled, but somehow it seemed that the plaza was bright with the warmest sunshine.

'Sao-Iris?' The barista said hesitantly. The coffee shop had you write your own name on the cup when you ordered, and I was surprised Lilah had opted for the name they'd never pronounce correctly.

'It's Seer-sha,' I corrected the barista, then gave her a wink when she blushed. 'One of those wacky Gaelic names.'

'I ordered you a coffee,' Lilah informed me. She took the two cups from the barista and gave her an icy smile, which contradicted her polite, 'Thank you very much.'

She passed me a cup and as I read the description scrawled beneath her name, I was relieved to find she'd ordered me full-cream cow's milk instead of almond. I took the handle of the suitcase from her and we joined the swell of commuters heading through to the wharf.

'Why not write *Lilah* on the cup?'

'Because last time I was there that barista was a total bitch to an old lady in front of me and I wanted to see her make an idiot of herself.' Lilah giggled like a schoolgirl and I couldn't help but smile at her delight. 'You had to spoil the fun and give her sympathy.'

'Note to self: beware—Lilah is vengeful.'

'Oh, absolutely. You should see what I'm going to do to this bloody mining company if they mess with my endangered species again.'

'Do you work on one case at a time?'

'*One* case?' she snorted. 'I have dozens going at any one time. I have a brilliant legal secretary and two paralegals or I wouldn't know what day it was. I couldn't even tell you how many cases I have open at the moment—the staff and my computer juggle it for me.'

'And why do you think this particular evil mining company is about to take another shot at you?'

'I don't know,' she shrugged. 'It's a half-billion-dollar development and I doubt they'd let a few frogs and insects in the next paddock slow it down, let alone stop it altogether. We could only find one ecological guy to testify against the development at the hearing, but it was embarrassingly obvious how clear-cut the science was. Our usual experts were either bought off or scared, which tells me this might get ugly. I need to be ready.'

'Morning, Lilah.' One of the ferry attendants called across the deck as we boarded and Lilah flashed a smile and a bright greeting.

'That's Rupert,' she told me. 'Do you know him? He works the morning ferry.' I shook my head. 'He's a great guy; his wife is expecting their third baby in a few weeks.'

I'm not sure I'd ever noticed any of the staff on the ferries, let alone learned their names or personal circumstances. We took seats side by side, nestled against a window which would take us past the northern side of the harbour. I wanted to say something to spark the conversation again, but there was a sudden heaviness in my gut and it took me a moment to identify it.

Disappointment.

For the very first time, it occurred to me how different Lilah and I really were. Oh, sure, the novelty of our differences had amused and perhaps intrigued me, but as I sat on the ferry and thought about the morning so far, I wondered if those differences might just be too extreme. What was I really looking for here anyway?

'Hey, are you okay?' Lilah asked suddenly. 'Did I upset you?'

I glanced back at her, and swept my gaze over those bright blue eyes, the soft freckles sprinkled over her nose, the high cheekbones, the glossy lips. The uncomfortable twist in my gut untwisted and retwisted in a much more pleasant way. Who said we had to be the same, anyway? Maybe we were somehow a perfect complement.

'Nope. I'm just fine,' I said softly, and took her hand in mine. 'Tell me about these frogs.'

❊ ❊ ❊

A pattern was emerging. Who knew the ferry could become so central to my happiness? Lilah told me she was just about overwhelmed with work, but we managed to at least share the ferry rides for the next few days.

For the trip home, she convinced me to take the slow ferry with her.

'Yes, I know it makes no sense; yes, I know you need to buy an extra ticket even though you already have a commuter pass; and, yes, I know it takes *forever*,' she said, as she linked her arm through mine and dragged me to the ticket stand. 'But if we take the fast ferry, we're back in Manly in fifteen minutes and then I'm obliged to get back to work. Besides which, you *told* me you loved the slow ferries.'

I didn't resist very hard. We sat at the bar as the ferry chugged its way across the harbour and we debriefed the day passed. Lilah told me all about her case, in extraordinary detail, although I could barely understand a word of the terminology and I didn't even know where the national park in question was until she told me. I became familiar with the people in her life at work and even the tone she'd use when she spoke of them. Alan was the managing partner, and she seemed to revere him as a father figure. Bridget was her legal secretary, and whenever Lilah said her name her whole demeanour would brighten—I could see the affection and respect she had for her.

And then there were the paralegals, Anita and Liam, who were much more of a mystery to me, given that although they comprised half of her team, Lilah usually was cursing them when she spoke of them.

'They just don't get it,' she told me one evening, when frustration bubbled over. 'We *know* the Hemway guys are going to appeal our injunction, and Bridget and I are working like maniacs, day and night, trying to be ready. And Anita and Liam can just get up from a task midmorning and go for a walk to find a chocolate muffin? It's just a *job* to them. They drive me crazy.'

I loved her venting to me. I loved the furious narrowing of her eyes and the wild hand gestures, and the way her hair was inevitably down around her waist by the time we caught up after work and the fiery halo it gave her when she was ranting. The passion and energy she had for her job was astounding.

We didn't just chat about work, of course. Sometimes during those early days we'd swap silly tales about our youth as we passed time crossing the harbour. I was learning her by degrees, every anecdote and giggle revealing more of her to me, and giving me a sketchy timeline of her history. I learned that she'd been to a uni not far from mine, and that she'd lived in the CBD for a long time too, and that she'd been to every continent at least once, including Antarctica, which she travelled to for her thirtieth birthday. And then there were the hints of a busy romantic life, given that many of her anecdotes featured boyfriends.

'He was built like a semi-trailer,' she told me. 'A two-metre wall of muscle and abs and gorgeous Greek charm.'

'Well,' I snorted, 'by the sounds of things it's a wonder he scored himself a girlfriend at all.'

'Ah, but looks and charm are definitely not everything. I was doing a sociology subject at the time and over beers one night I asked him if he thought gender was innate or cultural. And he looked at me just like this,' she squared her face up against mine to force uncomfortable eye contact, 'and he said, *are you telling me you're a dude?*'

'I can top that.' I was triumphant. 'A long time ago I took a woman I met through work to the theatre to see a political satire production. And then on the way out she told me she hadn't realised the prime minister was a comedian.'

So, maybe there were some half-truths in my anecdote, like the *lovely young lady* was actually a twenty-four year old beauty therapist I knew because I regularly went to her salon, and maybe it had been the previous year, rather than years earlier as I'd implied. But after Lilah's description of Nicko-the-Greek-God, I didn't want to admit that my tastes in women were apparently only recently maturing.

Those trips across the harbour were the highlight each day, and the moment when we separated to go to work or to our respective homes the lowlight. I wanted to stay with her, and when we parted, my thoughts did. She was occupying my mind, squatting in my consciousness, and even if I'd wanted to evict her I wouldn't have had a clue where to start. I was nervous about that, because every now and again, Lilah would let slip with a sudden burst of insecurity.

'We're spending too much time together,' she would say from time-to-time as we crossed the harbour, and the words always burst from her lips like she'd suddenly remembered in a panic. I tried to counter her panic with humour, often with a dismissive exaggeration.

'Yes, Lilah, I realise sharing this ferry ride is a commitment akin to buying a house together, but I promise that if things break down before we finish, I will only want weekend custody of the tickets.'

Or I'd mock her unbalanced attitude to intimacy, which always made her grin.

'So you're saying that all of this chit-chat is moving too fast, but what we did last weekend was fine? Noted and appreciated.'

But although our fragile relationship was staggering forward, its roots little by little cementing in our lives each time we saw each other, I was nervous about her continued hesitancy. Her enthusiasm for the shared commute and her affection while we were together just didn't match up to those words, and I was increasingly nervous that at some point she might pull the pin altogether.

❄ ❄ ❄

On Friday, I was walking down the stairs to coffee with Karl when my phone sounded. I glanced at the screen and stopped.

'Lilah wants to have lunch with me.' There was a sudden sinking dread in my stomach.

'Uh-oh. That doesn't sound good.'

'It doesn't.'

'Lunch?'

'Yeah.' I quickly texted her back to suggest a time and place then slid the phone into my pocket.

'No, I meant your *tone*,' Karl laughed. 'She just wants to have lunch?'

'Yeah... I don't know. Call it instinct.'

Maybe I'd been waiting for her to retreat, after her disappearing act and then her comments the previous weekend. It had all been too easy to spend the hours with her over the week, even though she'd made it abundantly clear that she wasn't looking for a relationship. Perhaps this was where it all broke.

There was a cafe on the corner between our offices. I arrived first and early, and waited a few minutes for a table to become free. Lilah was a few minutes late and looked a little frazzled.

I kissed her cheek and she dropped into her chair with a heavy exhale.

'Big day?' I asked, and she groaned.

'Too annoying to recount. How's yours going?'

'It's going well.' So far. 'This was a nice idea, catching up over lunch.'

'Yes, I'm starving.' Lilah reached for the menu, scanned it quickly then dumped it back onto the table.

'I think we order at the counter. Can I get yours?'

During the brief hesitation, I saw the way her independence battled the practical needs of the moment. She surveyed the busy café, the handful of people waiting for a table, and finally the sign at the front of the room proclaiming *please order at the counter*. Only after taking all of this in did she glance back to me and nod.

'Greek salad, please, no feta, but can you ask for extra olives? Thanks.'

As I ordered, the nervous rhythm beat in my stomach. There was a peculiar energy to her today, and I wasn't sure what it meant, or even how to decipher it. When I joined her again in the upholstered bucket chairs, she crossed her legs and gave me a stare like I was on the witness stand.

'I was thinking…' Here it came. I braced myself. 'Tomorrow, let's go bushwalking.'

'Oh?'

'You're startled. Not a good idea? I thought you might bring your camera. There are so many walks up in the Blue Mountains; we can catch a train up and then…' I tuned out from her words and just stared at her face, at the animation of her sales pitch for a day of exploring together, and only managed to focus back in on her words when she was wrapping up. '…and the best part of all, I'll *have* to wear shoes, so I figured you'd like that.'

I glanced at her feet and noted the black heels she wore. She kicked them towards me playfully.

'Yes, I know, but I do generally wear them all through the workday. This is just the first time you've seen me at lunch. So what do you think—shall we go bush tomorrow?'

'Oh… yes… absolutely,' I said. My words ran into one another, and she paused.

'You don't have to.'

'No, I would *love* to. Honestly.'

'You…' The tiny wrinkle appeared between her eyes again. When she was angry or confused, or even concentrating hard, it seemed to come from nowhere, and it would disappear just as quickly when she smiled. 'Is something wrong?'

'Not a thing,' I smiled and tried to reassure her. 'Really. It's a fantastic idea. I'll charge my camera tonight. I'd love to bust it out again—it's been years.'

'Okay.' She settled back in her chair, her gaze still on mine. 'You're sure you didn't have other plans?'

'Lilah, all I was hoping for this weekend was to spend some time with you,' I said. 'Honestly. And a walk in the mountains sounds perfect.'

'Great, we can get up early and be there by about nine...'

And Lilah was off again, chattering excitedly about all of the possibilities of a day of trekking. After we'd eaten, she kissed me and disappeared back around the corner to her office, and I stayed for an extra coffee alone to try to pull myself back into orbit.

It occurred to me that when I'd stopped reaching for new things in my life, I'd effectively circumvented both risk and fear. And now that a new possibility had erupted right before my eyes, and I was fast becoming addicted to the drug that was my relationship with Lilah, I was exposed and vulnerable. So she'd called lunch to make plans this time—next time it could well be to remind me that she wasn't looking for a relationship and to end whatever it was that was happening between us. If I was going to keep seeing her, I had to be prepared for that possibility. Already I had experienced firsthand the way that Lilah's approach to life had her taking left turns and right turns without warning, jumping all over the place in the name of *making the most of it*. Who knew if, or when, she'd take a turn away from me?

Given that every single time I saw her I fell for her just a little more, I knew I had to make a decision. If I was *going* to keep seeing her, I had to accept that it was entirely possible that we might reach a point where my hopes for our relationship did not match hers.

I would proceed with my eyes wide open, and take the calculated risk. Just like Lilah walking on the beach at night with no shoes, I'd focus on enjoying the moment.

❈ ❈ ❈

A new noodle bar had opened up on the Corso, and after we met at the wharf again that night, Lilah suggested we stop in for a quick meal. I'd ordered a laksa. Lilah stepped up to the counter to order when she noticed a canister of vegetable stock powder on the stainless-steel bench.

'Your menu says no MSG,' she frowned. 'That brand has MSG added.'

'MSG?' I repeated.

'Monosodium glutamate. It's a fucking neurotoxin.' Lilah's voice was raised, ever so slightly, but the tone was ripe with disgust. The line of people behind us all quietened and I had a sudden feeling that I was about to witness some kind of explosion.

'Lilah—'

'The menu says *no added* MSG,' the middle-aged woman behind the counter said flatly. 'Small amounts may be present in some of the ingredients. If you're allergic, I can leave the stock out.'

Lilah took a menu from the counter, opened it with force and slammed it in front of the woman.

'*No MSG.*' Lilah read aloud. 'You need to change your stock, or reprint these menus.'

'Come on, Lilah,' I tugged gently at her arm. 'Let's just leave, hey?'

'Studies have consistently shown that MSG is poison to the human brain—it has a cumulative effect and can cause brain lesions. Plus it's quite a common allergy. You can't just include it in food and not tell people.' She'd taken a deep breath and was calm again, but clearly determined to educate the woman. 'Do you understand how serious this is?'

The woman behind the counter was unimpressed.

'Lady, do you want the noodles or not?'

'Oh, *hell* no. I wouldn't eat here in a million years. But I *am* going to come back here in a week's time. If that stock or these menus are the same, I'll be making a call to the authorities.'

Behind us, I noticed movement, and when I glanced behind me, several people had left the back of the line and exited the shop. Those who hadn't yet left were watching Lilah with interest; some were talking quietly between themselves. The woman behind the counter noticed too and gave an exasperated gesture towards the door.

'I think you should leave now, or *I* will call the police.'

Lilah raised her eyebrow at the woman. Before she could open her mouth again, I pulled again on her arm.

'Lilah, let's *go,* please?'

Lilah turned to me, sighed, and then stepped away from the counter. Outside, she growled in frustration.

'You can't mess with food additives. I checked the menu online before we went there. I knew she was wrong.'

'So we don't eat there. Why is this such a big deal?' I hadn't really seen Lilah angry, but she was almost vibrating with furious energy.

'Callum, it is illegal to misrepresent a product, and that's exactly what that shop is doing. Do you not understand why that's so frustrating to me? Today she sneaks MSG in—what's next, a chunk of radioactive steak?'

I held my hands up, aware that she was still livid, and that this was an argument I had no chance of winning. 'Maybe we can go have a pizza instead? Or we can go home and I'll make you…'

I hesitated. Given her limited diet and my exceptionally poor culinary skills, I really didn't stand a chance of cooking for her. She raised her eyebrow at me.

'…a soy smoothie?' I suggested. A reluctant smile crossed her face. She slipped her arm through my elbow and we continued down the Corso.

'It is really important to me that I don't eat MSG, okay? I'm sorry I blew up. I just *hate* people underestimating this stuff.'

'Okay, Lilah. I get it.'

I still didn't really understand the issue, but it was enough for me that Lilah felt it was important she avoid whatever the hell MSG was.

'There's another noodle shop further down the Corso,' she said, 'I can eat there. Is that okay?'

'Absolutely.' I was just relieved that she was starting to calm down. Angry Lilah was a force to be reckoned with. We made it all the way to the other restaurant and had ordered our meals before she exhaled and glanced at me.

'Were you embarrassed?'

'At you nearly tearing the head off the server and scaring away half of their patrons?' I laughed wryly. 'Why would that be embarrassing?'

She winced a little.

'I'm not really a fiery redhead.'

'I can see that,' I raised my eyebrows at her.

'I'm really not.' Lilah insisted. 'But some things are worth fighting for, and I honestly believe that truth in labelling is one of them. I avoid MSG on principle but some people are actually anaphylactic to it. There's a reason those laws are in place: it protects people's lives.'

'Will you really go back and check on them?'

'I absolutely will. I have an obligation to now.'

'What if it's not your problem?'

'How is it not my problem? I *know* about it now.'

'It is not your responsibility to solve every problem in the world that you happen to know about.' The very idea amused me.

'That attitude is part of what's wrong with the world today,' she frowned. 'A simple thing like that, where people's health and safety is at stake, and all that's required of me to help fix it is a repeat visit and a single phone call? Wouldn't you?'

'When you put it like that, I guess I should. But under normal circumstances, honestly? I wouldn't even have noticed the menu said anything about MSG, and even if I did happen to notice, I don't think it would ever occur to me that I could or should do anything about it.'

'Are you seriously suggesting I should drop it?' Thankfully, there was no indignation in her tone, just confusion and maybe a little hurt. We were sitting in some waiting chairs, her hand on the arm-rest beside me. I picked it up and entwined our fingers.

'I'm not saying that at all. Firstly, I wouldn't *dare* to tell you what you should or shouldn't do.' I feigned fear and she gave me a look that left no doubt in my mind that she was not in the mood for jokes. 'I don't know. Where do you draw the line? We need more bike lanes in Manly and although I barely drive, I've nearly hit two cyclists in the last year or so. I think *someone* should address it, does that mean I have an obligation to lobby the local council? What about when I see those ads for starving children on television? I'm aware of the problem and apparently all I have to do is give my money over, but where do I stop? Is the right thing to do to keep giving until I bankrupt myself? You can't fight all of the world's battles.'

'But Callum, you *have* to fight *some*. Not for the world, but for you. When you find something that stirs a passion inside you, some injustice or some beauty or... or... *something*—you *have* to go after it, regardless of how big or small it is, because that's all there is in this life. There is nothing else worth wasting your time on.'

I didn't know what to say to that. I didn't even know what to *think* about it. We fell into silence, and even after we'd picked up our meals and quietly agreed to eat at my place, and Lilah seemed to recover from all of the fury of the evening and resumed an animated chatter about the week that had been, I still felt distracted. This woman, who apparently stood for everything that stirred a feeling within her, was the only thing that had stirred a passion in me in years.

'I should go home,' she said after she'd finished eating. She rose and I rose too, but instead of walking her out, I took her hand and pulled her silently towards me.

Even after just a week of knowing Lilah, there was so much change happening inside me that I felt I was being enlarged. I wanted to tell her so, but I knew my words would be clumsy and that she'd run like a frightened kitten, so instead I let my kiss and my embrace tell the story.

'Stay,' I whispered.

'But…' Her voice was weak, but her protest even more so because her eyes pleaded with me to convince her.

'Stay, Lilah. Please.'

She swallowed. I saw the flickering emotions in her gaze, the internal battle between whatever it was within her that held her back from me, and the opposing force, the bond between us that pulled her to stay. I even saw the moment I won, when the tension in her face relaxed and she wrapped her arms around my neck.

✳ ✳ ✳

She roused me at the crack of dawn, and before I had even fully woken, we had been past her house for casual clothing and a backpack she filled with food. Then we were on the earliest fast ferry, headed back to Sydney to catch a train.

Lilah had plotted a trek for us, starting at a lookout in Katoomba, looping around something with the ominous name of the Giant Stairway, through some rainforest and back.

When we arrived at Echo Point Lookout, the sun was still low, and there were only a handful of tourists around. It was freezing, but Lilah had told me that even by nine a.m. the area would be teaming with people and tour groups, so the best way to enjoy the area was to get there before they arrived. She stood right at the safety rail and surveyed the panoramic view of dense bushland and immense space, the valley stretching as far as we could see in both directions. The famous Three Sisters rock formation was just below us, shrouded in the low line of fog that ran through the very bottom of the entire valley. Lilah inhaled, as if she could breathe it all in, then turned to me with a grin.

'If anything is going to make an environmentalist out of you, surely this is it.'

'It's amazing.' I'd visited the area before, but couldn't remember being so awed by the sheer magnitude of it. I took my camera and snagged a few shots, including one of Lilah as she gazed outwards. She caught me and flashed a grin my way, so I snapped an extra shot. When I looked at the photo I'd taken, I was struck by the full force of the wonder I'd felt for photography as a child. I could capture a moment in time, and freeze it forever, and now I'd done it with something really worthy of such magic.

'Come on then!' Lilah walked ahead. 'We have a big day ahead of us!'

❄ ❄ ❄

She wasn't kidding.

We walked for hours. From Echo Point we headed down the Giant Stairway, and when we'd finally descended all nine hundred metal and stone stairs, found ourselves beneath the treeline at the bottom of the valley. Signs posted us towards various options to return to the top, including a railway and an overhead carriage, but when I pointed these out, Lilah laughed at me and turned me with some determination towards a longer trek.

'Where exactly are you taking me?' I asked her as we left the other tourists and headed deeper into the bushland. There was a well-defined and signposted track, but we were now alone, except for the teeming birdlife I could hear in the canopy above us.

'Leura Forest. This is the Dardanelles Pass. We'll return via the Federal Pass and then head back up the stairs.'

'*Up* the stairs?' I gasped, 'No! Up?!'

'Yep. Up.'

We walked for the next few hours, over blessedly flatter terrain, stopping to snack on the fruit she'd packed and rest very briefly every now and again. As we walked, we talked at first about the area and the wildlife, but then as our footsteps wound into deeper territory, so did our conversation.

'The first time I came here, I was with my dad,' Lilah explained. 'I think Mum might have been teaching back in Katoomba—maybe she was doing a one-off workshop. I don't think we were here for long. I just remember it took forever to get down the stairs, and some point near the bottom I just flatly refused to go any further, so Dad had to carry me. He scooped me up in his arms and then sat me on his shoulders right on top of the backpack he was carrying. At some point he convinced me to get down and we walked all the way to Leura Forest. On the way back up the stairs he was so positive and so encouraging that I actually made it all the way back up by myself. The smile that had settled on her face was transformative. She glanced at me. 'My Dad was amazing. He was one of those pure souls, who just loved with his whole heart. I think if anyone else had married my mum, she'd have eaten them alive; she's always been ninety-nine per cent music. But Dad, he had this way of bringing out the other one per cent in her, and that was the best part of her. He went to the most extraordinary lengths to support her, because making her dreams come true became *his* dream.' She was quiet for a long moment, then she admitted, 'I miss him every day.'

'Do you think you take after him?' All I knew about him was the simple story she'd just told me, and already I could see the similarities. Lilah laughed and shook her head.

'Dad was tall and stocky, and he had a broad Scottish accent. He came here when he was a teenager to live with his aunt and uncle. He was a quiet guy until he warmed up to people, and then he was the loudest man in the room. He'd build up to this enormous, booming voice and he seemed to use a burst of laughter to end every sentence. I inherited his hair, and maybe a few other traits, but I actually think I'm just like Mum. She has her music, I have the law—we're both obsessive, just in different ways. Who are you more like, your mum or your dad?'

I grimaced.

'I'm not really sure. I look like a lot like Dad, except I've still got Mum's hair. By my age Dad was starting to go bald.'

'You do seem to appreciate your hair.'

'It's my best feature.'

'No way. Your eyes and your jaw are your best features. Your hair is fine though.'

'Oh, thanks,' I laughed. 'I think.'

'What did your mum look like?'

'She was beautiful,' I said. My throat tightened. 'Even as she aged, she had this softness... a kindness about her.

You could see it in her eyes. I think that was so startling that even if she'd had a wart on the end of her nose, no one would have noticed.'

'Did she have a career?'

'Her career was our family. She used to say the three of us boys were each a full-time job. I think she spent about two decades playing referee to the twins.'

'Not you?'

'Oh, no,' I chuckled. 'I was *not* into rumbling. I was into hobbies: reading or drawing or photography, depending on how old I was. Ed or Will would often try to drag me into their scuffles and I'd get up and walk away.'

'It really sounds like you had a wonderful upbringing.'

'I know. And it was, in so many ways. I was lucky. Ed and Will were so close, and Mum and Dad were so close…'

The path curved around to a clearing, alongside which a small creek trickled down a mini waterfall. The gentle sound of the water joined the symphony of life playing around us, and automatically we stopped to watch the flow of water for a moment.

Lilah stepped a little closer to me. She looped her elbow through mine and prompted me, 'Did you feel left out?'

'I knew they all loved me. And I knew I wasn't a bad kid; I was never in trouble, and Mum and Dad were always proud of me. But I still felt like the black sheep. It's ridiculous because I'm sure it was all in my head. The bond the twins had with each other was just so different to the one they each had with me, and Mum and Dad… well, they were in love—like absolutely besotted, even after decades. I can vividly remember a few times talking away at the dinner table about the things I'd done at school, and looking up to realise that Mum was just staring at Dad and it was like I wasn't even there.' It suddenly struck me that here I was complaining about my stable, love-drenched childhood to someone who'd lived in seven countries before she turned twelve. I hastily tried to qualify my comments, 'Which is, you know, it's all fine. It's just the way it was.'

We were deep in the valley now, and hadn't seen anyone else for quite a while. For all I knew, the universe could have been reduced to just the two of us and a million birds and unidentified animals scuffling near us in the shrubbery. I thought about the things I'd just said, the private fears and insecurities that I'd never given voice to before. Maybe I'd never even admitted them to myself. I had a sudden memory of lying beside the first girl I'd ever slept with. I remembered trying to catch my breath, afraid to open my eyes in case I saw disappointment on her face.

'I think that everything has a good and a bad side—everything, even though at the time most things that happen in life seem to be entirely good or entirely bad,' Lilah murmured, and I finally looked at her. Her expression was thoughtful, and there was compassion in her face, instead of contempt. I breathed a sigh of relief. 'Living like a gypsy as a kid was an amazing adventure, even while it totally screwed up my education and my understanding of normality. And it's the same for your family, Cal. Even though it was beautiful and stable and you adored your folks, it must have been very isolating being the fifth wheel in a family of pairs. You don't have to pretend it wasn't.'

'I like talking to you.' I blurted, perhaps channelling a little too much of that awkward teenage memory. Lilah's arm was still looped through mine, and she leant her face into my upper arm for a brief moment. It was a strange gesture, almost reminiscent of that moment earlier in the morning when she'd stood before the valley and inhaled so very deeply.

'I like talking to you,' she said after a moment, and then she shifted herself so that she could stand in front of me to lean back into my chest. I wrapped my arms around her waist and rested my chin on her head, and together we watched the waterfall.

❊   ❊   ❊

It was late afternoon when we finally wound our way back to the stairs. I'd nearly filled the card on my camera, we were just about out of water, and my thighs were burning before we even started the ascent. It had been a full day, but Lilah refused to even entertain the idea of catching the railway back up.

'That's cheating!' she protested when I suggested it. I was exhilarated, but exhausted too, and although I could see she wasn't going to admit it, she was also tired. She'd stumbled a few times on the return path, and although she was still grinning like a mischievous child, I could see the weariness on her face.

'If I can make it back up there as a kid, you can surely do it as an adult,' she teased me. And so we climbed, squeezed in among a throng of tourists heading back up to the lookout. Most of the crowd was silent as we tried to focus all of our energies on the exertion required for the nearly vertical stairway. It was fast becoming cold as the sun left the valley, and there were white puffs of steam visible when people exhaled.

It was as I saw the top before us, and just as a final burst of energy and relief came over me, that Lilah slipped. She didn't fall far, just a few stairs down, and I reacted quickly enough to catch her and stop her tumbling further. She ended up on her backside against the cliff, and I could see immediately that she'd actually injured herself.

'Lilah?'

She was wincing, and pointed vaguely towards her left ankle.

'I think I sprained it.' There was genuine pain in her voice. The surging crowd was moving around us as if we were a rock in a stream. I shifted her back into a standing position and she tried to put her weight on the foot. She immediately cried out and leant into me.

'Uh-oh,' she said. She looked at me with pleading eyes. 'I don't think I can walk the rest of the way.'

I lifted her high against my chest and started very slowly walking again. It didn't matter that Lilah was tiny and thin; the extra weight made my already tired muscles burn, each step demanded a monumental effort. Lilah pressed her face into my neck and wrapped her arms around me.

After a few steps, I said between gasps, 'You shouldn't have told me about the time you made your dad carry you down. I know you're only putting this on to get out of the walk.'

She kissed me on the cheek.

'And yet... you're still carrying me.'

'What can I say? I can't resist a pretty girl.'

I carried her all the way back to the café in the tourist centre at the lookout, then gently removed her shoe to investigate the damage. Between the swelling and the bruise that was already visible, I could see that Lilah wasn't going to be walking anywhere for the rest of the day. I propped her foot up onto her daybag on the opposite chair, then went to fetch some warm drinks and supplies.

For the next little while, we stared out into the valley we'd conquered together. Lilah alternated between a cup of tea and a bottle of cold water. I sat beside her, hugging a latte towards my chest as I tried to warm my fingers up. I was thinking about the situation we were in, her foot and the best way to get home without causing her any further pain.

'We could catch a cab back to the train station? Or even back down to Manly if you want—I'll get it,' I suggested. The taxi fare would be hundreds of dollars, but the journey from the mountains to Manly otherwise involved at least a train and a ferry transfer, not to mention the blocks we'd have to walk back to either of our homes.

'Let's stay the night,' she said suddenly. I looked at her blankly.

'But you're hurt.'

'Oh, it's just a sprain,' she dismissed my concern with a wave of her hand before she pointed to the east. 'There are some gorgeous hotels over that way. Let's go find one and stay.'

'We didn't even bring clothes. Or deodorant. Or tooth-brushes.'

'We can re-wear these ones. You *will* survive without de-odorant for one day, I promise. And I'm sure we can find toothbrushes.'

'What about pyjamas?'

'Callum, I *never* wear pyjamas. You'll survive one night without them,' she laughed. 'You do realise that we're making a terrible habit of me bullying you into having fun. Come on, go find us a taxi.'

The idea was growing on me and my protests suddenly seemed ridiculous. We could find a romantic nest for the night, and I could nurse her back to health.

'I suppose it makes sense. The trip back might be a bit easier tomorrow?'

Lilah grinned. She sat her hand over mine on the table.

'Absolutely. I'm *way* too injured to sit on my backside and travel an hour back to the city, so we best stay here in this magnificent wilderness so I can rest. Taxi, please.'

❋ ❋ ❋

The helpful taxi driver took us to a heritage-style building on the edge of a cliff, and I left Lilah in the car while I ran in to enquire about a booking for the night. They had several options for rooms, including a deluxe suite with a spa, overlooking the valley.

'I'll take the king room—' I began automatically, but then changed my mind and withdrew my credit card. 'No, actually, can you give me the suite, please?'

The room had an open fireplace and a king bed, and the receptionist was more than happy to arrange toothbrushes and an icepack and some pain relief for Lilah. Once I had the room key, I returned to help Lilah out of the taxi and to the elevator.

By now, the sun was starting to set and the valley was aglow with late-afternoon light. The fire was only freshly lit, but the underfloor heating had the room toasty anyway. We both sighed as we stepped inside and felt the ambient temperature.

'That's better,' I breathed, walking straight to the fire. Lilah, on the other hand, hobbled awkwardly to the balcony and opened the doors. 'Lilah, what the hell are you doing?'

'Can you get some bubbles from the minibar?' Lilah stepped outside to survey the valley, and then called back, 'Was there a restaurant downstairs?'

'There is, but—' I'd had visions of room service and her resting her ankle on a pillow while we ate.

'Let's have a drink and watch the sunset, then go get some dinner.'

'But your foot—'

'There's an elevator,' she shrugged.

Her mind was apparently made up. Again. I laughed.

'You're a four-foot bulldozer, you know.'

'Oh come on, Cal. I'm not *that* short. And you only live once. When are you going to be here again? Let's just enjoy the moment.'

I popped the cork from the champagne and poured us each a glass, then carried it out to her. I sat the glasses on the coffee table and pulled Lilah down into a seat.

'Rest,' I instructed her. 'I asked the receptionist to send you up an ice pack. If you rest for a while, I'll help you limp back down to the restaurant and we can eat, okay? But it's a fancy place and we're both dressed like bushwalkers.'

'Who cares?' She raised her glass towards me. 'To adventure.'

'To adventure,' I echoed. 'Also, to taking the railway back up next time.'

'If we'd taken the railway, my ploy to trap you here in a romantic suite overnight wouldn't have worked.'

'You could have just asked.'

❊ ❊ ❊

Much later that night, something woke me. Maybe I bumped Lilah's foot accidentally and she made a sound, or maybe I rolled in my sleep and triggered a sore muscle of my own. For whatever reason, I found myself wide awake, and as minutes ticked by, I realised I wasn't going back to sleep anytime soon.

Conscious of Lilah sleeping on the bed beside me, I rose. The hotel had taken our clothes to launder them overnight, so I donned a fluffy white bathrobe and walked to the windows. We'd pulled the curtains shut earlier, but now I opened them just a crack and stared out into the valley.

I thought about staring at the stars the previous week with Lilah, and her comments about the city washing out the detail.

Surely here the view would be even better? It was far too cold outside to go out though, especially in just a bathrobe; I could feel the chill just standing by the window.

Some strange impulse triggered and I opened the door and quickly slipped out onto the balcony anyway.

The air was utterly still outside, and the valley was again shrouded in mist. When I looked up, though, I saw the creamy swirl of the Milky Way and the thousands of stars that had been hidden by the light pollution of the city. If the cold air hadn't already done it, the sight would have taken my breath away.

The balcony door cracked open, just a little.

'Sorry, Lilah, I didn't mean to wake you.'

She stuck her head out the door, peered up at the sky and then gave a little squeak of protest at the cold.

'Now that's more like it,' she said, still looking up to the stairs. 'And believe it or not, it's even better at my place up north, where there's almost no light from houses. But as much as it warms the cockles of my heart to see that you're freezing your balls off just to look at the stars, I'm going back to bed.'

'I'll just be a few more minutes.'

I stayed out on the balcony until my fingers and toes became stiff with the cold, and then I went back in to crawl into bed beside Lilah.

❄ ❄ ❄

Even Lilah managed a sleep-in the following morning, but still looked pale when she woke.

'Do you need to see a doctor?' I tried to gently prompt as we made our way back to the city on the train, but she made a dismissive sound out of the corner of her mouth. It was after lunch when we finally found ourselves back at the Manly

Wharf. By then, she couldn't bear weight on it again, and I could see she was never going to be able to walk the three city blocks home.

'That's it,' I said firmly. 'I'll go get my car and drive you back to your place.'

'I really—' There was genuine pain on her face. Protesting her independence was such a habit to Lilah that she couldn't help but do it, even when she didn't want to.

'Lilah. It's *my* turn to be the bossy one.' I sat my hands on her shoulders and looked directly into her eyes. 'I'll let you drag me to get dunked in the frozen ocean or torture me up and down nineteen hundred stairs any time you want, but just this once, you have to let me take care of you. I'll take you to the coffee shop and you can wait for me to get back.'

She pressed her lips together and nodded curtly.

CHAPTER SIX
Lilah

7 September

I have waded into dangerous territory.

Oh who am I fucking kidding? I'm *scuba-diving* in dangerous territory.

I made a mistake, and then a bunch of other mistakes which have just compounded my first stupidity. I am full of good intentions nearly every day, promising myself that I will immediately put some distance between me and Callum and get things back to normal.

But this relationship is like a compulsion for us both. Callum makes jokes about me being a bulldozer all of the time, but it's really not me that he needs to worry about. It's this connection between us: the easy sharing, the simple laughter, the fun in the normalcy and the spark when our eyes meet. I can see his mind ticking over, looking to the future that we won't have.

A bond has formed between Callum and I, which I need to dissolve—and already it's going to hurt both of us.

I don't need him. Of course I don't need him.

I *cannot* need him, and there is no way I can continue to play with his emotions.

I don't want to stop seeing him, but I have to—or at the very least, I have to put the brakes on big time. The irony is of course that he's letting me lead on how often we meet, and I've just been selfish because I like being with him. I've been telling myself that these cheeky catchups on the ferry and even our daytrip on the weekend wouldn't do any harm. *More friend territory than boyfriend*, I remember thinking Friday morning as I was plotting the trip to the mountains.

Stupid. Foolish. Reckless.

That stops tonight.

I stumbled yesterday. Exactly three times. It happened as soon as I started feeling tired, and it ended when I nearly fell all the way to the bottom of the valley while we were climbing the stairway. After that I barely walked all night, and I barely thought, because I knew if I let myself start thinking that, I would work myself up into the panic I'm feeling right now.

I've never had the misfortune of being stalked by an obsessed lover, but I can imagine the fear. He'd be there lurking in every shadow. I'd see his face in every crowd, and feel his breath on my neck even when I was alone. It's been like that for me these past five years, hearing the pounding steps of the sickness on the ground behind me when I run, seeing its fingerprints everywhere, even where it was not.

So I stumbled. Everyone stumbles sometimes, especially when they're tired. I mean, Callum was right there and he obviously didn't think anything of it. He wears every thought he has right there on his face for me to see and I'm pretty sure I'd have noticed if he was overly concerned about why I fell. It's probably nothing. It's probably the breeze in the curtains instead of a machete-wielding maniac. It's probably a coincidence that the black car has been behind me for the last twenty minutes. It's probably ordinary, garden-variety tiredness and clumsiness that had me nearly tumbling to the valley floor.

But what if it's not?

Callum has fallen asleep on my couch. He insisted on staying over, and he's been playing nursemaid to me since we got back, fetching me supplies from the chemist and dinner. I've tried to console myself with the reality that even Callum, who is definitely not sick, is exhausted even a day later and is now snoring like a buzz-saw even at eight o'clock at night. But Callum didn't fall over.

The truth is, the sprain will pass, and so will this anxiety. This isn't the first scare I've had since I've been well, not by a long shot. I've periodically seen signs where there were no signs and felt symptoms that were all in my mind and that passed as soon as I was distracted. It's a small part of why I need to keep so busy, because if I let myself be idle, I think too much and I talk myself into the worst-case scenario.

There is one thing, and one thing only, that I need to remember from the way I feel tonight. The nervous thud of my heart against my ribcage and twirling turmoil of the fear will probably be gone by the time the bruise fades, and that's why I had to hop over to my desk to write this down. Right now. While it's real.

I've been swept up in this Callum thing. In the last week or so I've gone with the flow of it, letting the chemistry pull us forward, thinking I could be good for him and he could be good for me and maybe we could just play normal for a little while and no one would get hurt. When we bumped into each other on George Street I remember thinking to myself that if I believed in *meant to be*, this would be it. I imagined myself telling Mum about how I tried to do the right thing and spare him the complexities of my life, and then he just popped up again right there in front of me, the very next day. She'd get that wise-old-sage look she likes to shoot for with her students and tell me that the universe was telling me something, and I'd laugh at her but I'd secretly love it because it's what I want to believe too.

But in spite of his protestations that he's a lifelong bachelor, all I see when I look at Callum is someone who wants to love and be loved. We're falling for each other. It's in its infancy, but every time we see each other, the words flow and the emotions are following them. Every day I prolong this is making it harder.

I'm going to distance myself as of tomorrow. I know I've been saying that to myself for a week, but I have to channel this scare into some action.

CHAPTER SEVEN

Callum

Lilah was much better the next morning. Her foot was obviously still tender, but she could limp around without too much difficulty. I made a joke about her having an excuse to forego shoes for the day. Lilah was different this morning: focused solely on getting to work from the moment she woke up. She kissed me goodbye when I left to go get dressed though, and as I walked home I convinced myself that this was probably just her usual weekday morning focus.

But she didn't answer my text that evening about the ferry ride home, and although I lay awake until nearly midnight waiting, she didn't respond that night. When I woke the next morning, there was a text waiting.

Sorry, Callum, the appeal I feared has happened. It's all systems go here for me at work. I'll call you when I have some time but I'm not sure when that'll be.

I allowed myself to acknowledge the bitter disappointment that rose within me. I wanted to see her, but of course I understood. She had frogs to save, or insects, or something vitally important to the ecosystem.

For the next few days, I texted Lilah every day, and she responded every day.

Busy with the Hemway case. Sorry, Callum. I'll let you know if things change.

Thanks for checking in with me, will catch up with you if it quietens down.

Sorry, Cal, still up to my eyeballs. I'll call you when I get some time.

I saw her case on the news. It was making headlines, and her name was often mentioned in the coverage, although usually with an old photo of her and a quote from a media release.

'Saoirse McDonald, senior partner with Davis McNally who is opposing the mining operation on behalf of several environmental lobby groups, had this to say: *Hemway Mining is well known for their dirty tactics and determination to pillage natural resources at their own convenience, and this case is a perfect example. Davis McNally, as well as our partners from the community, will throw the entire weight of our combined resources behind this case. The financial benefit to Hemway Mining does not offset the extreme risks to rare species in the Minchin National Park area.* '

I was impatient, but I recognised the genuine demand on her time, and I well understood that even if our relationship was increasingly important to her, I would always come second to a case like this.

❄   ❄   ❄

It was just after eight on Thursday night when I heard my intercom buzz. It almost never sounded, given how rarely I had guests to my home, and it took me a moment to remember what the noise was.

'Hello?'

'Cal, it's me.'

I buzzed her in, and while I waited for her to come through the small lobby to my apartment, I raced around tidying my lounge room. Unfinished renovations aside, I am something of a neat freak, so there wasn't much to do, but I had a sudden burst of emotional energy I needed to expend. There had been a strange tone to her greeting, a tension I didn't quite understand.

When she knocked on the door, I paused before I opened it.

'Hi,' I said. I was shooting for a warm, welcoming tone. I know my face fell when I saw her.

She was crying. There were heavy teardrops running down her cheeks, and judging by the red rims to her eyes, she'd been crying for some time.

'I tried to get another injunction and I lost.' She hiccupped and her face crumpled. 'I can't convince anyone to testify for me. I failed the frogs, Callum.'

'Oh, Lilah.' I pulled her inside and wrapped my arms around her. 'It's okay, Lilah. I know you did your best.'

'The fracking will raise the methane in the waterways and the frogs and the water bugs will die. I can't understand how I've lost this case.'

'Is this the end of the road? Are there other options left?'

I pulled her down onto my couch and she leant into my chest. Another sob loomed.

'No, I couldn't even get another temporary injunction so they'll be on site tomorrow. Not that I have any angles left to come at them with; without any experts willing to tell the court the reality of the situation in the ecosystem, it really is over.'

I didn't know what to say. I could feel the tension in her body. Her disappointment and sense of failure was palpable. I held her closer and just let her cry.

That's the thing about having a job with cosmic importance, I suppose. If I failed, I lost a client, maybe I got a wrap on the knuckles from the board—but that was about it. When she failed, something irreplaceable could well be lost.

I thought about this as I stroked the hair back from her damp face. Caring so deeply about her work meant she opened herself up to the highest levels of hurt when she failed.

'I'm so sorry to come here like this,' she said after a while.

'I'm really glad you did.' I genuinely meant it.

'I think I'm more frustrated than anything. To lose when we just should have won is so unfair. So many of my cases are in the grey areas…this one is black-and-white.' Lilah sat up away from me and wrapped her arms around herself. She was still in a black suit. I noticed now the mascara on her cheeks and realised she'd been in court that day. I hadn't seen her wear much make-up except for those first days, when I knew she'd been before a judge. 'I can't tell if I made a mistake or I missed something or I'm slipping or… or maybe this is just one of those unjust things that happen and even if I didn't miss any opportunities, I would still have lost.'

'Can I get you a water?'

She nodded and I walked through to the kitchen and slowly poured her a glass of water while I thought about my next move. When I returned to the lounge room, she was on her feet and looked as if she was getting ready to head back towards the door.

'I'm sorry, Callum. I shouldn't have come here. This isn't your problem.'

I extended the water towards her, and when she hesitated, I moved it towards her hand, and then I placed it in her palm and closed her fingers around it.

'Of course you should have come here. Even if we're nothing more, surely by now we're friends, and I want to be here for you.'

She took the water and stared at me, drank the glass in one long series of gulps, then passed it back to me.

'What do you want to do now?' I asked her.

Lilah looked from me to the door, and then back again, so skittish that I suddenly realised that, busy or not, she'd been avoiding me this week. I sat the glass on the coffee table and opened my arms wide.

'I'm all yours, Lilah. If you want to sit here and bitch at me, I'm up for that. If you want to watch dumb pay-TV shows, I'm up for that. If you need me to go buy you a few dozen bottles of wine, just say the word.' Again she hesitated. I reached forward and took her limp hand in mine. 'You came here because you wanted to see me. Now please let me be here for you.'

Lilah nodded and let me pull her close again. She rested her head on my chest.

'I don't suppose you have any decent vegetables in this place.'

'I'll have you know I have a pre-cut packet of stir-fry veggies in the crisper and some Hokkien noodles in the cupboard.'

She sighed and glanced up at me.

'I'm just hungry enough to eat that, even though your precut veggies have probably been washed in chlorine to stay crisp longer and if the Hokkien noodles can survive a cupboard, they're loaded with preservatives.'

'You're welcome,' I grinned. 'Shall I cook you a feast?'

I saw the way she clenched and unclenched her fists at her thighs. I saw the tension in her shoulders and the set of her jaw. And then suddenly the tightness seemed to drain out of her and she gave me a teary smile.

'I'd like that.'

❄ ❄ ❄

Lilah tried to nibble around the burnt patches on the broccoli and cauliflower florets I'd let stick to the pan. She had protested at the ingredients and binned the teriyaki sauce I'd tried to add to the stir-fry, and instead I'd attempted a creation based on some honey, soy and vegetable stock. Apparently I got the order wrong, or mucked the heat setting up, or maybe both—because what Lilah now had before her looked like it had survived a nuclear explosion.

'You know, you're really, truly, honestly a very shitty cook.'

'Yes, I did know that,' I muttered. She laughed and took a determined bite of a snow pea. While I cooked, she sat on the kitchen cupboard beside me and tried to explain the dangers of coal seam gas. After filling the charred wok with water to soak, I gently helped her down and led the way through to the couch.

'A shitty cook,' she repeated as she followed me, 'but you're one seriously sweet man.'

'Thank God,' I exhaled. 'I thought I'd blown it.' I watched her push the food around the oversized bowl I'd served it in and felt weak. 'I can go out and get you something, Lilah. I don't mind.'

'No, stay.' She took another almost-convincing bite. 'Some of these crunchy bits are almost...' She chewed, then swallowed. Hard. 'Almost edible.'

She curled her legs up beneath her as she sank into the couch. I turned back into the kitchen and retrieved a glass of wine for her and a beer for myself, then sat beside her.

'I still can't believe you live without steak.'

'I mostly don't miss it.' She motioned towards the plate with her fork and laughed. 'Except on nights like tonight.'

'I don't think I could give meat up entirely. I like it too much.'

'Of course you could. You can live without almost any-thing. In the scheme of things, food is a pretty small factor. Besides which, if you can live with half a kitchen, you can probably put up with anything.'

Her gaze drifted back to the kitchen, and I grimaced.

'What do you think the meaning of life is, Lilah?'

'Shit, Callum, that question is way too heavy to throw at me after the day I had and when I've only had half a glass of wine.'

'Do you think people have a purpose, or are we just here to enjoy what we can? Because it's not *really* your job to save the earth.'

Lilah propped the bowl between her knees and reached for her wine.

'It *is* my job to save the earth, actually. I decided that's my job, and so,' she shrugged, 'that's now my job. I can't do it alone, and I can't do it all, but I can have a serious impact.'

'What if it's not saveable?'

'I've wondered that.' She sat the wine glass down and looked back to me. 'I've wondered if all of these small victories are irrelevant, and if the world has passed the point of no return for the ecosystem.'

'And?'

'And what if it has—but what if it *hasn't*. This is quite literally the struggle of my lifetime: optimism against realism. I have had times when the odds have been stacked so high against me that I can't even see where the tower ends, and I've still come through. But my luck has to run out sometimes...' she sighed. 'Like today.'

'And still you're sitting here eating burnt broccoli when I have half a cow in my fridge which has already been raised, pooped and farted its little heart out, and been slaughtered.'

'I have to keep trying.' She was sad again and I realised I had to change the subject pronto. 'I feel like I am such a blessed person—not blessed by any god, just *blessed*, lucky, fortunate... whatever. I owe life my best shot at making a difference.'

'What's the ethical thing to do with my dead cow—can I donate it to a homeless guy?'

She laughed and nodded.

'Yes, when I finish this delicious accidentally barbequed stir-fry, let's go find some homeless people and gift them a freezer full of frozen meat they can't cook. That is definitely ethical.' Lilah wound a noodle around her fork and ate it slowly. 'The noodles are actually undercooked. I am almost impressed at the extreme contradiction in textures.'

I had run out of smart retorts, so I poked my tongue out at her, and she grinned.

'I didn't notice in your bathroom last time I was here… do you have a bath?'

'I do have a bath.' The bathtub was huge and, like the rest of the bathroom, an odd shade of bright blue. One of my 'to-dos' was to rip it out and expand the shower—finally now my procrastination was working in my favour. 'I probably don't have fancy bubble bath though.'

'Oh, please, Callum.' Her tone was positively bitter. 'Fancy bubble bath is like soaking yourself in a drum of toxic chemicals. Warm water would be more than fine.'

I chuckled and kissed her head as I walked past.

'I'll see what I can do.'

❅ ❅ ❅

After her bath, Lilah had relaxed and was calm and affectionate. We lay on the couch together and shared an in-depth debate on the health and environmental benefits of the vegan lifestyle vs Why *I* Love Steak. Of course I lost. Subjective taste versus the actual facts Lilah knew regarding the atmospheric impact of the dairy and beef industry alone was always going to be a tough battle, but throw in the fact that she was quite an experienced lawyer who had just lost an important day in court, and I was beyond doomed. We fell asleep on the couch, but I woke again at midnight to easily carry her through to my bed.

She didn't stir as I lay her down gently onto the mattress, nor as I climbed in beside her and wrapped my arms around her. As I drifted back off to sleep though I felt her gaze on me, and when I opened my eyes again, she was staring at me with a contented smile.

'Thanks, Callum.'

I kissed her softly.

'Absolutely any time.'

❋ ❋ ❋

Something had been set in motion the night Lilah came to me for comfort. There was a distinct shift in the tone of our relationship, and I was aware of it immediately. Suddenly we were lining up dinner every night and sleeping at each other's apartments more often than not.

When we had agreed to take it slow, I had genuinely meant it. That's not to say I wasn't out-of-my-mind overjoyed that Lilah and I had fallen into a pattern of spending every single night together—but it truly wasn't my intention to entwine our lives the way we did. As far as I can tell, it just happened. I am sure Lilah would say the same. I suppose we were both lonely in our own way, and the companionship and emotional intimacy we'd shared had become addictive. Nobody decides magnets will attract; it's just what they do.

We didn't talk about it—and we talked *a lot*. In those beautiful early weeks, we talked often until the small hours—but never again to try to name or analyse what was happening between us.

Instead, we kept things safe. I was courting a new client, a large-scale car manufacturer whose account alone would meet my revenue goals for the quarter. Lilah was initially dealing with the aftermath of the Hemway case. As soon as she seemed to finish with that, she ramped up in preparing to go to court on behalf of a group of residents concerned about a new shopping centre. There was talk about the centre necessitating the removal of what may have been an indigenous scarred tree, and Lilah was up in arms. I told her about the ad campaign we were going to pitch to the car company; she told me about the heritage studies she was commissioning into the origin of the mark on the tree. Somehow the conversation would wind its way around to her travels or my schooling or the hamburger I had for lunch or her thoughts on the stupidity of reality TV.

And the force of nature that was Lilah became a way of life for me, sooner than I'd have believed was possible.

'Let's go for ice cream,' she'd suggest when I was just about ready to crawl into bed.

'But... I just cleaned my teeth.'

'I'll shout you a tube of toothpaste to make up for the inconvenience.'

So, off we'd go for a walk around the suburb, inevitably finding our way to the one ice cream shop on the Corso that stocked a coconut soy blend she enjoyed. I may have taken some convincing the first few times, but I soon learned that there would be no early-to-bed when we were together, and I actually started to look forward to those late-night expeditions, especially when I discovered the waffle cones.

The ice cream bar had a high table and a set of stools at its front window. We'd sit there to eat, and watch and commentate on the human traffic that passed by on the Corso.

'This reminds me of a holiday I took with my family once,' I said to her one night. 'We went to Cairns and every single night my brothers and I snuck out and went for ice cream.'

'See, you weren't such a good boy,' she winked at me.

'The twins instigated it, and I'm pretty sure they only dragged me along so if they got caught they could argue that I was supervising them,' I said wryly. 'But it was still great fun. Doing this lately almost makes me feel like I'm on a permanent holiday here.'

I was still working long days, and my job was still full on. The difference was, when I came home now, I had something else to occupy my time and my thoughts, other than still more work. As for Lilah, every night after the ice cream expedition, whether we were at my place or hers, she'd set up her laptop and work while I either fell asleep on the lounge or just went off to bed. The woman was a machine.

During the week, she'd often suggest a midday rendez-vous. Several times I arrived at lunch to find she'd picked up a homeless guy or pair of random tourists on the walk from her office, and they were now joining us for the meal. After one such incident, I asked her if she realised how dangerous that was, and she laughed as if I'd made a hilarious joke.

'I walk past that guy every single day. So do you—he lives at Circular Quay. If he was going to mug and murder me, he'd do it one night when I'm rushing for the late ferry alone, not in a crowded café at lunchtime.'

As for the tourists, apparently she'd been walking behind them as they discussed in Spanish where they might find a train station, and after spending so many months in Mexico on her world trip, she understood the chat and couldn't help but offer directions. From there she realised that they'd only flown in that day and she offered to take them out for lunch.

And given the way she smiled at me expectantly after she finished telling me that, apparently that explanation was supposed to be enough for the random lunch guests to now make perfect sense.

It was impossible to argue with that kind of logic, because that was born of someone who genuinely wanted to engage with the world. And they weren't stupid risks; there was no bringing the homeless guy back to sleep on her couch or giving the tourists her address in case they needed anything else—but given that I'd never even *registered* the homeless guy until he turned up on my lunch date, even these small gestures had a way of blowing my mind.

It was on the weekends when Lilah really let loose. I'd always loved to sleep in, but lazy days in bed became a distant memory. I suggested, almost every Friday night, that we just turn off the alarm clocks and close the curtains and sleep. Lilah would stare at me as if she'd never heard such nonsense before, and bombard me with ideas for how we could maximise the hours before we found ourselves back in our respective offices.

Having lived in Sydney for my entire life, and rather enjoying my lazy weekends doing not much at all around my home, I'd never really seen the city as a teeming hotbed of things to do and see. Lilah, on the other hand, seemed to know of every cultural and recreational pursuit happening across the broader city space. I was like a tourist in my own home, discovering all of the ways and means a person might explore a city. My camera, neglected in its case literally for years, was once again getting a workout, and I quickly invested in some new equipment to better capture our adventures together—new lenses and storage cards and filters. At night, I started to play around manipulating some of the images we'd taken together, instead of working. And it was *fun*.

'Have you ever parasailed?' she asked me innocently enough one Friday evening, and twenty-four hours later I was at the end of a rope behind a boat on Sydney Harbour, 100 metres in the air with Lilah in the tandem seat next to me. The nerves I felt as we rose disappeared as soon as we were at full height, with the twinkling depths of the harbour below us and the golden sunset behind us. It was utterly peaceful, except for the sound of the wind in our faces. I wondered if Lilah was onto something after all with her continued insistence that it was possible to be busy and relaxed.

The following day she suggested we head to the city for breakfast, and after we ate, casually mentioned that the Harbour Bridge rock climb was just behind us and had I ever done it?

And so, up we went, and again I saw a whole new side to the city I'd professed to love. From the top of the bridge, Sydney looked bigger and bolder than I'd ever known it to be. In the obligatory climb photo that the tour guide insisted we have, my arms are around Lilah and I look somewhat shell-shocked, as if I'm holding on to her out of fear from the height. I wasn't scared, though—I was astounded and amazed.

Over the next few weekends, the bombardment continued, until my weekends plateaued at that same exhausted exhilaration I'd felt for the first time at the top of the valley in Katoomba. I was loving every second of it, but also longing for at least a *day* when I could convince her to just *stop* and lounge around in house clothes while we watched mind-numbing television.

One such Sunday, we drove to a community day at Camperdown before an afternoon wandering around a photography exhibition at the Museum of Contemporary Art. As dusk fell, Lilah had another sudden idea and we headed over the bridge to the Luna Park. Having never been one for theme-park rides, she almost had to drag me onto the rollercoaster, and when we stepped off I suggested it be renamed *Lilah's Ride*.

'And why,' she asked pointedly, 'would you name this rickety old thing after me?'

'You misunderstand me,' I grinned. 'It's not the age of the thing that reminds me of you—it's the way that it gets to speed in the blink of an eye and turns this way and that without warning. It's the thrill of the ride, even while you're holding on for grim death.'

'Is that supposed to be a compliment?'

'Take it as you will.'

'You're trying to tease me, but I saw how much fun you were having. Even though you did scream like a baby for most of the ride.'

And there behind the macabre grin of the Luna Park entrance, she kissed me quickly and moved to skip ahead to the next ride.

❈ ❈ ❈

I called Lilah as I walked from my office the following Friday.

'Hey, you.' There was a smile in her greeting. She was pleased to hear from me. I smiled to myself.

'Hi, Ly. What are you up to?'

'I'm at the wharf waiting for the five fifteen. How about you?'

'I'll see you in a minute; I'm just walking down now. Do you have dinner plans?'

'I don't know—do I?'

'I was hoping you'd want to eat with me. I promise not to cook.'

I passed through the turnstiles and saw her, sitting at the edge of the wharf in a chair by herself. She was staring out at the Opera House, her phone on her lap and her headset in her ear. I walked slower as I approached, soaking in the expression on her face. If I could forget for a moment that I was on the other end of her call, I could have been absolutely certain that she was speaking with someone she cared for deeply. There was a soft, satisfied smile on her face, and twice as I watched, she reached up to twirl at a lock of the hair that lay over her shoulders.

'You've gone all quiet,' she said suddenly. 'Are you still there?'

I hung up and slipped the phone back into my pocket, and she realised I was right beside her and rose.

'How was your day?'

'Productive.' She brushed a kiss over my cheek. 'Yours?'

'Same old. So, dinner? How about we eat in tonight?

'Okay.' She flashed me a brilliant smile, but it only lasted a second. I almost knew what she was going to say because of the shadow that passed over the sunshine in her eyes. Already I recognised these moments when she tried to pull away from me; they still came with astonishing regularity even though we'd been spending much of our spare time together for nearly a month. 'This isn't a girlfriend duty though, is it?'

'Girlfriend duty?' I repeated the words as if I was surprised. 'How presumptuous of you to assume so. I'm just hungry.'

'I just... I know we're spending a lot of time together, but you do still realise I'm not your girlfriend, don't you?'

'Lilah, even if you *wanted* to be my girlfriend, which I am well aware that you don't, we are *far* too old to define a relationship with terms like that.'

The ferry was docking beside us. We automatically joined the crowd and watched the passengers arriving from Manly as they disembarked.

'What are we, then?' she asked.

'Is that a trick question?'

'I don't know.'

'We are two grown adults who enjoy each other's company. Do we have to be more or less than that?'

She thought about this for a minute.

'You do realise that's the perfect answer, right?'

'Has anyone ever told you that you *way* overthink things?'

'I just want to do the right thing by you.'

'Then let's get a seat on the ferry, have some dinner, and you can do the right thing by me all night long.'

'Eww, Callum.'

'I'd like to remind you that I said the perfect answer less than sixty seconds ago.'

She was laughing. Lilah pushed me playfully towards the ramps.

'Get on the ferry, Callum.'

❄ ❄ ❄

We stopped in at the supermarket off the Corso. I carried a grocery basket while Lilah picked supplies from the shelves, and then I steered her via the deli where I picked up a pre-cooked BBQ chicken.

'Not going to comment on the chicken?' I remarked as we continued our journey around the aisles.

'I wouldn't even know where to start,' she rolled her eyes at me. 'Besides which, after what that piece of supposed food has been through between conception and now, you can hardly call it 'chicken'. Maybe antibiotic-modified, artificial-hormone-laden, fat-injected, salmonella-riddled, protein-food-like *stuff* would be more accurate.

'Hmm, you're making me hungry,' I winked at her. 'I hope it's got extra artificial hormones—they're my favourite.'

The supermarket was busy, teeming with people as it always was of an evening. We joined a line for the self-service checkouts behind a grey-haired woman pushing an almost-empty trolley. After a few minutes, her equally grey-haired partner joined her, arms laden with bread and biscuits and cleaning supplies. He dumped it all into the trolley.

'Where's the toilet paper?' the woman said suddenly.

'Sorry, love, I forgot.'

'Oh, for God's sake,' the woman snapped, and the tension in the words suggested that this might just be the final straw in a long list of failures. 'Would you get it then?'

Lilah and I watched silently as the man disappeared back into the market. When he returned with a packet of toilet paper, his wife snatched it from him and tossed it into the trolley. The man leant over to kiss the woman playfully and she swiped at him with a frown.

I grimaced at Lilah, and she gave me a wide-eyed glance that told me she'd overheard the interchange too, but it was well after we'd exited the checkout ourselves that I commented on it.

'That's exactly what I don't want, you know.'

'What, a grumpy old bitch for a wife?'

'No, the whole "death by commitment" thing. Why the hell would you stay with someone like that? Let's say they've been married for forty years—maybe they should have been divorced for thirty-nine of them.'

We walked a few steps in silence again until Lilah looked over to me. 'Maybe it was just a bad night for them. Everyone has them. He might be blissfully happy most of the time.'

'What on earth about that exchange makes you think either one of them could possibly be happy?'

'There's a reason most cultures have some version of marriage, some kind of lifelong commitment. People need the security of knowing their partner will stick with them regardless of what kind of uptight ogre they turn into in old age.'

I thought about this as we continued the walk home. It wasn't the first time Lilah had made me feel like my skull might cave in with the way my brain shifted into overdrive at some of her ideas. I couldn't quite grasp her point this time though.

'Surely you aren't *defending* marriage? You? Really?'

'It's a beautiful thing, Cal,' she insisted. 'I'm not saying you shouldn't get married, I've never said that. I think you'd be a great husband—you're loyal and stable and considerate.'

'So why can't I be *your* husband then?!'

'Fuck, don't go proposing on me.' The brakes slammed on in her tone and I chuckled. This was the Lilah I knew. 'Firstly, I don't necessarily believe in *legal* marriage. Of course, I completely understand that the law has to manage matters of family law, property ownership between partners, and so on. Informal partnerships bring much the same rights as an official marriage certificate these days, why bring the government into it? But I do wholeheartedly believe that monogamy is a beautiful, wondrous thing for most of the population.'

'But not you.'

'Nope. Definitely not me.' She shook her head. 'It's not something I want for myself.'

'Why not?'

'Why don't *you* want it?'

'I saw you deflect that question.'

'What's really so bad about those two having a tiff in the supermarket? He forgot the toilet paper. She got angry. He was already trying to make it up to her when he came back— did you see the way he kissed her? It was sweet. And later on she'll probably kiss him back and they'll share gross old-people kisses on the couch while they watch reruns of 1980s comedies. I'll bet they are both more rounded personalities now than they were when they met, and if they hadn't made some kind of commitment that this was love and that they were in it for the long haul, they'd have lost all of that at the first argument, *let alone* surviving the thousands of arguments they've had since then. '

'Lilah, you are bloody maddening.'

'You could do with a wife, actually.' She was warming up to the topic, climbing up onto her soapbox. 'Someone to challenge you and round you out a bit. She could nag you into eating better, and finishing your renovations, and she could make you take holidays,' Lilah proclaimed, but the longer her rant went on, the more I heard the edge to her tone. *Jealousy.* I looped my elbow through hers and stopped walking, pulling her back to stand in front of me.

'I should find myself a challenging lady and settle down and marry, hey?' I spoke softly. She met my gaze and nodded. 'And if I find this lady tomorrow, what do I do with you?'

'Well, you know from the outset I've said I didn't want anything long term...'

'Are you honestly telling me that if I shack up with someone else tomorrow you will be absolutely fine with that?'

She nodded without hesitation.

'Liar,' I dropped my voice to a whisper and saw her eyes flicker downward.

'I told you from the outset...' Her tone was weaker now though. She cleared her throat, took a deep breath and then looked up at me. 'I'd be sad to see you leave my life at the moment. But if you really met and loved this lady, I'd be happy for you and I'd tell you that you were making the right decision.'

'And if I did meet someone who challenged me, and who rounded me out, how do you suggest I proceed?' I was lowering my head, going in for the kiss. The air around us had become thick and the conversation felt startlingly intimate. Was I really gaining ground with her? How had I started a conversation arguing *against* commitment, only to feel I'd won just by bringing the discussion around to whatever was happening between us?

Lilah snapped her head back and disentangled our hands.

'In the case that you do meet someone who at first glance seems a suitable match, the very first thing you should ask her is does she want a lifelong partner. And if she makes it clear that she doesn't, and she doesn't want any kind of commitment and is only in the relationship to take things day by day, well, then you should respect that.'

I smiled even as I sighed.

'So to summarise—marriage sucks, and that's a beautiful thing, which I should definitely want, but you're allowed not to.'

'Exactly.' She gave an exaggerated sigh of relief. 'You *do* understand me. Did we say we're going to your house tonight or mine?'

'Come back to mine.' It was a primal sense of possessiveness that I didn't often experience, but there'd been something so delicious about waking up with her in my bed that morning and I couldn't wait to feel it again. 'I'll make you breakfast.'

'How about you *buy* me breakfast?'

'Deal.'

We started walking again.

'You confuse me, Callum,' Lilah said softly. 'Everything you've told me about your life makes me feel like I'm missing something. I know it was tough being left out as a kid; I spent enough time trying to assimilate into schools to really understand how that is. But if I met you and got to know you, and you hadn't told me otherwise, I'd assume you were a jaded divorcee. It sounds like you grew up with amazing role models for commitment, so why are you so cynical about it?'

'Because it doesn't work that way in the real world, Ly. My parents made love look easy, and it's just not.'

'Maybe you're looking back with rose-coloured glasses. They can't have been that great, Callum. I love my parents too, but I'm not blind to their faults. My mother's a narcissistic nutjob.'

'But my parents' relationship really *was* perfect,' I shrugged. 'They loved us. They nurtured us. They pushed us just the right amount. I still feel all warm and cosy inside when I hear an American accent, just because I have such amazing memories of Mum's gentle voice, all through my life until she died.'

'But.'

'But?'

'Well, the question wasn't *how fantastic were your parents?* It was *why are you so fucked up with relationships*, and you automatically started talking about your parents—so on some level you know what the answer really is.'

It felt disloyal to say it aloud, and I felt conflicted admitting my suspicions, even to Lilah. The words came slowly at first.

'They didn't *fight*, Lilah. They never argued, or disagreed, or even shared opposing opinions. They were just two halves of the same whole. And it was a stable loving home—the perfect childhood safety net. But how does a person *aspire* to that? You can't set out to find that person. It's the impossible dream, isn't it? What if I hung my hat on finding the person who made my life begin and I never found anyone like that?

And even if I did, do all of these decades suddenly count for nothing?' She pondered this for a moment. I guess I was on a roll now though. 'I have never met a *single person* I agreed with on everything. Not even *you*, you crazy, vegetable-loving weirdo.' She grinned at me and I felt bolstered by her attention. 'I guess it's not that I don't believe in marriage, but maybe more that I only want it if it could be perfect. And it just can't, so no, I don't want it. My parents bombarded me with a false version of love. Of course they disagreed; they must have—they just never let us see it. Dad had a perfectly good career and some grand adventures right up until that famous day at the supermarket, but the way he used to talk about it, his life was pointless before he met Mum. Whenever I think of them and how great things seemed to be, I automatically want this crazy perfect life that I just can never have. I've had plenty of perfectly good girlfriends and not one of them measured up. It's not fair to anyone.'

'I *knew* it,' Lilah was quietly triumphant. The particular light had sprung into her eyes that told me she felt she was about to win. 'I knew you were a romantic at heart. You're not a commitment-phobe. You're a *perfectionist* and you'd just rather be single forever than stuck with the wrong person. You just won't let yourself risk disappointment.'

'Exactly.'

'So what the fuck am *I* doing in your life? Like you said, we disagree on everything. You must have *really* given up if you're wasting your time with me.'

'I've had plenty of people in my life whom I disagreed with.' I shrugged. 'You're the most disagreeable so far, of course.'

'Seriously, Callum.'

We were nearing my apartment block, walking towards the unit that had never felt like a home until these last few weeks. I shifted the grocery bag from one hand to another while I debated how much to reveal.

Surely by now, after the amazing weeks we'd shared together, Lilah realised that there was a reason we kept coming back to one another. I'd sensed and even seen the hesitation in her, and had so far been very conscious of not pushing her too far and scaring her off, but maybe it was time to stop playing games. There was a reason we were falling into this easy pattern of sharing ferries and meals and conversations that felt like they originated at new depths to my soul.

'The fact is, Lilah, you're the closest I've come to the impossible dream. And when I'm spending time with you, all of that cynicism seems ridiculous. When we're together, I can't help but wonder if it *can* be easy to be with someone, and that maybe I *do* want that after all.' Her face fell and I hastened to qualify my words. 'Don't freak out, Ly. I haven't asked you for a commitment, have I?'

'No, you have not.'

'The way things are is perfect to me.'

'Except you'd like it to be this way forever.'

'I only met you a month ago. You could still be a complete nightmare—maybe we just need to give it more time so I can see through this whole most-amazing-woman-on-earth-act.' She was staring straight ahead now as we turned the corner towards my apartment block, and she didn't even smile at my pathetic attempt at humour. I took a deep breath, and added softly, 'If we take it day by day, and the days tick over, and we happen to get to old age, would that be such a bad thing?'

'That won't happen, Cal,' she shook her head as she whispered the words.

'Maybe it will, maybe it won't. If it doesn't, we haven't exactly lost anything. Besides which, I've just had ten minutes of you grilling me about why *I'm* so anti-commitment—what about you? You've just tried to convince me that I need to find a wife, and yet if I dared to even refer to you as *girlfriend* right now you'd probably karate-chop me and feed me to the sharks in the bay.'

'We're not talking about me.'

'We are now.'

'There doesn't have to be a reason for everything.'

I laughed and shook my head at her.

'That's hardly fair. If you get to play therapist with me, I should get to with you too.'

'It's different for me, Callum. For me, aloneness is a choice.' She was frustrated, the furrow between her eyes deep. 'I'm at peace with it. I don't think you are.'

'If you aren't happier spending time with me than you are spending time alone, why do you keep coming back to me? Every time you tell me you need space, I respect that. It's usually *you* who initiates our next meeting.' And then I saw something I hadn't seen before in Lilah. I saw the stricken panic on her face, then a burst of pure guilt, and I thought she was going to drop her grocery bag and sprint away from me down the street. I'd cornered her, and I hadn't meant to. Maybe I'd pushed her just a little bit too far. 'I wasn't complaining,' I added weakly.

Lilah took a deep breath and shook her head slowly. We were at my front door and at least now I had the distraction of unlocking it to let us inside, so I could avoid the discomfort on her face for a moment.

'Callum, I really like you. But the truth is I really like steak too.'

'You do?' I fumbled my keys on the lock and then gave up and stared back at her. 'Are you joking?'

'I do. And I really miss it sometimes. Last week when we had dinner here and you cooked yourself that juicy scotch fillet… I nearly ripped your fork out of your hands. But I've *chosen* not to eat it. Do you understand what I'm saying to you?'

'I can understand you avoiding steak, the methane and carbon and… and all of that other stuff. It makes sense. But how the hell is having a boyfriend bad for the environment?' We were inside now. We walked side by side to the kitchen and Lilah sat her bag on the counter-top.

She began unpacking in silence, her back to me as I sat my own food on my dining-room table. She left my question hanging for so long that I assumed she was going to ignore it, and it was my time to panic. Most of her food was out of the fabric bag when it slipped from her hand. The premade falafel fell to the ground and she swiped for it and missed.

'Fuck,' she muttered. I could hear the frustration in her tone, the emotion far exceeding the irritation of her clumsiness. I tried to grapple with the topic to bring it back on course, because it felt a whole lot like I was driving at top speed and headed right for a tree.

'We've really only been seeing each other for a few weeks, you know.' I tried to use a sensible, rational tone, as if the outcome of all of this didn't matter anyway. 'With any other woman I've ever been with, I'd probably be getting dressed for our second or third dinner and hoping I'd get her into bed soon. So considering we're apparently both—what did you call it? commitment-phobes?' Lilah simultaneously nodded and shrugged, her back still facing me. 'Well, things have just naturally moved fast for us, but that doesn't mean we have to negotiate the future tonight.'

Lilah turned around and leant her hands on the counter behind her. She exhaled slowly and finally looked at me again.

'My work is my partner, Cal, and while-ever you and I are…whatever we are… well, I'm just having a sneaky little love affair behind work's back. You won't ever have first place in my life, and I won't ever promise you a future. Not *ever*. So if you find that you're starting to hope for more than that, then just give me a sign and we can go our separate ways.'

'That sounds just fine to me. We said we'd take it day by day, and I'm happy with that. *You're* the one who started banging on about marriage.' Again I tried to inject some humour into the otherwise tense room, and at least this time Lilah gave me a wry half-smile.

'I just want to see you happy.'

'I *am* happy.' I pointed towards my chicken. 'And hungry for fat-injected-food-like stuff. Can we *please* eat?

CHAPTER EIGHT

Lilah

31 September

The night Haruto died, I sat right here on this balcony with a journal just like this one. It was the night I decided to start my pot-plant collection, and the night I first promised myself two things.

It was in a single heartbeat that I decided I'd ditch commercial law and take up his life's work to actually do something for the earth. The environment wasn't my fight then—but I felt I owed it to him. I enrolled in a postgrad environmental law qualification and within weeks I'd convinced Alan to let me found a new environmental wing to our firm when I'd completed it. Over time, I stopped doing it for Haruto and started doing it because I cared. But it did take time, and that first year I felt a fraud every single day.

The second promise was more a gift to myself than out of any loyalty or debt of gratitude to Haruto. I sat here with a bottle of fruit wine Nancy had made at the farm, wept my way through a box of tissues, and swore to myself that I would never let anyone build their future around me.

Haruto Abel was not my first serious partner, and if I'm honest with myself, I didn't love him as much as I could, or maybe *should* have. He was a good man—once upon a time, he was a great man—but the love we shared was comfortable and convenient, not passionate and deep. We met at a difficult time in both our lives—I am sure he saw me as someone to rescue, and I saw him as a beacon of optimism and hope. Of course I gravitated to him; Haruto loved to stare down bulldozers and emerge victorious. He was an environmental superhero, seemingly invincible... until, of course, he wasn't.

It's only in hindsight I see how immature I was, how needy I was, how little of him I ever actually knew. He was not much more to me at the time than a reason to wake up in the morning when I felt I had none, and then a source of hope that there might be a future for me after all. He could have been anyone. Actually, I'm fairly certain that if we'd met at any other time in my life, I'd barely have spared him a second glance.

And in spite of all of that, losing Haruto almost crushed me. I didn't anticipate the weight of the guilt and the loneliness I felt after he died. He had been sick for so long before his death, and I'd been more bedside nurse than lover, but maybe that made things worse. I had been so busy with caring for him and then he was gone and I was lost. The reality is I only found my bearings again by defining a new purpose for my life via his work.

I have been thinking of Haruto a lot over these past few weeks, which is probably strange given that I'm finally seeing someone else. I wonder what he would think of Callum, and then I smile to myself when I imagine how mortified he'd be. The companies Callum designs marketing campaigns for were the ones Haruto would coordinate letter-writing campaigns *against*. I abandoned animal products altogether when we came back from Mexico, but before then, Haruto had been violently outraged when I drank even organic cow's milk in his presence. Callum's diet probably had Haruto turning in his grave.

I am starting to realise that I'm wearing my own resolve down every time I see Callum. I keep promising myself that I will hold him at a distance, to protect him, because I know it's for the best. It takes so little to weaken my good intentions with him though. The sight of that careful, pretentious haircut across a crowd at the wharf, or the jingle of my phone when he texts me, it's just a flash of Callum into my day— my stomach turns to butterflies and somewhere inside I'm a thirteen-year-old schoolgirl with her first crush. Ludicrous and lovely, somehow all at once.

He tells me that day by day is fine and that he's not looking for a commitment either. I know on some level he's really hoping and expecting that the days will turn into decades and we'll be clucking over photos of the grandkids together before we know it. I see it in his eyes and hear it in his voice, although if I ignore the subtext, he's saying very convincing words to the contrary.

If I was a better person, I'd ignore his next phone call. Or better still, I'd sit him down and end it now. Logically, I know this situation is bad, but I keep wanting more and more. It's the old head-versus-heart battle, and my heart keeps winning out every time.

It's more than a silly crush, although that's definitely a part of the problem. No, there's something about Callum that drags me back to live in the moment. I *want* to make the most of the now, but lately I have such a tendency to be thinking about the future—when will I get sick again? How quickly will it happen? Is everything in place for when it does? Can I do any good for the world before I go? How much of life can I squeeze into these months or years or decades before it's lost?

And then Callum enters the room and I'm just here, and it's just now, and that's entirely enough for me. He has this remarkable ability to look after me and to provide me with the kind of help and support I've struggled to accept from anyone in my life. Just being with him makes me feel healthier.

So just for now, I'm telling myself some lies. I tell myself that he understands that this is a temporary arrangement and we will just quietly go our separate ways when we have to. Hell, maybe the novelty will wear off with me and Cal will even end things. I tell myself that he needs me, that he's starting to learn about his own capacity to care for someone, and he'll use this time as a springboard onto something concrete later on with a woman who's definitely going to stick around for a few decades. I tell myself that when he's ticked off some of those 'works-in-progress' and lived a little, that I'll quietly exit and leave him be with the memories of us.

I tell myself that I'm not doing any harm, that I've been upfront with him, and if he gets hurt it's not my fault. I tell myself that I'll do the right thing.

And then, when all of those lies echo in their own hollowness, I tell myself that I deserve happiness too, even just for this brief window of time.

CHAPTER NINE

Callum

Every relationship has its sticking points, and her refusal to consistently wear shoes was my biggest bugbear with Lilah. I could handle the dishes inevitably piled high on her sink, or the total chaos within her wardrobes, but I just couldn't fathom how such an intelligent, socially aware woman could feel it appropriate to go barefooted in just about any circumstances.

On my lunchbreak one day, I happened to walk past a shoe-shop and had a sudden brainwave. When I met Lilah at the wharf that evening, I held a paper bag in my hands. I offered it to her with a grin.

'What's this?' She seemed delighted and I made a mental note to surprise her more often.

'Just something to make your commute more comfortable.' I watched the delight drain from her face as she opened the bag and withdrew the expensive black sandals I'd purchased for her. 'They're flat… so you can carry them in that big handbag you take your laptop in, and if your work shoes are uncomfortable you can just swap.'

Lilah took a few breaths before she slid the shoes back into the bag and handed it back to me courtesy of a semi-violent slam against my chest.

'Wrong size?' I guessed, although I knew the size was right. I'd seen her remove her shoes so often that I'd inadvertently memorised it.

'Don't try to change me, Callum.'

'I wasn't—'

'This is me. And me is often barefoot. Deal with it or fuck off.'

'Hang on, Ly.' I held up my hands as if that would placate her. The sharpness and the venom in her tone were completely new. 'I thought this would be the best of both worlds. You can be comfortable, and you can have clean feet.'

'It should be blatantly obvious to you by now that I don't give a shit if my feet are clean or not. And frankly, I don't care if *you* care if my feet are clean or not. You might also want to know that those overpriced shoes were made by teeny tiny little children in Bangladeshi sweatshops and I've come up against the parent company more than once in a courtroom displaying their gross disregard of basic environmental protection principles.'

Lilah was staring towards the harbour, apparently willing the ferry to hurry up and take her away from the odious gift I'd attempted. I tried to reassess the situation. Had I overstepped the mark? Caught her after a bad day? Both?

'I'm sorry, Lilah. I thought it was thoughtful.'

She groaned and ran her hand through her hair.

'It was thoughtful, Cal. But I have a feeling it was more thoughtful to *you* than it was to *me*. Are you embarrassed when I take my shoes off?'

I *was* embarrassed at that moment, given that she had been swearing like a soldier and the wharf was, as always, packed to the brim. But was I embarrassed when she kicked her shoes off day-to-day? There was some truth in that, but I was also sure that the gesture had come at least in part from a purer place.

'Sometimes, a guy just wants to take care of a girl. Even if she doesn't need it. And apparently even if she doesn't *want* it.' She didn't respond, and I waited a long while before I prompted her. 'Ly? I'm sorry I upset you. Are we okay?'

'I don't know.'

She was silent all the way across the harbour, and I wasn't sure whether to push her or not. I thought about the outburst in the noodle shop all of those weeks earlier, and realised that although I didn't see it often, my Lilah could be volatile. Like those hot Sydney afternoons when thunderclouds came from nowhere, she had trigger points that you'd never know of until you accidentally pressed one and felt the force of the explosion. I was gradually accepting that I'd probably overstepped the mark buying her shoes, but her reaction still seemed disproportionate to my crime. I just didn't know how to point that out to her without reactivating her fury, which had at least settled to a fierce silence.

We stepped off the ferry and walked through the wharf, and although she was still in step with me, she hadn't said a single word. It was only as we got to the entrance that it struck me how full her life was, how busy she was, and how little rest she got. She was always on: during the week she was entirely focussed on work; the weekends were all about these crazy days full of action with me. It was no wonder, no wonder *at all,* that her emotions were on a hair trigger sometimes.

'Lilah, I'm sorry I upset you,' I said quietly. I took her hand but it sat limply in mine. She looked into my eyes, her gaze impenetrable.

'I'm sorry I flew off the handle,' she said.

'So we're okay?'

'We're okay.'

I took the shoes back to the store the next day and got a refund. The only part of the whole event that I couldn't erase was the nagging concern at the back of my mind, which I could only settle by promising myself that I'd try to find ways to help her slow down.

❇ ❇ ❇

We were eating at her house one night when her mother called. Lilah motioned towards me to be quiet while they had a brief discussion. From Lilah's end, it was almost monosyllabic.

'...yep, thanks... soon... no, I'm well... yep, just work...'

When she hung up, I raised my eyebrow at her.

'Someone's keeping a secret.'

I was shooting for the same teasing tone she seemed to use on me every five minutes, the one I was becoming familiar with but that still made me feel like I was somehow the centre of the universe and a loveable larrikin all at once. I missed the light-hearted lilt to it though, and it came out as an accusation. In spite of her porcelain complexion and the fiery hair, Lilah almost never blushed. That night was a rare exception.

'I haven't mentioned you to her,' she admitted. 'Mum wouldn't understand.'

'Your free-spirit, hippy mother, wouldn't understand your non-boyfriend?'

Lilah cringed and rose from the dinner table, her salad half-eaten.

'She's still Mum,' she said softly. She'd picked up her phone and was staring down at it, almost absentmindedly. 'Her relationship with Dad wasn't as *Mills and Boon* as your parents was, but it was still intense, and she'd have followed him to the moon. She wants that for me, I know she does, and if she knew I was seeing you, there'd suddenly be this immense expectation, and I'm too close to her to deal with that shit.'

'Surely you've told her about boyfriends in the past.'

We hadn't swapped detailed romantic chronologies, but there were photos of Lilah with a few different men on her walls. One stocky Asian man seemed to feature a lot, in various exotic locations, so I knew she'd done some travelling with him. Surely if they were together long enough to travel the world, her mother would have been aware of him? Lilah turned back towards me and sat the phone down.

'Of course I have. She knows about all of them. You're different.'

I could sense *blunt Lilah* was winding up, and I braced myself.

'I didn't mean to be an arsehole about it, Lilah. Forget I said anything—it's up to you what you say to your mum.' The reality was, I hadn't told anyone about her either—only, of course, Karl. But I barely spoke to my brothers, and my social life had been achingly hollow since I got my promotion. Somewhere along the line I suppose I'd accepted that and had just stopped fighting it—so in my case, I had kept Lilah a secret only by virtue of the fact that I had pretty much no one to *tell* about her.

'This relationship is *exactly* what she'd want for me.' Lilah ignored my semi-apology. 'It would be so easy to misinterpret—if she met you, and saw how we are together, she'd never understand.'

'You're forty years old, Ly. Does it really matter if she understands? We're happy with how things are. That's enough.'

When Lilah turned to me with a frown, I could see the pent-up energy in her, a palpable frustration that I wasn't grasping her point.

'Come for a walk with me?' she asked softly.

Spring was in full force and the cold in the night air was starting to fade. We'd left the balcony doors open after Lilah's nightly pot-plant watering ritual, and the breeze that floated through was pleasant rather than startling. It would be a good night for a walk, but she already looked so tired, and I knew that if we went for a walk we'd then go for ice cream and when we came home she'd sit at her laptop to work.

'Why don't we stay in tonight? We can cuddle on the lounge—maybe there's a movie on?'

She shook her head.

'I just need some fresh air.'

I decided to try a more direct approach.

'You look tired, Lilah.'

'I am tired. But a walk will help me sleep better.'

'Ly...' I suddenly felt helpless. 'I know you're a busy woman; I know you juggle at least a dozen tasks at a time and you like life that way, but you seem exhausted to me lately. Can't we just take it easy, just for one night?'

Sometimes I'd catch these moments of determination in her, where she was sure that she was absolutely right to be making whatever decision she was making at the time. This was one of those moments. There was a flare of pure doggedness in her expression.

'Cal, that's not how I do things.'

'But it is how *I* do things,' I said. 'I *need* downtime, and I want to share it with you. Just tonight, how about you curl up next to me, and make helping *me* relax your mission instead?'

'Maybe tomorrow?' she suggested. 'The night is just gorgeous; I really want to go out. If you're that tired, you can stay here.'

How could I refuse her? As I rose to don my shoes, I knew that I was stuck. For her own sake I needed to find better techniques for dissuading her when she defaulted to constant activity. In the meantime, all I could do was to go along for the ride.

❄   ❄   ❄

The next morning, Lilah woke me with a vigorous shake at five a.m.

'Come to the coast with me,' she said. There was no greeting or preamble, and the roughness to her voice told me she'd fought an internal battle over the issue while I was asleep. Bleary-eyed, I tried to figure out if I *was* still asleep and having a nonsense dream.

'Why?'

'Meet Mum. See the house and the garden. Meet Nancy and Leon.'

She was leaning on her elbow looking down at me, wide awake and beautiful. I cupped her face with my hand.

'If that's what you want.'

She hesitated, but then nodded curtly.

'I think it is.'

CHAPTER TEN
Lilah

24 October

So, yes, we're officially together and I've let that happen. And rectifying the situation now isn't as simple as just not seeing him anymore. I was going to sit him down in a café somewhere on a Saturday morning and, over a nice public brunch, I would quietly explain to him that we needed to take a break. I'd use words like that—*take a break*—so that he didn't realise how final my intentions were. Then I'd delete his number from my phone and stop catching the ferry and just never respond if he tried to make contact again.

When I write it down like that, it really does look perfectly simple. I'd tell myself, *tomorrow's the day*—and then I'd wake up in his bed and decide to wait *one more day* and the next thing I knew, another week had gone by.

All the while, his presence was spreading like roots across the soil of my life. My staff all know about him, Rupert the ferry attendant asked me where he was one morning when I commuted alone, and Jesse across the hall in my building asked me who he was.

He's been learning all of my likes, my dislikes, my loves and some of my secrets. Not all of them, of course.

Gosford is like my secret retreat. It's a world away from my apartment at Manly, which has always felt like a corporate shell for me to hide in when I'm in work mode. But the farm... God, the farm is like my inner sanctuary. I've retreated there to rest, to celebrate, to grieve, to lick my wounds and even just to reconnect with myself when life was too much. I've never taken anyone there before, not even Haruto, although he asked all of the time. It just never felt right. I guess I had so many reservations about our relationship that I didn't want to expose that part of myself. He did know everything else about me—absolutely *everything* else—and I just wanted to keep something for me.

But with Cal, I want to be exposed. It's a delicious game of cat and mouse we are playing, and I want to be caught. I want him to know the real me, or as much of me as he can in the time we have together.

And that's why I decided to take him home. Whenever this thing winds up, I want him to remember me there, safe within my sanctuary, fully alive and fully myself.

CHAPTER ELEVEN

Callum

Gosford is about an hour and a half from our apartments, down beautiful scenic highways that congested like hell of an evening. It took a few weeks for us to organise our weekend away because we'd need to take Friday off so we could drive up early to avoid the peak-hour snarl. Although we took Lilah's (inevitably hybrid) car, she was keen for me to drive.

'I can work if you drive,' she'd insisted, but her iPad and laptop sat untouched at her feet for the entire trip. Instead, Lilah looked out the window and talked about the national park that we passed and the waterways we saw.

Her relationship with nature was intense and her joy as we moved from the city into the greenery of the coast was tangible. She knew names of trees and types of forests and what species inhabited which creeks. She told me about the sand mines as we travelled north, and about the case she'd fought against the expansion of the motorway itself at one point.

Time and time again I knew that in another life Lilah would easily have lived off the land, growing her own food and being at one with the earth or some such nonsense. In that way, we were so different it was hard to imagine how we ever clicked at all. I ate with her so often now that I was fairly familiar with the foods she ate, but every time I bit into something plant-related that pretended to be meat, I felt cheated.

I loved convenience meals and technology and television. She used all of those things, but as a way to enable her to work more—which, when it all boiled down, was her way of connecting with the earth in the life and time she'd wound up in.

The 'farm', as she called it occasionally, was just out of Gosford. Once we turned off the highway, the roads progressively became narrower and rougher, until we were on a little dirt road which ran parallel to the ocean.

'There it is,' she murmured as wrought-iron gates came into view just before a bend. Across the road I could see a small brick home, well-shielded by shrubs and trees. 'And there's Leon and Nancy's house.'

I turned into the gates and we began a cautious journey down a long dirt driveway, lined on both sides by enormous grey gums.

Lilah's beach home was the quintessential Australian beach house, without any flair or fanfare, right down to the deep blue weatherboard exterior and white trim. The one outstanding feature of the property was, as Lilah had described in painstaking detail, the orchard and market garden that Leon and Nancy tended for her.

'How old are these caretakers of yours?' I asked as we stepped from the car. I had vastly underestimated the size of the land and the amount of work involved.

'They're in their sixties, but they're workhorses,' she grinned. 'They're making enough money off the garden to put their grandson through uni.'

'Wow.' I took a few steps and looked beyond the small home. 'That's another ocean view?'

'Yep.'

'Just how much money do you earn?' I asked, turning back to her suddenly.

'I inherited this, you goose.' She flashed me a grin. 'I do okay, but if I hadn't changed specialities, I'd be well and truly loaded by now.'

I was well aware that she was a partner at her firm. And I'd seen how hard she worked—Lilah could work for eighteen hours, sleep for three and then go for a run before starting all over again.

'Come see the house,' she half-jogged towards me and took my hand, and led me up the steps towards the small porch. After she'd unlocked the security screen and then the heavy front door, we stepped inside.

Just like her home in Manly, the space was uniquely Lilah. I'd seen the photos of her grandparents at her apartment, but here those images were prominent—there was no mistaking that in some way, they lived on here. She showed me the bedroom she'd lived in as a teenager, the master bedroom she used now, and the compact home office she'd set up. The entire house was decorated in a crisp light blue, with nautical-themed items featured prominently, and semi-translucent white blinds on every window that did little more than reduce the glare. It was a sundrenched home, with its own twenty-four-hour soundtrack of waves crashing into cliffs and gum trees rustling in the coastal breeze.

'I tore up the shagpile carpet after Grandpa and Grandma died, had the floorboards polished, and eventually had the place painted,' Lilah told me. 'But beyond that... it's just as it was when I was growing up. There's a lot more that I could have done but... this place is just perfect to me.'

We stepped out onto the wide deck that faced the expanse of the ocean. The northern and southern ends were enclosed by walls of glass bricks, but the eastern face was open except for a low rail. One side of the deck sported a long timber table, the other a new cane outdoor couch set. Lilah opened one of the seat bases and withdrew a set of navy and white canvas cushions which she carefully placed over the seats, then a few hurricane lamps which she sat just so on the table. Next, she took my hand and led me down the steps towards the cliff face.

There were a few dozen metres of sparse grass and shrubs leading from the house, and then the rickety fence before a very sharp drop, straight to the tumbling water below. We wandered to the fence and I leant over it warily. A small patch of sand nestled between rocky outcrops, but there was no obvious way down or beach to break a fall, just a view that seemed as big as the earth itself.

'So... truth be told, Callum, this is home. This is *really* home.'

'It's beautiful.' The house was really nothing special—not compared to her magnificent apartment in Manly. What was extraordinary about this place was the joy she so obviously found here. I felt beyond humbled that she was sharing it with me.

❋ ❋ ❋

Peta MacDonald didn't walk into a room. She *arrived*.

She had the air of an aging diva about her, minus of course the success or fame. Lilah's mother was beautiful, in an aged way. She had an elfin crop of hair an artificially deep shade of burgundy, and the same piercing blue eyes as Lilah, framed by subtle lines, and *un*subtle brown eye shadow and heavy blue eyeliner. I couldn't miss her elaborate artificial talons and I wondered what Lilah would make of the chemical exposure her mother suffered having them applied. When Peta entered the house that night, she was obviously not expecting Lilah to have company, and did not quite manage to hide her shock.

'What's for dinner, lovey—oh, shit.'

I rose from the breakfast-bar stool where I'd been shelling fresh peas for the salad and enjoying a glass of red wine. Lilah didn't miss a beat.

'Mum, this is Callum—Callum, this is Peta. Let's eat.'

'Callum, such a pleasure to meet you at last,' Peta said. She took the hand I'd extended in anticipation of a shake and pulled me in for a hug. 'I assume this is an *at last* type situation, although I've not heard a single thing about you.'

'Lovely to meet you, Peta,' I said. 'I can see where Lilah gets both her beauty and her subtlety from.'

'I made stir-fry, Mum. With that satay sauce you like. Callum made you a salad, and I even have black rice and mango for dessert.' Lilah had already lit large candles beneath the hurricane lanterns and carefully placed an arrangement of foliage between them. I'd wondered at Lilah's flurry of activity over the afternoon; I realised now it was the beginnings of a burst of nervous energy which was snowballing right before my eyes. She clearly had no intention of dwelling on or even explaining my presence, and even as Peta and I were disentangling our embrace, Lilah had served the stir-fry and was on her way outside.

'I take it this means I don't ask if you're a boyfriend,' Peta asked me, voice low.

'I'd suggest you make up your own mind on that topic.' Peta and I shared a grin.

'Well, then, Callum, you'd best be getting me some wine; I'm not an easy mother hen to impress.'

I quickly complied and Peta and I followed Lilah out onto the deck, where she was impatiently looking at the bowl of stir-fry and apparently trying not to meet her mother's gaze.

I sat close to her and sat my hand on her knee under the table. Peta sat opposite us and took in the view for a moment.

'You can relax, Lilah,' Peta said. 'I'm not upset that you didn't tell me you were seeing someone. I'm sure you have your reasons, although I can't even *begin* to imagine what they would be.'

'Lilah tells me you sing?' I offered.

'Oh yes, I do. Do you like music?'

I had an inkling that Peta would be easily distracted, and I just wasn't sure what my role was supposed to be if the two women were going to have an awkward argument about why Lilah hadn't mentioned me. And I was onto something, as for the next hour Peta did something of a non-musical performance about her musical interests and experiences.

Peta on stage would surely be much like Peta at dinner: animated and alive, glowing with a vitality and charisma that drew *all* of the attention to her. She was a fascinating woman, albeit a completely self-absorbed one, and I could easily imagine her dragging her young family around the world in search of a brighter spotlight. I wondered why she'd never hit the big time. She certainly seemed to be a likely candidate for fame.

'We lived in London for a year, you know, Callum, while I was working in West End productions.'

'How old were you, Ly?' I asked.

'Oh, God, maybe ten. Dad was working for the City of London, so the main thing I remember about those months was wandering London unsupervised while *you* were at the theatre all day and night and Dad was travelling the city tending gardens.' Lilah laughed then rolled her eyes. 'Bloody negligent parents you were.'

'We knew you could handle yourself, Lilah. You've always been able to handle yourself, even as a toddler. God help us if you didn't want to do something—it took me nearly a year to toilet train you.'

'So you keep telling me.'

'She was breastfed until she was nearly three, Callum. I tried again and again to wean her; she'd just wait until I was asleep and—'

'Which musical did you say it was? Did you have a major part?'

'I was in the chorus of the first production of *Cats*.' Peta shrugged with what I assumed was feigned nonchalance. I had a feeling she slipped that little titbit into conversations a dozen times a day. 'I'm sure I would have had a major part but my dancing just wasn't quite up to scratch.'

'We went to New York with *Cats* too, after that,' Lilah told me.

'And then we went to India.'

'*Cats* went to India after New York?'

'Oh no, I left *Cats*. We went to India to stay at an ashram so I could recharge. I was exhausted. It was the same place Lilah was born, so it seemed fitting.'

'Callum had the same bedroom his whole life until he left home for uni.' Lilah informed Peta.

'Yep, dull as a doorknob comparatively,' I agreed.

'Jesus. You poor child.' Peta reached for her wine. 'And what do you do now?'

It was the first question she'd asked of me all night, other than to enquire about who I was to Lilah. I was caught off guard.

'I'm in marketing.'

'I thought about going into advertising at one point—well, I entertained it for a moment. I have fantastic ideas; I think I really could have made it.'

The dynamic between Lilah and her mother was fascinating. It seemed to me that with every story, Lilah had more than enough reasons to resent her mother for the crazy, unsettled life they'd led. Instead, she was totally at peace with it, and the fondness in her gaze towards Peta was genuine.

As the breeze off the ocean became cool, we moved back inside. Peta and I sat on the lounge while Lilah prepared dessert and coffees.

'So, it is serious?' Peta asked me, as soon as Lilah was out of the room. Her voice was low again, but the tone was urgent and serious. I hesitated.

'I think you and Lilah should talk about that, Peta.'

'Lilah would have talked to me about it already if she intended to. I'm not sure how to read this *keeping you a secret* bullshit. '

'We're very new to each other. Maybe she was worried that you'd get ahead of us.'

Peta thought about this for a moment and her smile was almost grateful.

'Thanks, Callum. I'll back off.' Before I even had a chance to breathe a sigh of relief, she pinned me to the chair with an icy scowl. 'Just know that if you hurt her, I will find you, and I will make you wish you were dead.'

'Lilah, do you need a hand in there?' I half rose, and Peta grabbed my hand and pulled me back down, her expression instantly soft and warm again.

'No need to run away. Just consider yourself warned.'

CHAPTER TWELVE

Lilah

29 October

I've had a few glasses of wine tonight, so my ramblings in this entry will probably be even more flowery than usual.

When Mum met Haruto she was cold and rude. Which was unfortunate because he was cold and rude too, and I ended up spending the entire lunch talking for the both of them. When Haruto got up at one point to go to the bathroom, Mum leant forward and whispered to me something along the lines of *have you lost your mind?*

I'll give my mum one thing: she always lets me make my own decisions. If she disagrees, she will certainly let me know, but she always supports me anyway. At so many crossroads, she's begged me to go left when I wanted to go right, and then she's walked with me even when I went right anyway. She never warmed to Haruto, but after that first meeting, she always made an effort. She didn't want me to go to uni—she said there was almost no point me spending four years of my life studying when travelling the world could offer me so much more. But then, when the time came to move down to Sydney for classes, she bought everything I needed for my dorm room, and over the years not a semester went buy when she didn't try to buy my textbooks. All for something she thought was a waste of time. That's just how Mum works. Peta's biggest fan has always been Peta, but her pet project has always been me.

I knew she'd like Callum and I wasn't wrong. He listened to her talk for hours tonight, he refilled our wine glasses, and he was affectionate with me— as he always is. And all the while there was a glint in my mother's eyes that I've never really seen before. I think it was approval.

I like him she whispered to me as we embraced when she was leaving. *Lilah, he is really fabulous. I'm so happy for you.*

And I'm happy too. Truly happy, maybe for the first time in my entire life. It feels right to have Callum here, meeting my family, deepening his place in my life. He fits here, in spite of the fact that he doesn't know a carrot from a gum tree.

In another life, in another time, I'd marry Callum.

We'd get married somewhere scenic, maybe in the Blue Mountains, up near Mount Tomah where the botanic gardens are. There is a grassed clearing in the bush, way up high, overlooking an immense valley. We'd plan the ceremony for late afternoon, just as the golden sun was setting over the mountains behind us. Eucalyptus would hang heavily in the spring air. Callum would wear something fairly casual—a pair of dark grey slacks and a collared shirt, but no jacket or tie. He'd be nervous waiting for me, but he'd wait with his brothers, and they'd pat him on the back and make jokes to distract him. There'd be a small crowd there, not more than a dozen or so people, standing around us in a circle. I'd invite Bridget and Alan and maybe the paralegals if they hadn't pissed me off that week. It could *be* that fluid because we wouldn't plan some four-ringed circus. Cal and I would talk it out a few months in advance and then we'd email around a few days before and invite people to join us if they wanted to. Minimum bullshit.

I'd arrive on foot and I'd wear my hair out, in loose curls, and I'd probably don some make-up—but not a lot. I'd want Callum to *see* me while we made our vows, not some fake version of me. I'd wear a light-blue dress. Sure, it's not to everyone's tastes, but I always thought blue looks amazing against this forever-white skin and against my hair, besides which, I'm not exactly going to wear white. The dress would be heavy silk, fitted close to my body with a cowl neckline.

I wouldn't wear shoes, and Callum would laugh riotously when I stepped onto the grassed clearing and he noticed. But as I walked towards him, I'd feel the soft grass under my feet and I'd be so very grateful for every part of the moment. I'd probably cry, maybe I'd weep in an undignified fashion and Mum, who would be walking me down the aisle, would roll her eyes. And she'd insist on singing a song for us too. Mum and her bloody singing.

The celebrant would keep it simple; in fact she'd probably only say a few words here or there. Callum and I would do most of the talking.

Afterwards we'd have a meal at a hall nearby. We'd set it up the night before over a few wines, decorating the rustic setting only with beautiful blue tulle and a few fresh flowers in recycled jam jars. The meal would be entirely plant-based, of course. Not an animal product in sight, except that Callum would probably sneak in some disgusting deli meat and eat it under the table when he thought I wasn't watching.

Later we'd retreat to be alone at an isolated cabin somewhere lost in the national park, just me and Cal and a million trees and birds and bugs. He'd lose himself in me, and I'd lose myself in him, and we'd plan a life together, right down to how we'd expand the garden at the farm when we moved there to retire. Callum would have to learn how to tend it, because Leon and Nancy won't be around forever, and God knows I'm no green thumb.

In another life, in another time—and lately when I find I can't sleep—that other life and that other time is where I go. It's at night that I'm at most risk of lying awake and looking for reasons to be scared. When I try to clear my mind for sleep, it rushes to speculate. Was that a twitch in my hand today when I was slicing the tomato? Did I forget the meeting because I'm busy, or because something misfired in my brain? Are my moods becoming erratic, and would I even know if they were?

I don't miss the irony of it. I'm avoiding thoughts about the reason I *shouldn't* be with Callum by *being* with Callum, and even distracting myself with fantasies about him. I suppose that shows the extent of the comfort I find in our relationship—that even when I could work myself up into an anxious ball of fear, I can calm myself down by daydreaming about a version of our life that cannot even be.

Six months ago, the thought of getting sick again passed my mind maybe once or twice a week, and it usually flittered past without leaving much in the way of concern. But these days, I think about it daily, and it's increasingly easy to slip into a driving sense of anxiety about it. The shapes in the shadows keep morphing into monsters. There have been no definitive symptoms, nothing that I can't explain away as being all in my imagination or just a side effect of pushing myself too hard. And maybe all of this fear is just because I have something to lose now. If I really was to slip out of remission, well…

It doesn't bode thinking about, but my I keep looping back here anyway. If I wasn't such a coward, I'd make an appointment at the clinic and have an assessment done. That might give me some peace of mind—but then again it might mean just the opposite, and that would mean that I would have to say goodbye to Cal.

I just can't do that yet.

CHAPTER THIRTEEN

Callum

The east-facing glass doors in the bedroom at the beach house led straight to the deck over the ocean. This meant a beautiful breeze was on offer day and night, but it also let rays of light beam into the room from the small hours. Apparently the orientation of the house was the natural enemy of the sleep-in.

While I woke as soon as the room was flooded with sunlight, Lilah slept on, and I was amused by our role reversal. She slept on her back, with her hands beneath her pillow and her elbows wide. I watched her sleep for a while and listened to the soft breaths she took, and wondered if here was the mysterious key I'd been searching for to helping Lilah find rest. All I had to do was bring her home.

She slept until well after eight, and given that at Manly she was generally out of bed and doing something by six, I considered this a significant lie-in. And even once she was up, instead of her usual million-miles-an-hour race to productivity, Lilah made a coffee and then sat at the breakfast bar wearing only one of my shirts. Then, to my shock, she sat and read for leisure for the first time since I'd met her, even though it was just the news on her iPad.

'No work this morning?' I prompted. She raised an eyebrow at me.

'It's the weekend.'

'You always work on the weekend.'

'Not when I'm here.'

After a while, she dressed in a loose-fitting T-shirt and shorts, and left her hair in a long plait over her shoulder. There was a special glow about Lilah at the coast and she was beaming and radiant, excited about the day ahead.

'Leon and Nancy want to meet you; they've invited us over for breakfast.'

'You told your caretakers about me but not your mother?'

'Just go get dressed,' she grinned. 'You're going to love them.'

We wound our way down the driveway and across the road, to the small brick home Leon and Nancy occupied. They greeted Lilah from their front porch like she was a long-lost family member.

'Lilah, it's so bloody good to see you.' Leon walked down the cement steps to embrace her in a bear hug. 'This must be Callum.'

'Nice to meet you.' I shook his hand, and his grey eyes twinkled.

'And it's just lovely to meet you. A friend of Lilah's is a friend of ours. But, good lord, please tell me you eat bacon and eggs.'

I laughed and winked at Lilah.

'Now *this* is more like it.'

Nancy wore heavy-canvas camouflage-pattern cargo pants and a singlet shirt, and I couldn't quite figure out if she was trying to dress like a teenager, or if this was the practical uniform of someone who would spend the rest of the day in a garden. The weathered lines in her tanned face told me she was no stranger to the sun.

'Don't you worry, Lilah. I'll make you vegetable tortillas for breakfast.'

'Thanks, Nancy.'

'We grew mushrooms under the house.' Nancy explained, leading the way along the veranda to the front door. 'It's true what they say: you really do treat them like a husband.'

'Like a husband?' Lilah prompted, although I suspect she knew where Nancy was headed.

'She means you grow them in the dark and feed them on bullshit.' Leon sighed, but his sigh was almost contented, as if this was a joke fondly held over decades.

'If you grow them in manure, does that make them non-vegan?' I asked. Leon and Nancy laughed. Lilah raised an eyebrow at me.

'Oh, you're a purist vegan now, are you?'

'Hey, with a bit of luck I'm about to eat half a pig—don't call me a vegan. I was only looking out for your best interests, Ly.'

'I like you already, young Callum,' Leon said as he offered me a seat at the laminate teak dining table. The chairs were lemon vinyl, and the carpet was mottled brown shag. It was like I'd stepped back into my childhood home, which is probably why Leon's use of the word *young* didn't strike me as odd. 'I'm guessing you're not an environmentalist like our Lilah.'

'I work on the other side of environmentalism. I keep the environmentalists in business by feeding the corporate machine.' I said, and at his blank stare, I clarified, 'I'm in advertising.'

'How exciting.' Nancy had stepped into the kitchen and I heard the click and whir of a gas stove firing up. 'Leon used to work in the corporate world before we retired.'

'Really?'

'Yes, I was managing director for a manufacturer. My, those were the days, back when whitegoods lasted a lifetime or more,' he chuckled and rose. 'Tea? Coffee?'

'Coffee, please. And what did you do, Nancy?'

'Me? Oh, I just raised the kids.'

'Just.' Leon repeated. 'Yep, Nancy *just* stayed home with our five children while I worked. I tell you what—I used to get a forty-hour-a-week holiday compared to what she did for a living.'

'Five kids, hey?'

'And eleven grandchildren now, and five great-grandchildren—so far; I'm sure there'll be more.' Nancy was busy with a frying pan, but she gestured towards a vague point behind herself with a shoulder. 'There's a picture up there.'

I glanced past Lilah to a large framed photograph in the middle of the dining-room wall. Standing in the centre of a sea of people, Leon and Nancy beamed. I looked from their middle-aged children and their spouses to the broader smiles of the younger generation.

'Wow.'

I wondered how it felt to be able to look at a frame on a wall and see the sum total of your life's legacy within it. I looked at Lilah and found her staring right back at me. When I smiled, she looked away, and I wondered what she was thinking.

'It was easier to have a family back in our day. You kids these days get to a point in your life where you try to have babies; we spent pretty much our whole life trying *not* to have babies—and sometimes we failed.'

'Oh, Nancy,' Lilah finally broke her silence. 'I have a feeling you've never made a single move in your whole life that wasn't premeditated.' She glanced at me. 'Don't let the sweet-old-lady act fool you, Cal—Nancy is one of the smartest people I know. '

'I can hear you, you know,' Leon feigned offence.

'And Leon is one of the second-smartest people I know.' Lilah winked at him.

'That's better. I think.'

'One egg or two, Callum?' The bacon was beginning to sizzle and the salty smell was tantalising, so thick that I felt almost like I could fill myself up just by breathing it in.

'Just one, please.'

'They're from our chooks,' Leon said. 'The free-est free-range you'll ever taste. Nancy just about handfeeds the bloody things.'

'How on earth do you have time for handfeeding chooks when you look after that mega garden across the road?' I asked.

'Well, the garden just about takes care of itself these days,' Leon informed me. 'I mean, we spend a few hours here or there pruning or weeding or what have you, but it's really no bother and we make a lot of money selling the produce at the farmers' markets. We get more out of the deal than Lilah here does.'

'Yeah, I get a really rough deal,' Lilah laughed. 'You spend hours every day tending the garden, and I pop up for a weekend every few months and fill up my car with fresh veggies. Poor me.'

'It's keeping us young,' Nancy said. 'We'd be withering up like prunes by now without that garden. We used to wonder how your grandparents stayed so spritely Lilah—maybe there's magic in the dirt there.'

'Maybe it's less magic than it is excellent diet and hours of strenuous exercise.'

'Whatever it is, we're grateful for it. We're making enough money from the markets to pay for Zach's board and tuition at uni.'

'Zach is your grandson?' I prompted.

'He's going to be a doctor. Says he's going to go work in Africa when he's qualified,' Leon slid mugs of coffee in front of both Lilah and I.

'He'll do it, too,' Nancy added. 'He's got a one-track mind, that child.'

'What's on in the garden, Leon?' Lilah asked.

'Strawberries have gone nuts this year; there are thousands of them. The salad greens are ready now too; wait till you taste this season's cucumbers—so sweet they should be a dessert.'

'Yum.'

'We made a small bucketload of money selling zucchini flowers last week at the market,' Nancy added. 'All these crazy young people with silly haircuts and old-style clothes. Who eats flowers? Not that we mind, I suppose.'

'I eat flowers all the time,' Lilah pointed out.

'That's different: you only eat a few things, you're entitled to make the most of them. At least you're not stuffing them with quinoa and pork liver or some such rubbish.'

Lilah grimaced.

'Ha, I feel sorry for you guys and your crappy, salt-and-fat-laden bacon and eggs,' she snorted.

'I'll take your pity as long as I get some of that bacon soon,' I said.

'Not long, Callum,' Nancy assured me. 'We'll fill ourselves up and then take you two for a show-and-tell of where the produce is up to. Then I hope you realise you'll be getting to work.'

❄ ❄ ❄

She'd worn plastic garden shoes to Leon and Nancy's house, but as soon as we'd crossed the road and were back in her own garden, Lilah kicked them off. I opened my mouth to point out the risks of sunburn to the top of her feet or injury from rocks or god knows what in the garden, and she raised her eyebrows at me.

'I give up.'

'Finally,' she grinned.

'If you can't beat 'em, join 'em?' Leon suggested.

'The soles of Callum's feet are so soft and delicate that when he walks on tiles, he weeps.' Lilah took my hand in hers as she teased me.

'Differences make relationships interesting.' Nancy was still a few feet in front of us, mostly because she walked as if she was on a life-critical mission. Leon was behind us, strolling and stopping constantly to look closely at leaves or pick up stray bits of bark. I wondered how the two of them ever managed to arrive at the same place at the same time. As we meandered around the garden and through the orchard, I stopped wondering and started marvelling. Leon and Nancy constantly finished each other's sentences and moved from sharp disagreement to contented laughter in a heartbeat. The tension of difference swung to the comfort of sameness and back constantly. Leon and Nancy together formed a mosaic, each piece of their life reflecting compromise, negotiation, warmth, passion—and overall making up the picture of a unique but remarkable relationship

I'd been carrying my camera with me all morning, and finally began to take a few photos. I tried to focus on the garden itself, but the three people sharing it with me begged for my lens's attention. I took candid shots of Leon brushing a leaf off Nancy's shoulder, and Nancy embracing Lilah spontaneously as they reminisced about the time she got stuck at the top of a pecan tree as a teenager.

'Leon and Lilah's grandfather were debating whether to call the fire brigade when Lilah here decided she'd had enough of tree life and climbed back down as if it was nothing. That was not long after you came to live here, Lilah, and you were finding it very difficult to settle in at school. If your gran and pa hadn't already been grey, they would have been by then.' Nancy shook her head. 'But then again, we knew you'd be trouble the day you were born. No newborn should have that much red hair.'

'Yeah, yeah. Bash the redhead,' Lilah sighed. 'I'm not nearly as fiery as you are, you old goose.'

They hugged easily in spite of the barbs. I quickly caught a shot of them mid-embrace.

'And don't think I haven't noticed you taking photos of me, Callum. I'm hardly at my best,' Nancy raised her eyebrows at me. 'We have a saying in this garden: it's an hour's work for every photo—and I'm about to call your debt in.'

'Please do. I'm eager to get my hands dirty.'

'But not your feet,' Lilah laughed, and it was contagious.

'All right you two, go weed the vegetable patch. We need to go pick some fruit for the market tomorrow so we'll see you later.'

'Absolutely. And thanks for breakfast,' Lilah kissed Leon and Nancy on the cheek and took my hand. 'Let's see what you're made of, city boy.'

❄ ❄ ❄

We worked quietly for a long time, side by side on the ground. The vegetable 'patch' was immense, but it was obviously maintained with military precision. The sparse weeds were all new, I'd guess only a few days old at most. As I plucked them from the moist dirt, I thought about Leon and Nancy and how much they reminded me of my parents.

'They say the things that attract you to a person eventually become annoying,' Lilah said suddenly. She was standing across a row of seedlings, her bare feet on either side of the plants. When I looked up at her from the weed I'd been removing, she wriggled her toes in the dirt and then raised a filthy foot to me and laughed.

'That was annoying from the first moment I met you,' I assured her.

'You have some annoying traits too, you know.'

'Oh, really?' I threw a small weed at her, and she fumbled to catch it and sighed when it landed on her lap. 'At least I'm not clumsy.'

'Yeah, yeah. But your hair doesn't grow.'

'Of course it grows.'

'It's always the same length.'

'I have it cut pretty often. The curls get frizzy if I let them loose.'

'How often is *pretty often?*'

I cleared my throat.

'Does it matter?'

'Fortnightly?'

'Weekly.' There was a little salon opposite my office; I visited on my lunchbreak on a Friday and had done for years.

'Callum!' Lilah was laughing a little too hard. 'You've had more haircuts this year than I've had in my entire life.'

'I have no problem at all putting effort into my appearance.'

'You wax your chest, don't you?'

'Does *that* matter?'

'Of course it doesn't. Do you?'

'Maybe.' I hated chest hair. And back hair, but if she hadn't noticed that, I wasn't about to point it out to her.

'I knew it!' she squealed, almost with delight. 'Do you ever get the feeling that I'm the male in this relationship?'

'On more than one occasion the thought has crossed my mind. Having said that, I hardly expected *you* to stereotype.'

'You have manicures and facials too, don't you?'

'I don't have them like *regularly*, but I've had a few. Haven't you heard of the metrosexual? I'm just on-trend.'

'Whatever floats your boat, Cal.' Lilah was still laughing. 'Do you know that you fold your briefs and group them by colour—and you do the same with your socks?'

'Like a normal person.' I knew she was mocking me, but I was enjoying it—mainly because Lilah was inadvertently reminding me how well she knew my life.

'That's not normal, Callum. It's anally retentive. You also line your shoes up, from what I can tell, in order of formality.'

'It's in order of preference, actually.' I was surprised she'd noticed *that* level of detail. 'Have you been snooping when we're at my place?'

'I didn't need to snoop—it's right there in plain view because you don't have a bloody cupboard.' She was right. I really needed to get around to that, but the finish on the wardrobe doors had undone me. 'And, of course, you spend more time getting ready than me. Even though my hair is at least fifty times longer than yours, and getting longer than yours by the day, because I never cut mine and you cut yours every hour on the hour.'

'Is this an official complaint or are you just ego bashing me to keep me humble?'

Lilah laughed and shrugged.

'I'm not complaining. Just don't you think it's hilarious how we seem so compatible in some ways, and so utterly opposite in others?'

'We have a lot in common too.' I stood and arched my back, which was already beginning to ache, not that I'd have admitted it aloud. 'We're both successful and focussed on our careers, we both work too hard, we both have no social life worth noting. We both chose to live in the same city, even the same suburb. It's the areas where we're different that make things interesting, and the areas we have in common that meant we found each other.'

Lilah fell quiet again as she abandoned the weeds and picked up some sheers. She wandered here and there through the vegetable patch, cutting various plants for a salad. When she returned to me a few minutes later, her arms were full.

'Do you think we have a good mix of same and different?'

The vulnerability in the question surprised me. Lilah had wiped her cheek and there was a smear of dirt over it. Her hair had been contained in a pony tail but was beginning to frizz in the heat. I hesitated just a second before I wiped my filthy hands on my otherwise clean jeans and picked up my camera. Lilah self-consciously smiled while I snapped a few photos. As I put the camera back into its case, I tried to keep my tone light.

'I actually can't imagine a better blend.'

❆ ❆ ❆

After the weeding was done and we'd eaten the fresh salad Lilah had picked, we retired for a lazy nap on the deck. Lilah suggested it, which nearly floored me. She barely slept at night at home, let alone during the day.

It occurred to me that during our visit to Gosford I'd actually found a few ways to make her slow down and rest. I was pleased with myself, thinking forward to the positive impacts the downtime would have on her.

I worried about Lilah sometimes. I couldn't put my finger on it, but I had a feeling she was headed towards some kind of burnout. The only concession I saw in her towards her own physical health, other than the borderline-obsessive diet, was the way she always squeezed in at least a powerwalk every day. Some days she worked from sunrise to sunset, long after I'd fallen asleep myself. And she slept fitfully, jumping around her in sleep as if even in her dreams she couldn't be still.

If I could have frozen in time a single instant in our relationship, it would have been that half-doze on the cane chairs over the ocean. Our conversation became ever slower, and she snuggled into me as her eyelids grew heavy, and then her breathing slowed into a deep and steady rhythm. I half-slept, not really giving into slumber as she did, but mainly because I was so transfixed by the moment. The softness of her red hair against my arm, the scent of her perfume in the air, and the sound of her breath in time with the waves below—it was intoxicating, and as drunk on her presence as I was, I was also in love.

The realisation wasn't a shock, although it did slip into my consciousness for my first time that day. I'd loved my parents, I loved my brothers, maybe I loved my work. But this—this was different. The love that had blossomed between Lilah and I, even in the space of just a few months, started from the very centre of my being and it was as solid and real as the earth itself.

When I was in my twenties, Dad would sometimes talk to me about settling down. He worried about me, and sometimes his well-intentioned chats would diverge into long-winded sermons about how much finding Mum had changed his life. I think—*hope*—I was respectful, but I was so frustrated with his fairy-tale view of the world. By then, I'd known enough girlfriends to know how the system worked and what the emotions involved were.

Until Lilah, I had never understood Dad's insistence that the right partner could really kick-start my life. After decades of dismissing his thoughts on the matter, I suddenly realised that I was a lot like my dad after all. We were men who fell hard and fast into love, even though it had taken me half a life-time to meet someone suitable and discover that about myself.

I wondered if—*when*—I could tell her. Maybe it would be still more months or maybe years, and maybe the words would bud within my throat thousands of times and wither and die at her insistence that we take it day by day.

It wouldn't matter what she did or said from that afternoon on, not really. She could be barefoot for the rest of our lives and I'd love her disgustingly filthy feet with every bit of strength I had.

I was hopelessly, beautifully lost to her—and at last, that day, I knew it. All that I had to do now was to make sure she didn't slip away from me.

❋ ❋ ❋

I'd been wondering about the Asian man in Lilah's photos since the first night at her apartment. Sometimes, when she wasn't looking, I'd stare at the photos of them together looking for clues as to how close they were. There was a definite romance vibe there, I'd concluded, and they'd been together long enough to traverse at least three continents together. After so many weeks of staring at him, he started to look familiar, and it was driving me crazy wondering who he was.

One night, Lilah was out on the balcony. Darkness had fallen but she'd bought a new plant that day and it was looking a little wilted so she'd decided to repot it then and there. There was a gentle breeze and I had been watching her work through the waving of the light curtains in the wind. I had also been making an attempt at reviewing the day's emails on my laptop, but the task had failed to catch my interest. I got up to get a glass of water, and on my way back to the chair as I passed some of her photos, I tried to slip a casual question out.

'Looks like you did a lot of travelling with this guy—was he a friend?'

Lilah turned to see who I was referring to, then returned her focus to the pot plant.

'No. He was a lover.'

She'd have left it at that, if I didn't push her. I continued back towards the lounge and kept my tone light.

'Were you together long?'

'A year or so.'

I waited but she fell silent again. It was like pulling teeth.

'And…'

'And… ?'

'And… I don't know. Something?'

'Are you jealous?'

'Nope. Just curious.' Of course I was insanely jealous. Especially now that she'd told me they'd been together for a *whole damn year* and she usually got jumpy if I tried to get her to commit to something a week in advance.

'His name was Haruto Abel. We were together for a while, and then he died. End of story.'

Her words hit me with force. It wasn't just the shock of what she'd said, but the quick-fire casual way she'd spoken, as if she was hoping I'd miss it altogether. *And then he died.* I'd been about to sit back on the couch. Now I stopped and stared at her.

'Lilah, shit. I'm sorry.'

She shrugged and dusted off her hands over the plant, then poured some water onto it from her watering can. It didn't escape me that I was having this conversation with her back and had no way of judging how upsetting it was to her because I couldn't see her eyes.

'People die, Callum. It's not nice, but it is life.' She sat the watering can down on her balcony table and turned back to me. 'I'll just wash my hands then we can go—I could really do with that ice cream tonight.'

'Hang on a minute, Ly. You can't just drop that on me. When did he…' I couldn't even bring myself to say the word. 'When did this happen?'

Lilah frowned at me.

'About five years ago. I really don't want to talk about this. Can we just go please?'

'But… you've never even mentioned him.' I was bewildered. 'How has that not come up even once in conversation? We've talked about everything.'

'I've just told you what happened. We met. We were together. He died. Life moved on. That's really all there is to it.'

'But…' I swallowed and forced myself to press on, even though I wasn't exactly sure how to be sensitive on the issue, 'how did he die?'

'I *don't* want to talk about this.' The tension in her wound tighter and she stepped inside and pulled the sliding door shut with a little too much force. 'If you can't drop it, maybe I'll go for a walk alone tonight.'

She walked straight for the door and I hastily sat my glass of water down to follow her.

'Listen to me, Lilah, I want to understand. That must have been horrific for you, but you've never even said his name to me before. Can't you see why I'm curious?'

She slammed the door behind herself and I was left standing in her apartment. When I'd collected myself enough, I walked over to her wall of photos and looked again at the images of her with him. They were sitting on the floor eating noodles maybe in China, they were rugged up in the snow somewhere, they were standing before a sign that said Mexico City.

In every photo, his arm was around her shoulders and she was smiling.

I looked closer, closer than I ever had before, and, glancing between those images, I realised that there was something different about the Lilah captured within them. There was a dullness to her eyes. Maybe it was because she'd been travelling for a long time or maybe the trip hadn't been the life-affirming adventure I'd assumed it was, or maybe even the years between now and then had faded the photos and I was reading too much into it. But now that I really looked at those photos, I felt an instinctual concern surge.

It was easy to assume that carefree, million-miles-an-hour Lilah had *always* had it all together. But I'd seen cracks in her façade, only rarely, and usually she came out swinging rather than weeping. But just seeing the sparkle missing in those photos triggered an urge to comfort her instead of push her, and I scooped my keys from the bench and ran after her.

I was nearly at the ice cream shop when I realised that she wouldn't be there. Lilah was hardly the type to comfort eat—in fact, when she was stressed, I'd noticed that she barely ate at all. Crossing the road, I headed north along the beach, and wasn't at all surprised when I found her sitting on the sand just down from her unit. Her legs were crossed and she was lifting handfuls of sand and watching it fall through her fingers.

She didn't look up as I approached, and I sat beside her silently. The waves rolled on before us, and Lilah quietly shifted closer to me. It was an apology, and a plea for comfort, and her own admission of guilt. I wrapped my arm around her shoulders and rested my head against her hair, answering her wordless conversation with a silent apology of my own.

'He had an accident.' Her voice was tiny once she'd settled into my embrace. If I wasn't holding her so close, the ocean would have drowned it out altogether. 'In Mexico. They transferred him back here, but he was in a coma for months and then he died. I don't like to talk about it; I don't even like to think about it if I can avoid it.'

'Thanks for telling me.'

That night, I naively thought I'd figured it out. There'd always been an undercurrent, even as we settled into something of a stable relationship, some part of herself she was always holding back from me.

It made such sense that she'd be resistant to commit to someone after she'd lost a partner like that, and I even felt a smug satisfaction that I finally understood her better. She'd *had* a partner, someone who had seen the world with her, and he'd been cruelly taken from her. Maybe she'd even seen it happen, or maybe she'd been first on the scene and had tried to save his life. There were enormous blanks in the story she'd told me; I knew only the barest details, but my fertile imagination was happy to fill them in with a few possibilities—I suppose my way of feeling in control of the situation.

And in the flood of thoughts as I digested the discoveries of that evening, it eventually occurred to me that in some way, Lilah was still hung up on Haruto. I heard the thickest of emotions in her voice in the few words she spoke about him, and I remember being sick to the stomach with my jealousy and disappointment.

'I finally did it,' she said after a while.

'Did what?'

Lilah slid her leg forward and rubbed her bare, sand-encrusted foot against mine.

'I got you to the beach with no shoes on.'

CHAPTER FOURTEEN
Lilah

November 17

I fell today. I had been out talking with Bridget and I was carrying a folder back to my desk to review a document. I went to sit down, missed my chair altogether, and wound up on my arse under the desk.

No one saw it. No one heard me go down. I didn't hurt myself; in fact I got up without too much hassle and sat on my chair successfully the next time I tried and then I opened the folder as if nothing had happened.

But the words swam on the page. I wasn't crying—I was fighting the panic so hard that I think I forgot to see or breathe. Dread rose in me and threatened to overwhelm me, and I battled it down until I could get back to the task at hand. For the rest of the day, until tonight, I did not spare one single thought on the fall.

Cal thinks it's hilarious that I'm so clumsy and I laugh along with him. But every single time he says anything about it I realise again how obvious it must be for him to comment. Has he noticed a deterioration in my coordination? Or have I been clumsy since he met me but now he feels safe enough to poke fun?

It's four a.m. and I'm sitting alone in my apartment. I can't sleep and for once I can't blame Callum's snoring, because for the first time in weeks we're sleeping apart. We've alternated between his place and mine for a while now, and I've grown accustomed to the comfort of having his arms around me, as if that could actually keep me safe.

I told him I really had to focus on work tonight and he was supportive and decided to go work on his wardrobe project. I haven't even turned my laptop on; instead I've just been worrying. I need to get checked out. If I rang Lynn now, even though it's the middle of the night, she'd take my call and she'd see me first thing.

I can't do it.

When Dad got sick, and Mum sent me to live with Grandma and Pa, I was suddenly a fish out of water. I remember my first day at high school in Gosford, looking at the sea of classmates and trying to wrap my mind around the reality that I would have to spend six years with them. Six years felt like eternity to me. The longest we'd ever lived in one place was the year in California, and we'd moved house twice during that time.

But I was never the kind of kid who hid from the worst of life. Those first few months at Gosford were brutal, but I faced them head-on, with Grandma and Pa right behind me like my own personal cheer squad. I didn't disappear into daydreams or television or books. I learnt the hard way how to manage friendships and worked my arse off to catch up with my schooling.

I could never pretend that things were good when they weren't. I don't shirk confrontation; in fact at work I find it somewhat addictive, and I know it makes me difficult to work with. When I came back to work after Haruto died, I went through five legal secretaries in four months before I finally found Bridget, and she's threatened to resign a dozen times. I still lose paralegals, all of the time. Alan says I confuse them with my friendly attempts at break-room chats after chasing them into the toilet yelling when they've dropped the ball on a case. So, fair to say I'm no coward under normal circumstances… but since I met Callum… well, here we are. Three and a bit months in, and not only have I let this casual encounter turn into a relationship, I'm now playing head-in-the-sand about my health.

I think I'm going to ask Callum to go away with me for Christmas. He's not exactly subtle about his thoughts on my activity levels, which is fine, because I've not exactly been subtle with my thoughts on his. Most of the time I tend to think we do balance one another out; he calms me, I motivate him, and the push/pull of that dynamic is where so much of the fun lies.

But then again, maybe he's just plain right and what I do need now is a break. I have become over-cautious with my health, and all of these supposed symptoms I keep seeing could also easily be explained by a little burnout.

Yes. A month at Gosford, just a month to recharge my batteries. I might well bounce out of there back at full steam dragging Callum behind me.

CHAPTER FIFTEEN

Callum

It was finally warm enough to snorkel, and I'd spent most of the day beside Lilah in Cabbage Tree Bay off Shelly Beach. I'd made a quick dash to the shopping centre for an underwater housing for my camera in the morning, and then our quick snorkelling trip had turned into an all-day event when I re-alised how difficult it was to take decent photos in the water and just how much there was to see under there.

As a result I had a nasty sunburn on the back of my neck and we'd tumbled into bed early, but were lying awake de-briefing the sights of the day.

There was a high window in my bedroom which directly faced a cool white streetlight in the alley behind. I'd hung heavy navy curtains over it, but streaks of light still cut across the bedroom at night. I was staring down the bed, traversing the brown, navy and white doona cover that blanketed our entwined legs. In the semi-darkness, beneath the doona, we looked like one entity.

'… that weedy sea dragon as it darted behind the rock— Callum, are you even listening to me?' She nudged me with her elbow and twisted to look up at me.

'Of course I was. You were talking about that seahorse thingy.'

'You weren't listening at all,' her tone accused me. 'I was talking about the crab you picked up in the rock pool.'

'Lilah, I *was* listening to you. You finished talking about that five minutes ago. When you elbowed me you were talking about the weedy seahorse thing and how I nearly got the photo of it but it ducked behind the rock.' The chill came over me, one that I was becoming familiar with. There was a now familiar beat to these odd moments. She'd say or do something that was just beyond quirky, and I'd tell myself she was probably exhausted. At least this time I had some evidence to back up my argument. She'd had as much sun as I, and I was feeling pretty rotten too. I tried to convince myself that she had a little sunstroke, then, to make light of it, 'How *tired* are you?'

'Oh. That's right,' she said, her voice soft and slow. And just when I began to relax she added, 'And they aren't sea horses. They're sea dragons, it's a different species.'

'I stand corrected.' I wanted to doubt the way I knew the nuances and inflections of her tone. She was correcting my terminology mix-up as if I'd never made it before, but she'd corrected me at least a dozen times over the course of the day and now when I said the word *seahorse* I thought I was making a joke with her. I was sure she'd been in on the joke earlier. She'd roll her eyes at me but then giggle a little anyway, which was actually the only reason I'd kept on with it.

A few moments went by, and her breathing deepened. I thought she was falling asleep, until she whispered, 'You should come to Gosford with me for Christmas.'

'But… that's weeks away.'

'So?'

'So we're allowed to plan weeks in advance now?' I felt instantly light inside; a helium-like joy had filled me up. 'I must have missed the memo.'

'I just thought you'd enjoy it. Leon and Nancy usually have some of their kids over; it's a lot of noisy, messy, fun.'

'It sounds fantastic. Thank you.'

'I'm actually going to take a few weeks off. I thought... maybe you might like to take a break as well.'

'Really?' Maybe we really both had had too much sun and now I was imagining things.

'May as well.'

'That sounds...' I was momentarily overwhelmed with happiness. A holiday with her? It was such a *couple* thing to do. The most positive sign yet, actually. 'It sounds bloody fantastic. What will we do while we're there?'

'Nothing.' The word came slowly, sleep slurring its edges. 'Absolutely nothing.'

'I could take some photos.'

'Hmm.'

'And I could help Leon and Nancy in the garden—they'd like that, wouldn't they? They'd have to show me what to do though.'

She didn't answer me, and I smiled to myself and wriggled to get comfortable on the bed. HR would be delighted to see me reduce my leave liability, and the timing was actually great—other than the traditional Tison's rooftop New Year party with our clients, I wouldn't miss a thing.

❋ ❋ ❋

The longest break I'd taken in my entire working life was two weeks when my parents died. So by the time we left to begin our month together at Gosford, I was actually nervous.

I had no idea what the days would look like without work to fill them. I knew Lilah had a case due to go to court only a few weeks after we got back, so she'd likely do some work here and there. My plans were simpler: I'd help Leon and Nancy out, read a book here and there, maybe take some photos and generally just do nothing. And for the first few weeks, that's exactly what I did.

I rose early and did some work on the fruit trees with Leon and Nancy before the sun was too high. The stone-fruit season was in full swing, and Leon and I were picking fruit as it ripened, stacking it into foam boxes ready for a Christmas Eve market day. Nancy was working her way methodically through the garden doing some light pruning.

'We used to only ever prune in winter,' she'd told me on the first morning in the garden. 'But now that the trees are a bit older, we also do some corrective pruning in summer. We need to keep control of the shape of the trees, and to make sure there isn't too much growth. Growth is good but it needs to be controlled; we want the tree to conserve its energy for fruiting.'

It turned out pruning the trees was a bit of an art form, and Nancy had no hesitation in guiding my 'art'. There was a structure they were aiming for, and by trimming the trees in the right places, they guaranteed the longevity of the tree.

'Not there!' Nancy exclaimed a few times when I went to make a cut with the sheers. 'Oh, heavens, Callum. Let me do that one.'

And so the sixty-eight-year-old caretaker would push me out of the way with her artificial hip and cut through thick green branches as if they were made of butter.

There was something organic about the yard work. I felt relaxation take hold a thousand times quicker than it might have had we holidayed at a resort and tried to find peace over cocktails and man-made pools. In the evenings, I wandered the coast line, reacquainting myself with my camera and the feeling of being totally off-line. I took a few cheeky shots of Lilah as she sipped wine on the deck, or when she picked fresh herbs from the garden.

Mostly I reminded myself that life wasn't always meant to pass by in such a blur of monotony that there was nothing worth capturing, and that realisation in itself was gold. I tumbled into bed beside Lilah those first nights, stiff and sore from unused muscles waking up, Tison Creative a billion miles from my mind.

❄ ❄ ❄

I've never been big on Christmas—at least not since I left home, and even less so since my parents died. Lilah and Peta, on the other hand, were like two children buzzing with energy about Santa's impending visit.

Trying to quell a growing sense of discomfort, I nursed a glass of wine while they assembled an ancient plastic Christmas tree. Peta sang carols as they decorated it with dated baubles and well-loved tinsel.

'Do you remember when we were in New York, and there was such a dump of snow on Christmas Day that the whole city ground to a halt?' Nostalgia interrupted her song and even slowed Peta's rapid-fire speech.

'I was just thinking about the year after when we were at Darwin and you were teaching at that high school, and we spent Christmas Day at that stinking bloody dam eating yabbies.' Lilah shuddered, but it was obviously a fond memory because the smile didn't slip from her face.

'Or the year your father died...' Peta started talking and I saw a look pass between them. Lilah's brow was furrowed and she gave a subtle shake of her head. I watched all of this, then tried to reinsert myself in the conversation.

'What happened?'

'It was a tough year,' Lilah said quietly, and although I knew that was surely true, I also knew instinctively that there was more to that glance she'd shot her mother. Peta, with her never-ending stream of words, would no doubt have freely shared a blow-by-blow description of the awful time, and Lilah obviously didn't want to relive it. 'We had Christmas here and we gave each other plants. I gave Mum one of the roses that she has in her garden where she lives in Gosford, and she gave me a bonsai which is on the balcony back at Manly.'

'I also gave you that adorable little ceramic pot with that flowering thing, the one I found at the market.' Peta smiled to herself at the memory.

'The plant was dead before you even gave it to me!'

'Yep,' Peta winked at me. 'Well, it seemed fitting.'

'Peta!' I looked to Lilah, but both women were laughing, and Lilah waved off my horror with a tinsel-wrapped hand.

'She was kidding, Cal. Apparently plants in teeny tiny pots need lots of water. Mum and I had no idea. We still have no idea.' Through her giggles, she flashed a look at her mother, a brief moment of shared sadness. It seemed remarkable to me that the women could make a joke about the death of their obviously much-loved husband and father.

They resumed their decorating, but I rose and walked silently out to the deck where I stretched out on the outdoor couch and stared towards the ocean. It was late evening; the sky was tinged with purple and orange, the chapter of today closing before my eyes.

Behind me, I could hear Lilah and Peta laughing and swapping Christmas memories, an emotional intimacy between them that I marvelled in. I knew very little about Lilah's father, but I just didn't think I needed to know details to know the depth of their loss. What was confronting to me, and all that I was focussed on at the time, was that they seemed to have come through their grief so much more intact than I had. A decade on, I still couldn't think of my mother's passing without my chest constricting, and I sometimes feared I'd never be able think about Dad without feeling irrationally angry that he hadn't been able to carry on without her.

It struck me that the difference was the way they shared it. I saw it in the way they could joke about the period of their deepest grief now, and in the glowing embers of warmth which existed between them.

Ed and Will, always so much closer to each other than to me, had spent many of the days after Mum's death together and with Dad. They were with Dad when he collapsed while writing thank-you cards to the dozens of people who'd attended the funeral. Dad had been silently staring out over the backyard, resting in the floral recliner that Mum had often sat in to read. Later Ed would tell me that he suddenly slumped forward and the twins both assumed he was crying—until the stillness registered and they realised he was in trouble.

I was alone at home at the time, not yet ready to go back to work, but somehow the idea of sitting around reminiscing for days on end had been unbearable. I'd told the others I was too busy to take time off and I'd just visit in the evening, even going so far as to don a suit each day so I wasn't found out. I think I was actually watching a marathon of some terrible television show when the call came.

I've never really been sure if I regretted the decision to stay away. The very thing that would have made being there preferable—spending Dad's last moments with him—was the same thing that would have made it agonising. I remember him as he was at dinner the night before, sad and subdued, but alive.

Ed was sobbing when he called me shortly after the ambulance arrived. The paramedics were still trying to resuscitate Dad. I always imagined that as Ed and Will watched their efforts, they would have had their arms around each other, twins with a bond between them so much stronger than the one they collectively shared with me. After Dad's funeral and wake, Ed and Will had begged me to come back to our parents' home for a drink. We'd held the wake at Dad's regular pub, just a block away from the house, the place he'd walk to every Friday afternoon for beers with his mates.

I stayed for the wake of course, but then I went home. I sat alone in my unit and felt, more than ever before, the weight of my self-imposed isolation. And the next day, I did go back to work. It was both a punishment and a comfort.

'Cal?' Lilah was at the door, a quizzical look on her face. I sat up and raised my glass to her.

'Just wanted some fresh air. You two carry on without me.'

'Oh no, we need your help to put the menorah on top of the tree.'

'You put a menorah on top of your Christmas tree?'

'Doesn't everyone?' she raised an eyebrow at me, but grinned. 'When we were in New York, we lived across the hallway from a Jewish family. They didn't celebrate Christmas of course but we celebrated Hanukah with them and Mum felt it was appropriate to invite them for our Christmas dinner. Guess what she served them?'

'Please don't say roast pork.'

'Oh, Lilah, you make it sound so crass,' Peta called from the living area. 'I made an effort, Callum, I really did. I roasted a chicken *and* some pork, and I put the menorah on top of the Christmas tree to show I respected their culture. They didn't eat the pork of course but they devoured the chicken and they had the time of their lives.'

'It was awkward,' Lilah assured me. 'But somehow after that the menorah became a bit of a tradition. It's probably horrifically offensive. But it needs to go up regardless and you're the only one tall enough to do it.'

The menorah was plastic, spray-painted gold, and some-one had clumsily glued a funnel-like piece of cardboard to the bottom so that it could slide over the top of the tree. I didn't even need to stretch to fix it. When I stood back to admire my handiwork, Lilah slid her hand around my waist and leant into me.

'It's beautiful. Don't you think?'

I hadn't had a Christmas tree in decades. The chaos of the decorations, the lop-sided distribution and the crazy colour scheme jarred my sense of colour and style. The tinsel was so old that I could see long stretches where only cotton was left, not just around the tree, but all over the room—someone had hung it on every doorway and over most of the photos too.

And that bloody menorah was absolutely ridiculous.

I put my arm around Lilah's shoulder and squeezed gently.

'It is beautiful. You two are certifiably crazy, but your tree is definitely beautiful.'

❄ ❄ ❄

Lilah and I weren't really the gift-buying type of couple. After the disastrous shoe incident, I hadn't dared attempt a gift, and she'd never bought me anything either.

It made Christmas all the more challenging.

We hadn't discussed it, and initially I hoped that Lilah's dislike of all things wasteful might let me off the hook. But as I watched the hype build around Christmas over the first few days at Gosford, I realised that wasn't going to be the case, and I had no idea what to get her.

Peta called around to pick up some fruit for gifts for her last few students of the year, late one afternoon when

Lilah was working in the study. As we packed stone fruit into cane baskets, I asked her for some ideas, but Peta was equally clueless.

'I bought her a scarf. An angora scarf,' she informed me.

'Isn't angora animal fur?'

'It the hair of a beautiful rabbit native to China,' Peta explained. 'Sometimes they rip the hair out while the little bunnies scream for mercy. But it's an insanely soft fur and it makes just divine clothing.'

'But... why would you buy that for Lilah?' Even if it was a joke, I couldn't imagine Lilah being amused.

'Because Lilah is going to buy me a series of vegan cookbooks or vegetable juicer or a large donation to some environmental charity.'

'So...'

'So we do this every year. We buy each other elaborate and expensive gifts we would like to receive ourselves. And then we exchange the gifts, act delighted, and quietly swap them before the day is out.'

'You are the strangest mother and daughter I've ever met.'

'You'll get used to us. Buy her an engagement ring—she'd love it.'

'Yeah,' I half-laughed, but the idea had crossed my mind a few million times. 'I'm sure she would.' I had visions of her shot-putting a jewellery box over the deck and into the ocean on Christmas morning. 'What about some other jewellery—some earrings maybe or a necklace?'

'Absolutely,' her sarcasm was thick. 'That's a great idea, Callum; give the woman who spends half her life fighting the mining industry the products of it for your first Christmas with her. You could gift-wrap it in the skin of an endangered rhino. The jewellery she wears is made from renewable materials. If it's not, you can be sure she inherited it from my mother.'

'*Help* me then, Peta. What would she like?'

'Well, I don't really think I *can* help you. I mean, seriously, I've given up trying to please her. Every year I used to put a whole lot of effort in and she'd end up hating what I bought anyway. This new system works much better.' At my pleading gaze, she sighed. 'She won't like most of your typical gadgetry or novelty gifts. No, I think you need to go with something thoughtful.'

'Like?'

'You're the one trying to be thoughtful; you'll have to think of it yourself.'

'Thanks, Peta. You were a great help.' I shouldn't have been surprised.

And with only a few days left to Christmas, I was out of time and options. I'd either have to head back into Sydney for a day, or try to find something in Gosford.

❄ ❄ ❄

'Going out for a while!' I was already at the door the next afternoon, keys in hand.

'Where to?' Lilah called back from the study.

I mumbled something about groceries and made a mercy dash for the car, then headed away from the house. I didn't really have a plan; I was hoping that now that the pressure was really on, my brain would suddenly kick in and I'd get a brilliant idea.

I parked at Gosford and for the next two hours I wandered the shopping centre looking for something suitable. Evaluating potential gifts through Lilah's eyes was frightening. I could almost hear her commentary in my mind, *so much waste! It's all feeding the corporate machine! The horror!* And yet, knowing that magical, dream-like quality that leapt into Lilah's eyes whenever she passed that silly Christmas tree, I knew the holiday still had real significance for her.

I *had* to find something.

I knew she'd notice my absence soon, and so I picked up some soy milk to back up my lame excuse about groceries and told myself I could always come back the next day. Defeated, I headed back to the car, idly browsing window displays as I went. The sparkling gems in a jeweller's window caught my eye, and I stood for several minutes, trying to think how I could justify such a purchase.

But… how could you buy me this? Don't you know me at all? inner Lilah would gasp in my mind.

I want you to have something beautiful. And it was already out of the ground when I found it, I tried to argue. *I want to spoil you. Can't you just enjoy it to make the damage the mining did worthwhile?*

No way would she buy into that idea—but, regardless, I had to get her something. I stepped inside.

❄   ❄   ❄

'Merry Christmas, Callum.'

She was excited. I could hear it in her voice before I opened my eyes. When I did open them, I could see she was lying right beside me, propped up on one elbow with a cheeky grin on her face. I kissed her and sank back onto the pillows.

'Didn't you get me a sleep-in for Christmas?'

'No time for sleeping in today. We have to help Leon set up the marquee and I want to give you your present before we go.'

'Ah, okay.'

She leapt out of bed and bounded towards the kitchen. I sat up and stretched, then followed her in my boxer shorts. She was sitting under the tree, surrounded by rectangular presents. When we went to bed the previous night, only three small gifts had been there: one from Lilah for Peta, and two boxes of gourmet chocolates I'd found for Leon and Nancy.

'Did Santa visit?' I asked her, confused.

'Call me Mrs Claus.' She passed a rectangular package towards me and I sat slowly beside her.

'I only got you one thing, Ly.'

'This is only one thing,' she assured me, but I could see at least ten parcels. 'It's a set.'

'I hope this wrapping paper is recyclable.'

'Of course it is,' she sighed impatiently.' If you must know, it's both recycled *and* recyclable. Now open the damn presents.'

I knew from the weight and feel of the gift that it was a book. As I tore back the brightly covered paper I caught sight of a logo I recognised.

The Lonely Planet Guide to France.

There was one for a country on every continent, along with a book on marathon training, a renovation encyclopaedia and a photography manual. When I opened the last, she clapped her hands and informed me with obvious delight, 'You might still have a million excuses but I took at least one away—now you have the *how to* guide for everything you ever wanted to do.'

I paused, the display of books all around me. I looked from the books to Lilah's twinkling blue eyes and felt a swell of emotion stir within my chest.

'Cal?' She was suddenly worried and rose to sit somewhat awkwardly on my lap. 'I'm sorry if you don't like—'

'I love them. I love it.' I didn't know how to explain myself. There was a promise to her gifts, an unspoken hint to our future together. I could see us visiting Ed in Paris and reminiscing about her last disastrous visit, or running a marathon together. I'd finish hours before her, but that'd be even better, because then I could be waiting for her at the finish line. She had reanimated me, and in the process she'd reminded me of the dreams I'd put down when I picked up my career. I pulled her close, buried my face in her hair and shut my eyes. 'I don't think anyone has ever known me like you do, that's all.'

She relaxed and returned my embrace.

'Phew!' Lilah said. 'You had me worried for a minute. Do you want a coffee?'

'I'd love one. But not until you open *your* gift.' The receiving was a mere afterthought for Lilah in the gift-giving equation. She looked under the tree and then back to me.

'Where is it?'

'I hid it.' I kissed her forehead as I rose to return to our bedroom. The tiny gift box was hidden in my toiletries bag. 'I didn't want you peaking.'

When I returned with the tiny box in my hand, I saw the panic. I noticed the way her gaze narrowed and her shoulders bunched. I watched as the suspicion wound its way along her body and caused such a deep tension within her that her toes curled beneath her feet.

I grinned and passed her the box.

'Settle down, Lilah. It's not going to bite you.'

She shot me a warning glance and tore into the wrapping paper.

'*This* better be recyclable paper,' she warned me.

'Of course it is. Not sure that it's recycled *and* recyclable, but it's definitely one or the other.'

The grey jewellery box she uncovered did nothing to allay her fears. She paused.

'Callum.'

'You could fit a lot of things in a box that size,' I pointed out.

'Callum—'

'Just open the bloody box, Lilah.'

She sighed and cracked it open.

'Oh.'

'Now, I know you might already know this, but mining gold is disastrous to the environment,' I gently mocked her as she lifted the necklace from the case. 'Apparently to produce that pendant and chain would have created fifteen tonnes of mining waste, not to mention a bunch of nasty chemicals released into the environment in the process. Which is why *this* particular necklace is handcrafted from 100% recycled gold. The sapphires were mined ethically right here in New South Wales, and the diamond in the middle is recycled too. It's actually an heirloom. Apparently.' I reached down and carefully pulled the necklace from its cradle and moved to sit it on her neck. 'Two crazy young kids fell in love in the late thirties. They got married and had two nights together before he was sent off to war. There was no time for rings, or a reception, or any of the fanfare—but he promised he'd make it up to her when he came back. Little did they know he wouldn't come back—but he had left her with a son. And when the son grew up, he bought *this* diamond and had it set in a ring for his mother, to honour his father's promise. And then of course, time went on and the mother passed away and the son didn't ever marry so when he passed away too, the ring found its way back to the jewellery store.'

'That's beautiful,' she whispered, her hands fluttering to her neck to gently touch the pendant.

'The designer works only with ethical and environmentally friendly jewellery and she designed the piece with the history of the diamond in mind, whatever the hell that means.' I fastened the clasp and gently kissed her neck before I dropped her hair back over it. 'I just wanted you to have something beautiful. And something that you wouldn't hurl over the cliff in a fit of rage.'

'I'm not that hard to please, am I?' She turned to me and wrapped her arms around my neck. I kissed her and smiled against her lips.

'You are a massive pain in the backside almost all of the time.'

We rested our foreheads together.

'Merry Christmas, Callum.'

'Merry Christmas, Lilah.'

❄ ❄ ❄

It was tradition for Leon and Nancy to host their family for Christmas Day lunch, and Peta and Lilah usually joined in. This year, for the first time, all of the grandchildren were coming, and there was magic in the air. Even though I'd not really celebrated Christmas in at least a decade, I felt the excitement and the joy of it.

Nancy was glowing, at least in part from the exertion and heat in her kitchen. When we arrived, Leon took us straight to her to see the spectacle.

'She's been up cooking since four a.m.,' he told us. 'Crazy old woman she is.'

'You won't be complaining when you taste these potatoes later.'

'I wouldn't dare. Just don't skimp on the butter for mine. Give me Lilah's share.'

'I'll decide about butter rations when I see the job you two do on the marquee.'

Leon motioned towards the door.

'I think that's our marching orders, Callum."

'I'll help too,' Lilah offered. The necklace was around her neck, and she kept touching it and smiling. Given how difficult buying for her had been, I was pretty sure I'd nailed it in the end.

'Lilah, if he wanted a tiny vegetable-powered munchkin to help, he'd have enlisted one of the chickens.'

Lilah slapped me playfully and I winked at her as I followed Leon out of the stifling hot kitchen. The marquee had been constructed by a hire company the previous afternoon, two interconnecting spaces in an L-shape, with enough room for all of us to sit comfortably and an open space for the children to play. An industrial air conditioner fitted in at one end and was already pumping cool air inside. It was a cloudless day so it would be scorchingly hot—a typical Australian Christmas.

Leon and I set up two long tables parallel in one wing of the marquee then placed chairs all around them. We hung tinsel around the plastic windows and set wine glasses at the adult seats and coloured plastic cups for the children. There was a packet of red and green balloons, half of which I fully inflated and left on the ground in the open space. The other half I inflated to varying sizes and stuck to one of the plain white walls of the marquee, so that they looked like bubbles rising. Peta arrived as I was finishing.

'Well, aren't you man of the hour?' she remarked. 'I can't think of the last time I saw my daughter look so chuffed. Good thing you ignored me and bought her jewellery anyway.'

'It's not ordinary jewellery, though. It's Lilah-friendly environmental, ecological hippy jewellery.'

'She told me. Sounds to me like it's a marketing ploy to trick you into paying premium price for second-hand shit. I would have thought you of all people would have seen through that,' Peta laughed. 'I'll give you one thing, though: the marquee look fabulous.'

'Thanks, Peta.'

'We're missing music, though. Let's get some carols happening!'

It didn't take her long to find an iPod dock and crank loud her playlist of carols. The cars had started arriving, and from thereon it was like a tidal wave of cheer was upon us.

In the lead-up to Christmas, I'd been thinking so much about the past and about my family. Christmas lunch with Leon and Nancy's family, though, was so hectic and chaotic that I found myself fully absorbed in the moment. Faces and names escaped me; there were too many people, each introduced rapid-fire as they arrived. Being the outsider, everyone knew my name, and everyone wanted a chat. I met the social worker from Melbourne and her public-servant husband early and went all day before I finally worked my way around to their teenage son. He showed me the illustrations he'd been quietly working on in the corner, including a brilliant one of Lilah and myself, which I asked to keep. I chatted for over an hour to the young medical student who Leon and Nancy were financially supporting, and was impressed with his focus and determination to work in medical aid to third-world countries. I met Leon and Nancy's youngest daughter, who was working as a firefighter, her softly spoken partner and their adopted daughter, Yi-Liang, which strangely enough was the only name I managed to remember all day.

There was an endless array of delicious meat-based foods (Lilah inevitably picking away at the vegetable side dishes beside me), and the never-ending loop of Christmas carols on the sound system. And Lilah, flitting about like a butterfly around stints at her plate between Peta and I, and chatting to Leon and Nancy's descendants as if they were her siblings.

I've never had a day like it. When the eating slowed and the cleaning began, Nancy directed Lilah, Peta and I to supervise the children while the other adults cleaned.

We settled into seats near the kids as they tore around Leon and Nancy's garden squirting each other with water guns and laughing hysterically. As Peta sat down, she held herself gingerly, as if she was tender.

'Too much lunch?'

'Always,' she said, but she said it quietly and that in itself was a shock to me. I didn't realise Peta knew how to be reserved. I glanced at Lilah, who was watching the children play, a far-away look on her face too.

'Are you two okay?'

'We're fine,' Lilah shook herself a little to smile at me, then drew in a deep breath. 'Fantastic day, wasn't it?'

'Amazing,' I said.

'Was it like this at your place when you were a kid?' Lilah asked me.

'It was,' I said slowly. 'It was exactly like this. A crazy volume of noise and too much fun and just people making the most of each other.'

I remembered the look on Mum's face as we opened our gifts, the excited expectation that she was about to delight us with exactly what we'd asked for on our Santa lists—which she always did, regardless of how obscure our requests were. I thought of Dad, pretending to be grumpy to be woken up so early, then wrestling the twins for the right to hand out the gifts, even though that always ended up being his job anyway.

I thought of the camera they bought me when I turned thirteen, even though they cost an absolute fortune at the time, and the car that magically appeared in the driveway on Christmas morning when I was seventeen. Mum always made a full roast with all of the trimmings, including a turkey, most of which wound up in the bin. Hardly anyone in Australia ate turkey back then, let alone a whole turkey, but Mum never stopped missing the cold Christmases she grew up with or the enormous family she'd left in New York. And even as we got older, right up until Mum and Dad died, not one of us boys had dared to miss a Christmas. Not even me, even as I'd grown comfortable in the idea that I was a token add-on to the family somehow.

But suddenly I saw my family life from a much broader view, and the good memories—the great memories—seemed so much bigger than my feelings of exclusion. For the first time in years, I felt a pang of longing for my brothers. There had been great times in amongst the tension. Maybe, looking back at my family life through the lens of adulthood and the filter of decades, I had the ratio of those things mixed up.

'Surely it's time to exchange gifts,' Peta prompted, her slightly uneven voice interrupting my reverie. She slowly withdrew a Christmas gift from her bag, and Lilah did the same, a cheeky grin on her face.

'Merry Christmas, Mum.' Lilah extended her tiny package and Peta did the same with her larger, soft one.

'Merry Christmas, my darling.' Peta whispered. There were tears in her eyes and she clutched Lilah's little gift close to her chest.

'Oh, come on, Mum.' Lilah tried to laugh. 'It won't be that bad—come on and open it.'

Peta swallowed and nodded, and I wondered if Lilah and her mother had somehow squeezed an argument in among all of the fun. I rubbed Lilah's shoulders, and she smiled at me and began to unwrap her gift.

'Oh, how lovely.' Lilah held the scarf up by the very tips of her fingers, as if it might contaminate her somehow. 'Real angora?'

'It is, darling.'

'It's… beautiful.' Lilah dropped it onto her lap and pointed to Peta's package. 'What do you think of yours?'

Peta was holding a key ring in her hand. She raised her eyebrow at Lilah.

'It's pretty?'

I took it into my hand and turned it over. The plastic case contained a photo of a beautiful vista, a deep valley with endless gum trees beyond it. The other side was similar, but in tiny, hard-to-read text, stated *Proud Platinum Donor of the Fight Coal Seam Gas Coalition.*

'How much did you donate?' I asked Lilah quietly.

'You don't want to know.' Lilah was delighted. 'But it's the gift that keeps on giving, literally for generations.'

She went to take it from me, but Peta reached out and snatched it back.

'Hey!' Lilah protested. 'That's not how this works. I don't want your tortured rabbits and you can't keep both.'

'I can,' Peta said. She frowned pointedly at Lilah and I wondered what the hell I'd missed that had spurred such a fierceness between them. 'And I will.'

They glared at each other for a moment, and I winced to myself and reached into my pocket.

'Maybe you can give Lilah her crappy key ring in exchange for this. Merry Christmas, wicked non-mother-in-law.'

As I'd expected, Peta was distracted, at least enough to take the parcel from my hands and stare at it for a moment.

'Callum! I didn't even think to get you a gift. I feel terrible.'

'Not at all,' I said. The day was already full for me. I didn't need a single thing more.

'From the same designer who made your necklace,' I told Lilah as her mother withdrew two very large, sparkly earrings from the package and immediately placed them in her ears. They were flashy, gaudy and ridiculously shiny—the perfect match for their new owner. Like Lilah's pendant, they were made from repurposed materials, but, unlike Lilah's pendant, featured oversized glass quasi-gemstones.

'These are amazing, Callum.' Peta had tears in her eyes, and then to my surprise choked back a sob. She pulled me close for a hug and I felt her trembling against me.

'Are you okay, Peta?' I hesitantly patted her back.

'Just give me a minute to collect myself,' she whispered. 'I don't want the kids to see me crying and get upset.'

'What a bloody drama queen,' Lilah looked suspiciously misty-eyed herself, but she rose and pointed to the water fight. 'You two girls can sit here and weep; I'm going to go wage warfare on innocent children.'

It was a little awkward when she left, but I tried to comfort Peta as best I could given that I could only assume she'd over-indulged in the champagne at lunch or perhaps was thinking about her husband.

'Sorry,' she said after a few moments. She righted herself, wiped at the streaky mascara that was all over her cheeks, and watched Lilah chasing the kids through the garden. 'It's been a tough day. But your gift was so thoughtful. Thank you, Callum. And thank you for making my daughter so happy. I never thought I'd see her this happy, actually.'

The tears were welling again. I patted her hand, hopefully without condescension.

'She's a special lady,' I said softly. 'And a stubborn, obstinate nightmare sometimes. Did you two have a fight?'

Peta swallowed and rose.

'I think I have just enough room in my stomach for another glass of champagne. I'll be back shortly.'

Alone now, I looked around, to the children and then back to the chaos of twenty adults all trying to clear the table at once, and sighed with a kind of stuffed contentment. It had been unforgettable.

❄ ❄ ❄

Peta decided to sleep at the beach house. She muttered something about having too much wine over lunch to drive home, and walked with her elbow looped through Lilah's as we made our way back across the driveway.

They were walking slowly and I was distracted, thinking about how much I'd enjoyed the chaos of the day and how little I'd expected to. I thought again about my brothers, and wondered what they were up to. Ed would no doubt spend Christmas with his wife, and maybe her family. What about Will—did he have a partner, or did he spend Christmas Day alone like I'd tended to, his only nod to the holiday an overindulgence of convenience food?

And then my mind turned to the future and I wondered if I'd be back in twelve months' time, and what Lilah and I would be doing by then. My apartment would be finished. Would I sell it and move in with her? Could I convince her to reconsider children? Would we decide to marry?

The future seemed so golden, every possibility more delicious than the last. I had changed so much over these months and was slowly arriving at peace with my warped idea of family, beginning to dream of a clan of my own for the first time in forever.

My thoughts meandered, but my footsteps didn't, and as the women dawdled on I walked ahead. It was easy to fall out of the conversation when Peta was there, especially after the tension between them over lunch.

I was at the front door when I glanced back to see Lilah and Peta in an embrace. They'd stopped quite a distance from the house and it took me a minute to realise that they were trembling with that whole-body shake that only comes from crying. I smiled to myself, assuming they were sharing some touching mother-daughter Christmas moment as they cleared the air, and turned back into the house.

CHAPTER SIXTEEN

Lilah

25 December

There's no doubt now.

I liked the doubt. I liked the possibility that my remission—my miracle—did not come with an expiry date. No one had ever had a remission from this disease before, which meant no one knew what to expect. I liked to think that I'd been cured. I needed to live as if I had.

Mum reached over at Christmas lunch and grabbed my hand. Her grip was too firm and I didn't understand at first, until she released it just as suddenly and we both saw that my hand was jerking ever so slightly on the table. I could never feel the chorea unless I was watching for it. It's minute today; most people would probably think I'm just burning off excess energy. But it's not a nervous habit. I can't control it. It will get worse. It will consume me.

I suppose, though, now that the hope is fading away, I can be honest with myself. Six months ago, most of the time I was sure that I was well, and since then I've felt differently. On some level, I knew, which makes it all the more dastardly what I've done to Callum.

People live with Huntington's for decades and they lead fulfilling lives. They have children, they have careers, they have marriages, hobbies, achievements, fun. If I told Cal right this very instant, he'd be gutted, but then he would do one of his goddamned Google searches and within half an hour he'd be full of hope and plans again. It'll be a slow decline, he'd argue, and we can make the most of the time we have together. We could try more experimental treatment. We'll find a way. Together.

If I hadn't already watched two people I cared about disintegrate into this disease, I'd buy into that, and I'd continue to entrench him in my life. I'd stop pretending that I was anything but crazy in love with him. We'd move in together, probably travel, and maybe I'd actually marry him after all.

The one indulgence I've allowed myself with this disease is to let Callum into my life. It was a slippery slope, this relationship. It gained momentum so damn fast and by the time I realised what was happening, I didn't want to stop falling. It was like a luxurious reward to myself for having survived these years so well.

But enough is enough. The reward to me, the comfort I'd take in my final months or years, would not even come close to the pain for him. I've seen light and life grow in Callum over these months as he's crawled out from his shell. I refuse to be the thing that puts it back out again.

And I'm not playing the martyr. I don't want him to see me decline. I want him to remember me like I am today. I'd like Callum to take the thought of all of these months with him into the rest of his life, and to continue to grow himself. If in ten years' time he happens upon photos of us together here at the beach house or snorkelling or parasailing or at the art gallery, I want him to smile to himself, to think of me with fondness, to miss me. I can't bear the thought of him seeing that same photo and his mind shuddering back to a hospice where I lay twisted and writhing and drooling on my pillow. I don't ever want him to change my catheter bag or feed me through an NG tube or remind me constantly what his name is.

And yes, maybe it's selfish of me, but I love the look in his eyes when he stares at me. There's adoration there, and I shine it right back at him. It's sacred. I want to remember these good times with him, not what comes after.

When I told Mum that I have to let him go now, she begged me to reconsider. She wanted me to tell him the truth and to let him figure it out for himself. We were walking down the driveway and he'd wandered up ahead and disappeared inside. Mum and I stayed outside for an hour and we both wept and she argued for a long time that his love in my life will do me good. I think even she could see my point by the end though. She, of all people, should understand.

Later on I realised that Cal had been texting his brothers while we were arguing. He was so excited to have touched base with them, and I was so proud of him. They're baby steps, but he's reaching out, making connections for himself, and I hope that in some small way I've been a part of that. What a brilliant legacy to leave behind, maybe my best—Callum Roberts, this intelligent, giving, nurturing soul, has realised that he has something to offer to others.

For both of us, I will fix this now, before I put the wheels in motion towards this new, last stage of my life. But first, I'm giving myself a few last days to say goodbye.

CHAPTER SEVENTEEN

Callum

I'd questioned and prodded Lilah about the tension with her mother on Christmas Day. It was like a cloud had settled over Lilah's head, and I had no idea what to do about it.

She was resting a lot, which I suppose was what I'd wanted her to do for a long time, but this was not what I'd pictured. I'd imagined her reading books on the couch with the sea breeze blowing and a contented smile on her face. Instead, she was sitting in the study, staring at her computer for hours on end. When I asked her if she was okay or if she wanted to do something with me, she'd snap. The fierce temper was cocked and ready to fire, simmering just below the surface all of the time.

But she still came to bed at night and still cuddled up to me like she always had. I knew Lilah was upset about something—but it seemed that the *something* wasn't me. I actually thought I understood because, for all of Peta's quirks, she and Lilah were particularly close, and I could easily imagine any rift between them causing Lilah angst. It seemed my suspicions were confirmed when I overheard her on the phone to Peta one evening when I was returning to the house from a walk.

'...I just want to be alone with Callum right now, okay?'

Her hushed whisper carried in the dusk stillness, and I slammed the door extra loud so she knew that I was home.

She hung up her phone and growled, and I tried again to prompt her to vent. 'Maybe you'll feel better if you talk about it, Ly?'

'Callum,' the growl returned, this time directed at me, 'I don't want to fucking talk about it. I will let you know if I change my mind. Can you please stop asking me?'

'If that's what you want,' I sighed. 'I care about you, so when I see you're unhappy, I want to help. I'm sorry if that annoys you.'

I braced myself for the impact of her anger, and was surprised when her expression twisted. Her breaths were heavy and tight. She was struggling to contain herself, but instead of anger, there was agony in her eyes.

'I just need some time to myself. I have a lot to think about.'

There was the faintest ripple of unease somewhere very deep inside me. It was something about the slump of her shoulders, the confused pain I could see in her, the way she was holding herself back from me. It seems naive looking back, but I brushed the thoughts away as soon as they arose. I was so sure I'd found my happy ending, and so confident in the bond between Lilah and I. If something was seriously wrong, Lilah would tell me when she was ready, and we'd work through it together. In fact, even if I was right and her strange withdrawal was just related to a fight with her mother, she'd tell me about that soon enough too.

'I'm trying to give you space,' I said, as gently as I could.

'You are. I know. I appreciate it.'

'If you need anything, I'm here for you.'

Lilah swallowed and walked slowly closer to brush a kiss against my cheek.

'I know.'

But she walked past me, out of the kitchen out to the deck. After a while I uncorked a bottle of wine and followed her. I silently poured her a glass and sat beside her.

We sat that way for a long time until well after it was completely dark. Without speaking a word, Lilah finally took my hand and led me down the stairs to the patch of grass between the house and the cliff face.

She lifted her head to stare at the sky. I looked up too.

'See,' she murmured. 'No light pollution. You only see it for what it is when there's no city haze over your view.'

It seemed every time I looked up at the night sky I realised there was more to see. Lilah was right; the night vista we could see from the Gosford property was beyond compare. We stood there for a while, until a distant shooting star flashed over the ocean. Was there some folklore about making a wish on a shooting star? I wasn't sure, but I made one anyway.

When I looked back down to her a few moments later, Lilah's star-lit expression was calm and I felt like whatever had been going on, the worst of it had surely passed.

❄ ❄ ❄

The remaining days before New Year were different again. Lilah was still spending a lot of time on her own, but the anger seemed to have passed. She had space for me now, and although it was often in silence, she'd sit with me while I read or help me as I did jobs for Nancy and Leon in the garden. I thought she was healing. I thought it was only a matter of time before she explained.

'It's your birthday tomorrow.' Lilah's sing-song reminder was almost a surprise when it came. I suppose I'd been aware that the date was drawing near, but it wasn't a priority. I was distracted by the tension of the days that had passed, and focussed only on her and our break together. Turning another year older seemed a minor detail.

'Yep.'

'You don't seem very excited. You're forty tomorrow, you know.'

'I'm well aware of that,' I laughed and rose from the breakfast bar where I'd been reading a book and eating my breakfast. I rinsed my dishes in the sink and headed for the front door.

'I've organised a surprise.'

'Really no need, Lilah. I'm not interested in celebrating it,' I said as I picked my hat up off the hallstand and pulled it onto my head. I was secretly pleased though—not so much with the surprise, but with the happiness in her voice.

'Are you having a mid-life crisis instead?' Lilah called after me.

'Isn't that what this holiday is all about?' I called back, and let the door slam behind me as I went to do some weeding.

❄ ❄ ❄

I woke on my birthday to find Lilah in the kitchen frying bacon.

'Oh, dear God. You've lost your mind.' I was stunned.

'Happy birthday, Callum.'

'Bacon? You?'

'And eggs. I'm not going to eat them, of course. But you can.'

I stood behind her and wrapped my arms around her waist.

'What an unexpected treat.'

'Yes. I would hope so,' she grimaced as she turned the sizzling meat over. 'Did you sleep well?'

'I did indeed.'

'Good. It's going to be a long day.'

'Oh?'

'I have a surprise for you tonight.' She twisted to kiss my cheek.

'I have to wait until tonight?'

'Yep.'

'What if I can't wait?'

Lilah shrugged. 'Too bloody bad.'

❅ ❅ ❅

Nancy had asked me to turn the dirt over in part of the garden to prepare it for planting. The area was shaded by the shadow of the house in the morning, so after breakfast I spent a few hours getting my hands dirty. It was nearly forty degrees by the time the sun was high in the sky and after a quick shower I set myself up under the fan in the living room with my *Lonely Planet* guides and an icy drink. Lilah had been cooking all day, and I had realised with some amusement that she'd planned some kind of dinner for me.

Just after four, she disappeared into the bedroom. I yawned, stretched and followed her.

'So, what's the plan?'

'Plan?' Her tone was light, teasing. There was a blue cocktail gown on the bed, and the necklace I'd given her for Christmas beside it. I raised my eyebrows.

'You are going to look amazing in that.'

'I do,' she confirmed. 'You'd better get dressed, we need to leave soon.'

'Leave?' Given all the cooking, I had assumed we were eating in.

'You heard me. Wear something fancy.'

'I didn't bring anything fancy.'

'Then take a bloody shower and wear something clean,' she laughed.

❄ ❄ ❄

I realised pretty quickly that we were headed back to the city. Lilah had packed the back seat of the car with a small esky and a box containing a few bottles of wine. She insisted on driving, and was chatting away as the car headed south, blatantly ignoring my questions as to what exactly we were doing.

The CBD of Sydney is a nightmare on New Year's Eve. Over a million people crowd the shorelines of the harbour to see the fireworks, and traffic was gridlocked even at five thirty in the afternoon. It took us forty minutes to find our way to Lilah's building.

'We're going to your office?' I laughed. 'I've just guessed your plan. You're going to sit me at the back of a meeting room with the wine and food to entertain myself while you have a meeting.'

Her smile was sly. She pressed a remote-control gadget on her key ring and the underground basement roller door opened. Beside the elevator door was a parking space with her name on it. She parked the car and pointed to the back seat.

'I hope you brought your muscles.'

'Why's that?'

'We've got a bit of a hike ahead of us and you need to carry the wine.'

❄ ❄ ❄

We joined the masses of revellers on the streets. Lilah pointed me towards Circular Quay, only a few hundred metres away, and we walked slowly towards the harbour. She was wearing strappy sandals with a small heel, and before we'd even left the block she stopped, sat on the esky and silently removed them.

I laughed.

'I'm sorry, Callum. I know it's your birthday and I really did mean to wear them all night, but...'

'It's fine.' I grinned. 'I might even be used to it.'

She looked at me in surprise, then slipped her sandals into her handbag and continued towards Circular Quay. When we neared the ferry wharf, she headed right instead, walking towards the eastern side of the quay beside the Opera House. The crowd was incredibly thick, barely moving as people lined up hoping to find a place within reserved shorefront areas to watch the later fireworks over the harbour. There were children so excited that they bounced beside their parents as if they were standing on trampolines instead of cement, and teenagers trying very hard to look casual. And in the midst of all of the youth and excitement stood adults, trying harder to play it cool, but even they carried a smile on their lips and a light in their eyes.

I loved the city, and I loved the way it partied at New Year. It was all of the joy at Leon and Nancy's Christmas dinner, on a city-wide scale.

I still had no idea what Lilah was up to, until she pointed to a water taxi stand.

'Intriguing.'

The taxi skipper helped us into his small boat and Lilah quietly murmured to him our destination. We headed out into the harbour, making a beeline for North Sydney on the other side of the Harbour Bridge. It was still warm, but the water taxi was such a small craft that it provided almost no protection from the wind as we moved, offering a slightly bruising relief. Thousands of vessels were already on the water, jostling for the best vantage spots for the famous fireworks display, and the taxi darted here and there to avoid them.

'What *are* you up to?' I asked Lilah. 'I didn't think you'd be one for the fireworks. If the expense doesn't mortify you, surely the resulting smoke does.'

'Tonight isn't about me,' she said with a shrug. 'It didn't seem fair to have you turn forty, on New Year's Eve no less, sitting on a farm eating rabbit food with me.'

'That would have been absolutely fine. Divine almost.'

She shook her head. 'I thought of something better.'

The water taxi docked at the wharf at North Sydney. Once we had alighted, Lilah pointed to another craft further along it.

The boat was small, a luxurious but tiny flat-bottomed pontoon with a circle of padded leather chairs along the rear. A woman in a uniform was waiting on the wharf, a man in casual clothes seated up the front beside the steering wheel. A small table was in the middle, and beside it an open box of ice, waiting for our wine.

'Bloody hell,' I whistled. 'That's amazing. How did you organise this?'

'Personal favour from the owner,' the skipper said as she took the esky from Lilah and kissed her cheek. 'Happy New Year.'

'Callum, this is Paige; Paige, meet Callum.'

'That's some favour,' I said. 'Lovely to meet you, Paige.'

'Lilah and my boss went to uni together,' Paige informed me. She took the box out of my hands and climbed down into the vessel to sit the wine in the cooler.

'He's also an old client from my commercial days. I helped him out with some legal issues a few years ago. He owed me big time; I thought it was a good chance to call it in,' Lilah said. 'Do you like it?'

'This is amazing,' I said, and I pulled her close for a kiss. 'I can't believe you did this for me.'

'I even cooked you more meat,' she said, grimacing. 'So you'd better bloody appreciate it.'

'I do,' I said, and I looked at the boat and the harbour again and shook my head. 'You're a marvel.'

'I'm nothing if not well connected,' she agreed.

'This is my partner, Lewis.' Paige informed us, and the young man on the boat waved and called back a greeting. 'I hope you don't mind; he's going to sit up front and keep me company.'

'I cooked enough for you two as well,' Lilah said. She squeezed my hand and stepped cautiously forward onto the pontoon. 'Let's go! I want to see the harbour before we have to line up and wait for the fireworks.'

❊ ❊ ❊

We spent the next hours darting here and there over the harbour, waving to party-goers on other vessels, eating the picnic Lilah had prepared, drinking the wines she'd arranged. Paige and Lewis kept to themselves for the most part, occasionally pointing out interesting landmarks or vessels, or joining us to eat before returning to the front of the boat.

'I spent New Year on the harbour when I was at uni,' I told Lilah. The sun was starting to set and the bite had gone from its rays, leaving only the golden glow of the impending dusk. All around us, party boats and smaller crafts were alive with the sound of celebrations. There was something remarkable about New Year on Sydney Harbour. As one of the first places in the world to see in the new day, it was always a massive event. 'I wasn't on a boat this plush; it was actually one of those nasty seafood buffet jobs, an all-you-can-eat-and-drink deal. One of my friends vomited on me.' It had been a girlfriend actually, but I couldn't remember her name, only the red wine stain on the front of my shirt.

'Classy,' Lilah chuckled.

'Don't you just love the way this city goes all out for New Year?' I murmured.

'Honestly? The waste… nearly does my head in,' Lilah grimaced. Her expression softened though. 'But… remember when you told me this city energises you?'

I nodded. Of course I remembered, but I was amazed that she did too.

'I just knew you'd like this,' she swept her arm before her. 'Being a small figure on a small boat, dwarfed by the enormity of the city and the crowd. It seemed like the perfect way to ring in a new year full of possibility. My office usually has a rooftop party for clients—I nearly took you there,' she grinned when I grimaced. 'But then of course I remembered that I actually *like* you. Does Tison's do the New Year party thing too?'

'Yeah, they do. It's kind of an institution. I'm glad I'm on leave; it's one of those endless networking events where you really want to medicate yourself with alcohol to numb the pain of small talk with dozens of clients but you have to be on your best behaviour.' I'd been at the Tison's party every year since I graduated. It wasn't the kind of event I could ever have opted out of, except for this happily timed block of leave.

'My firm's is low-key, but it's still arduous. Only clients above a certain level are invited, and the food is all lobster and caviar and baby cow. It's a nightmare. When we decided to go to the farm this year, I told Alan I wouldn't make it so he insisted that Bridget, Anita and…' She trailed off, frowning suddenly.

'What's up?' I prompted. I followed her gaze but she was staring at the containers of food on the picnic table, and nothing seemed out of the ordinary there. I looked back to her face, which was twisted, contorted with the effort of whatever thought had caused her to stall.

'Anita and...' She repeated, then again. 'Bridget, Anita and...'

'Liam,' I said, referring to one of the two paralegals she was forever complaining about. 'Don't you think it's funny that I know his name but I've never met him? I think you either need more wine, or less, Ly.'

'More. Definitely more. Refill me?'

I did as she asked, but a shadow passed over the light-hearted bubble I had been floating in. I'd been explaining so many tiny, little things over these past few months as Lilah being exhausted and burned out. Together, they formed a bigger picture that I couldn't quite decipher—I just knew that something wasn't right with her. We'd been at Gosford for two entire weeks and she'd done little more than laze around, in that strange way she had of just switching off when we were at the farm. I had genuinely expected to see her sharpen again. I thought the rest would refocus her and she'd be firing on all cylinders, but there was no denying that she still she was stumbling, if not with her feet, with her words.

We both fell silent for a long moment, and I glanced at her.

'Are you okay, Ly? You've not been yourself lately.'

She didn't seem at all bothered by my question. Lilah shrugged her shoulders and said, 'Neither have you, you know. You've been renovating and gardening and taking photos and actually texting your brothers. It's been a big few months for both of us.'

'So do you think you're just worn out?'

'You've been trying to get me to relax more, I know you have.' She gave me a pointed glance. I chuckled and nodded. 'And if there wasn't something in that, I'd never have let you get away with it. I'm taking it really easy over this break. You don't need to worry about me, okay?

'I like worrying about you.'

'Don't you dare ruin this elaborate birthday surprise with serious chats about slowing down and taking it easy,' she said suddenly. 'Pour the champagne and let's get back to partying.'

She was right, and I was sure that there'd be another time. I reached for the champagne.

❅ ❅ ❅

Darkness fell just before the nine p.m. family fireworks. The cheers of the hundreds of thousands of people on the water and the shorelines were the soundtrack to a spectacular light show that kicked off above us. The Harbour Bridge was awash with colour, a rainbow of light. Maybe the New Year's fireworks were Sydney's way of dressing up for her lovers— people like me who saw her beauty every day but stopped to appreciate it just one night a year.

'This has been incredible,' I said softly. I glanced down to Lilah, the reflection of the rainbows above us dancing in her eyes.

'You're looking the wrong way!' she protested. She was giggly from several hours of wines and the hype of the atmosphere just from the crowd, and there was a childlike wonder on her face. Maybe the environmentally sensitive part of her mind could be sedated by Moet, because she was truly enjoying the fireworks, and I was literally loving watching them through her. I cupped her face in my hands.

'Thank you, Lilah.'

I bent to kiss her. All of the things I knew she wasn't ready to hear—how much I loved her, how grateful I was for the joy she'd brought me, how happy I was at that moment—it was all in my kiss. And better still, I could feel in the way she kissed me back that she felt exactly the same.

❊   ❊   ❊

We returned to the farm the following afternoon. In the car, Lilah was quiet and I told myself it was just the late night, but as we ate dinner I finally acknowledged that she was back to barely speaking again.

'Fuck it.' She suddenly dropped her fork and rubbed her face with her hands. 'I'm sorry Cal, I'm just distracted... just... I really need to do some work on the new case to-night. Do you mind if I skip the rest of dinner and go try to make some headway before bed? It's prep work. Pre-reading. Needs to be done and leaving it undone is driving me insane.'

There it was again, the tiniest blip on my instinctual radar. In spite of the stereotype of her profession, Lilah was not a great liar.

'It really can't wait?'

She shook her head slowly, the ridge between her eyes deeper still. I hesitated, an internal debate happening in dou-ble-time as I tried to figure out if I should call her out and push her more about whatever was really going on, or just leave it be.

'Then go for it, Lilah. Whatever you need to do.'

She pushed back her chair and left. I watched a silly com-edy on television only for a while before the long day caught up with me and I realised I needed to go to bed. I stopped at her study door and saw her sitting at the desk, one foot tucked up underneath her, staring at the ceiling.

I asked what I thought was a logical question.

'Problems with the Internet or problems with the case?'

She startled and turned back to me with a semi-scowl. She'd wound her hair up with a pencil into a messy knot on top of her head and, make-up-free, suddenly looked exhausted. The scowl disappeared quickly and was replaced by sadness that I didn't like one bit.

'The Internet is actually playing nice today. I just wish it wasn't.'

The screen behind her did contain hundreds of lines of tiny text, so I decided that I must have misread the signals earlier and maybe she'd been telling me the truth after all. I knew the case she'd return to after the break was a big one.

'Is there anything I can do?' I offered gently.

The hand fell from her face, but her eyes were closed, and she gave another silent shake of her head, knocking a lock of hair from its precarious bun and onto her shoulder.

'Are you okay?' Now I was really worried. Lilah looked almost as if she would cry. I hadn't seen her cry other than that night she lost the Minchin case, and I wasn't sure I'd handled it well then. The blue eyes flung wide and she offered me a shimmering smile.

'Sorry, Cal. Everything is okay. I just—*God.* I just wanted something *different* for these weeks. I think I'll have to go into the city tomorrow.'

'Just for the day?'

She nodded.

'Okay, love. I'll let you focus. Goodnight.'

'Thank you, Cal. Goodnight.'

❄ ❄ ❄

Lilah left early. While she was gone, I pruned, I walked, I read, I slept. She returned after the sun had set, and seemed her usual self.

'Did you sort out your problem?' I'd asked when she returned. She barked a harsh laugh.

'If only.'

But that was the end of our discussion. We went to bed together, and we made love. It was always amazing with Lilah—but there was something poignant about that night, and even at the time I knew it. She'd rested on my chest afterwards, soft tears falling from her eyes onto my skin. At first I didn't feel I should draw attention to it, but within minutes, tiny little tremors were shaking her body that couldn't be ignored.

'Are you sure everything is okay?' I'd asked her. I was stroking her back, kissing her hair, hugging her extra tight. I just wanted her to know I was there, although of course there seemed to be no way I could help her with her work, and I still assumed that was the problem.

'Sometimes things aren't okay, and there's nothing you can do about it.' Her voice was miserable and weak.

It was louder now, and growing louder by the second, that instinct that told me that something was not as it should be. I'd tried to find the perfect balance between pushing her to talk to me and letting her work it out in her own time, but something about the distress in her voice almost panicked me.

'Talk to me, Lilah, please.'

'What do you want me to say?'

'If you could just tell me why you're crying, I think that'd be a great start.'

'I'm crying because I want life to be a fairy tale and it's not.'

'Do you remember what you said to me a few months ago, about everything in life having both a good and a bad side?'

'I didn't know what I was talking about.' The self-derision was not a natural fit for her, and her words sounded hollow.

'Of course you did. You always do. Take tomorrow off. Forget about your reading; you can do it later. You might just need a bit more of a break from work, and you are technically on a holiday, you know.'

'No. There's no more avoiding it,' she said softly. 'I need to get this done.'

'Well, maybe the day after then.'

'Do you remember that night when we went to Shelly Beach and I goaded you into joining me in the waves?'

'Of course I do. I'll never forget it.'

'That night was *all good*. For me, I mean.'

'And me too.'

She kissed me one last time, then said goodnight. I knew Lilah often had insomnia and I'd frequently heard her up and about in the middle of the night. That night, she either feigned sleep immediately or genuinely drifted off, and it was I who lay awake staring at the ceiling.

❋ ❋ ❋

It was at breakfast that I finally realised that Lilah was not upset about an argument with her mother. She was not distracted by her case. There was something wrong, and it was wrong between us.

We sat at the kitchen bench, as we usually did for breakfast at the beach house. She was quiet again, and once we'd finished our coffees and I mentioned heading out to prune, she put her hand on my arm.

'Callum,' she said. This tone was new—it was as cold as she had been warm all of these months. Business-like Lilah was back, and I was suddenly aware that she had returned to break my heart.

'What's wrong?' My voice was strained. I cleared my throat.

'We've been kidding ourselves. I told you this wasn't going to be a forever thing, and we need to end this now before anyone gets hurt.'

'Before anyone gets hurt?' I couldn't believe my ears—not her words, or the achingly embarrassing sound of my own high-pitched whine. 'You really think we could end this now and neither one of us gets *hurt*?'

'You can't say I didn't warn you.'

God, she was so cold. I stared at her, trying to figure out who this icy stranger was and where the passionate, emotive woman who'd laid on my chest the night before and wept had gone.

'So how does this play out, Lilah? You're calling the shots here.' I felt the anger burgeon in my chest. 'Do I leave now? Not contact you again? Let you cut me out of your life without even an explanation?'

'I don't *need* to give you an explanation because I warned you from day one,' she hissed at me, but then she shifted on her stool and it fell backwards. She grasped for the breakfast bar to keep herself from falling with it and I automatically moved to catch her. Lilah shook my arm off furiously. 'Don't touch me, Callum. Just get your things and go.'

'It's been a big few weeks for us. Let's just take it easy today and talk about this later—'

'You're not hearing me, Callum. There is no later. You need to leave.'

'Why are you doing this? Do you really think I will let go of what we have without a fight? Because I just won't.'

'You can't force something that isn't here. *What we have* might seem perfect to you, but it's obviously *not* to me.' I wondered who this cold woman was, and where Lilah was hiding. She suddenly softened her voice and the change again caught me off guard, 'I know this is hard to hear, but I just don't want to be with you anymore, Callum. You aren't going to change my mind. I want you to leave and I don't want you to come back.'

'I don't understand.' I tried to keep my voice level, to stop any escalation of the discussion into a screaming match. I thought of Lilah's hair-trigger temper and I knew I had to tread lightly. 'Can we please just talk about this, Ly? We've been so happy together; I can't understand why you want that to change. Is something else going on here?'

'I told you all along, Callum. I don't want to play happy families. I don't want to settle down. Not with you, not with anyone. I'm sorry if you've come to believe otherwise over these past few months. That really wasn't my intention. I need to focus on my work again now.'

It was her closing argument. The language and her presentation were all business; her courtroom demeanour was on in force.

'You're afraid.' I was clutching at straws. She was really going to throw me out—just like that. I knew the truth of what she'd said—she *had* warned me—but her actions had spoken so loudly that I'd ignored the words.

'I'm not afraid.' The polished façade slipped and the look she cast me was pure scorn. 'Of what, *love*? Is that what you think this is? You make an emotional connection with another human being for the first time in your life and you assume it's love?'

The cruelty was so brutal that it took my breath away. Of course I wasn't going to beg or cry in front of her, but this was so sudden that I shifted into a state akin to shock.

'I'll go,' I said. I was defeated. There was no coming back from that, not in this conversation. Maybe once she'd cooled down we could talk, and maybe things would be different then.

But for now, she'd fired a shot in this battle that I couldn't recover from quickly enough to keep fighting.

'Take the car,' she said. I couldn't see her face now, but going by the sound of her voice, she wasn't the least bit upset by what was happening. She could have been discussing the weather. 'Just leave it at my apartment.'

'No. It's better if I don't.'

'How will you get home?'

'I guess that's not your problem now,' I said. My throat was constricting. I walked out of the room and into the bedroom—our bedroom—and I packed my things, feeling as if I was trapped in some horrible nightmare that was rooted in all of my darkest fears for our relationship. I packed my suitcase, my camera, my laptop, loaded all of those things into my arms and walked back into the kitchen.

I wanted so much to hear her call me back that I could almost sense the words in the air. But although I hadn't heard her leave the house, Lilah was gone, and the empty rooms just mocked me. I thought about waiting for her to return, trying to talk it out without the emotion, but even in my grief, I understood that she had made up her mind, and the door was already closed.

I called a taxi and I went home.

CHAPTER EIGHTEEN

Lilah

3 January

I don't know if everyone does this, but sometimes I attach a memory to the setting the moment it happened, and I can't unstick it. The memory and the temperature and the light and the breeze become entwined and I can't think of the event without reliving the exact moment.

So when I think back to the night Haruto died, more than anything else I remember the cool breeze and the golden sunset. He was comfortable and stable, but his parents had gone to get some dinner and I didn't want to leave him alone. The nurse told me that on her way in for night shift she'd seen the most amazing cloudless autumn sky and that I just had to get some fresh air and enjoy it. And I did. I walked around the park near the hospital and I watched the ducks huddle together for warmth and I soaked in the last rays of the day's sun and I loved every second of being out of that godforsaken room.

And then when I went back into the fluorescent lighting and the corridor outside his room was in chaos, I knew I'd inadvertently discovered yet another thing to feel guilty about forever.

The purple twinkling twilight of Sydney Harbour at dusk takes me instantly back to the night Callum and I met, where the sense of wonder hung so heavily in the air that I could barely force myself to breathe. I can close my eyes even now and I'm back there, the smog and the salt in the air, the tension of a fascinating exchange waking up my body and my emotions after the longest drought. I knew almost from the moment we spoke that I'd sleep with him, probably that night, and that we'd be great together, if only I could let us.

Today I made a new memory and it bonded immediately to the shock of a blazing summer sun, midmorning on the coast. There's nothing like it in all the world I've found, where in spite of the cool breeze off the ocean, the sunlight is still hard enough that you know you'll burn within minutes. As I walked from the house, away from Callum, I knew that the dual shock of the heat and the absolute coldness in my heart would forever be entwined.

I blame hope for this. I went along with her for too long, even though I knew she was lying. Her tumbling twirling promises whispered that somehow everything was just going to work out—yes, in spite of the odds. She was so effortlessly confident that everything was going to be okay. Her relentless optimism wore me down and I bought into the lie of an eternal summer.

Winter came anyway. I managed to ignore autumn, to look aside from the browning leaves and the looming chill in the air. But then I woke one day and I knew hope had left me.

The danger in self-deception is the hunger afterward. It commands a sense of loss, a gap inside that just can't be satisfied. I knew love, and it changed me, and I found a new baseline of happiness that I won't ever experience again. I've moved from a technicolour world back into a black-and-white one, and while I never thought to question black-and-white before, I realise now what I'm missing.

Oh, Callum. If only there was another way.

I can't think of a single thing in my life I wouldn't give to sit him down and explain why I had to do this today, why it had to be so final, and why I had to be so cold. But as much as I trust Callum, I trust the way I know him, and I know that I finally did the right thing for both of us.

CHAPTER NINETEEN
Callum

The very worst of it was I had two weeks of leave still stretching before me, the endless barrenness of my life before Lilah—without even the distraction of work. It was as if Lilah and the universe itself had conspired to remind me of just what sunshine she'd brought to my world.

I could barely bring myself to get out of bed those first few days. I'd had breakups before, bad ones even, but this… I was lost.

I hadn't seen it coming. As I lay in bed, I replayed the days and weeks leading up to that awful morning over and over, looking for signs. I'd been so sure I understood the situation I was in, that we'd found each other and we'd build a future now, and that any little hurdles along the way could be explained away by Lilah working too hard or Lilah's past history or Lilah's quirks. Now it occurred to me that Lilah had never reciprocated the level of feeling I had for her, and maybe her stress over all of these months had been because I'd pushed her into a relationship she really wasn't interested in. I sank further into myself, and wondered how I was supposed to pull myself out of the hole she'd left me in and get back to life again.

And so there were days and then weeks of me letting the filth pile up in my apartment, not eating or bathing, generally wallowing in utter misery. Every few days I'd drag myself into the kitchen, make a stiff espresso, and try to face the day and

the world. Then I'd decide it was all too much, and I'd slink
back to bed, defeated and desolate.

I felt the absence of friends and family. Someone should
have been knocking on my door, demanding I find my boot-
straps and pull myself up by them. No one knocked, and
although I checked my phone a hundred times an hour, no
one called—least of all Lilah. There were people who *might*
have called, maybe my brothers, maybe even Karl, if only I'd
let them know I was back and I needed to be checked in on.
But that wasn't my style. And so I waited alone with the damn
phone never far from my hands.

My self-control wavered only once. At eleven a.m. one
weekday morning, I scrolled through my phone contacts and
looked at her listing.

Lilah.

The word held such beauty to me that staring down at it,
my vision had blurred. Before my brain could kick back in, I
sent her one text message.

Are you sure this is what you want?

Her response was immediate.

Yes.

There was no arguing with that. I'd given her a long window of opportunity to cool down and call me back to her,
and she was refusing me again.

So… that was that.

❋   ❋   ❋

Although they were the longest weeks of my life, my leave did
end, and I went back to work.

'So glad to have you back. The place has been falling down
around my ears without you here,' Karl greeted me as we met
at the stairwell for coffee. 'How's Lilah?'

I just shook my head. In the unspoken way of long-term friends, Karl had learnt everything he needed to know.

❅ ❅ ❅

Life became about getting through one more day.

Every day I knew the ache was easing, but it wasn't easing fast enough. It was at night I missed her most. Our comfortable companionship had been such a revelation to me—the first time in my life I'd been able to just sit in the presence of another human being and feel connected. I could fill some of that space with work, but when the work had to stop, I'd lie awake and feel the ache deep in my soul. There was no way the wound would ever heal, I knew. There would be a scar there that was a part of me now, because at last I understood what it was I'd been missing.

❅ ❅ ❅

My phone rang early on a Tuesday morning, twelve weeks and three days after Lilah threw me out of her house and her life. It was an unknown mobile number, but work calls often were and I didn't think anything of it.

'Callum Roberts.'

'Cal, its Peta.'

I only knew one Peta, but even if I knew two, I'd have known that voice. Peta's syllables were rounded from a lifetime of travel, and there was a musical lilt to her tone, even just in a greeting. For a long moment, I couldn't even breathe. I spun slowly in my chair and looked out to the harbour. Clouds had gathered since my sunlit ferry ride, and the day was ominously grey.

'Cal?' Her prompt was hesitant. Uncharacteristically hesitant.

'Yes, I'm here. '

'I'm so sorry to do this to you.' Peta sounded genuinely heart-broken. 'But can we meet?'

Peta was in the city—she was actually in the coffee shop on the corner between the street I worked on and the one Lilah worked on. Lilah and I had met here for lunch more times than I could count—and I did try to remember them all as I walked from my office. But I was nervous, and I walked so slowly that when I arrived, Peta looked as if she might be getting ready to leave. She had her handbag on her lap and she was staring at the door.

'I'm just not sure anything good can come out of this conversation,' I said by way of greeting as I sat down opposite her in the embroidered bucket chairs of the corner cafe.

'Hello, Callum,' she said as she smiled at me. Peta looked beyond tired—exhausted was probably a better word. For the first time it occurred to me that maybe Lilah had been injured.

'Is—Lilah okay?'

Saying her name hurt my throat. I swallowed as I awaited Peta's response. I willed her to provide me with the answer I wanted. *Of course she is. I just wanted to catch up with you.*

'I'll get us some coffees,' Peta suggested instead and my stomach sank. I wanted simultaneously to hasten and to prolong this moment. Potentially, this was the last moment before I knew that Lilah was *not* okay—that she'd been hit by a car, or fallen ill, or married someone else.

Married someone else. It seemed the worst possible outcome.

'A latte please,' I said.

Peta rose and walked to the counter, and I watched as she placed our order and made her way back to me. She didn't smile at the server, and she didn't make eye contact with me as she returned. Once she'd taken her seat again, her eyes finally filled with tears.

Oh God, oh God, oh God.

'Is she…' I didn't finish my sentence. I couldn't. Images of Lilah lying in a morgue had filled my mind and I was frozen.

'No, no.' Peta shook both her hands and her head violently. 'No, she's not dead. But, Cal, Lilah is very sick.'

'She can't be.' What a stupid thing to say. I wanted to breathe the words back in. 'I'm sorry, Peta—I just mean—she's so healthy.'

Even as I said it, I knew I didn't fully believe it. There had been signs that all wasn't entirely well with Lilah. I'd explained them away and with an almost arrogant hope had believed that I could fix whatever ailed her. I remembered the blind innocence of my thought that just a measure of rest would do the job.

'I assume Lilah never told you about James.' Peta's voice was a whisper and she didn't bother waiting for me to confirm I had no idea what she was referring to. I knew Lilah's father's name was James, and that he had died, but that was about it. Whenever she did speak about him, it was generally about his life, not his death.

'James had a genetic disorder. We are pretty sure his mother had it too—she was the original Saoirse. I knew we shouldn't have given her that stupid bloody name.' Peta smiled weakly. 'She died just before Lilah was born, back in Ireland, and all that James ever knew until he got sick was that she went crazy and had been institutionalised.'

I had been looking at Peta, waiting for the blow to fall, knowing that there was an understanding coming that I'd never be able to unknow. Suddenly, though, I couldn't bear to see Lilah's mother; it was bad enough to have to listen to these words, but to see those familiar eyes was just too hard. I looked out onto the street beside us and watched the flow of traffic as the soft rhythm of her story continued.

'Lilah was only eleven or twelve when James started having problems. I actually remember the first time he told me about it—he was just having trouble using a shovel. Decades of doing garden work and suddenly he just couldn't dig.' She laughed softly. 'I thought he was making excuses… being lazy or a coward… he never wanted to travel; he just wanted to be with me. I know he worried about Lilah and our lifestyle. I actually thought he was trying to trick me into settling down somewhere in some desk job, just when my career seemed to be taking off.'

A waitress silently slipped our coffees onto the table. I stared down now at the creamy milk and the swirl in the shape of a leaf on top of it.

'And of course, not only did I not believe him, but even if he would go to a doctor—which, incidentally, he very rarely did—he never would have gone for something so vague. After a few months, he started this nervous twitching in his fingers.' Peta was whispering now. 'And then his personality began to change. He became depressed, angry, confused…'

She sighed, physically shook herself and reached for her coffee. Now I looked directly at her and she was shaking and pale.

'It's called Huntington's Disease,' she told me. I'd never heard of it, but that didn't stop me from making wild assumptions.

'And what's the cure for it?'

'There is no cure.'

'There *has to be.*'

I had raised my voice and the café fell silent. Peta reached across the table and put her hand over mine. Her hand was warm, and mine felt cold, and I realised I was shaking too now.

I wasn't in touch at all with the emotions that were pummelling my body. Maybe I was in physical shock.

'I'm so sorry, Callum. There just isn't.'

'We'll find someone,' I said. 'If she needs help, we have to find something—there just has to be something.'

'Sweetheart, there are therapies, they help with the symptoms.' She was speaking to me as if I was a child, and strangely, I needed that. 'But nothing takes the condition away. It's a mutation of a gene—there's a protein that is missing from their brains. Over time, usually in middle age, the brain becomes damaged. It can't be stopped.'

I pulled my hand from hers and rubbed my face with it. It was almost funny how those last few miserable months suddenly seemed blissful in comparison.

'Is there nothing?' I whispered. 'Nothing at *all*?'

'Not at this stage. Well, not that we know of.' Peta sipped her coffee. 'Lilah knew she was going to get Huntington's; she'd been tested after James died. She only started getting sick maybe… I don't know… five or six years ago. Somehow she went into remission.'

There it was. The glimmer of hope I needed to hold myself together. I stared at her.

'So she did it once—she can do it again.'

There was pity in Peta's eyes, and it was beyond frustrating.

'Has she told you about Haruto, Callum?'

Oh, great. Now I had the ex-partner rubbed in my face too, the lover who had lasted a whole *year*.

'She mentioned him.'

'She told you he died?' I nodded. 'Haruto had Huntington's too. They were travelling, in Mexico I believe, and he was injured somehow and left completely brain damaged. It happened at the same time she miraculously recovered.'

The meaning in her tone went over my head. I stared at her, and when she didn't elaborate, my words were too harsh.

'I'm not following, Peta.'

'It's just a theory, but Lilah's doctor and I have wondered if she and Haruto attempted some kind of experimental therapy while they were over there. And yes, maybe whatever they tried helped Lilah, but it's likely the same treatment all but killed Haruto.'

'Have you asked her?'

'She denies it. Of course,' Peta sighed. 'Whatever happened over there is not something she's willing to share, and if it cost Haruto his life and they should never have been doing it in the first place, I can understand why.'

I'd convince her to talk. And then I'd convince her to get back on a plane and find whatever magic potion she'd swallowed all over again. I just had to see her, and before I did that, I needed to know what to expect.

'So what's happened to her now?'

'At Christmas, the chorea—that's the medical term for the twitching—started back again, like it had all of those years ago. The progression of the disease is usually pretty predictable—but no one knew what to expect after a five-year holiday from the symptoms. Mainly of course because no one has ever had any kind of holiday from their symptoms before.' Peta idly wiped a smear of lipstick from her mug with her fingertip.

'And now?' I asked. She twisted the cup this way and that, and although she didn't look at me, I saw her eyes finally fill with tears.

'Her doctor tells me it's like her body is making up for lost time; her progression has been unusually rapid. I don't know how long she has, Callum. She's had pneumonia three times in the last month. Every time she tells me she's going to let it take her so she doesn't have to die from the Huntington's, and every time her damn body claws its way back. I can't help but feel she has some unfinished business, and I think you and I both know what that is.'

'So she twitches? She's clumsy? What else?'

'Her gait has changed and she walks differently. Her speech… I don't know, it's hard to explain. She just sounds different, maybe she slurs a little. The worst of it is that she's having some issues with swallowing which is why she keeps getting chest infections. As it progresses, she will progressively lose cognitive function—there will be psychiatric symptoms—James had severe depression and crazy, impulsive mood swings. It's a neurological disease…' Peta bit her lip and stared at me for a moment before the finished her sentence, 'Callum, her brain is basically going to melt down.'

'Are you sure this is why she ended things with us?'

Everything hinged on that. Everything. I would need time to process this, time to research it, time to understand. But before I could even decide what my next steps would be—I had to know that Lilah had really not wanted me to leave her to deal with this in her own way.

'There is no dignity in this death.' Peta wiped at her cheeks as the tears spilled across them. 'It took James ten years to die, and we both wished him dead a thousand times a day by the end. We sent Lilah to live with my parents and we tried to *live*, but it was impossible, especially in the last few years. Life became about managing, and waiting for release. The only thing I can imagine worse than this disease is to die from it alone. I suspect for my daughter the only thing she could imagine worse than this disease was to put someone else through the pain of having to watch her suffer it. But I wasn't sure that you'd feel the same way.'

I suddenly pictured Lilah, alone in a hospital bed, and I stood, the motion violent with urgency.

'Where is she?'

'You need to be sure, Callum. Go away, think about this, do some reading. I can't have you trying to reconcile with her and then running away when things get ugly.'

'Things *are* ugly.' I sounded harsher than I meant to. Peta recoiled a little. 'I haven't slept a full night since—' I took a breath, a hard breath, and finally met the older woman's eyes. 'If I can have a few more moments, or days, or weeks even, with Lilah, I will treasure that time far beyond whatever pain I go through watching her get sick. You wouldn't have come here if you didn't already know that.'

Peta nodded. She drank the last of her coffee.

'Let's go then.'

CHAPTER TWENTY

Lilah

10 March

It's time.

I've put this off for five years. I never used to put things off. I need to do it now. It's slipping—I'm slipping, and no one knows the truth. Once I'm gone, it will be gone with me, and that doesn't seem right.

I used to write in a journal like this so that I could make sure I wasn't losing the parts of me that mattered most. After I first developed symptoms, I kept a journal so I could track them and note down when I had taken my medication. It evolved into a way of reflecting on my personality and my decisions, a way of ensuring that I was still able to connect with myself. I knew the disease would take my memory. I wanted to make sure I had a way to remember who I once was.

I met Haruto on my first trip to the Huntington's clinic at Newcastle. His appointment was just before mine, but Lynn was running late, as I now know she almost always is. He was reading a *New Scientist* magazine and like almost everyone else in the waiting room except me, jerking uncontrollably at irregular intervals. I somehow wound up sitting beside him and as the minutes ticked by, every spasmodic movement of every patient felt like it wound the pressure within my chest tighter and tighter, until a somewhat strangled *hello* burst from my lips in his direction and he offered me a sympathetic smile. I think his first words to me might have been, '*You're new to this, huh?*'

Haruto had never known his biological parents. He was abandoned as an infant, bounced around a few foster homes until he was a toddler, and then he somehow found his way into the home of Janice and Ryan Abel, who immediately set about building their lives around him. The fresh start of an adoptive family gave Haruto every opportunity he otherwise might have missed, but the one thing it couldn't do was restore the defective gene lying dormant in his DNA.

Unlike me, Haruto had no idea he might have Huntington's, and no time to simultaneously dread and prepare for its onset. He was in his thirties when he started getting sick, and the first signs for him were psychiatric. He was at the absolute top of his game at the time—a high-profile environmentalist who had a number of very public wins under his belt, he was achieving everything he'd always dreamt of. He sank slowly into a deep depression and began systematically alienating his friends and colleagues, until an accidentally helpful psychologist suggested he might make some peace with his adoptive past if he had his DNA analysed to understand at least something of his history. And so he ordered a kit online and had a run-of-the-mill analysis done, some genetic heritage tracing and a routine review of DNA for likely genetic issues.

The DNA analysis confirmed what he'd already suspected—Haruto's parents were both Japanese. It also flagged that he had the Huntington's gene, and the game changed overnight. A few easy blood tests later and he finally knew he was a walking time bomb which had actually already gone off.

He was forty-four when I met him, and furiously determined to find a way to beat the disease. I was a decade younger and for every shred of anger he possessed, I held only fear. My hands were beginning to twitch, my speech was already suffering—but worst of all I felt my mind bogging down as if my thoughts had to wade through treacle before they came clear. When I thought about the future, I saw a terrifying hurricane of uncertainty.

Not so for Haruto. He had a master's degree in environmental science and knew *stuff* about genetics and stem cells. He seemed to have spent years researching breakthroughs in rare genetic diseases and he was absolutely, positively certain that there was a way to beat this. He just had to convince Lynn to try something experimental—and if he couldn't, he was going to go around her.

I latched onto him like a parasite. He went in for his appointment, and when he emerged, I slipped him my business card and all but begged him to call me. My appointment that day with Lynn was futile as all of my future ones would seem to be—but Haruto called me that night, and we met for coffee, and over the next few weeks and months somehow wound up living together. He lived in a shoebox in the CBD and the walls were lined with journal articles and post-it notes of ideas and email addresses. Our bathroom cabinet was full of medication.

Haruto was something of a household name by then. He had been active in the environmental scene for a long time—a passion he'd inherited by osmosis from Janice and Ryan. They did crazy things like chain themselves to trees in rainforests with him in tow while they raised him, and their passion had left an indelible mark. He'd worked for worldwide environmental organisations, campaigning to save whales and bees and patches of foliage other people saw no value in.

By the time I met him, though, the only passion he had left was to save himself. He was living off savings initially, but before long I was supporting him financially. I didn't care—I was working in commercial law and I could afford it—why bother saving now anyway? Besides which, it was almost like we were trading precious commodities. I paid his mortgage and he gave me hope.

He found Dr Charles' website after countless dead ends, people who didn't seem to have the science to back up their claims of a cure. What Haruto was looking for was a clinic and a neurologist who would attempt a stem-cell therapy that was illegal in just about every country. Thousands of patients with terminal illnesses do that same desperate search for a lifeline every day, but unlike most desperate patients seeking a back-alley service, Haruto knew his stuff. He sent Dr Charles a list of questions and when the answers were all satisfactory, he interviewed him several times via Skype. And then he turned to me one night and announced that I needed to sell some shares and take time off work.

Janice and Ryan begged us not to go. Ryan had great hopes that if we continued the regime prescribed to us by Lynn and the Huntington's clinic, we would have years, maybe decades, before the disease stole away our quality of life. Who knew what could happen in that timeframe? It was a slow decline ahead of us both, plenty of time for opportunities to arise for clinical trials. Maybe someone would even stumble across a cure. Janice, understandably, just wanted Haruto under her wing. She adored him, and I think she would have contentedly nursed him at home right to the end if he'd allowed her.

I remember feeling sick to my stomach the day I went in to tell Alan I was going to take a year away. I hadn't told him about the Huntington's, but he knew I was sick. *Everyone* knew

I was sick. My work was slipping, and although I knew it, there didn't seem to be a damned thing I could do about it. I was no longer arguing in court because not only could I not handle the pace of thought required; my speech was thick and when I was tired, words only came in waves, with long pauses in between. Most insulting of all to me somehow was I was beginning to lose the feeling in my feet, and I'd shifted from wearing sky-high stilettos to ballet flats just to maintain my balance. Alan had been concerned, but supportive, even when I refused to tell him what was wrong. The day I finally took leave he shocked me by embracing me as I went to leave his office.

The clinic was in Mexico. It was booked out for months though, and Haruto and I made the most of the time before we could be treated. We stopped taking our medication and we travelled, criss-crossing over Asia and Europe and finally stumbling our way into Central America.

I had totally lost fine feeling in my feet by the time we flew into Mexico. So, I could still walk, but I couldn't manage uneven terrain at all. There we were—me, hopelessly clumsy and blindly following Haruto, who was suffering less physically but really deteriorating mentally. In any ordinary morning he might swing from euphoric to violently angry and all the way back again, sometimes without any warning at all. His short-term memory was still reasonable, but his long-term memory was terrible—at one point he argued black-and-blue with me that we lived in Perth, not Sydney. I'd lay awake at night and wonder if I had let him lead me all over the world based on a delusion that Dr Charles could cure us, but even if I had, I had nothing else to live for, so I figured that I may as well see it through.

Dr Charles was American. He lived in Chicago and travelled to Mexico only a few times a year to perform the stem-cell treatment. We would never know his real name. *Just call me Dr Charles.* His stem-cell patients never saw his Chicago clinic, and he never referred his Chicago patients to Mexico—it was his way of protecting his reputation back home.

Although he'd impressed Haruto, the first time we met him, I knew we'd made a terrible mistake. He was like a late-night infomercial up close, all bad spray tan and artificially white teeth framed in a collagen-plumped mouth. And after our initial greeting, Dr Charles just took over, with an endless spiel of pie-in-the-sky promises and nonsense statistics. Haruto, for all of his smarts and caution back in Sydney, now lapped the gold-plated promises up. The clever scientific questions via email had disintegrated into naivety. I remember watching the excitement dawning on his face when Dr Charles spoke, even though with absolutely no scientific training to that point, I could easily see through the unlikely guarantees and the overtly simplified science he was pitching us.

I went ahead anyway. On some level, maybe I hoped the supposed cure would kill me.

Haruto had the first treatment. They harvested cells from our skin and conducted an experimental induction process. Dr Charles told us he might win a Nobel Prize one day for his process, but he also assured us the medical establishment was going to take some convincing and widespread use of his groundbreaking technique was years away. It took weeks before the cells were ready, and then they took Haruto into an operating theatre. I met him hours later in recovery, where he was resting comfortably, his condition unchanged except that he now had a tiny hole in his skull. The procedure was, I suppose, as non-invasive as brain surgery could possibly be, and they hadn't even shaved his head, just a tiny patch around the little wound.

I had my first treatment the next day. I remember rising from the anaesthetic sleep. Before the mild pain in my head or the grogginess or the IV in my arm registered, I felt a tidal wave of disappointment. I had been so sure I would die.

And when the clinic cleared us both of infection, we went back to our hotel, and we waited.

At first, I thought it was just my imagination—perhaps more likely wishful thinking—that the sensations in my feet might be returning. Haruto was also sure his symptoms were easing too, but I couldn't see any evidence of it. There was a tension that simmered just below the surface with Haruto, and increasingly it would bubble out of him in the form of frustrated outbursts and irrational ranting. I remember more than once sneaking out of the hotel while he was in an overwhelming, unseeing rage, and walking around the streets of Mexico City, waiting for the storm to pass. Early in our relationship I'd console him, or reason with him, or try to distract him—but by the time we were in Mexico, there was no way to reach him when the fury rose. His anger and confusion were an ever-widening gap between us, and my only option was to avoid him until he found his centre again.

When he went for his follow-up treatment a month later, I wasn't at all surprised that his assessment showed further degeneration rather than improvement. But mine... somehow, *mine* showed a marked improvement. My cognitive function really was returning, I was gradually regaining the sensation in my feet, and the twitching in my hands had all but stopped.

Dr Charles was excited, very excited. He promised Haruto that his improvement was only a treatment or two away and recommended follow-up treatments for me too.

We were to have the second treatment on the same day, and we were first and second on the theatre list. Now when I held Haruto's hand, mine was the steadying force, and he was looking at me like he could drink the improvement right out of me and into himself. He had been my hope, and now, somehow, I was his. He had volunteered to go first again, but the nurse called my name, and so we exchanged a shrug and in I went.

When I woke up in recovery, I expected Haruto to be next to me. He wasn't, and time passed, and he didn't appear. None of the nurses spoke English, and Dr Charles was nowhere to be seen, so it was days before I found out what had happened.

We knew the risks. Even Haruto, for all of his blind optimism, knew we had placed our lives in the hands of a doctor who was essentially treating us with a combination of theory and luck. Maybe the luck ran out, because when Haruto was having his second treatment, something went horribly wrong. I never saw Dr Charles again, and I never found out exactly what happened, but when I finally found Haruto in the intensive care unit of another hospital several days later, he was drooling on his pillow and he didn't react to my presence.

The cruellest irony was that, overnight, the last of the feeling in my feet was back. While I tried to figure out how the fuck to get Haruto some help, I paced on the gravel outside of the hospital and the sharpness of the rocks in my soft skin was more mystical than sex.

Eventually I made up a story about a car accident and managed to get him medevacked back to Sydney and under Lynn's care. When the doctor overseeing his transport asked me why Haruto had wounds on his skull from surgery, I feigned confusion and said the hospital had operated when they were treating his concussion.

Lynn wasn't so easily fooled though, and neither was Mum. At first, they hammered me for answers. It was impossible that my symptoms had disappeared—just as it was impossible to her that Haruto's brain injury could possibly have been caused by a car accident. My hair was shorter then, but it didn't matter; I easily hid the tiny scar with a ponytail. I never told them, and in spite of journaling just about every other thought that crossed my mind after Haruto's accident, and even more so after his death, I've never written this down before. I was genuinely scared that if I put this on paper, it would suddenly become real, and the guilt would destroy me.

But once again I find myself in a position where I have literally nothing left to lose, and it actually feels good to get this out. The memory will dissolve soon enough, like all of my memories, and it's cathartic to confront it before it fades away. Maybe I'll get up the courage to leave this journal for someone, so they could know the things about me that no one has known. My love for Callum. My failure for Haruto.

Time caught up with Dr Charles, just as it has caught up with me. Months ago when I realised that the chorea had returned and my hand was beginning again its godawful dance, I spent days at the farm trying to track him down. With Callum enjoying his supposed holiday around me, I forgot all about my work and began to hunt Dr Charles like a stalker. I know it was crazy, given Haruto's outcome, but it was an automatic reaction—or maybe just a way to keep myself busy until I figured out what to do about Callum.

I found Dr Charles after a few days, and as soon as I knew his fate, mine was sealed. His real name was Charles Morgan, and he's serving a life sentence in a Chicago prison. Judging by the news reports, Haruto's outcome was much more standard than mine.

When I was well, there were times where my brain would get stuck on a mantra which would fuel a frenzy within me. *You got Haruto's miracle, Lilah.* And I've always known it to be true. But it was a one-time-only deal, and it seems only to have delayed the inevitable, given that I've wound up in exactly the same place I was destined for all along.

CHAPTER TWENTY-ONE

Callum

I stood outside Lilah's room and watched her through the doorway. The bed was at a half recline and she was propped up on all sides by pillows. Her flame-red hair was loose and matted, around her shoulders, over the top of her chest.

She was pale, so pale, and above the sheet I could see she was wearing a hospital gown—white skin against white sheets, and then two straps of an ugly green gown. Lilah hated sleeping in clothes, and there was obviously a reason for the attire—but I struggled against an irrational impulse to run in and strip the gown from her, at the very least to reclothe her in something beautiful.

Her hands were over the sheet, and even as she slept, I could see them move sporadically. It wasn't a constant movement, just the occasional twitch; had I not known, I would have thought she was just dreaming. It was a slightly familiar movement too, and I wondered if I'd seen her doing it back at Gosford and just not registered that it was anything more than an idle habit.

'Don't wake her,' I said as Peta reached for the door. Peta turned back to me and, to my horror, I started to cry. 'Please, Peta, let me just go for a walk before we go in there.'

I didn't give her a chance to respond. Instead, I turned and walked as calmly as I could down the hall, back to the elevator we'd rode upon. I took it down to the ground floor and pressed my fists into my eyes in the privacy it offered as it descended.

Lilah did not yet know that Peta had contacted me. In spite of my bravado at the coffee shop, now that I was close to her, I realised I had a choice—a real choice. Now that I knew she was sick, I would have to grieve her again one way or another—but I could choose not to watch her slip away from me, piece by piece, losing the person she had been.

The last thing I needed was more coffee but I ordered one anyway, and I placed a call to the office, explaining that an emergency had arisen and I didn't know when I'd be back. Then I sat at the table in the cafeteria and watched minutes tick by.

Minutes you could spend with her, a vicious voice in my mind reminded me. If she was going to progressively lose herself, I needed to spend every second I could with her now, soaking her in, before the disease stole her away.

Or, I could go home. I could go back to my half-renovated apartment and eat a steak and drink some milk and watch silly TV, or work until all hours. I could find ways to fill the emptiness. Staying with Lilah would mean watching the void left by her absence gradually return and ever expand.

Time passed. Tears periodically rained from the corners of my eyes. I noticed strangers staring, but I didn't move. At one point, an elderly man in a clerical collar came and sat opposite me.

'Is there anything I can do, son?'

I looked up at him, stared into the faded blue of his wrinkle-framed eyes, and asked, 'How do you believe in God when the world is so fucked up?'

The priest smiled sadly. 'You've got it backwards. It's *because* the world is so fucked up that I believe in God.'

I was choking. I shut my eyes. 'If I had faith at all, today I'd have lost it.'

'Can I sit with you a while?'

'You may as well.'

He sat with me for a long time, not saying a word, probably praying I suppose. Eventually he slipped a card onto the table, reached across and squeezed my hand, and then silently left. Shortly after, Peta returned and sat opposite me. She looked at the card on the table and laughed softly.

'I remember when James was diagnosed. It was such a shock, and I fought. God, how I fought. I dragged that poor man to doctors and specialists and therapists, faith healers, mystical healers, herbalists, naturopaths, kinesiologists, spirit guides…'

She bent the card in two and sat it like a tent on the table.

'The worst thing was that no one could help. Sure, I could understand that the doctors couldn't fix it. And I could understand that the various healers each weren't quite up to it. But what I couldn't quite grasp was that absolutely *no one* could help. Not even a little bit. Not individually, not collectively, no matter how much I begged or rallied or fought. This was just happening, and there was no force in the universe big enough to even slow it down.'

I reached out and picked up the priest's card and crushed it into my fist. Peta reached over and enveloped my fist in her hand.

'If you want to go, I will completely understand. Truly I will, and better than anyone, Callum.' She was strong. There was a resolve in her face that I envied. 'I'm so sorry to even put you in this position, but I couldn't let *her* go without giving you the choice.'

I looked back to the tabletop. It was scratched, worn in one patch right near my coffee cup. The laminate was loose all around the scratch and under my fingernails. How long had I been sitting there, scratching aimlessly, lost in my misery? The disconnect between my body and my consciousness was startling.

Fuck.

Peta squeezed my hand again. One more glance into those achingly familiar blue eyes, and the choice was made for me. I remembered that moment on the ferry all of those months earlier, where logic tried to intervene and I wondered if Lilah and I were suitably matched, and how my emotions had just quashed that thought like the tiniest of irritants. Here I was coming up against some much stronger logic, and the very same thing was happening.

'Let me go to the bathroom and clean myself up,' I said. My voice was strong and I had no idea how. 'And then we can go back upstairs.'

❋ ❋ ❋

Lilah was awake this time, sitting up in bed, an oxygen tube under her nose and a scowl on her face as she stared down at afternoon tea on the tray before her. As Peta opened the door, I watched Lilah poke at a packet of sweet biscuits as if it was a diseased animal. I felt angry for her, and frustrated—I knew she was so easily pleased with food. They could have tossed her a carrot or a banana and she'd have been content. Why give her long-life biscuits? *Idiots.*

She looked up and our eyes met. A million emotions flickered across her face. Guilt, shame, sadness, grief, misery—

Joy. Relief. Happiness.

'You are in so much trouble, Peta,' Lilah whispered, before her face crumpled and she pressed her hands over her mouth.

Her speech really had changed. It was thick, as if she was drunk maybe, and just a little stilted.

I ran to the bed and I cradled her like she was a broken bird. There were tears and sobs in the room and I had no idea how many were mine.

'You shouldn't have to watch someone die like this if you've only had a few months of them at their best. I can't ask you to be a part of this, Cal. I just can't.'

'I don't care. I just don't care about what I should or shouldn't have to do. And I don't care if you hate me for it. If you have ten good minutes left, I *need* to have them.'

Her face was in my shoulder, the jerking movements of her hands against my back were frightening, but no more than the heaving sobs of her fragile chest. I heard the door close as Peta retreated, heard the sounds of the hospital around us, the steady beeping of Lilah's heart monitor and the gentle hiss of the oxygen. In the most hostile, alien place in the world, in circumstances so uncomfortable that my worst nightmares couldn't begin to compete, I found myself at home.

'Please don't make me go again, Lilah. We can deal with this together.' I whispered the words, my mouth against her hair. I breathed in, looking for her unique smell, but the antiseptic sterility of the hospital drowned her out. I was already ready to steal her away from the hospital, back to her home, where she could be herself. 'Whatever is ahead of you—please let it be ahead of *us*.'

※　※　※

We were fragile that day. The rawness of the knowledge and the wound was too fresh—we just couldn't speak much. I held her hand and then I fell asleep on the bed with her in my arms. A nurse tried to send me home late into the night and

I told her she'd need to physically force me out if she needed me gone. After some negotiation, I allowed them to evict me as far as a stretcher beside Lilah's bed.

In the morning, the doctor came.

'Callum, this is Lynn Overly. She's my neurologist.' Lilah introduced a surprisingly young woman in a white coat. Lynn had enormous green eyes and a startling halo of white-blonde curls. As tall as me and with the broad shoulders of an Olympic swimmer, she was Amazonian almost, but her strong physical presence was strangely comforting. 'This is Callum Roberts, my partner.'

Partner. Oh, how I'd wished for her to label us with something as concrete as that. I didn't cry when my parents died— but now it seemed every time anyone spoke, I had a sob waiting to burst out of my chest.

'Nice to meet you, Callum. And you're looking much better, Lilah. Your chart is markedly improved on yesterday and I understand you finally accepted those antibiotics I've been trying to ram down your throat.' Lynn surveyed the clipboard she'd taken from the end of Lilah's bed.

'I feel a lot better. When can I go home?'

Lynn slipped the clipboard back into its holster and pulled up a stool, perching beside Lilah's thighs.

'I need to talk to you about that, Lilah. It's time for a frank chat, and a plan to move forward.'

'Move forward?' Lilah's smile was wry. 'You found a cure for HD and forgot to tell me?'

The depth of regret on the doctor's face spoke of someone who held a far closer attachment than her profession would have recommended.

'I wish that were the case.' Lynn looked to me. 'Callum, would you mind going for a walk?'

'No.' Lilah interrupted Lynn. 'If Callum wants to be here now, he needs to hear whatever you have to say.'

'I'm fine with that, Lilah. I was hoping *you* might have some things to say though.'

'Lynn, I'll tell you if you really want to know. I just don't see how it will help.'

'Tell her what?' I prompted quietly to Lilah.

'How I went into remission.'

'I know it was something dodgy.' Lynn's tone was wry. 'I just feel that now might be the time for us to swap specifics.'

Words hung in the air, unspoken. They were words which held no form as yet, but which I'd be pulling together as soon as I had some detail. *How do we get you back there to do it again and how soon can we arrange it?*

'I won't put you in an awkward position, Lynn. Is there any point to this disclosure?'

'I've never heard of a Huntington's case going into complete remission—let alone for five years. I'm desperately curious, Lilah—but more than that, what they did might give us a clue as to what we can expect next.'

'There's no point,' Lilah sighed, sitting up straighter on the bed. No oxygen tube in her nose today, and her colour was better. I wondered about the doctor's comments about the antibiotics and if I was responsible for that decision. 'It was stem-cell therapy. An American doctor did the procedure in a hospital in Mexico, and he is now in jail.'

'Is that all you know?'

'Of course not.' Lilah was annoyed and offended at the question. 'The neurologist who did the procedure injected pluripotent stem cells into the basal ganglia.'

'What kind of surgery was it?'

'Stereotactic.'

'How many treatments?'

'Two. I started getting better after the first; the second seemed to send me into immediate remission.'

After a moment, an expression of pure concern settled on Lynn's face. She looked at the floor, then shook her head.

'That procedure is ten years away still, Lilah. Maybe more.'

'I had nothing to lose,' Lilah shrugged. 'I had literally nothing to lose.'

'They injected something into your brain that they told you were stem cells, but it could easily have been toilet water. You'd never have known.'

'If I died, I died. What did I have to live for? Decades of slow decline? It was worth a shot, and I got five great years out of it, so it paid off.'

'And...' Lynn asked the word hesitantly, and then thought better of it. Lilah sighed as she stretched her neck this way and that.

'Yes, Haruto had the same treatment. I don't know what went wrong. It was our second treatment, but he hadn't responded like I had. He never woke from the surgery so I assume the doctor slipped or a mistake was made with his anaesthetic.'

'Let's go back to Mexico,' I said. A sudden flare of hope had been birthed in my gut. 'We can get a flight as soon as you're strong again. We can go back to that hospital—maybe there's another neurologist—'

Lynn waved her hand towards me, politely dismissive.

'Other than Lilah and Haruto, I can think of seven patients off the top of my head who've gone overseas to a country with looser medical regulation, in the hopes of a cure.'

'So do you have contacts we could use?'

'You misunderstand me. Out of the seven, five had no improvement, one died, and one other was severely brain damaged.

Even Haruto… I assume you know that he came back in a vegetative state. That Lilah happened to find someone who did what he said he was going to, and did it successfully, without damaging her brain during the surgery or leaving her with an infection—well, honestly, it's nothing short of a miracle. Hell, this isn't even an exact science as yet, nowhere near it—I'll bet even if you could get that same neurologist to repeat the procedure he couldn't replicate these results.'

'I'm not even entertaining the idea of trying again.' Lilah was looking directly at me, and when I opened my mouth to protest, she continued with determination. 'Last time around, I hadn't come to terms with this. Now, it's different.'

She squeezed my hand and I knew she was referring to me, but that was just nonsense. I was surely all the more reason for her *to* fight.

'You can't give up,' I said. 'You just can't. Even if we just have to hang on for a few years, the procedure might be available safely here. '

'Even if they perfect it and somehow it's approved that quickly, I don't have a few years, Cal.' Lilah's blue eyes pleaded with me to understand. The pleading didn't bother me—the complete and utter peace I saw within them did. She really had come to grips with this, and that meant that she'd given up.

'You can't *know* that.'

'I do know that. I feel it. I can hear it in my fucking voice, for God's sake.' She pulled my hand to her face and rested her cheek against it. There were tears in my eyes and my jaw was flapping like a fish. I wanted to argue with her. I just didn't know how to start. When she spoke again, her words were softer. 'We did a swallowing study a few days ago. When I swallow, a tiny amount of saliva is slipping into my lungs. That's why I keep getting pneumonia, and that's why I'll keep getting it, until it kills me.'

'But pneumonia is *treatable*.' I was so frustrated that I had
to stand, and I began to pace the length of the room. 'You bull-
dozed your way into a one-in-a-trillion miracle cure last time;
this time you're going to let a bloody cold take you down?'

'If the *bloody cold* takes me down, it's a mercy,' Lilah
shrugged. She'd had years to prepare for this—I'd had hours.
But I couldn't fathom ever being as calm about this topic as
she was. 'If I wait for the HD to do it, I will forget how to
swallow altogether, and smile, and wipe my bum. One day
Mum will come into the room and I won't remember her
name, and because my brain will have lost the connection
between her name and my memories of her, even once you
remind me who she is, I won't care. That's *exactly* what happened to my father. So I get a fever and I cough and I die?
That sounds *divine* to me at this point.'

'Do you two want some privacy?' Lynn asked. I was still
pacing up and down beside Lilah's bed, from wall to wall,
looking for a tiny glimmer of hope and feeling like I had just
found one, and Lilah or Lynn had immediately shot me down.

'I just need to understand, Lynn. I need to understand
why, with all of the resources of this hospital and your training and this whole damn industry, that there is absolutely
nothing that you can do to help her.' My voice broke.

'There is plenty we can do to help her, Callum. I have an
entire team of specialists ready to treat the symptoms as they
arise.' Lynn rose and her expression was sad as she watched my
pacing slow. 'The only thing we can't do is change her DNA.'

❀ ❀ ❀

Over the next few days, I could barely leave the hospital room.

I sat with her and slept beside her and shared her disgusting hospital food. We held hands in silence, we talked about

the weather, and we read the newspaper together. There'd be time for explanations and deep conversations—this wasn't that time. All I could do was soak up the wonder of having her back beside me.

And then I began to search for answers, to try to find a way to understand. Lilah, Peta and even Lynn sat with me for hours, showing me academic studies and textbooks and silly line drawings to try to help me understand what was happening. Lynn showed me the sequencing they'd run all of those years ago that had shown the genetic mutation that caused the disease. She explained patiently and repeatedly the basics of measuring trinucleotide repeats in genes, which basically put a number on how bad the Huntington's mutation was in Lilah's DNA. This was then fed into a model which predicted the onset of symptoms, so Lilah had known to expect to get sick in her early to mid thirties. Although HD symptoms could start at any time, Lynn's experience was that the earlier the onset, the worse the decline. Some HD patients didn't get sick until their sixties. Failing another miracle, Lilah wouldn't live to see her sixties.

Lilah's quirks suddenly made a lot of sense—her paranoia about MSG, for one. There were a few disparate journal articles that suggested that one of the ingredients in MSG was somehow related to neurological disorders, and that was enough for her—she'd eliminated it religiously.

'I wanted to give myself the best chance. So I read, and I read, and I read, and I turned every novel idea into a dogma,' she explained softly. 'Haruto was a strict vegan. I only adopted the diet after he died, but I always felt better for it. And there's no shortage of science suggesting that a plant-based diet is better for general health.'

She was still adhering to her diet in the hospital, and I took that as a sign that on some level, she did still have a degree of hope. Why anyone would endure the hospital's pathetic attempt at vegan food without a genuine belief that they would reap some greater benefit was beyond me.

And of course I did my own research. While Lilah rested, I bombarded Google with search after search. And just like I had the day after we met, I was looking for the right combination of keywords or characters to give me what I wanted: hope.

It didn't matter how I cut it, though, the situation was dire. Research was underway all over the world, studies and trials and ideas being worked on and worked out all of the time. There were genuine possibilities for the future, too: research into stem cells was obviously promising, and studies in animals had shown some potential in a DNA-based drug which might disable the mutated gene for a period of time, causing a break from symptoms, much like Lilah had experienced already.

I showed Lynn my research when Lilah was off having a test.

'Down the track,' Lynn told me, very gently. 'There's definitely hope that in my lifetime we will see a cure for this disease. It might well be that concept, the DNA-based one, that cures it.'

'But what about Lilah's lifetime? The article said the drug trials are only a few years away. '

'Yes, Callum. The antisense drug trials in human patients are at least two years away.'

Two years. Twenty-four months. Ninety-six weeks. It was nothing, a blip in time. Surely Lilah could hold on that long? When I said as much, Lynn shook her head silently.

'She has to, Lynn. She's come this far.'

'You'll keep reading and you'll keep researching,' Lynn told me softly. 'No matter how pessimistic Lilah or I or anyone else is, you'll keep going, because you love her. '

I nodded. She was right. I couldn't stop wishing or trying if my life depended on it.

'But if you want the truth from me, Cal—it's this: I don't know how the Mexican clinic triggered her remission, or why it ended, and I don't know why she's deteriorating this rapidly. But as hard as it is to hear and accept, I'd say we're talking about months for Lilah, not years; and I'm pretty sure she's okay with that.'

'I can't just give up.'

'Of course you can't. But I think you need to find a way to focus all of this fantastic, positive energy on making the most of the time she has left.'

Lynn left me alone after that. I stared at the laptop screen until my eyes ached, tossing theories and possibilities this way and that in my mind. There was a university in China conducting animal trials on the antisense concept. Could I take Lilah there? Bribe someone to try to help her? Try to steal some of the drug? How could I convince Lilah? Would Peta stop me?

I put the idea on ice when Lilah came back to the room. She was tired and she needed me to be calm and supportive, not bouncing crazy ideas off her. As I left to retrieve her an alternative dinner—*any* alternative to the limp salad the hospital had delivered—I promised myself that I'd come back to it, maybe in a week or two once things had settled down.

❆ ❆ ❆

We had some visitors during the hospital stay. Peta was in and out, trying to maintain her private singing classes back at Gosford, staying overnight in a nearby hotel when she could. Nancy and Leon brought a few fresh salads in and a box of fruit, and sat and had morning tea with us as if we were in a café instead of a hospital ward. They came with all of the news of the family and the farm, and of promises for astounding preserves from the winter crop.

On Wednesday afternoon, a group of four people appeared at the door while Lilah rested. I was reading a newspaper at the time—rather I was *rereading* for the tenth time the previous day's edition—and I rose and quietly slipped into the corridor.

'Can I help you?'

'You must be Callum.' The oldest man in the group stepped forward as if he was going to shake my hand, but then shocked me by embracing me. 'I am so relieved that you're here. I'm Alan, one of the partners at Lilah's firm. This is Bridget, Anita and Liam.'

'We're—we were Saoirse's team.' Heavy tears swam in Bridget's eyes. She was young, maybe in her early twenties, and seemed overwhelmed. 'I'm her legal secretary… I was, anyway.'

'And Anita and Liam were Lilah's paralegals,' Alan explained quietly, although he didn't need to because I'd heard their names dozens of times—usually in between curse words, given the brutal disappointment Lilah seemed to experience in their work. I surveyed the faces of her colleagues and saw the misery within their eyes. 'How is she doing?'

'Much better,' I said. And in terms of the pneumonia, she really was.

'I'm so, so happy that you and she…' the tears spilled. I was suddenly uncomfortable with the sympathy in Bridget's eyes and I shifted awkwardly, uncharacteristically self-conscious.

'Me too,' I said.

'Would you idiots get in here?' Lilah called from the room. I pushed the door open and Lilah's colleagues followed me inside. 'Fuck me, you do realise this is a hospital, not a nightclub. Why are you all here at once?'

The disdain in her tone shocked me, but it didn't seem to faze her visitors one bit.

'Was Lilah an awful boss?' I asked suddenly.

'Oh, God yes.' Anita said, and we all laughed a little nervously, except Lilah who grimaced.

'I miss you.' Bridget neared the bed and tried to take Lilah's hand. Lilah shook her away and motioned impatiently towards the chair I'd been sitting in.

'Sit down, Bridge. This isn't a deathbed farewell you know. You don't need to weep all over me.' Lilah's sharp tone lightened the mood in the room considerably, until she added quietly, 'Yet.'

'I have great news, Lilah. We managed to recruit Ann Jenkins; she's going to start in a few months' time.' Alan unbuttoned his jacket as he sat on the end of the bed.

'Ann?' Lilah repeated. 'As a partner?'

'She's going to buy in.'

'That is brilliant, Alan. Congratulations.'

'I thought you'd approve.'

Lilah glanced at me.

'She's a lawyer. A much better one than me. She'll run the environmental practice.'

I looked at Alan and frowned.

'Lilah's job?'

'It's not my job anymore,' Lilah said. 'Alan has bought me out of the partnership.'

She began a cross-examination of her previous team, enquiring about various cases and staff members, while I stood silently by the door, digesting the news that she'd given up work. After a few minutes I glanced at my watch.

'I might just… I'll just duck home and pick up some fresh clothes. Will you be okay, Ly?'

'Of course I will.' She smiled at me. The work discussion had animated her, and as I drove home, I thought about that. Of course I could understand why Lilah had given up work, but it was still a surprise and not a pleasant one.

I made it all the way home and back to the hospital before I realised why I was so upset about the news. I was looking for signs that Lilah was fighting, hanging all of my hope on little signs of life. She was maintaining her diet. She'd taken the antibiotics. She seemed genuinely thrilled that I'd found my way back to her. At the same time, almost all of my focus had been on understanding the disease and how we could access a cure. As long as I did my job and found the miracle, and she did her job and kept trying, somehow, surely, she'd be fine.

But Lilah had given up work and sold her partnership. She was finalising her affairs, getting ready to say goodbye. For her, the battle was already lost. I had been so focused on her illness and what it all meant that I hadn't spared much brain space for the reality that she was actually going to die. I was never going to be ready to let go of Lilah. Not even if she did manage to hold on for a decade or two or three.

Her teammates had left and Lilah had showered while I was gone. She was sitting on the bed drying her hair with a towel. I noticed that her IV had at last been removed.

'Lilah, you have to go back to work.'

She looked at me blankly.

'Well, firstly, no I don't. And secondly, I can't, even if I wanted to.'

'Look.' I sat beside her and took the towel from her, and she spun around so I could finish for her. As I blotted and rubbed her hair, I struggled to form the right words. 'You need to work. You just have to work. Maybe Alan can give you a few small cases to do from here or from home.'

She was silent and I wasn't sure she'd heard me. She turned around eventually and took the towel back. Her expression was blank.

'Lilah?'

She dropped the towel in a heap beside the bed and leant against her pillows, her gaze on mine. Her skinny hand reached up to brush against my cheek.

'Do you know, Cal, until I met Haruto, I'd never had any interest in environmental law.'

That shocked me, almost winded me actually. I found it hard to imagine Lilah without the green-hippy environmental bits. I knew she'd worked in corporate law at some stage, but I had assumed it was a stepping stone to the real, noble profession she'd always dreamt of, saving the planet and all that. Besides which, I really didn't want to hear about her dead lover, especially now that I knew how he'd died.

'I changed my specialty after he died because the environment was his passion, and I felt so guilty that I'd survived and he hadn't. I felt like I owed it to him to try to make a difference. And the fact is, I came to love it. I'm a hippy at heart even if I didn't really understand that myself until five or six years ago.'

Her hand dropped to my thigh, and she entangled our fingers.

'But, Callum, I have HD. Even if I wanted to, I can't go back to work, and the fact is, I *don't* want to. When I realised I was getting sick again, once I'd processed the grief of it, a weight was lifted off me. No more obsessively looking for signs that it was back, no more feeling like I'd robbed Haruto somehow of his chance to change the world. I got five years, five wonderful, unexpected years, and I made the most of them for him. But these last days or weeks or months, they're *mine.*'

'But what will you do?' My lips were numb. Lilah brushed her thumb against the back of my hand.

'The main thing I'm going to do, Callum, is get sick, and then I will die. You need to understand that.'

I brought her hand back to my cheek and hid behind it. I didn't want her to see that I was on the verge of crying like a bloody baby. Again.

'I want to go back to Gosford with you,' she whispered. 'I want to laze about the house and eat fresh greens and talk shit as if we have all of the time in the world.' Her hand jerked against my face. I shut my eyes tight. 'I want to pretend this is the middle of our life together. I want to pretend we've had decades and we have decades left. I want to pretend that we know everything about each other but we haven't run out of things to talk about, because we just like to *hear* each other speak.'

It sounded lovely. Truly lovely. She sat up straight, and when I opened my eyes and looked back to her, her gaze was hard.

'But we do this on my terms. When it's time for me to go, you let me go, even though it's too soon and you don't want me to leave.'

'Jesus, Lilah. You can't ask that of me.'

'I'm strong now. I'm as strong as I'm going to be. Tomorrow morning when Lynn does her rounds, I'm going to discharge myself and go to the apartment. We can spend a night there so I can water the plants and pack some things up, but then I want you to take me to Gosford. And when I get sick again, I'm not coming back to into the hospital. Do you understand?'

Maybe I'd change her mind, maybe I wouldn't. She'd never convince me to stop trying. I opened my mouth to tell her as much, and she clamped her hand over it.

'And that is all there is to it, Callum. If you can't deal with that, then go. I want you here, but I won't *have* you here if you can't do it my way.'

Her hand was still over my mouth, but our eyes were locked. She was scanning me, looking for resistance, ready to turn me away again. I reached up and gently shifted her hand away from my face.

'I understand.'

I didn't. *Of course* I didn't. It was all too new, and I was a long way from even understanding this strange place I found myself in, let alone her demands. But I needed time to grasp it all, and this conversation couldn't survive a month-long pause.

'Good.' Her smile was satisfied, until a sad thought crossed her mind. 'It'll be a relief to get back to the apartment. What was left of my pot plants is probably dust by now.'

❊　❊　❊

Lynn didn't resist when Lilah asked to be discharged the following day, and I'll admit it was a relief to walk her to my car and drive her home.

And Lilah was right about the garden. It was all but dead.

'I just wish I could do what my dad did,' she sighed as she walked among the pot plants with a watering can. 'He really had a gift for making things bloom. No matter how hard I've tried over my life, I just can't do it.'

'You can't do it with plants,' I murmured. 'You did it with me.'

She looked up at me, and we shared at wry smile at my corny line.

'Did you *bloom* these last few months?' A flicker of guilt crossed her face.

'I don't want any secrets between us anymore, Lilah. So I'll tell you I have been utterly, hopelessly miserable since we said goodbye at Gosford.' I looked out to the ocean beyond her balcony. 'You could have just told me, you know.'

'I thought I knew how you'd react,' she said, and gave me a sad little laugh. 'And now I know for sure that I was right. It was only fair to give you an out before you knew you needed one.'

'I think you've lived a big life, and you've seen the four corners of the world and you've known fascinating people and achieved a lot. Maybe to you this relationship is just another part of all that, but to me, this has been a mind-blowing, soul-changing revelation. And to have you take that away from me because you could see things were going to get rocky up ahead, well, I appreciate the sentiment. The fact is, when I imagine the pain of watching you get sicker and compare that with life without you, I know immediately that I'm going to stand by your side withering in helpless frustration even while I feel embarrassingly grateful that you are still a part of my life.'

Lilah's hand jerked and the watering can moved with it, spilling water all over her leg and the balcony floor. She carried on as if nothing had happened.

'How did you know it was back?' I asked her. Lilah plucked a weed from a pot plant and shrugged.

'I suspected for a while, maybe even since before we met. Knowing this guillotine was looming over my head, I've always seem symptoms even when there were none, but the last year or so… there was just a change in my ability to keep up at work…' She tossed the weed over the balcony onto the street below and went back to watering. 'I think that's part of why I tried to tell myself I'd just keep you at arm's length.' She looked up at me and flashed a cheeky grin. 'See, I was delusional already. We both know this isn't the kind of relationship a person can control.'

'Don't you think it's brutally unfair that you've been well all of these years and we meet just as you're getting sick again?'

'Chance is chance, Cal.' She watered a completely dead plant, as if there was hope for it yet somehow. 'After we met the first time, I decided it *wouldn't* be fair to you to let this thing between us solidify. I actually drove to work after that first night so that I wouldn't see you, and then—bang—there you are, walking past my office at just the right time. Part of me wants to believe this was meant to happen, but most of me believes it just did, and once we knew each other...' She trailed off and turned back to me. 'Have you taken leave from work?'

'They emailed me this morning.' I had actually read the email while she packed up the hospital room, but then I'd forgotten all about it. Funny how work really was the least of my worries these days. 'The directors have given me three months' paid leave, after which we'll reassess.'

'Reassess,' Lilah repeated softly. The flow from the watering can had slowed to a trickle and she turned back and held it towards me. 'Refill?'

'You know you're watering dead plants, right?'

The dozens of pot plants on the balcony contained mostly leafless sticks in dry dirt. She shook the watering can anyway and raised her eyebrows at me.

'We're in last-chance bucket-list territory, shithead, and being an amazing gardener is on my bucket list, so get hopping.'

CHAPTER TWENTY-TWO
Lilah

17 April

I'm not sure that I'll ever forgive Mum for contacting Callum.

I *am* sure that I'll be forever grateful.

I'm on the last part of my journey. These are the last days and weeks that I'll be here, and I thought I knew what it would look like. I've been anticipating this point in my life for nearly six years. Everything is in place; all of my affairs are wrapped up—all except one. What's left is the best loose end, the love knot I'll be slowly tying until I go. What Mum and Callum have given me is an unexpected beauty and warmth—and complication—during this very last period of time.

I still daydream about marrying him sometimes. I still retreat to that garden in the mountains and promise him the lifetime that I don't have to give. It is a beautiful and delicate dream, the calmest part of my mind. Maybe it will be the last part left. I'd like that, for everything to fade away now, and for my last thoughts to be of Cal.

But now… I get to live the honeymoon. I'm the luckiest woman in the world, given that, right down to the very strands of DNA that compose me, I have been fucking un-lucky since literally the moment of my conception.

If it was just the swallowing, or just the chorea, or just the way my balance is failing, I'd be fine. There are solutions to those things. Give me a feeding tube. Pump me with an-tispasmodics. Hand me a walking frame. I could deal with that. I really could.

But the treacle is returning. The sense that my mind is becoming muddy and my thoughts are jumbled in amongst the mess. I search for ideas, and find only concepts. It's a fine distinction, I know, but it's an important one. What is that thing called, the thing I want to pick up my food on? I could tell you everything about it. It's cutlery and it's got four prongs. It's sterling silver and my grandparents were gifted the whole set on their wedding day, which means it's nearly seventy years old—maybe I could even calculate down to the day how old it is, given I know their anniversary. I've eaten a thousand meals with it at the farm, some of which I can remember in vivid detail. It's sharp and cold and surprisingly heavy because it's such a high-quality set. It belongs to a knife and a spoon.

And then I will sit and stare and hold it and finger it and still minutes might pass before I can assign it the name fork. It's happening more and more. Not every day yet, but every second day. The fog has returned, and it's thickening in front of my eyes.

It's just too much, too much altogether. That's why I can't handle it. Or so I tell myself. The truth is, I'll never know what I could or couldn't deal with, because these were the cards I was dealt.

CHAPTER TWENTY-THREE

Callum

It was almost a relief to be back at Gosford, even given the circumstances. I think I'd always have missed closure if we'd left things the way they were.

I was getting used to being with Lilah again, the initial delirium and shock of the week in hospital wearing down. I was learning not to see the jerking movements of her hands or the clumsy way she walked now. There was an awkwardness to her steps and a stiffness in the muscles in her legs. She was still very much mobile, and if it was only a few steps she might just have been rigid from sitting too long. But when I watched Lilah cross a room or in the garden, it was clear that she was struggling.

And that was bad, but not nearly as difficult for me to see as her choking. She let me know in her typically unsubtle way that I couldn't panic when she tried to swallow and coughed instead, because I only made things worse when I leapt to my feet and rushed to her side.

'For *fuck's sake*, Callum. Give me some fucking space!' She'd barely be finished choking before she'd let loose on me. I retrained myself to eat very slowly so that I didn't finish a long while before her. I learned to focus on my breathing while we ate, and if she did seem to gag, I'd take two long breaths before I tried to help her.

I also found ways to be beside her almost twenty-four hours a day. She was clumsy, and her coordination was already suffering. If she went to the toilet, I casually lingered within earshot, in case she fell. When she showered, I'd wait until she was in the bathroom, and as soon as I heard the water turn on, I'd stand at the door and listen to make sure she was okay. When the water turned back off, I'd quickly walk away so that she didn't know. She was more open now with me, about our relationship and her feelings for me, but she still refused to be coddled. I knew instinctively that Lilah would refuse to be treated like an invalid long after she really had lost her independence. For now, I was part guardian angel, part stalker.

I'm sure part of my subconscious motivation was to soak up every second in her presence while I could, but mostly I was just scared. Every room, every activity, every moment brought potential danger, and somehow I needed to enjoy every second of it. The days were gloriously long, so much time to enjoy her, and so much to do to keep her safe.

❊   ❊   ❊

Once we'd adjusted to the new normal, I began to encourage Lilah out into the garden. She was at her best in the autumn sunshine. I'd pack a picnic basket with a blanket and some books and snacks, and take her to a soft patch of grass. This naturally lent itself to her wanting to work in the garden again, and although this was a nerve-wracking exercise for me, I could see that she needed it.

'What do you think happens when we die?' she asked me one afternoon as we harvested from the vegetable plot.

I didn't know how to answer her, and I guess the silence that became awkward answered for me.

'Same as me,' she surmised correctly. 'Nothing.'

Don't get me wrong; I wished with all of my being that my rationality was wrong and there was some beautiful afterlife waiting for Lilah. The problem was, I just didn't buy it, not even now when it would give us both some desperately needed comfort.

'My belief is that we only have this life,' I admitted. I tossed more celery into the cane basket we were harvesting into. 'So you're the same?'

'I lean towards humanism,' she admitted. Suddenly she snapped a stalk of celery off the plant I'd just cut and bit into it with some force. 'I expect that when I die, it will seem like falling asleep and that will be the end of it—a relief, just like dozing off when you're super tired or going under anaesthetic.'

'Aren't you scared?' I asked. I was amazed and bewildered, and too fascinated by the turn in conversation to continue with my physical work.

'I'm not,' she shrugged. 'I'm not scared at all, which scares me, in case that's a symptom. Dad was wildly impulsive once he was really sick. Once, Mum found him climbing down the cliff face in front of the house here; when she asked him what he was doing, apparently he had just thought he might paddle in the water for a while. The connection between activity and danger had come apart in his mind.'

I made a mental note to reinforce the fence one night while she was asleep.

'But I think I'm being rational about it,' she continued quietly. 'I just expect I'll get sick with a flu and maybe there'll be a fever, and I'll slip in and out of consciousness until there is only darkness. My brain won't be awake enough to feel fear.' She gave me a smile. 'Darkness. Peace. What's there to fear? I won't even *know* to be scared.'

I had to go back to cutting the line of celery plants before me; the image she painted was too depressing. After a moment, she jumped over the lines of plants to cup my shoulders and I had to look into her face again.

'But, hey, if I'm surprised and I die then wake up among fairies and there is some kind of afterlife, I'll sneak back and mess you up somehow. Maybe I'll pop into your room to tip your underwear basket out, or reorder your shoes so they aren't even in *pairs* anymore.' She feigned horror and I laughed, in spite of the agonising way my gut twisted.

'I can more easily imagine waking up one day to find my bed covered in leaves or flowers or something.'

She giggled too, and bent to kiss the top of my head.

'You're right. I would like to hope I'd be more subtle, but quite frankly, if I drift off to sleep and wake up a fucking fairy, I'll make you look like you just stepped out of the Mardi Gras.'

✼ ✼ ✼

'The symptoms started just before my thirty-fourth birthday,' she explained to me as we lay in bed one night the following week. The anxiety I'd felt the first few days had passed, and finally I could just enjoy her again. 'I'd had the genetic test just after Dad died and I knew it was coming. I knew I'd be young too, because of my CAG repeat size. Do you remember what that is?'

'I remember yours was high.'

'Forty-eight.' Lilah said, and it was clear from the tone she used that she had considered the number at length over the years. 'It's high, but it doesn't mean the HD is worse. It just means the symptoms are likely to start earlier and progress quicker—and mine arrived, bang on time.'

'And your dad?'

'He was a bit older when he got sick, and my grandmother was a bit older still. There are some cases where it gets worse with every generation. That's why I was never going to have kids. It stops here.'

'How did you know you were sick?'

'Most people have psychiatric symptoms first. Often it's anxiety or depression, but I don't think I did. My feet just started going numb, and I *knew*, and I was just so furious. I had read that keeping my brain stimulated would lessen the motor symptoms so instead of seeing a doctor, I just started working like a maniac. I worked and I researched, and I was just livid with the whole universe.'

'Is that when you found the neurologist in Mexico?

'No, first I found Lynn. I did what you did that morning in the hospital—I tried to talk her into giving me the cure,' she laughed softly. 'I just had some crazy feeling there was some breakthrough she was withholding from me. And via Lynn's clinic, I met Haruto.'

We drifted into silence. I brushed the hair back from her face and listened to the ocean for a moment.

'Do you want to hear about him?'

Her voice was small. Of course I didn't. I didn't want to know anything more than I already knew, but there was a thread of longing in her tone, and maybe she needed to talk about him. I forced down my jealousy.

'Absolutely.'

'You never talk about your exes.'

'My exes aren't very interesting.'

'I'll bet they talk about you.'

'All of my notable exes would be happily married by now and at some point each of their husbands would have said the words *Callum Roberts is an arsehole.*' We both laughed softly.

'Tell me about one.'

I sighed.

'You're a demanding wench. I'll tell you about Annalise.'

She was my last girlfriend before Lilah, a silly, giggly little girl, really.

'Can I guess? She was a gym instructor.' It sounded like Lilah had me pegged anyway.

'Wrong,' I said, and I was smug, until I realised how much worse the truth sounded. 'She was a beauty therapist.'

'Oh, this is perfect. Let me guess. She was *your* beautician?'

'Only for a while.' I pretended to be defensive because it seemed like a hitherto heavy conversation had suddenly turned light-hearted and teasing, and even if it was at my expense, that was preferable to the previous topic.

'Isn't that a conflict of interest on her part? I mean, lawyers and doctors can't date clients.'

'It was handy, actually. She never made house calls until we were going out.'

'And Annalise the house-call-making-beautician, was she beautiful?'

'Not like you,' I said, and I meant it. 'But she was attractive. Pretty is a better word for her than beautiful.' All of my ex-girlfriends had been pretty. It had seemed so important, once upon a time. No wonder I'd never settled down.

'What went wrong?'

'We went out for a few months. It never actually went wrong; more… I don't know. I knew it wasn't going anywhere.'

'Because she wasn't perfect.'

'No,' I said, and then it felt like my heart was going to leave my chest as I realised I could say the words and it wouldn't do any damage at all to what was already a rock-bottom situation. 'Because she wasn't *you*.'

The playful light disappeared in Lilah's eyes. She bit her lip and settled back against my chest. I knew she wasn't upset, and I knew she wouldn't retreat. She wanted me there, and she had no secrets to hide behind anymore—I could be open with her now.

We lay silently together for a moment.

'I hate this disease, Lilah.'

'The thing is, Cal, it's not a disease. It's my DNA. That's what *I* hate most. It's not something that happened to me, or something I caught. It's the way *I am*, so when I try to hate it, I'm just hating a part of myself. That's what's most awful about it.'

'What did Peta think of all of this? You never told her you were going to Mexico?'

'No, we told Haruto's parents and they tried pretty hard to talk us out of it. So I left Mum in the dark. She has always been behind me one hundred per cent but I couldn't ask this of her. It didn't seem fair.'

'Really? It's hard to imagine either of you pulling any punches.'

'Mum absolutely *lost* it when I did the genetic testing and we knew I had the gene,' Lilah sighed.

'It must have been hard for her.'

'Oh, I know, Cal. I'm sure it was horrific for her—but, Jesus, it was *worse* for me. Grandma and Pa had both died by my final year of high school, and then Dad finally died too, so we had both been battered and bruised by life and I just think she'd reached the end of her rope. She insisted I have the test, I think looking for a ray of sunshine and believing I'd somehow dodged the genetic lottery, and then I didn't. So to cap off the worst year of our lives, I got accepted into law and the world was briefly my oyster, and the next week found out I had HD, that my CAG repeat was high, and that within twenty years I'd be well on my way to hell. And just when I needed support to process it all, Mum went totally off the rails, so I was alone with it.'

'I'm sorry, Lilah.'

'I survived. And I got past it. I had to because I knew life really is too short, at least for me.'

I think she was trying to be funny again, but this time I didn't laugh.

'So you went to uni anyway?'

'Mum didn't want me to. She thought, if I only had fifteen or so good years left, that I should make the absolute most of them. She proposed selling the farm and travelling the world while I still could. She even offered to come with me.'

'You went to uni anyway, obviously.'

'I'd already seen the world. I knew what was out there. I wanted knowledge, learning, challenge, stability… mostly I wanted something normal before all of the twitching and insanity started.'

'And you had it.'

'I really did. I've had a great life, Cal.'

'Your mum obviously came round.'

'She did, and once she got over her meltdown, she was, and is, unfailingly awesome. But I didn't tell her when I started getting symptoms; I just left it unsaid. I knew she'd figure it out for herself. She didn't exactly love Haruto, so when we decided to go and try the stem-cell therapy, I just told her he and I were going travelling. I kept in touch with her via email but for the time we were away I just let her think I was making the most of the time I had left.'

Lilah shifted slightly on the bed beside me, snuggling closer at the memory.

'So you lost the feeling in your feet, and then you got it back. Is that why you never wear bloody shoes?'

'I missed the feeling of the earth beneath my feet. But no, I don't have an excuse, I've always done that. I just fucking *hate* shoes.'

I felt her grin in the darkness.

'How long was Haruto sick for before he died?'

'A few months. He was breathing on his own, but otherwise he was a vegetable, and he didn't ever regain consciousness. I lied to everyone and told them we had a car accident. I didn't even tell his parents the truth. I just said the stem-cell therapy didn't work and we decided to make a holiday out of the trip and were travelling around Mexico and that's when he got hurt. It was such a fucking stupid lie. They must have known the truth. But they were just such great people and I couldn't bring myself to draw attention to the fact that he was dying and I was actually living.'

'I'm sorry, Lilah.'

'The worst of it was I never contacted them again. He died, I went to the funeral and we cried together, and I told them I'd keep in touch. And I didn't. It was too hard.'

'I'm sure they understood.'

'Maybe.'

'And what was your plan from there? Just go on lawyer-ing?'

'That's the great thing about being in a totally hopeless situation: you don't need a plan. I don't think I had any expectation that the treatment would work; I just couldn't bear the thought of doing absolutely nothing but sitting around waiting for my brain to dissolve.'

I thought about that for a long moment and tried to imagine how I'd feel in her shoes. I was beginning to feel like an expert in HD, although I still couldn't bear the thought of witnessing her decline.

'Did you see much of your dad when he was sick?

'Yeah, enough.' I heard it then, the shift in her tone. It seemed when Lilah spoke about her own experiences, even with Haruto, she was matter of fact. As soon as I mentioned her father, though, a heaviness sank over her. 'It was awful. He went from this vibrant, life-giving man, to... he couldn't sit or lie or stand still. The chorea got so bad that he would move constantly, but he was totally unaware of it. And then he began to lose his mind, and eventually he was just a twisted, soulless body in a nursing home.'

Oh, how I wished I hadn't asked. I'd seen only a few photos of James McDonald, but now I could see him vividly in my mind, and he suddenly looked a lot like his daughter.

'The worst thing about them dumping me with Grandma and Pa was that every time I saw him he was worse, so to my stupid teenage brain, it seemed like it was happening overnight. And now here I am, and it's my turn, and it really is happening overnight, just like I always feared. It's like all of my teenage nightmares are coming true. If I let myself, I could be really, really scared right now.'

We were both silent for a long time after that. I shifted so that she lay partly over my chest and I could stroke her back. After a long silence, she spoke again, and when she did, her voice was hoarse.

'It was a long, slow march to death for Dad. Mum wouldn't put him into a nursing home; Grandma and Pa had to force her to when he was beyond even knowing she was there. And he was a there for months, until finally he died from a heart attack. And instead of grief, all we felt was relief because we'd already grieved him a hundred times over.'

There was nothing I could say to that, and we lay silent but for the sound of our breathing, until we were both asleep.

❀ ❀ ❀

A few days later, she was in the bath and I was reading a book on the bed nearby.

I was listening for sounds that she was in trouble. I particularly hated it when Lilah decided to take a bath. There were so many potential hazards in that bathroom. When she'd renovated years earlier, she'd installed an enormous freestanding bathtub under the window. It wasn't close enough to the wall for my liking, and there was nothing for her to hold on to getting in or out. And those damn floorboards in the bathroom were an absolute nightmare; she always filled the bath too high so it was always overflowing when she got in, and they were slippery at the slightest hint of moisture. I'd been putting down towels and bath mats, but Lilah kept picking them up and throwing them in the hamper.

After a while, I realised I was turning the pages but not absorbing a word of the storyline, so I stood and walked to the bathroom door.

She was so beautiful and frail, humming out of tune to the music playing from an iPod dock on the window sill.

'Hi there,' she smiled at me. 'Good book?'

'Not really. Do you think we should get married?'

She didn't miss a beat.

'I'd love to marry you, Callum Roberts. If I wasn't me, I'd marry you in a heartbeat.'

'But given that you are you…'

'This has been the problem all along, you know. The only problem, actually.' She lifted her hand from the water and watched the droplets fall back into the bath. 'I'd love to promise a lifetime to you. I just don't have one to give.'

'Of course you do,' I said. 'It might not be as long as we'd like, but it's still a lifetime. And while it's very noble of you to try to save me from your shortened life expectancy, Lilah, the whole way along you've been missing one important factor here.'

'And what's that?'

'That I love you. And I'll love you forever, whether you're sick or well, or here or… not.' My eyes filled with tears, and then hers did too.

'I love you too,' Lilah whispered, and she pressed her hand over her mouth as if she could stop the sob that soon escaped it. I walked to the bath and dropped to my knees beside her.

'I know you thought that you were saving me from having to be a part of this, Ly. But you were also taking these moments from me, from us, and I wouldn't trade them for the world.'

'I just want you to be happy, Cal.' She slurred worse when she was upset, and the words were barely distinct.

'I want that for you too,' I said. She fumbled her wet hands for mine against the edge of the bath and as our fingers entwined I rested my cheek against them to stare at her. 'You, in *all* of your perfect weirdness, are the love of my life. I can't fix this for us, Lilah, even though I want to more than anything else on this earth. But I can promise you that I'm yours no matter what happens next.'

'I love you so much, Cal. I feel exactly the same. I'm sorry that… I'm sorry that this is all of the life we will have together. But I'm so glad you found your way back to me.'

For a moment we were silent, except for the rough-drawn sounds of our breathing and the periodic drop of her tears into the bathtub.

'That sounded a lot like a set of wedding vows to me,' Lilah whispered. I squeezed her hands and nodded.

'None of that legal bullshit, right?'

'This is almost exactly how I dreamt it'd be, except I wouldn't be naked and you wouldn't be kneeling in a slippery puddle next to my bathtub.'

She sat up and we shared a soft, lingering kiss. I could soar now, just for a moment. She loved me too, and she'd said it. Everything else slipped out of my mind and I was fully there, and fully alive. I didn't want to move, not ever, because I didn't want to shatter the spell.

The floorboards undid me. My knees went numb, then my feet, and then I realised that her bath was getting cold. Damn reality would not be put off, not even for a few more minutes. I kissed her again.

'So, what do you want for our reception dinner?'

'I'll get out in a minute and help you cook.' It was code for *please let me do it myself.* Not only because she was still so damned independent, but time had not improved my vegan culinary skills one iota. She brushed a stray curl back from my forehead. 'I *knew* you were a romantic deep down inside.'

'You caught me.'

❊   ❊   ❊

We instituted a tradition at the farm. Every Sunday, we'd spend all day exploring the garden looking for ingredients, and then researching recipes that would best suit them. I bought insanely expensive wine matched to the food, and even had a bucket of the coconut soy ice cream Lilah liked so much couriered up from Manly.

As the sun set, Leon and Nancy would walk down the drive and Peta would arrive soon after. We sat on the deck and ate and swapped stories and drank until the laughter and companionship almost drowned out the reason we were all there. It was like a mini Christmas Day every Sunday night, and for those brief hours I lived fully in the moment, just being there with Lilah and *her* people, who collectively had become my family.

I watched the joy on Lilah's face in the flickering candle-light, and I tasted the depth and richness of the food and the wine. Although she'd be exhausted, we would cautiously, tenderly make love in the bed afterwards—with the French doors open just a crack, and the cold winter breeze and the sounds of the ocean washing over us. It was those nights, more than any other, when I would lie awake in the quiet afterwards, thinking about who we were, and where we'd come from, and as little as possible about where we were going.

❄ ❄ ❄

It was a cool morning and we'd decided to go for a walk, out the long driveway and past Leon and Nancy's. If Lilah was still up for it, we'd planned to keep going and have a look at the neighbouring properties up close. We hadn't yet made it to the end of the driveway but I could already see her tiring.

'Have you told Ed and Will about me?'

'I mentioned you at Christmas when we were chatting,' I admitted. 'But... as for everything else... I don't really speak to them all that often, so there hasn't been the opportunity.'

'You should ring them.'

'Why?'

'You'll need them sooner or later, Cal.'

That did not bode thinking about.

'I've gotten this far without them.'

'What are they like?'

She stopped for a rest and I automatically stopped with her. All of the hundreds of hours of conversations with her, and I'd only mentioned them once or twice. I kicked at the gravel driveway with my feet as she leant against a gum tree with her hands behind her back.

'They're not like me,' I said. 'They don't wax their chests, for a start.'

She grinned.

'Nor do you these past few weeks.'

She was right. I felt like I was becoming a slow-motion werewolf. It had been weeks since I'd had my hair cut, and it felt unruly and long—out of control—just like my life.

'I have higher priorities at the moment. And frightening re-growth. But that's beside the point. No, my brothers are...' I searched for words. 'They're manly men. Does that make sense?'

'Blokey blokes, huh.' She raised her eyebrows at me.

'I might have said meatheads, once upon a time. They were a barrel of fun and fights as kids; I was studious and focused. While I was studying, they were usually wrestling each other or entertaining girls in their bedroom and getting caught and chastised by Mum. Whereas I *was* just studying, and I only discovered how much fun girls could be by the time I got to university.'

'Which was probably a good thing.' She watched me thoughtfully. 'I reckon you were an awkward teenager.'

I laughed.

'Oh, you have no idea. I felt like when I walked my knuck-les dragged along the ground behind me—not because I was a Neanderthal, just because my limbs were so long and it took me years to grow into them. But I made up for lost time with the ladies once I hit my early twenties though, I promise.' I winked at her and she raised her eyebrows at me.

'I'm sure you did. But you never mended bridges with your brothers before they both moved away?'

'It wasn't even that we didn't get along, so there were no bridges to mend. It was just they were so different to me, but they were so similar to each other.'

'What do they do?'

'Ed is crazy on sport. He was on a short-term contract as a soccer coach in France when he met his wife and now he's settled there permanently. I think he's coaching some famous team, not really sure. And Will is a mechanical engineer; I think he works with car engines or something.'

'So he stopped wrestling long enough to do some studying.'

'They both did. Ed has a degree in sports psychology or some such nonsense. But you see the problem: I can tell you seventeen ways to sell a car and I can manage to drive one, but if it stops working, I don't even know how to change a tire. And as for sport...well, I watch it sometimes, and I do like squash... but it's not my thing. '

'You'd much rather look at drafts of artwork for ads, or drink fancy wine, or get your hair cut every five minutes so you look neat all of the time.'

'Exactly.'

Lilah stepped away from the tree and continued her awkward shuffle along the driveway.

'Did you ever figure out what Ed's wife's name is?' she asked me as I fell into step beside her again.

'Karen.'

'No way! I thought you said it was Lizette or Suzette?'

'I'm kidding—I still don't know.'

'You're an arse.'

'So I've been told. But surely I'm an adorable one?'

'You have your moments.' A few more steps down the road, she turned to me and frowned. 'Did you ever figure out what Ed's wife's name is?'

I swallowed. Hard.

'Lizette.' I said. 'I'm pretty sure it's Lizette.'

CHAPTER TWENTY-FOUR

Lilah

11 May

If my mind were a tide, it would be pulling away now. It would leave a damp shoreline, because I know I've made some kind of impact here. But the next wave that crashes here will not be me, because my moment will have passed.

This morning Callum stopped me from taking my antispasmodic medication a second time because I forgot that he'd already crushed it up and given it to me in honey. I spent at least twenty minutes trying to figure out how I used to get the hand towel to hang on the bathroom vanity before he quietly came and took it from me and hung it simply on the hook. Callum doesn't really leave my side. He thinks I don't know he's lurking outside the bathroom or watching like a hawk from the windows if I go out for fresh air.

Mum quietly told me yesterday that I'm snapping at him, and asked me to try to keep it in check. I don't think I'll be able to, because I'm literally not aware I'm doing it. Just like I'm not aware of the chorea until someone points it out, the agitation simmers somewhere below my consciousness.

And it's awful, beyond awful, because I have been in Callum's shoes with Haruto and I know the pain and the frustration of watching someone you care about suffer these exact symptoms.

Callum tells me he loves me dozens of times a day, but he doesn't need to. Even if he was mute, I'd still get the message loud and clear, because his eyes and his hands and his kisses say it. The fact that he is still here says it. When he wordlessly chops peas in half so I can swallow them, I know he loves me. When I see him pretending to remake the bed for the fifth time when I go into the en suite to pee, I know he loves me. When I realise he's cluttered up my bathroom floor with improvised floor mats—again—so that I don't slip, even though it's driving me completely insane to be babied like that—I know he loves me.

I worry for Cal. I'm going to die, and I know it's going to rock him. Losing Haruto nearly killed me, and the connection I had to him was loose, sporadic at best. I think Callum will probably go immediately back to work, and he'll stick his head up in about twelve months' time and suddenly realise he's lonely again.

If I could make a dying wish and know that it would come true, it wouldn't be to save myself, it would be for Callum. I'd wish into existence a wife for him, someone bursting with fertility and gentleness, a curvy woman—I think he'd like a curvy woman. She'd pull him into her cushiony bosom and soothe his loss, and cook him dead animals and give him beautiful babies. She'd make him ring his fucking brothers. And he'd move into a big house with her and their children would have the one bedroom each right up until they leave home.

Oh, God, I'd wish that for him. I'd wish him happiness, all of the happiness I've compressed into our short time together, spread out over the decades that he has ahead of him.

There are no magic genie bottles here though. Just bottles and bottles of pills.

CHAPTER TWENTY-FIVE

Callum

For seven glorious weeks, we relaxed together by the ocean, enjoying all of the carefree moments we were supposed to share the first time around. Maybe Lilah was choking more and more on her food and even water; maybe the chorea movements were becoming more noticeable and more sustained; maybe she was becoming forgetful and everyday tasks were more difficult; maybe she was stumbling more and more—if I noticed, I didn't ever acknowledge it, even to myself.

Peta visited each day. Sometimes she came for breakfast and brought me bacon, and although Lilah rolled her eyes at us, Peta and I would sit and devour the meat as if we were children raiding a lolly stash. We saw Leon and Nancy all of the time too because they spent their days in the garden right outside our house. Nancy seemed to have developed a terrible habit of accidentally cooking too much and asking us to take suspiciously fresh-looking vegan 'leftovers' or baked goods off her hands. Karl called from time to time. They were our only connections beyond the beach house, because I was totally focused on Lilah, and she was totally focused on me. We did a lot of living in those seven weeks, especially for two people who only ever left the property to buy supplies.

It was a golden time; all was well with the world except for the very distant band of storm clouds on the horizon, and

I was absolutely determined to ignore them until I no longer could.

Lynn had been Skyping in every few days, but after one of these sessions, suddenly decided she needed to see and reassess Lilah, and we reluctantly packed our bags and headed back to Lilah's apartment in Manly. As soon as we stepped inside, I looked through the French doors to the utterly barren garden on the balcony, and I resisted the urge to shield Lilah's eyes.

'Fuck, it stinks in here,' was all that she said. She walked immediately to the doors and flung them open. 'Don't you hate that musty smell? Your apartment must be even worse— Jesus, it's been six months since you were there.'

But it hadn't. It had been seven weeks, the same seven weeks I'd been fully immersed in her world, and wouldn't have given a toss even if my apartment had burnt to the ground. I watched her silently.

'It's bloody cold too, isn't it? I'll let it air for a while then we'll crank that heater up.' She stepped back into the living area, wiped her hand over the top of a couch and sighed. 'Fucking dust. Cal, could you grab a cloth and wipe a few things down? I need to find a jumper.'

Lilah didn't wait for an answer. Instead, she walked through to her bedroom.

Over the next hour, I waited for comprehension to dawn, and for the disappointment to set in on her face. She donned a jumper, but was still cold. She tried to add tracksuit pants, but her hands were too unsteady, so I had to help her, and eventually I settled her in on the couch with two pairs of socks and a blanket, and I thought surely now she'd see the balcony and I could console her.

Instead, she started flicking between channels, the dead pot plants just a metre behind her and still unnoticed.

Several minutes later, I tried to force the issue.

'I'm sorry about the balcony, Ly.'

She looked at me blankly.

'The plants?' I prompted.

When comprehension still failed to dawn, I physically pointed to the dead pot plants. She turned around and looked at the balcony, then she shrugged at me as if we were talking about the weather.

'Shit happens. We can replace them.'

There had been worrying signs, and troubling symptoms, but I'd managed to avoid them all, until that very moment. Right there in her apartment I finally admitted to myself that the honeymoon was coming to an end.

❄ ❄ ❄

Over the next few days, Lilah underwent a battery of tests, and Lynn's take on the situation was bleak.

'Her memory is shot,' she told me. 'And her cognitive tests show significant decline… reasoning, sequencing and problem-solving have deteriorated. The swallowing study was even worse. Surely she's been choking more and more?'

Of course she had been. I just didn't want to say it aloud. I had taken to preparing only meals that consisted of tiny portions to encourage her to take smaller mouthfuls, but it wasn't helping.

Lynn placed her hand over mine.

'Callum, I'm sorry, but you are just going to have to bring her back for reassessment more often—there is a weekly clinic at Newcastle I can meet you at, which might be easier. At this rate, I'd say we will need to consider withholding nutrition and hydration by mouth and utilising a feeding tube in the short-term future. It's a miracle that she hasn't had pneumonia

again, and you guys have already had your share of miracles—
we can't push this any further.'

❋ ❋ ❋

While Lynn and I met, Lilah was at an MRI, and all the
while I knew the worst was yet to come—telling Lilah herself. When she joined us, she was tired from the back-to-back
tests, and before Lynn could speak, she held up her hand.

'I know. I know we're on the last downhill run here and I
know it's happening faster than we hoped. Everything is beginning to fade, and I know you're going to want to do more
and more to alleviate the symptoms but...'

We hadn't talked about any of these things, and I had
assumed Lilah was unaware, as I had wished she were. She
looked at me; the darkness in her blue eyes tugged hard at
my soul.

'We've had our time, Cal. The next time I get pneumonia,
I'm refusing treatment, and I'm going to let it take me. Do
you understand?'

It was amazing how strong she sounded. Even the thick-
ness to her voice seemed to improve as the stubbornness rose.

'That's entirely your choice, Lilah,' Lynn said softly.

'*Callum* needs to understand, not you.' Lilah's gaze was
sharp and focused on me. 'And you need to make sure Mum
understands. I do not want you two to override my wishes
when I can't speak for myself.'

'I understand.' I could barely force out a whisper, let
alone a sentence. I fumbled for her hand and the tears spilled
from my eyes. Only a brief few months with her facing this,
and I couldn't refuse her. How people managed decades of
this decline I'd never understand. 'I will make sure that your
wishes are respected, sweetheart. I promise.'

Lilah was crying too. She pulled me close, pressed my face into her neck as if I was the sick one, and her fingers clutched at my hair.

'Thank you,' she whispered. 'Thank you, Callum.'

She pulled herself back from my shoulder suddenly and wiped away the tears with an almost violent determination. When that failed to work too, she shut her eyes and took a deep breath to compose herself.

When she opened her eyes again, they were twinkling with mischief. She grinned, and then winked at me.

'All right then, take me to the Manly Inn, my friend. I'm in the mood for some teeny tiny bites of steak.'

❀ ❀ ❀

I knew somehow that this would be the last time we'd be at Lilah's apartment together. She must have known it too.

'I just need a few minutes here alone, Cal.'

The bags were by the door, and I couldn't think of a single excuse to refuse her. I hesitated anyway.

'What if I just…'

She rolled her eyes and pushed me towards the door.

'Go for a bloody walk, Callum. Grab a coffee or get your damn hair cut or buy me some ice cream. I just need ten minutes to myself. I promise I'll still be here when you get back.'

I caught the elevator downstairs, staring at myself in the mirror and knowing I'd never forgive myself if anything happened to her before I got back. When it stopped on the ground floor, I walked across the lobby to the front door. I remembered my first visit there, how shocked and out of place I'd felt when I saw how new and exclusive her building was. Now home was wherever Lilah was. How would I find home after she was gone?

Don't think about it. Don't think about it.

I walked back to the elevator and pressed the fifth-floor button, once, twice, three times, trying to hurry it up. The doors opened and one of the other occupants stepped out, offering me a faint smile as I pushed past him.

The elevator doors opened on her floor just as she kicked the last of our bags out into the hallway.

'I said ten minutes.' She was exasperated. 'Jesus, Callum. Did you even leave the building?'

'I…' I looked at the bags. 'You should have let me do that.'

'It's done now.'

'What were you even doing in there?'

She frowned.

'Do you think we could go get some ice cream?'

Was it a deflection? I didn't know, and I knew I couldn't push it. I picked up a bag in each hand.

'All right. Can you walk?'

'It's only a block away.' She was impatient and irritable. 'Of course I can walk.'

Bags safely stowed in her hybrid, I took her hand in mine and we walked along the beach towards the Corso, as we'd done so many times over the early months of our relationship. As we neared the ice cream shop, she released my hand, flashed me a smile and pointed to a clothing shop.

'Remember that day?'

She'd tried on hats, and I'd waited on the bench outside and watched her through the glass. She looked like a world-class model that day, and I'd been overtaken by a strange urge to play-act with her—so unlike me, especially back then. As if we were two playful kids, I pretended I was holding a camera and she laughed at me and played along.

'I remember that black felt hat. No one else in the world could pull that off except you,' I murmured.

'Remember the noodle shop?'

'I thought you were going to get yourself arrested.'

'Ah, now *that* would have been fun.'

'What flavour ice cream do you want?' I asked her.

'Coconut soy—'she began, then paused. 'Triple chocolate sundae please, with extra whipped cream and chocolate sprinkles.'

I kissed her forehead and helped her into one of the low chairs out the front. We'd always sat in the higher bar stools along the window, but that would be too risky now. We could re-enact our ice cream runs, but we couldn't pretend things hadn't changed.

I'd get Lilah exactly what she asked for, although we both knew she'd be licking only a few mouthfuls off the spoon before it became too much work to swallow it. It didn't matter though, not one little bit. She'd enjoy those mouthfuls and I'd soak up the joy on her face as she did.

❅ ❅ ❅

It all happened too quickly from there. It was as if Lilah had possessed the strength of mind to hold off her demise for a while, but then even her resolve broke.

She got a mild fever less than a week after we saw Lynn. I wasn't worried at first; she seemed comfortable and assured me she wasn't in pain. The only sign of trouble was a slight glassiness to her eyes, and when I felt her forearm I was surprised at the heat there.

I insisted she take some paracetamol and slept fitfully beside her as the fever came and went, and by morning she was coughing a little.

And then the fever came back, but this time it did not let up. Lilah just wanted to sleep, and when woke, she was still exhausted. I rang Lynn, who sent around a local palliative care GP. As she slept, he listened to her chest then looked up at me.

'It's pneumonia,' he confirmed very quietly. 'I understand she's refusing treatment?'

I stared down at her. Her cheeks were flushed. It was so rare to see colour in her chalky complexion.

'That's what she's said.'

'I'll come back in the morning. If she gets any worse in the meantime, call me and I'll come back and we can talk more serious pain relief.'

'Will she just sleep like this now?' Had my chance to converse with her, to share moments of enjoying each other, to say goodbye… had it already passed without me knowing it?

'It's hard to say,' the doctor shrugged. 'If we hook her up to some morphine, she might sleep on. But… she's a long way off leaving you.' His expression softened. 'You should have time yet to say goodbye.'

✳   ✳   ✳

Lilah woke later that afternoon and slowly ate some soup. She seemed a little better somehow, well enough even to ask to move to the lounge to watch some television for a while.

I was channel surfing, looking for something that might vaguely interest her, when she suddenly grabbed my arm with a grip that was so tight it literally elicited a howl from me.

'You need to call Mum and get her to come.'

I did as I was told, and within minutes Peta was there, bag in hand, ready for the long haul. She let herself in and walked straight to Lilah on the couch. She crouched before her daughter, fumbled for both hands, and they stared at each other for the longest time. Such emotion passed back and forward that I felt awkward being in the room.

Then, without a word, Peta rose.

'I'll make up the bed in the spare room.'

❄ ❄ ❄

In the days that followed, I got my first taste of Lilah's absence. She was still there, but our days were entirely filled with her illness, and she was too sick to do anything but rest. The days were pain-filled—physically for Lilah and emotionally for Peta and I—punctuated only by medication to administer and visits from the doctor.

'Has she ever been this sick before?' I asked Peta, while Lilah moaned and half-slept on the bed before us. I knew she'd had pneumonia a bunch of times while we were apart, and somehow had clawed her way back. Oh, that this would be a false alarm and she'd sleep fitfully for days and then wake up and demand green tea.

'No,' Peta said softly. 'I think this is it.'

When I called, Lynn drove up from the city immediately, and after examining Lilah she pulled me out onto the deck.

'I don't know how long this will take, Cal. I've just set up an IV for fluids and a self-administering morphine device because she's in so much pain but—' She looked tired and emotional. I understood too well. Physically, I felt like I no longer slept with my whole mind, in case I woke to find Lilah had stopped breathing beside me. Emotionally, though, I was so tired, just knowing that my love was fading before my very eyes, and there was nothing at all I could do to stop it. 'At some point over the next few days, she might just go,' Lynn whispered, and to my horror, she was suddenly crying. 'I'm sorry. I know this is unprofessional, but I've been treating her for years and—'

Lynn took some sharp breaths and swatted at her face with her hands, turning away from me for a few moments, pulling it all together before she faced me again.

'It never gets any easier, trying to treat the untreatable,' she murmured. 'It's not a nice way to die, untreated pneumonia. She will probably be feverish for long periods, and eventually she'll lose consciousness. Her breathing will become more laboured, her respiration rate might increase and decrease, it might sound like she's gasping for air or like her chest is rattling... but these are just reflexes, and part of the process. Just keep the morphine up so she's not in pain; the device won't allow her to overdose. Once she passes, call an ambulance as soon as you can and explain the situation.'

I suppose I knew that we were at that point, but seeing the finality on Lynn's face and in her words, I suddenly crumbled.

'Is there—what can we do to keep her comfortable?' I couldn't resist Lilah's will, not after watching her decline. How could I insist she stay with us, knowing she would slip away anyway, leaving only indignity? My arrogance, my confidence—it was all gone. I would be compliant to Lilah's wishes now. I had seen enough.

'I'll arrange some oxygen,' Lynn promised. 'And I will drop everything and come here if you need me.' She reached for her pocket and withdrew a piece of paper with a phone number already scrawled upon it. 'This is my home number and my personal mobile. I'm willing to be here at any time, day or night.'

'Thank you.'

I took the paper and slipped it into the pocket of my jeans. The ocean continued to roll in below us, and I heard the inevitability of the waves and wondered where the bigger picture of all of the comings and goings of the universe fit into the pain that lay before me. Lynn suddenly took my hand.

'You didn't sign up for this, Callum. If it's too much, go home. Peta has done this before, and she will cope.'

I wiped at my face and shook my head.

'I want a part of every breath she has, until the end, whatever that looks like.'

Lynn nodded and then left, but I took a few minutes on the deck before I dared take myself back into our bedroom, where my so deeply loved Lilah seemed to be teetering on the very edge of leaving me forever.

✳ ✳ ✳

Peta and I were spending a lot of time sitting in Lilah's room. I suppose we were keeping vigil, but it felt like we were nursing a child.

We took turns on the bed, lying beside Lilah while she rested. She slept a lot; even when a fever took hold and she sweated and fidgeted, she slept. We spoke things to her that were so intimate and private that I could never repeat them. Peta spoke as a mother who'd had carriage and adoration of this human for forty years, but I spoke as a lover who wanted nothing more than forty *more* years with her. A web of privacy formed, the triangle between us so tight that we could each say anything and know that it was okay.

Such an awful situation only brings out the best in humanity. Peta and I are obscenely self-absorbed personalities—that day was entirely about Lilah, and pushing words of comfort and love through whatever delirium she might be experiencing.

I thought Lilah seemed better by the next day. She was lucid enough to eat tiny bites of scrambled egg here and there, and we had some light conversation as the afternoon progressed. Best of all, her coughs seemed to ease, and I wondered if this wasn't actually going to be her final war, but just another battle that her body would fight.

'I don't want to see that local doctor today,' she announced out of the blue at midday. Peta frowned.

'Lilah, is that wise?'

'What's it going to do, kill me?' Her grim humour felt flat. She shook her head. 'No, Mum. This isn't the time for strangers, and he can't do anything for me.'

'I can ask Lynn to come again?' I offered, and Lilah shook her head.

'No. I just want to be with you two now. The GP can come back tomorrow.'

Peta gave me a helpless shrug, and I sighed and rose to make the phone call to cancel his visit. Lilah had us read to her from a few of her favourite books and listened to some music as she rested. As darkness fell, Peta retreated for a break, and Lilah cuddled up against me.

'Are you in pain now?' I asked her. She hadn't used the morphine pump in a while, or so I thought, but maybe I'd missed it.

'I'm okay,' she whispered. Her voice was still hoarse. 'I'm so glad you're here, Callum. I know this is awful for you.'

'The thing is,' I said, my voice deceptively strong, 'I have no idea what happens after you go, but it will be better because I knew you.'

'You have to marry someone.' Her voice was light, teasing again—and then in a heartbeat, deadly serious. 'You have to find someone, Cal. You *have* to marry and have babies. You just have to.'

I shook my head and the tears threatened.

'Saoirse, don't talk about that now.'

'Oh, for fuck's sake, I'm minutes from death—don't go pulling out my *in trouble* name now.' It was a weak laugh, but it was a laugh, until she was serious again. 'Promise me.'

'I can't promise that.' That she was even asking me to seemed obscenely cruel. For a moment I wanted to rage at her. *Do you really dare to ask this of me? I have to find you, love you and watch you die—let you die—and in the midst of all of that you demand I think about moving on?*

'Of course you can. You met me, you cared for me, and now I'm dying. I need to know you'll find someone else—I can see just by looking at you how much happier you are having someone to adore in your life.'

'You're a once-in-a-lifetime deal, Ly.' Tears were threatening. She slapped my chest with real force and it stung.

'Bullshit! And stop with the waterworks. We don't do that "true love" rubbish, remember? You'll find someone else, and when you do, I want you to be with her without guilt and marry her and make some beautiful babies with her, and be sickeningly happy for the rest of your sickeningly long life.'

How could I possibly answer that in any sensible way? We lay silent together, in the darkness of her room, for a very long time. Eventually she elbowed me weakly in the chest and I pretended that it hurt. She was weak now, exhausted from the conversation and her exertion in trying to beat me into bending to her will.

'I promise,' I whispered, although I couldn't even begin to fathom how I would fulfil that. Maybe it didn't matter. Maybe just making her think that I meant it was enough.

'Good,' she whispered back, and even though I felt her skin was beginning to burn up again, I felt her breathing was slowing as she relaxed.

❅ ❅ ❅

It was not even five a.m. when she woke me with another sharp elbow to my ribs.

'I need a mandarin.'

Groggy and confused, I sat up.

'What? What time is it?' The digital clock beside our bed answered me when she didn't. *4:48 a.m.*

'You need to get a torch and go to the mandarin tree,' she said. Her voice was hoarse, her breathing was laboured, and her skin against mine under the blanket was scorching hot.

'It's on the other side of the garden,' I argued automatically.

'Callum, there isn't much time. *Go.*'

So, half asleep, I left the room and found the torch and went out into the garden. It was cold—winter was almost upon us—and I could see the frost of my breath as I walked. I knew the landscape like the back of my hand and I found the best tree easily even in the darkness, and spent only a moment or two finding the most ripe mandarin. As I walked back through the predawn night, I pictured her peeling it and enjoying the sweetness of each segment. Her abrupt waking only reminded me of that night when she'd awoken me with the same shock to invite me to the coast, and it seemed appropriate and fitting.

When I got back to the house, Peta was still asleep, and Lilah was sitting back on the bed. I assumed she'd been to the bathroom and was furious she'd attempted it without me. The lamp near the desk was shining, and the one beside the bed was also lit. She took the last step towards the bed and accepted the mandarin eagerly. Lilah ate it segment by segment without choking, as if it was some sinful delight to be savoured, some pleasure greater than her physical shortcomings.

'So good,' she whispered on the last bite. 'Can you wake Mum up?'

'It's too early, Lilah.'

She took my hand and pressed it to her lips.

'It's time, Cal. You need to wake her up and carry me out to the deck.'

❄ ❄ ❄

She talked me into taking her out to watch the sunrise. The actual request wasn't a big one, given that she was tiny and weak and, while I was in the orchard, had pulled out her IV—but I distinctly remember resisting hard, in case the icy cold air somehow did her more harm.

But those beautiful blue eyes were pleading. If she'd asked me to find a way to bite off my testicles, I'd eventually have done it, so the short walk out to the deck was no real ask. It was so, so cold outside—so I rugged her tiny, frail body in the doona, and I do remember as we passed her laptop on the desk she leant over, nearly unbalancing us both, and slammed it shut. As we walked through the living areas she hollered for her mum, and then I opened the French doors and sat her on the cane chair as if she were a baby bird. The darkness was giving in to frail rays of light from the sun right on the horizon, and she couldn't stop smiling.

'This is perfect,' she whispered against the muscles of my upper arm, as I hadn't dared release her since I sat her down on the chair. She was feverish but, compared to the day before, didn't even seem all that sick. Certainly her breathing had improved, even in the icy air. This wasn't what Lynn had described.

'Perfect for what?' I asked. I was confused by the contradiction of her words and her very vibrant, mandarin-scented breath in my face, and, most of all, the fact that she was lucid and seemingly quite comfortable.

Peta chose that moment to step out onto the icy deck in the darkness.

'What's going on?' she asked. She was so groggy that her words slurred and she sounded just like Lilah.

'I don't know,' I answered when Lilah let the sound of the waves breaking on the shore below fill the gap after the question.

'I'm going soon, Mum,' Lilah whispered eventually—and just like that the entire tone of the morning changed for me.

'You can't know that,' I said automatically, and my muscles contracted around her. She shook her head weakly against my shoulder.

'I know it, Cal.'

Peta took the tiny space on the other side of Lilah, and I felt her arms snake around her.

'Goodbye, my beautiful baby,' she whispered. 'I'm so proud that you've done this your way.'

And then we all fell into silence. Mine was a tortured, confused, half-asleep silence—until I realised that Lilah's breaths were gradually slowing, the gaps between exhale and inhale increasing with each cycle. Right within my arms, the one thing I'd wanted to hold on to in my life was slipping away. I held her closer and pressed my face into her hair.

'Please, Lilah,' I whispered. For the first time, I was actually weeping in front of her—these weren't a few leaky tears; I had altogether lost control. She woke again as the first rays of the sunrise were breaking the horizon, only enough to look up at me and manage a smile.

'It was worth it, Cal. It was worth sticking around a few extra years just to meet you.'

Her voice was so weak, and when her eyes fluttered closed again, I shook her. Peta squeezed my arm—hard. Over the top of Lilah's head, her mother shot me a glance that silenced me.

This was happening, and there was nothing I could or should do about it.

'I love you,' I said. Maybe I shouted it, I don't know. Her sleepy face registered the faintest smile only one more time, and then the distance between her shallow breaths increased exponentially. They slowed from then, until every few seconds. I was sure she was gone.

I waited again and again for the next breath, as the sun breached the horizon. We were sitting in silence now, and just as the sun was halfway up into the day, I found myself holding my own breath and waiting for her to give another one, but her next breath would never come. Eventually the air left my lungs in a rush and with a wail that would stain my ears for months to come.

Lilah, my sweet, unique Lilah, had gone with the sunrise.

❄   ❄   ❄

When I could move again I carried Lilah's tiny body back to lay her on the bed, and it registered that she somehow felt even lighter than when I'd carried her out there only half an hour before.

There was a numbness that settled over me. It was probably shock, but at the time there was a whirling turmoil of loss—and then there was just peace. I lay her on the grey sheets, crinkled and ever-so-slightly sweat-stained from that last, unsettled night. I gently straightened her limbs. She was still wearing a light-blue dressing gown over cotton pyjamas, and she was pale of course, but Lilah was always pale. I left her only long enough to find a clean washer and wet it with warm water, and then I sat beside her on the bed. I ran the washer over her forehead, smoothing the hair that had frizzed during the night, and then over her face so gently, and then

over each hand. Then I waited, as if she might open her eyes
and laugh that I'd fallen for her prank, or jerk suddenly because she'd only fallen asleep.

When I heard the door to the deck close and realised
that Peta had at last joined us inside, I finally called the
ambulance.

Peta went straight to the couch in the living room, and I
while I waited beside Lilah, she began weeping as if her heart
had left her body. While I sat holding Lilah's hand, I thought
about Peta and all of her flaws, and the fact that she was surviving this for a second time. Lynn was probably right, Peta
would cope somehow—but for now she was just an empty
shell like Lilah, and like me.

❋   ❋   ❋

When the ambulance came, I met them at the door and the
two officers followed me inside. There was paperwork to do,
and we did it quietly at the breakfast bar to a soundtrack of
Peta's continued sobbing, and then I led them into the bedroom and lifted Lilah onto their stretcher myself. The officers
are blurred shadows in my memory, but I remember being
almost overcome with gratefulness at how they treated her
with such dignity.

When she was gone, there was a gaping hole in the house—
and I felt it immediately. It was a grief-drenched day, the kind
of day where the hours drag and dissolve into nothing all at
once; the kind of day when you wake the next morning and
think it was just a bad dream, until the grit in your eyes and
the heaviness in your chest remind you otherwise.

It was days before I realised how lucky we were. All Lilah
had hoped for was a pain-free passing and she got that. And
even as I missed her so much that I felt an agonising physical

pain within my chest, I knew that her end had been as perfect and as beautiful as she—and I—could ever have hoped.

❅   ❅   ❅

Time now rushed past as a train rushing through a station. I couldn't stop the minutes, but I wanted to. Every minute I breathed through was taking me further away from the last I had with her. The only blessing was that I was in no state to register the details of each hour. At some point Peta told me she'd called the funeral director, and he came to the house the day after she died. He sat at the dining-room table and Peta made us all cups of herbal tea.

'Lilah was in contact with me before she passed.' He opened a manila folder and laid it on the table before us. 'I know this is going to be uncomfortable to hear, but she has signed her body over to a university research program. She wanted her brain to be studied... something about understanding the experimental treatment she underwent?'

'I knew,' Peta rubbed her swollen eyes, and then looked at me. 'She was worried you'd argue, Cal. I'm sorry that she didn't tell you her yourself.'

I looked from Peta to the overweight, balding man whose name I'd already forgotten, and then back to Peta. I *did* want to argue. I wanted to lay her to rest somewhere, not let the thought cross my mind that some clumsy medical student might be cutting her open even as we spoke. I was outraged that she'd made this decision without me, embarrassed that she'd spoken to Peta and this stranger about it and that I had to only hear about it now. It was unfair, it was brutal, it was wrong. I was immediately terrified that she'd once again placed me in a position where there would be no closure. A sudden end to the sentence of the life of our time together, but no full stop. *Again.*

But the problem was, I was already defeated. I didn't want *any* of this to happen, and this was just one more shitty thing in a run of utterly, utterly shitty things. I didn't even have it in me to raise a protest.

'So when there's nothing to bury or cremate, how do we hold a funeral?'

'We hold a memorial service.' The funeral director shuffled the papers and picked up his pen. 'Tell me about your Lilah.'

✳ ✳ ✳

Peta and I sat on the couch that night. The television was off. For a while she held my hand and we stared at the floor in silence. Then she got up and filled two glasses with the $500 bottle of wine I'd purchased for our next Sunday dinner. It was rare and reputedly spectacular, and I'd been excited for Lilah to try it, and now she never would. Was it enough if I tasted it in her honour? Was I allowed to enjoy it if it was amazing?

We sipped the wine for a while in silence. It washed over my tastebuds like water, no pleasure at all registered within me. I looked at Peta.

'Would you do it again?'

She was staring at the wine glass in her hand. When I spoke, she smiled at me very gently.

'Do what, sweetheart?'

'If you could go all the way back to that first day when you met James, before you were too attached, before it was too hard to walk away. Would you stay with him knowing all of the years that would stretch before you and all of the heartache they would contain?'

Peta smiled. God, she looked so much older than she had the first time I met her, but I saw the strength returning to her. Hour by hour, Peta was already healing. I felt like I was still being torn open, like every moment the pain was getting worse.

'You might not feel it now, but you will soon enough. When the rawness heals, there'll still be pain, but a thin layer of gratefulness will shield it. Eventually you'll think fondly of the good times you shared with her, and how she changed you, and how it was all worthwhile. I promise, Callum. This is something I know with all of what's left of my heart.'

I sat the wine down on the coffee table and buried my face in my hands and wept.

❋ ❋ ❋

When the afternoon of the service came, I stood in the house and watched the cars arrive. The funeral director had arranged for staff to direct people, but I'm not sure any of us had anticipated the size of the crowd. The hire company had set up a large screen and hundreds of chairs, but even with half an hour left before the service was scheduled to start, the chairs were full and there was still a throng of people standing.

I hid behind a curtain, watching the shock of people fill Lilah's favourite space and wondering who they all were. It felt strange that Lilah had been central to my very happiness, but I knew so little of her day-to-day existence beyond our months together. I bitterly regretted the shortness of our life together, and as I stood there watching the sum total of her relationships mingle outside without me, I felt more alone than I had in my entire life.

'Come on, lovey.' Peta approached me, dressed in an outfit that would have made a rainbow cringe. She wore bright red pants, a yellow shirt, a multicoloured neck tie, and as my gaze drifted down I noticed her feet—bare except for garishly bright polish on her toes. For a long moment I stared at her feet, and then sighed and bent down to remove my shoes.

'Seems fitting, doesn't it?' she whispered.

'I suppose it does.'

Alan Davis approached us as soon as we stepped outside. He was wearing a black suit and looked as though he could just have stepped from a court somewhere, except for the box of tissues in his hand and the fact his feet, too, were bare.

'I had a feeling today would be rough.' He choked the words out as he embraced Peta. 'But I don't think I had any idea how hard it would be.'

'I know.' Peta held him close, like he was a brother. 'It's like she's looking down on us, cursing the electricity we're wasting with the big screen and the PA.'

We all shared a weak laugh, and Alan shook my hand.

'Are you holding up all right, Callum?'

'I am.' Was I lying? I wasn't even sure; it just seemed the polite thing to say. 'Are you ready to deliver your part of her eulogy?'

'I learnt that if Lilah told me to do something, I did it, or suffer the consequences. So when her mother asked me to do this, I had a feeling I'd better not cross her.' His puffy eyes crinkled when he smiled, and I smiled too.

As we walked to our seats at the front of the crowd, I met dozens of Lilah's colleagues and opponents. There were judges and barristers and CEOs in suits, farmers in chambray shirts and canvas trousers, activists in hemp shirts and dreadlocks. A startling number of people made comments about her being a terrible thorn in their side—one that they were so very sorry to lose.

Just as the celebrant suggested I start to move towards my seat, I saw a small group of familiar faces on the other side of the large crowd. I watched them in silence for a moment, wanting to be sure that I wasn't imagining their presence, then I pushed my way to them.

Will and Ed were standing side by side, stiff and awkward as they looked at the garden. Karl's hands were behind his back and he was staring at the ground. Not far from them, most of my staff, as well as the entire Tison Creative board and their spouses waited.

I approached my brothers first. It was hard to breathe, and harder to believe they were really there. The relief was almost overwhelming. It had actually occurred to me to call them, even since her passing, but what a conversation that would have been. *Hi, Will, Ed and Ed's wife whose name I can't remember. The girlfriend I loved but barely told you about just died. Fancy a visit?*

'What are you doing here?'

I'd always thought Ed looked a lot like me, if someone compressed him into a shorter package. He was nowhere near as tall as me, but much stockier. He embraced me as soon as I spoke and I held him close, trembling with emotion.

When he pulled away, Will took his place for a moment. Will was tall, like me, and just a little chubby these days, which surprised me. How many years had it been since I last saw them? I was sure they'd each visited Sydney since Mum and Dad died… but was that three years ago, or four, or had it really been a decade? When we ended our embrace, Ed cleared his throat and offered me an explanation.

'Lilah emailed her old boss and asked him to track us down. She didn't want you to be alone.'

I pressed my fist against my mouth and nodded. I should have known she'd take matters into her own hands if I didn't do something. *Lilah always got her way.*

'How you holding up, Callum?' Karl asked. I took a shuddering breath and shook my head.

'I'm okay… I just… thanks so much for coming.' It was a hoarse whisper, but it was the best I could do. 'Truly, I mean it. You have no idea what it means to me to have you all here.'

I had *needed* someone there for me, and now I had it—not just someone, but a whole team of people. Jesus, the twins didn't even know her, nor did any of my colleagues—they were here only to support me. I glanced back to the front of the chairs, where my slide show was flashing onto the screen. Lilah, so many breathtakingly beautiful shots of her, as a child, as a teen, as an adult—and then as the frail waif I'd loved these last few months.

I turned back to my brothers, and in their concerned gazes I saw my parents.

'Please, let's catch up afterwards. I think I'm going to need a beer.'

❄ ❄ ❄

The celebrant read some silly poems Peta had found and played a few songs for quiet moments of reflection, one of which Peta of course sung to. Her voice wavered but she didn't miss a single note, even as the tears coursed down her face. Time and time again I thought to lean over and whisper to Lilah about how her mother was *ever the performer*, even under these circumstances, and my next thought would be that Lilah was really gone, and my less-than-hilarious commentary would forever remain unsaid.

We had roughly divided the eulogy—Peta would speak about Lilah's younger years, Alan about her professional work, and it would be my job to speak about her as a woman.

When Peta took to the lectern to speak, she was surprisingly eloquent and stoic, and managed to hold herself together bar for a few dignified tears here and there. If Lilah had been sitting next to me, I had a feeling she'd be heckling her mother, demanding more. As heartfelt as Peta's eulogy was, the raw emotion I'd witnessed over the previous days was now well and truly restrained. She was only performing a part in a musical she'd written about the grief she'd suffered over the past days.

Alan followed, and through tears, rattled off a seemingly endless list of causes Lilah had taken on over the past few years. There were sad laughs from the crowd when he spoke of her less likely wins, and then a quiet hush when he spoke of the legacy she'd left at the firm.

'I didn't want an environmental law wing. None of the partners did. There's no money in it for a start, besides which, when she pitched the bloody idea, Saoirse was one of our top-earning commercial lawyers and didn't know a tree from a lizard. She just had a way of getting what she wanted... and it was probably the best crazy idea I've ever given in to in my life.'

When Alan sat down, everyone looked at me. The walk from my chair to the lectern was a marathon.

'I feel so conflicted, speaking for Lilah today.' I looked up at the crowd, and focused on the only faces I knew—Lynn, Leon and Nancy in the front, my colleagues and brothers at the back. 'I knew Lilah for less than a year, and I don't know many of you here at all.'

The faces before me blurred. I swallowed and looked down at my notes.

'But if I know anything, I know that the love Lilah and I shared was a beacon of light to both of our lives. We didn't have time on our side, but we did have a relationship that renewed my faith in pretty much everything worth believing in.'

On the screen behind me, a single image was now projected. It was Lilah, standing in the garden that day months earlier, with her arms full of vegetables, a smear of dirt on her cheek and her feet inevitably bare. She was a mess—her hair an unruly halo around her radiant smile. I turned back to the photo and that was it—I, the man who didn't even cry in the privacy of his home when his parents died, was weeping in front of several hundred people—and worse still, I wasn't going to be able to pull myself together enough to say any more of the beautiful words I'd written.

Not that it mattered in the end because I think my photo said enough.

❅   ❅   ❅

If you'd asked me six months earlier to list what mattered to me most, family wouldn't have even made the top ten. But everything had changed.

After the memorial, the twins and I retreated to the courtyard of a small wine bar in Gosford. Ed suggested we go inside the house, but I desperately needed a change of scenery and I didn't want to watch the garden drain of mourners and become empty again.

We made an unlikely group in the late-afternoon bar scene: me, red-eyed and fragile, sitting between my two brothers in silence. The bar was quiet, but the other patrons were all young professionals celebrating the end of the working week. We sat in cane chairs in what was left of the sun and I leant mine right against a brick wall so that I could feel the warmth radiating from it. I was colder than the day commanded and it kept reminding me that Lilah would never be warm again.

We ordered drinks and sat in silence until they arrived. Will raised his glass. 'To Lilah. It sounds as if she was a beautiful, remarkable woman. May her legacy live on.'

I raised the glass of scotch he'd ordered me and nodded. 'To Lilah,' I whispered. 'And to family.'

The scotch burned its way to my empty stomach and the conversation finally began to flow.

'When did you arrive?' I asked Ed.

'This morning. We only just made it in time for the service. I tried to call you to make sure this Alan character wasn't a lunatic before I got on the plane, but your phone was off.'

'I don't even know where it is,' I admitted. How strange to be so totally off-line and not to realise it. 'It's probably been flat for weeks.'

'We figured even if Alan was a lunatic, we'd better check on you,' Will said wryly. 'So we rang your office and eventually someone put us through to Karl.'

'And he at least knew who Lilah was, so from there we were able to connect the dots,' Ed murmured.

'And how long are you here for?' I asked my brothers.

'As long as you need us,' Ed said. 'There's nowhere else in the world we need to be.'

❄ ❄ ❄

Ed and Will wandered the house and garden with me in near silence over the following days. They cooked for me and made sure I ate and got out of bed and showered when I might not have done otherwise. When the weekend was over, they helped me pack up my things. We really didn't speak all that much. Of course there were bursts of conversation here and there, mostly about meaningless details—what particular plants were, what size the property was, was something edible. It didn't matter what we talked about or even if we talked at all. If they hadn't been there, I would have been alone. I just don't know how I would have been able to bear it.

When the time came to leave, Will loaded my bag into the boot and I did one last sweep of the house. I knew, at last, it was time to say goodbye—I didn't intend a return visit and I needed to be sure I had all of my belongings.

I hesitated at the door to our bedroom. Ed had packed my toiletries and clothing up, somehow understanding without an explanation my reluctance to enter the spaces where she'd last been.

As I stepped into the room at last, I *saw* her in the imprint on the bed, and pictured in rapid-fire images the fade of her vitality so fast over those last few weeks. I quickly reviewed the surfaces, confirmed there was nothing out of place, and then when I was almost ready to leave, saw the blinking light on her laptop.

'Oh, hell.' I remembered her awkward lean across me to shut it as I carried her to the deck. As I opened the lid to shut it down, her email client filled the screen.

It was only natural for me to be curious. There was an email stuck in the outbox, maybe because the Internet at the farm was so unpredictable, but maybe because she'd shut the damn lid too quickly. I clicked on it.

Dear Alan

By the time you receive this email you will be aware of my passing. This will be unexpected to you.

Please do not open the attachment unless further unexpected developments take place and there is a suggestion others are to fault. Store it in the corporate records system with security avail-

able only to you and know that I ask this with as much trust as I've ever bestowed upon a friend.

Thank you for so much over the years, and I wish you all the best into the future.

Saoirse

There was a large attachment, far too large to successfully send on an email, and my hand shook as I opened it. When I did, her face filled the screen.

The physical pain I felt at the sight of her was overwhelming. I sank into the stool under the desk as I touched the image with my forefinger. If I could have crawled into the damn screen, I would have.

'Hi,' she whispered. To my shock, I realised the shape under the blankets behind her on the recording was me. 'I'm Saoirse Delilah MacDonald and the person on the bed behind me is the love of my life, Callum Roberts.'

She inched back to the bed, painfully, coughing every few shuffles, clearly very sick. Once she'd slipped back into bed she shook me violently.

'I need a mandarin.'

I suddenly understood what I was watching, and it very nearly undid me. There was the conversation between Lilah and I, before I left to go to the orchard. As soon as I did, Lilah rose from the bed and shuffled back to the desk, and as I watched the video, I began to sob.

'I am Saoirse Delilah Macdonald. I am dying of Huntington's disease. Ahead of me is a long road of undignified suffering and the current laws of this nation do not allow me to circumvent that.'

She withdrew a small, unmarked vial from the desk below the webcam she was recording on and withdrew a handful of small pills. Her eyes had filled with tears.

'This is sodium pentobarbital. I obtained it illegally in Mexico more than five years ago, and within my hand at the moment is more than the accepted dose to end human life. I take these steps alone, without the knowledge of those present on this property at the time. It's my hope and plan they will be with me as I pass, but they will believe it is the course of pneumonia taking my life, as opposed to my own decision to end my life before I lose my very self.' Lilah's beautiful face contorted. 'If I had more time, I'd have fought for the right to do this. But it's too late; my mind and my thought processes and my memories are sliding already, and I *refuse* to fade away. I will go out on my own terms, with the presence of mind to know what it is I'm doing. And one last time— my companions, Peta MacDonald and Callum Roberts, have absolutely no knowledge of that which I'm doing. Namaste.'

She then, with obvious difficulty, swallowed several white pills one by one, before hobbling away from the webcam and back into bed.

I watched, my fingers still resting against the screen, as she lay in the bed waiting for me, and then as I brought that stupid mandarin back to her, and then when I left the room to wake Peta, I saw her sneak out of bed and stop recording. I knew too well what happened next.

There was no way to send the video, even if I'd wanted to. If she'd known to, she could have adjusted the settings on the recording so that it was a lower resolution, and the file would have been small enough to slip through her mail server without me ever knowing. Instead, I unplugged her laptop and carried it with me. I couldn't think about its contents yet. It was too much, and it was too soon. I filed the knowledge away somewhere in my mind and forced myself to leave the house.

❊ ❊ ❊

'What are your plans?' I asked Peta. My brothers and I had stopped to drop off the perishables from the house and to check in on her on our way back to my place in the city.

Peta was in surprisingly good spirits—she seemed at peace.

'I've never wanted to live at the farm,' Peta admitted. 'But now that she's gone... well... I don't know. I'm thinking about moving my business back there; maybe I could add a studio in the garden for my students. I just want to feel near her.'

'And the garden?' It was vitally important that the garden continued. Lilah had never said as much, but she didn't need to.

'Oh, shit Cal, I wouldn't have a clue where to start. No, Leon and Nancy can have that till they die, then I'll give it over to some hippy charity.' Peta smiled, the first humour I'd seen in her face since Lilah had passed. 'Make sure you're at the reading, won't you?'

'What reading?'

'The will.'

I grimaced.

'Peta, I don't need to be there. If there's anything I need to do, just give me a call.'

'No, Callum.' She was firm. 'Lilah will have made mention of you in the will. You need to make sure you're there.'

'I don't—'

'I doubt she's left you her secret collection of Picasso paintings, but I also will be very surprised if she hasn't left you at least something special to hold on to.' Again, those pleading blue eyes, so achingly familiar. I sighed.

'Okay.'

We embraced one last time and I kissed her on the cheek. Then I climbed back into my car and Will turned it towards the city.

'You okay?' He asked.

I looked out the window to the passing trees and water-ways that Lilah had so delighted in.

'It's going to take some time, but I will be.'

❋ ❋ ❋

Both Ed and Will flew out the following day. I drove them to the airport. Will's flight was earliest, and I shook his hand as he went to board.

'I can't thank you enough, Will.'

'I'm only sorry we were only here after, Cal. Please keep in touch. I know it's easy not to, but do it.'

I nodded and then pulled him close for an embrace.

'I'll do better, I promise.'

Ed's flight was a few hours later so we had lunch in the domestic airport before I travelled with him across to the in-ternational terminal. After he checked his baggage, I realised we were still much too early for his flight.

'I can wait with you a while.'

'Nah, I'll go through and do some duty-free shopping for Suzette. She's—' he paused. 'You're going to come visit us soon, aren't you, Cal?'

I'd been aware of the differences between the twins and I for their entire lives, but the weekend of quiet companionship and support had finally shown me our similarities. I knew I didn't need them—I'd functioned very successfully as an adult without them forever. Never in a million years had it ever oc-curred to me that my tough, strong, close-knit brothers might actually need *me*. But there was a colour to Ed's voice—eager-ness, a hope, a desperation. Maybe it had always been there, but I recognised it now because I finally felt my aloneness.

'I'll come,' I promised.

'This year?'

'Absolutely, Ed.'

'It wasn't the right time to tell you… I wasn't sure how to, and even now…'

'It's okay,' I frowned. 'Is everything all right?'

He nodded slowly.

'She's pregnant, actually. It didn't seem right to say it in an email, and we never seem to call each other anymore, and this is the last chance I have to see you face-to-face, so as much as I feel like a shit for telling you now, I guess I had to.'

I pictured his wife, Suzette; I'd seen a photo once and I was pretty sure she was a brunette. I imagined her heavily pregnant and then radiant beside Ed with their child. A happy family. The circle of life: Lilah was gone and someone new was arriving. I realised that I was actually jealous, but mostly I was thrilled for my brother—I couldn't *not* be when he was standing there beside me glowing with pride. I allowed myself to smile, a genuine smile.

'That's fantastic, Ed.'

'In a couple of months you'll be an uncle,' he pointed out. 'So visit us. Come whenever you want to. If you come during the season, I'll take you to training and my games, and if you come on the off season, we can travel or something. Just come.'

We embraced, and then he left. I stood and watched until he was out of sight and I was finally alone.

❉ ❉ ❉

I'm not the type to rage. Growing up, my brothers would stir each other to the point of furious sparring, but that just wasn't me. If Ed or Will tried to get a rise out of me, I was likely to fling out a lazy barb and walk away, back to whatever activity I was enthralled in at the time. I let go of anger quickly, and it never threatened to rule me, so I suppose I never learnt to control it.

I'd been home for a few days when the surge began. It was a king tide, seeping in slowly, and I didn't realise the heights it'd achieve until I was drowning. Where grief had been, there was now black, thunderous rage. I could handle Lilah being taken from me—just, just barely handle it—but she wasn't taken; she left, and she didn't even tell me she was going.

I was sitting on my couch one morning, trying to tune out with breakfast television, when it suddenly struck me how many chances she'd had to tell me. She'd had the drug since Mexico— long before we met. So many days and nights and weeks and months where she could have mentioned it, or hinted at it. Didn't she trust me? Didn't she realise that I'd have understood? I could have been prepared. I could have supported her.

I don't remember throwing my mug through the television, but that's apparently what I did. I remember only the groan, and the sensation of being overwhelmed by emotions which I had no chance of controlling and which I simply couldn't bear. I surfaced maybe seconds, maybe moments later, to find shards of ceramic all over my lounge room and the punctured LCD sounding ominous bursts of static.

It happened again and again over the early weeks. I couldn't bring myself to go near the beach, because there was no way to avoid the sight of her building, so I'd walk away from it instead. But often while I was out walking along the suburban streets, I'd miss her, and then I'd miss the sand and the brine air; my aloneness would seem insurmountable for a brief moment, until anger would replace it. And then, for a time, that was all that there was. I'd disappear into the rage and emerge later, my lungs burning and my legs throbbing, at the other end of the suburb, soaked in sweat. Or I'd be at the supermarket or a cafe, and all it would take would be the sight of a couple in love, and such a blind fury would strike me that I'd abandon my trolley or my table and walk away, blood thundering through my ears.

I was angry with Lilah and angry with myself. How could I not have known? Lynn had told me what her passing would be like, and it sounded violent and uncomfortable—why didn't alarm bells ring when she simply fell asleep and didn't wake up? Had Lilah given me clues that I'd missed? Had she not trusted me enough to let on to me… at all?

My internal chaos gradually passed. I was learning that everything passes. The emotion gave way, little by little, to the logic, which argued the reasons for her decision, and pleaded the case for her to find peace in her own way. And when the king tide of anger had faded, what was left in its place was a strange community of well-wishers.

Colleagues were sending me emails and texts, just letting me know they were thinking about me and offering condolences. Karl visited a few times and then bullied me into meeting him at the office for lunch twice a week. Leon and Nancy seemed to 'happen by my neighbourhood' every few days with a box of fresh fruit or vegetables.

And the brothers I'd thought of as strangers for years rang me or Skyped me at least once a day.

For forty years, I'd viewed the world as a hostile place, where even those close to me were aloof, and I was an outsider in every group. Somehow, in losing Lilah, my perspective had been broken down and rebuilt. I had decisions to make. I still had paid leave from work, but I wasn't sure if that was a smart move anymore. My life had been turned upside down and inside out, and I now stood in exactly the same place I'd always been, but the world around me had completely changed. I needed to get moving.

I sat at my computer and researched options for travel, new jobs, and some university courses. I bookmarked pages for marathons I'd once thought I might train for. I tried to buy new lenses for my camera online.

I've never been great at decisions, but this was impossible. It was too soon, too raw, too hard. What would I even photograph with new lenses? Who would be waiting for me at the marathon finish line?

The thought of selecting a new path for my life nearly overwhelmed me, until I picked up the phone.

'Tison Creative. You're speaking with Elise.'

'Elise.' There was genuine warmth to my tone. 'It's Callum.'

'Oh, Callum. We miss you. The place has gone to hell in a hand basket, I swear. How are you *doing*?'

I knew that my whole firm was well aware of why I'd been away, and it would be painful and tedious for me to return. But I was ready to get back to work, to have a real distraction to focus on, and to look for a kind of normal while I figured out what to make of myself. I closed my eyes, inhaled, and put my best game-face on.

'I'm doing okay, Elise. I need to arrange to come back.'

❊ ❊ ❊

I forgot about the will. The next month was all about getting back to work, getting back to running, and getting back into working on my apartment in the hopes that someone would actually buy it. Getting back to sleeping all night, to feeling like I might survive after all and getting back to normal were all a long, long way off yet—but at least I could go through the motions.

I was in a meeting at work when I got the text from Peta.

Will reading is tomorrow at the office. 1:00 p.m. xoxo

Not even a full day's notice. I sighed and reached for my iPad. Of course there were meetings which would be just about impossible to reschedule. I had such a great excuse to miss it. It wasn't even like I had to see Peta's disapproval; I could just text her back and say the timing didn't work for me. Easy.

I moved my attention back to the phone.

See you then. My fingers betrayed me. I watched the text send and then pretended to refocus on my meeting.

There was one appeal to attending the reading, and that was a chance to speak with Alan.

❊   ❊   ❊

Peta and I met in the foyer of Davis McNally, and after an awkward hug, simultaneously noticed the missing plaque on the wall where the partners were listed. The exposed cement had two visible screw holes and a squiggle of glue still attached, but no doubt it would be covered up soon when the new partner started. Lilah was being erased here, just as she probably needed to be, but it was still uncomfortable.

We had shared a silent elevator ride to Alan's floor. I had Lilah's laptop with me, in a spare case I'd found at home. I felt a little paranoid about it. If Peta asked me about it, could I convincingly lie and say it was my work laptop?

She didn't ask of course. Why would she? I'd come from work; it made sense that I might have a laptop with me. If I was outwardly jittery at all, no one would blame me or even think twice, given the circumstances.

'You're looking well, Alan,' Peta greeted him with a kiss on the cheek.

'My wife has me on Lilah's wacky diet. I've lost a few kegs' worth of weight.' He shook my hand and directed us into a boardroom.

'I'm sorry this has taken a while for me to get to.' He leant his elbow on the table. 'I just needed to get my head right before I came back. Saoirse was a critical part of our team here and I knew the morale was going to take a hit, so I needed to be on my game.' He looked down at the papers before him. 'But legally, as you might imagine, she'd left everything in A1 condition.'

There was so much preamble and my thoughts wandered. I thought about how many hundreds of hours Lilah had spent in this building, probably in this very boardroom. I wished I'd seen her there, in that crazy plum suit, with her hair tucked away in that no-nonsense bun.

'The Manly property shall be bequeathed to Callum Roberts…'

The words sank in belatedly and I looked to Peta, who was staring back at me in surprise.

'Shit, Peta—my apartment is on the market.' Embarrassment made me stumble over the words. 'You can have the money for your studio.'

Peta smiled and clasped my hand in hers.

'Don't feel you need to do that, sweetheart. Lilah wanted you to have her place, and she's given it to you.'

I needn't have worried. The Gosford property, and Lilah's car, and the shares and the savings we didn't know enough about, were all going to Peta. Lilah had made sure her mother would be just fine.

'Now, there were a few letters.' Alan opened another folder. 'There was one to her team, which I passed on this morning. Basically she apologised for being a slavedriver and thanked them profusely. I believe she also told those poor paralegals to quit immediately and find a job they actually liked.'

He picked up a sealed envelope.

'This is addressed to Janice and Ryan Abel. I'll track down their address later today and deliver it.'

I knew immediately what it would contain; an apology and an explanation. I was proud of Lilah for finding a way to make things right, even if she couldn't do it in person.

I looked to the folder, hoping for more.

'One for you, Peta.' He passed the second envelope across the table and closed the folder. 'And...there was one for me.'

It was awkward again in the room, this time Alan and Peta each avoiding my gaze. And I was disappointed—God, I was so disappointed. She had time to change her will to give me her house, but no time to write a few words to explain why, or to tell me what the hell to do next?

'I'm sorry, Cal.' Peta's eyes were brimming. 'She must have—'

'It's okay,' I interrupted her as gently as I could. 'It really is. I think I know where we stood.'

Peta nodded, swiped at her eyes, and clutched the envelope to her chest like a baby.

'That's about it,' Alan said softly. 'I can take the legal mumbo jumbo from here to transfer the properties into your names. Thanks for coming in.'

Peta was keen to leave, mumbling something about a choir practice back at Gosford, but I saw the death grip she held on the envelope and I knew she was probably headed home to read it. I remained in my seat as Alan walked her to the door, an unspoken request for a private audience with him, and one he clearly understood because he shut the door when she left.

'When did she name me in her will?' I asked.

'Months ago, when she first knew she was sick again,' he admitted.

After we broke up, before we reunited. I swallowed and forced myself to start the conversation I didn't know how to have.

'Did you know...' I wasn't sure how to convey the right meaning in my tone, and I assumed I'd failed, because Alan didn't react, not even a little bit. That startled me and when I spoke again, I was rambling, '...what she'd planned?...I found an email addressed to you with a video that I guess proved that Peta and I... didn't know how Lilah was really dying. The video was too big; it couldn't send.' I lifted the laptop case from under the desk and pushed it in front of him. Alan stared at it for a moment.

'I don't know what you're talking about,' he said hesitantly. 'But if I *did* know, we might have considered the relevant laws and ascertained that if she did self-administer the right drugs, that certain parties shouldn't be present, and in case it came to light, she should obtain video proof of her isolation at the time of self-administering to protect certain parties.'

It took a minute to decipher the sentences.

'The one thing that bothers me,' I whispered, when it all sunk in, 'is why didn't she just tell me?'

'You silly man,' Alan murmured. 'I can chart a direct course from the start of your relationship to now—and it was all about protecting you from pain, and then when that became utterly unavoidable, she was protecting you from prosecution.'

I shook my head and moved to argue, and Alan cut me off with a violent move of his arm.

'I sat with that woman in this very room and discussed for hours how we could indemnify you under the current law. She wanted to go out on *her* terms with those who loved her around her, without any risk of you suffering further after her death. Whatever video you found was her way of protecting you, in case she was found out. She was so determined to donate her body to the university, even though it was risky because of what toxicology studies might find, I think she saw this video as her—*your* insurance policy. She also, I might add, had drafted up some very strict conditions for what could and couldn't be done to her after her death, and one of those conditions was anonymity—the researchers who were to study her where to have no idea who she was. The point is, the chances of that video ever being needed were very slim.'

'Did Peta know?'

'I don't know, but I'd assume so. She'd seen James die, she knew what it was supposed to look like, and I'm guessing Lilah's passing was a whole lot more peaceful than that. But she's hardly going to make an issue of it, so I guess it's all over to you.'

He'd misunderstood my angst. I had no intention of going to the police or whoever would care about such a thing; I was just trying to understand her secrecy. I was too emotional to explain myself any better. I cleared my throat.

'She didn't want me to find it. She just didn't understand how computers worked.'

Alan and I shared a sad smile.

'That was our Lilah for you,' he sighed. 'Brilliant at handling the law, useless at handling a keyboard.'

'What do I do with the laptop?'

'Leave it with me. I'll keep it for a few more months, and then I'll have it quietly destroyed.'

❄ ❄ ❄

It took me weeks to get the courage up to visit Lilah's—*my*—new apartment in Manly. First, I had to grieve enough to face it without it breaking me. So I watched the days on the calendar tick past and I waited until I could again think of her without the sense of loss feeling overwhelming.

I knew it was time to go when the unsettling feeling that I was slipping back into my old habits grew stronger than the grief.

The morning I woke up and felt dread at the thought of another long day at the office hit my mind before thoughts of Lilah, I called in sick and went to the apartment instead.

I stood in the hallway with my key near the lock. My hands shook and memories of Lilah danced all around me. I remembered times she'd greeted me at the door, times we'd kissed as we said goodbye. I remembered that last day, when she'd behaved so strangely, and then the walk we'd taken back to the Corso, as if we were just any old couple wanting an outing.

As I'd expected and maybe even hoped, the grief resurged, bigger and stronger than it had been in weeks, and I pushed the key into the lock and opened the door.

The very first thing I saw, beyond the stacking doors but before the ocean, was a balcony that was fully in bloom. Plants that had been totally dead months before were green again, with blossoms at their most unbelievably perfect peak. Every colour of the rainbow was perched upon a pot, bulbs and succulents and perennials and every other kind of flower, burgeoning with life in spite of the season.

I had my travel bag on my shoulder. It slipped off and hit the tiles, and I stared.

Dead twigs were thick bushes, and scrawny seedlings held heavy-set flowers. The herbs were in full health, and the pansies were virtually glowing in their finest display. I quickly calculated, it had been almost four months since our last visit, and somehow in spite of the neglect of that time, those skeletal plants had become the brightest of examples of the beauty of life.

And then I knew that, somehow, Lilah was okay—and that in death, she'd found a way to be free.

❄ ❄ ❄

I found her diary almost immediately. She'd propped it on the kitchen bench, right between the kettle and the coffee jar. The necklace I'd given her for Christmas was hanging over it.

I sat on the balcony, with the waves lashing the coastline below me and a cool wind blowing a scattered cloud cover together into something which actually threatened rain. But I kicked my feet up on the coffee table and I read. I started on the first page, and I kept reading, even when my bladder threatened to burst and my backside was numb from pressure.

I read, and I cried, and I felt Lilah's skinny arms wrap around me to bring me comfort. I watched her handwriting and even her eloquence begin to slip. And then I found her last entry, which she must have written sometime during that last visit to see Lynn, and I understood why she'd left it for me.

CHAPTER TWENTY-SIX

Lilah

4 June

Dear Cal

Well, obviously I'm dead, so sorry about that. I can't imagine how it's been for you. If it were you instead of me, I'm not sure I'd cope. Please cope, Cal.

I've debated long and hard with myself about what to do with this journal. I destroyed the others when I got sick again, but this one... I thought I wrote it for me, but I think it's actually for you.

There were some things I needed to make right, and things inside my head are just too feeble for me to do it properly now. So maybe this is the coward's way—but, hey, if you have to die tragically, there has to be some benefit, right?

I loved you, Callum Roberts, you uptight, annoying, stubborn freak of nature. I loved every cell in your stupidly handsome body and every moment I had with you. I loved your stinky meat breath and your hopeless uncertainty about your life. And you know what? You loved me too, and I couldn't have doubted it for a second when we were together, because it was more real to me than anything else I'd known in my lifetime.

You're reading this, so you must be back here at my place, which I guess means you've read the will and you know it's now your place. It's worth a fortune you know, so do whatever the fuck you want with it, and get out there and *live*. Walk the Andes. Get Bali belly. Rescue an orphan in Romania. Go to fucking Paris. Pick up a gorgeous lady in Thailand and run screaming from the room when you realise she is actually a *he*. Just do something. You have so many days, Cal, so many days before you—and you know what's a bigger tragedy than me getting HD? You *not* getting HD and dying of inertia, or locking yourself away and pining over me when you could be living for the both of us.

So don't fucking do it, okay? Get your arse on a plane.

Love always, and forever, truly.

Your Lilah

EPILOGUE

I've spent a few months here, beside the ocean, amongst the foliage. From the moment we broke up until the moment I opened that door and saw the plants, I was craving peace, and although I will miss Lilah until I die, it's time to move on.

Behind me now, there are boxes and bags and all kinds of finalities. I'm done with this apartment for now. Lilah was somehow here with me for this time while I grieved her; I saw her every day in the garden on the balcony, and I soaked that essence in so that I could take it with me on the road.

If Lilah can live on, then—*hell*—so can I. It's time to embrace the world.

The movers come tomorrow, to take our shared things into storage, and a tenant will move in here soon. But for me, tomorrow I will go to a hotel near the airport, for a night in with room service and some scotch. Will flies in tomorrow, and then we will both head to Paris together, for a few weeks with Ed and Suzette and their beautiful new baby boy.

Beyond that, the entire world awaits us. I have income from Lilah's apartment and more than enough cash to sustain me while I explore the four corners of the earth.

It turns out Will is a lot more like me than I ever realised, and he's joining me for a year while we globe-hop. He wants adventure; I just want to live. I'm going to take every opportunity life throws at me and not waste a single moment.

If Lilah taught me one thing, it is that calamity could be hovering around any corner—but the timing of its arrival cannot be known, and the very same can be said for love. I'll find it again—I know I will—she will lead me to it with that stubborn, dogged determination that defined her entire life and death.

There is love that forms the pillars of a lifetime, and there is love that forms the foundations of a lifetime. My relationship with Lilah showed me all of the possibilities of living life awake. It's up to me now to do that in her honour.

LETTER FROM KELLY

Thank you so much for reading *Me Without You*. I sincerely hope Callum and Lilah's journey entertained, moved and inspired you.

While Lilah's scenario is entirely fictional, Huntington's Disease is unfortunately all too real. You can find more information and ways to help via your national Huntington's Disease Association.

If you enjoyed this book, I'd be so grateful if you'd write a review. I love getting feedback and your review can help other readers find my books.

Finally, if you'd like to receive an email when my next book is released, you can **sign up to my mailing list at my website**: www.kellyrimmer.com/email. I'll only send emails when I have a new book to share and I won't share your email address with anyone else.

Kelly